MIRRORSUN RISING

Also by Sean McMullen

CALL TO THE EDGE

VOICES IN THE LIGHT
Book One of Greatwinter

Forthcoming:

THE MIOCENE ARROW
Book Three of Greatwinter

MIRRORSUN RISING

BOOK TWO OF GREATWINTER

Sean McMullen

Aphelion Publications

All characters in this book are entirely fictitious, and no reference is intended to any living person.

First published in 1995 by Aphelion Publications
3 Pepper Tree Lane, North Adelaide, South Australia. 5006

Postal Address:
P.O. Box 619, North Adelaide, South Australia. 5006

Production consultant: David Harmon.

Printed in Australia by McPherson's Printing

Cataloguing in Publication Data

National Library of Australia

McMullen, Sean, 1948- .
Mirrorsun rising : book two of Greatwinter.

ISBN 1 875346 14 7.

I. Title. (Series : McMullen, Sean, 1948- . Greatwinter; bk. 2.).

A823.3

for

Trish Smythe, Chief Librarian

John de la Lande, Chief Engineer

Anne Holmes, Chief Edutor

CONTENTS

Paraline and Beamflash Networks

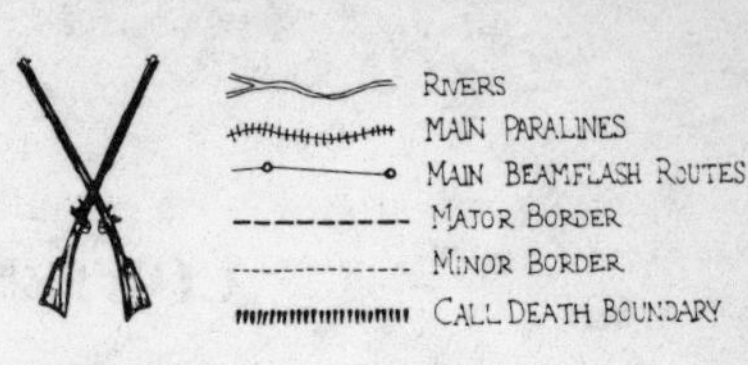

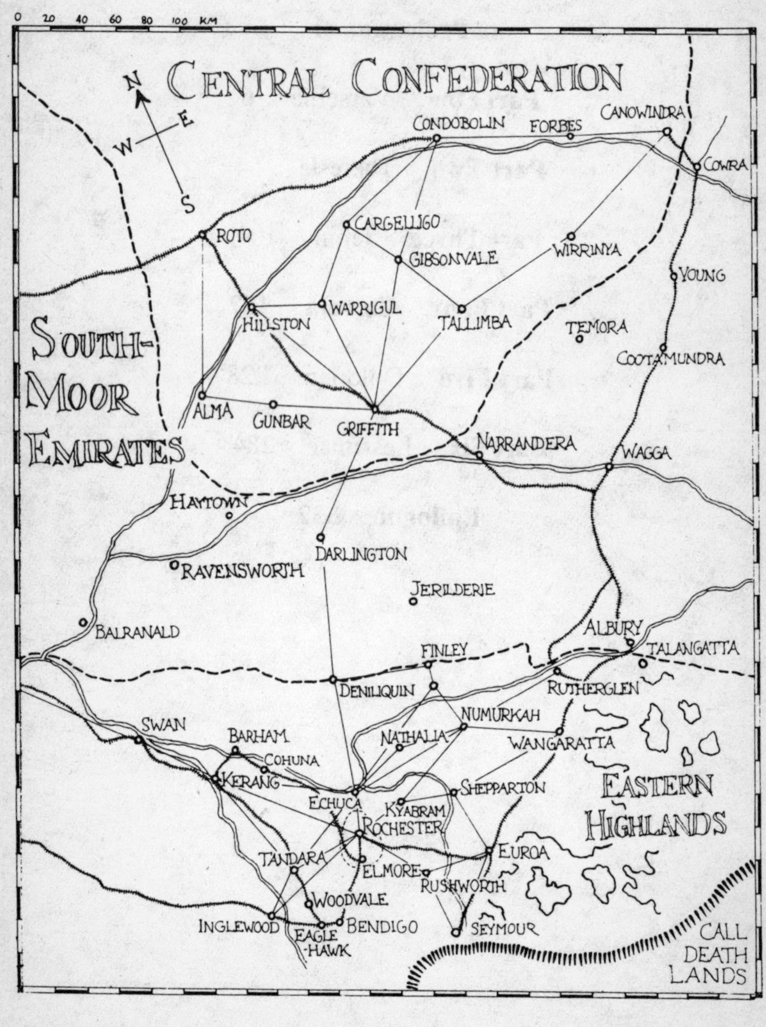

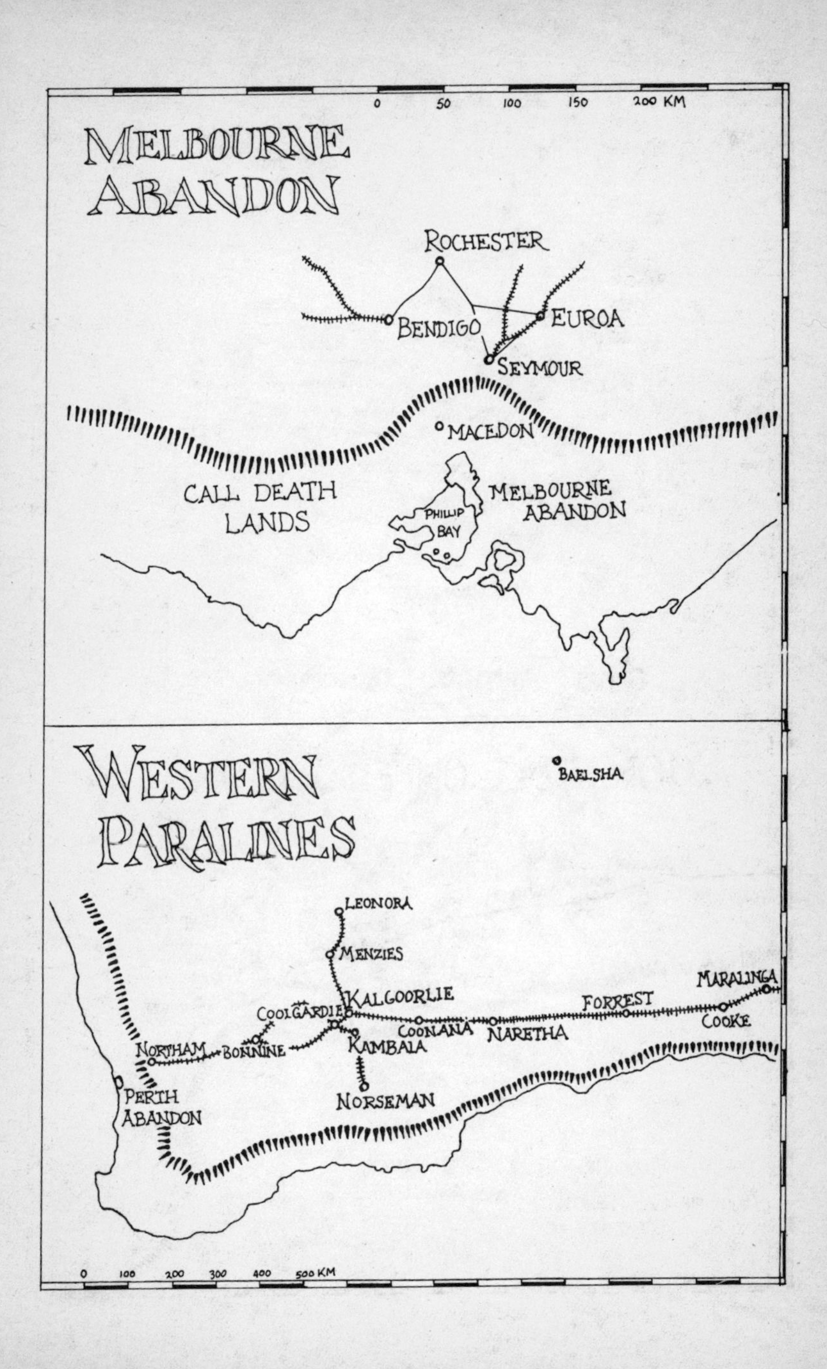
0 50 100 150 200 KM
MELBOURNE ABANDON
ROCHESTER
BENDIGO
EUROA
SEYMOUR
MACEDON
CALL DEATH LANDS
PHILLIP BAY
MELBOURNE ABANDON
WESTERN PARALINES
BAELSHA
LEONORA
MENZIES
KALGOORLIE
COOLGARDIE
FORREST
MARALINGA
COONANA
NARETHA
COOKE
NORTHAM
BONNINE
KAMBALA
NORSEMAN
PERTH ABANDON
0 100 200 300 400 500 KM

Alspring Cities

Camel Roads

Glenellen
Alspring
Gossluff
Ringwood
Tempe
Henbury
Pebble Desert
Erldunda
Ayer
Cavanaugh
Fostoria Oasis

Great Southern Desert

Woomera Confederation

Maralinga
Irmarna
Juwe
Warrion
Tarcoola
Kingworth
Wirraminna
Lake Tyers (Dry)
Lake Gairdner (Dry)
Woomera
Hawker
N
Peterborough
Paraline
Burra
Morgan
W
E
Call Death Boundary
Eudunda
S

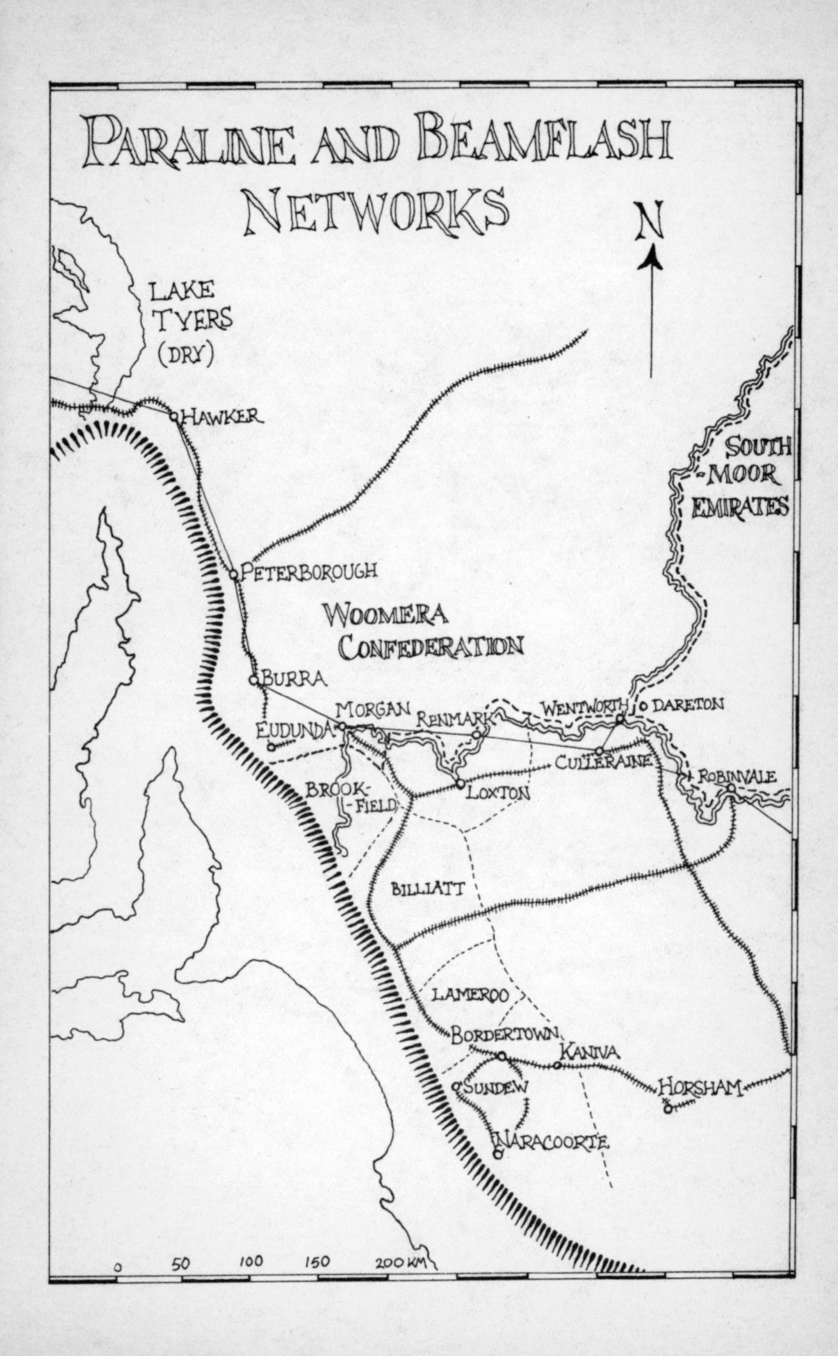
PARALINE AND BEAMFLASH NETWORKS
N
LAKE TYERS (DRY)
HAWKER
SOUTH MOOR EMIRATES
PETERBOROUGH
WOOMERA CONFEDERATION
BURRA
MORGAN
RENMARK
WENTWORTH
DARETON
EUDUNDA
CULLERAINE
ROBINVALE
BROOK-FIELD
LOXTON
BILLIATT
LAMEROO
BORDERTOWN
KANIVA
SUNDEW
HORSHAM
NARACOORTE
0
50
100
150
200 KM

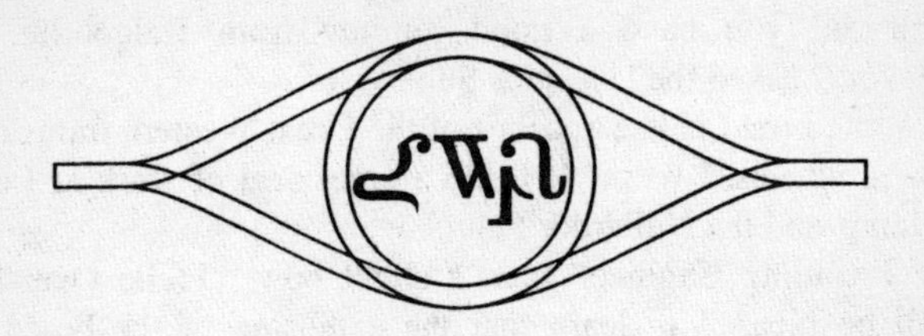

Prologue

The gusty wind of a late summer thunderstorm helped spin the great tubular rotors of the wind engine *Victoria* as it rumbled into the paraline terminus at Peterborough. The sun had been down for an hour, and the lamps of the terminus were all lit and glowing brightly, in spite of the wind and torrential rain. Waiting on the platform was a guard squad of Woomeran musketeers, and all of the senior paraline officers of Peterborough. Zarvora Cybeline, OverMayor of the Southeast Alliance and Highliber of Libris, was on this wind train, and there was no doubt that she would spend at least a few moments with them on the platform. The gauge of the paraline track changed from seven foot to four foot eight and one half inches at Peterborough, so she had to change trains.

The Overseer of Yards, the Terminus Master, the Presiding Engineer and the Logistics Supervisor stood around the door of the Great Western Paraline Authority coach as Zarvora stepped out onto the platform. She hurried under the platform awning to where there was an exchange of formal greetings, followed by an inspection of the squad of musketeers. The hood of her raincape was thrown back to reveal her black hair, braided and pinned by silver orbile combs. Her face was pale and gaunt, and she seemed weary.

"We had arranged a band to greet you as well, Frelle OverMayor Cybeline," explained the Terminus Master, "but this unseasonal storm ruined that plan."

"No matter, Fras," replied Zarvora. "This is no occasion of state. I am just at work here, like the rest of you."

"And did you have a good journey from Kalgoorlie, Frelle OverMayor?" asked the Logistics Supervisor."

"Yes, the broad gauge coaches of the Great Western trains are like palaces on wheels. I was able to do a great deal of work as I crossed the drylands and the Nullarbor Plain."

The Presiding Engineer gave a slight bow. "Frelle Over-Mayor, you will be pleased to learn that the extension of the broad gauge paraline is now within a few kilometres of Morgan. Within no more than a week the broad gauge wind trains will be able to run as far as the Morgan yards and railside. Thus the Great Western Paraline Authority will actually be operational from Southeast Alliance territory, and you will not have to change trains here in Peterborough any more."

"Good progress," she said, favouring him with a smile, "but rest assured, gentlemen, that I shall always stop at Peterborough for a few words with you. The paralines stitch my OverMayorate together as surely as the beamflash towers that transport its messages, and Peterborough is a major lynchpin of both networks."

They reacted with discreet smiles and sideway glances, and the Presiding Engineer drew breath for his carefully rehearsed reply. He was interrupted by shouted curses, and the sounds of a scuffle nearby. The Overseer of Yards snapped his fingers and pointed, and a lackey in parade uniform immediately dashed off along the rain-lashed platform toward a crowd of gearjacks and riggers.

"The usual problems with broad gauge and narrow gauge gearjacks fighting over which system is better," he said with a shrug and a graceful flourish. "The trains' captains have orders to keep them in good discipline, but still this happens."

"I cannot understand this," said Zarvora. "I have now witnessed half a dozen such fights on my many journeys between the Alliance and Kalgoorlie. Why do people become so emotional about the width of a paraline track? The Great Western trains give a fine ride, that is why I authorized the broad gauge extended to Rochester, but ..."

She was interrupted by the lackey returning, his uniform of green felt and gilt braid now soaked by the rain.

"Where are the captains, why hasn't that fight been stopped yet?" demanded the Overseer.

"It's the captains as is fightin'," replied the young lackey.

A squad of musketeers was despatched into the rain, and presently they returned with the two dishevelled, soaking-wet captains. Both were still cursing each other and struggling against their captors as they approached Zarvora and the group of officials.

"It's frogs and fishplates, and thus it's been for two thousand year thereabouts!" shouted the captain of the Alliance and Midlands Paraline's galley engine.

His opponent bawled back defiantly. "Fishplates! Fishplates! Fish don't use plates! As for frogs, if I comes upon frogs on my track I squashes 'em."

"Just as your overgrown brute of a windfarm damages all trackwork as it passes over."

"Broad gauge trackwork is all baulks, transoms and screwpins, it can't be damaged."

"It doesn't have fishplates."

"Replace your sleepers with baulks and you don't *need* fishplates."

"Replace our sleepers with baulks and it'd be easier for *your* poxy Authority to convert us all to broad gauge rubbish."

"And what's wrong with that? Mr Brunel invented baulk and transom trackwork two thousand one hundred years ago and —"

"Pox take Brunel!"

A scream of blind rage burst from the captain of the Great Western wind train, his standard reaction to any insult whatever to the memory of Isambard Kingdom Brunel. He did not so much break free of his musketeer captors, as drag them with him until he was close enough to deliver a solid left hook to his rival's eye. The musketeers took several more minutes to restore order, and had to form a line between the officers, gearjacks, riggers and pedal navvies of the crews of the two trains. Zarvora and the paraline officials remained beneath the shelter of the platform's slate-shingle awning as the musketeers did their thankless work.

When the captains suddenly began yet another exchange of insults, Zarvora decided to walk out into the rain and stand between them.

"Are you two quite finished?" she asked firmly as the noise of the struggle faded into the hissing of the rain and the rumbling of the free-spinning rotors of the wind train.

"He said my wind engine were fit only to grind corn."

"He called my navvies mice in a treadmill."

"Rats in a treadmill!"

"There! There! You heard him!"

"He started it."

"Both of you, stop it!" Zarvora shouted.

Suddenly realizing that the most powerful ruler in the known world was angry enough to shout at them, the two captains seemed to come to their senses.

"I have a wagonload of work waiting for me in Rochester, I have not been with my husband for six months, the Council of Mayors of the entire Southeast is waiting for me to preside over their annual meeting, and what do you two do? You, top-link captains of two of the most advanced and powerful machines in the world? You roll about in the rain trading punches and insults, and arguing about — what were they arguing about, Fras Overseer?"

"Frogs and fishplates, Frelle OverMayor."

"Galley Engine Captain Songan, Wind Engine Captain Parsontiac, call your crews to attention for me to inspect them."

"In the rain, Frelle Highliber?" asked the Overseer.

"In the rain, Fras Overseer, and on my behalf please thank your musketeers for restoring and maintaining order so patiently tonight."

Ten minutes later the standard gauge galley engine pulled Zarvora's standard gauge Mayoral coaches away from the terminus platform toward Rochester. Zarvora was joined by the Purser, a natty, efficient little man who looked as if he had a daily polish rather than a wash. She personally checked her boxes of equipment in the baggage van before allowing herself to be taken to the Mayoral coach.

"There's a fire in the grate, Frelle OverMayor, and refreshments are laid out for your pleasure."

"I am OverMayor of half the continent, yet here I am, cold, wet, tired and lonely," she muttered as they walked along the narrow, swaying corridor.

The Hospitalier was waiting in the Mayoral coach, and the Purser beckoned to her at once.

"I can attend the first two Frelle OverMayor. Here now, a warm, welcoming Mayoral coach. Frelle Hospitalier, a change of clothing for the OverMayor, if you please. Journeybox ZC/OM/12," he called with a snap and point of fingers.

The woman saluted Zarvora and departed at once. Zarvora shrugged off her rain cape and accepted a towel from the Purser.

"I didn't know that you were married, Frelle OverMayor," he remarked as she dried her braided hair and wiped her face.

"I am so busy that I almost forget it myself. I cannot even tell you the date of my wedding anniversary, Fras Purser, can you imagine that?"

The Purser smiled sympathetically. "I understand, Frelle OverMayor. I see a lot of the rich and powerful on the trains, and many confide to me that without a good invel-spouse their marriages would be unhappy indeed."

"Neither my husband nor myself have an invel-spouse, Fras Purser, we are far too busy for that. Now, will my dry clothing be long in arriving, please?"

The Purser left to help the Hospitalier unpack the OverMayor's luggage. Zarvora had just sat down in a chair of red and gold leather upholstery when the train began to slow down. It had run into a Call zone, a Call which had become stationary for the night, and would not begin to move again until the morning. Because the train was driven by pedal navvies, and because the Call had rendered everyone on board but Zarvora senseless, the train was now stuck just beyond the outskirts of Peterborough until just after dawn.

Zarvora cursed quietly, then rummaged around for some blankets in the overhead lockers.

"Were this a wind train, it would continue through the Call automatically," she grumbled to herself. Then she shook her blankets out, and settled down to spend the rest of the night as comfortably as she could manage.

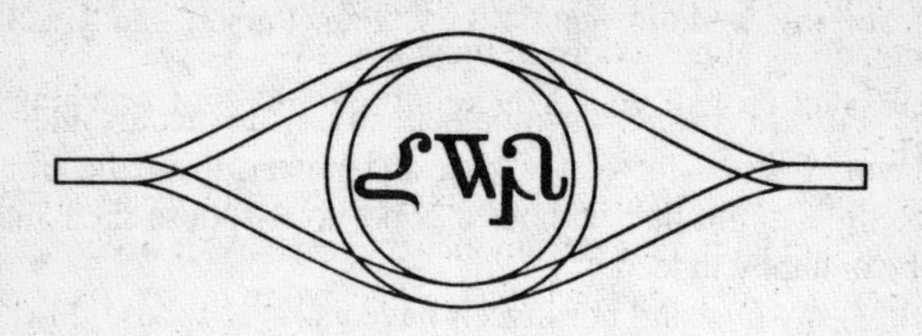

Part 1

VARSELLIA

The landscape below the red upland cliffs was laid out like a scatter of colourful cloth scraps on a Northmoor carpet of pink and olive designs. From their vantage on the clifftop three riders were observing the aftermath of the battle and making their own judgements about what had happened between the armies of the two Alspring cities. They were dressed as Neverlander nomads, swathed against the pervasive red dust in robes, veils and head shrouds of ochre, light orange, sienna brown and dappled olive.

"Glenellen is again victorious," said Overhand Genkeric as he lowered his brass-inlay telescope. "That infernal calculating machine fights their wars for them now. It has made them invincible."

The man on his right continued to scan the scatterings of colour on the landscape below, using one of the new twinocular devices that split the light from one lens into two eyepieces.

"The Glenellen battle calculor, I can see it!" he suddenly exclaimed. "It's off to the side there, just near those observation masts ... it's just a group of scribes at desks! Who would ever guess what they are, or what they can do?"

"An invincible machine, Captain Lau-Tibad. That's the nature of calculors. Whatever odds are sent against it, the damnable thing will multiply its men twenty-fold. What hope do we Neverland tribes have against it?"

"Folding desks. I can see them folding their desks away. The desks are white, no — about a third of them are red —"

"Gah, shut up will you! You're not with the bird watching convial now. This is war."

"My apologies, Overhand Genkeric," he said as he lowered the twinocular and let it dangle from the strap around his neck.

"We are nothing, that's what has protected us so far. As nomads we Neverlanders roam as no more than a minor bother to Glenellen's expansion, but the raids of our brother tribes must become an annoyance eventually."

"To Glenellen? We're the bite of a flea. There's plenty of room for all on the desert, and what do we Neverlanders have but our tents and camels?"

"The day will come when Glenellen begins to scratch its fleas. We must stop biting, and persuade the others to do the same ..."

His voice faded as he realized that the third rider had looked away for a moment from the patchwork of despair and triumph below the cliffs and was regarding them with an expression that was at the same time quizzical yet impatient.

"If only you could hear yourselves." The voice from behind the heavy red cotton veil was measured, sarcastic. While the two officers sat proudly erect in their saddle frames, the Commander turned away from them again, and hunched over, intent upon the scene below.

"But, Commander, our numbers are small and we are untutored in such advanced arts of war," replied Genkeric. "That machine multiplies their numbers twenty-fold, and their numbers already exceed ours."

The Commander laughed, and it was a long, mirthless, unsettling laugh with a light but hollow pitch. "That machine is nothing more than a highly developed book of tactics. I helped to build the first one, in the distant city of Rochester. I should know."

"But, Commander, I know how a crossbow works, but that will not stop an enemy shooting me with one."

"Oh so? Well I too know how a crossbow works, and that tells me where to stand to be out of range, and how much time I have to charge at the bowman while he is reloading. I say that any skilled officer could have done what that battle calculor has just accomplished. Any skilled officer could have easily defeated it."

"My most profound apologies, Commander," said Captain Lau-Tibad, "but if that is the case, why did Glenellen's forces triumph so convincingly just now?"

"Because there are few good officers among those dandified, overdressed lapdogs that pass for the military command of the Alspring cities."

"The Gossluff army was three times bigger —"

"The battle calculor down there is a strategic weapon. It has its uses as a tactical device, but they are limited. That's its secret. It's vulnerable, so very vulnerable that it could shatter its own army as easily as granting it victory."

The Overhand raised his telescope and began examining the battlefield again, as if looking for something he had missed earlier. Captain Lau-Tibad did likewise with his twinocular.

"Do you have those squadrons of lancers, archers and musketeers I require?" the Commander asked without turning.

"They await you within a day's ride, Commander," the Overhand replied, hastily lowering his telescope.

"Good, then we leave now. I want to begin training those lancers as soon as possible. If we delay, someone may realize that the battle calculor is a fickle ally and abandon its use on the battlefield."

"But, Commander, what advantage will that be to us Neverlanders? We want food, caravan routes and land."

"And we *shall* get land, my puzzled Overhand. All the land from here to Rochester."

*****

All the land from that cliff top to Rochester was mainly an immense sprawl of red sand and tough olive vegetation. An eagle soaring on the thermals and following a straight line two thousand kilometres to the southeast, would cross craggy ranges of red sandstone interspersed with walled cities, deep rock pools and reservoirs, palm groves, aqueducts, seasonal rivers, nomads with their flocks of sheep, goats and emus, then the flat, open plains of red sand criss-crossed with ancient roads and modern camel trails. Hundreds of kilometres along the line were the salty waters of the largest known lake in the land: Eyre lake's choppy waters were covered with pelicans and cormorants.

Further southeast still were the Flinders Mountains, then the Barrier Grasslands, crossed by the Barrier Paraline with its blue and white wind trains. The climate became wetter and more temperate and greener, and the land was covered in low eucalyptus forest. During the last few hundred kilometres to Rochester one crossed river galleys and barges plying the slow, broad waters of the Murray and Darling Rivers. The complex of Mayorates that was the Southeast Alliance was an intricate pattern of paralines, beamflash towers, cities, roads, farms, vineyards and Call fences. Rochester itself was the largest city, built on an island on an artificial lake, then spilling across paraline and road bridges into suburbs that surrounded the lake itself like a moat of bricks and terra cotta tiles.

Had either Overhand Genkeric or Captain Lau-Tibad been physically able to fly along that line to the southeast, they would have been quickly demoralized by the vast distances, and the size and wealth of the cities and Mayorates, yet Lemorel looked beyond all that to the roots of Rochester's control. That control was based in Libris, the huge library in central Rochester, and it took the form of two thousand men and women chained to desks in a vast hall with whitewashed stone walls, all working at abacus frames. Taken together they were the Libris Calculor, the great-grandparent of the machine now operating on the battlefield near the Alspring cities. Through a network of beamflash communications towers the Libris Calculor controlled the transport, communications and economic life of a third of the continent's people, and its rule had lasted ten years. The Commander observing that distant battlefield understood it all, and in the most intimate detail.

Tarrin Dargetty, Dragon Librarian, Class Gold, was escorting an important visitor through the complex of halls, corridors, bookbays, workshops, dormitories and cell blocks that was the interior of Libris. Jefton was the Mayor-Pretender, the deposed monarch of Rochester who had lost his throne to the Highliber of the library six years earlier.

"The place has changed since I was last here," observed Jefton, bending to duck under a pulley rack that was humming and swishing with taut wire cables.

"Those original systems of 1700 seem so old as to be unusable compared to what we have now," reflected Tarrin. "The Highliber can run the Alliance quite smoothly from 2,500 kilometres away to the west in Kalgoorlie."

"And she runs it a lot better than I ever did," Jefton said with a hint of annoyance. "Why should I ever bother to sire an heir? This machine will probably run the known world by itself within another decade."

"There is more to running a Mayorate than collecting taxes, controlling the army, maintaining the roads and paralines, and having the turds carted off to the farms. The people need a face for ceremonial occasions, a royal love life to gossip over, even a figurehead to complain about."

Jefton shrugged his podgy shoulders, sending tremors across the rest of his generously-fleshed body. "They can throw rotten fruit at felons in the stocks if they have anger to vent. What has this to do with me?"

Tarrin did not answer, for they had reached a guarded door, and the Mayor-Pretender had to be signed into a register. Beyond that door, and the door behind it, was a balcony overlooking the Calculor's hall. Jefton crossed to the edge of the balcony and looked down over the stone railing, at first silent with awe.

"It has grown to fill the entire hall," he observed after a time.

"Yes, and there is some dispute among the Libris planners on whether a floor should be added ten metres up to house any future expansions, or whether more calculors should be built elsewhere for specialized tasks."

"Why bring me here? Why show me all this?"

Tarrin made a spiralling gesture to the Calculor, then gave a parody of the Mayoral bow. "Would you be willing to sit on the throne of Rochester if the Libris Calculor continued to run the Mayorate, and the Highliber ruled you as OverMayor?"

In spite of his expanding waistline and general look of dissipation, Jefton had retained the sharpness of his mind. "She wants me as a figurehead? I'm to be restored as Mayor?"

"As Mayor-Seneschal, actually. She has the same arrangement in Tandarra, Yarawonga, some western castellanies and the captured Southmoor province of Finley."

"I'm not sure that I like the title of Mayor-Seneschal."

"So you prefer Mayor-Pretender?"

Jefton did not answer that, but glared away into the bustling complexity of the Calculor. Tarrin scratched at soup stains on the sleeves of his robes.

"The title is generally abbreviated to 'Mayor', even at most official functions," Tarrin explained casually, not wanting to give Jefton the impression that anyone was desperate to have him back. "When the Highliber is present and acting as OverMayor you would be announced as Mayor-Seneschal, and the title would be on all official documents and letterheads, but you could move back from your villa at Oldenberg and live in the Mayoral Palace."

"In the servants' quarters?"

"No, the rooms of the Mayor. There have been new rooms built for the OverMayor in Libris. They are impressive, take my word for it."

Jefton folded his arms on the rail and looked up at the skylights of frosted glass. "How often is the Highliber-OverMayor, or whatever she calls herself, actually in Rochester?" he asked.

"Of late she is within the city walls no more than six weeks of every year. Most of her time is spent travelling the other Mayorates, and across in the far west at Kalgoorlie. She is friends with the Mayor of Kalgoorlie, and is negotiating a trade and military pact that could eventually have her OverMayor of the entire south of the continent."

Jefton's decision was visible before he spoke it. He suddenly stood up straight and threw his shoulders back in a pose of Mayoral dignity that he had not allowed himself for many years. Tarrin actually heard joints popping.

"I accept!" declared Jefton brightly.

Tarrin was a little taken aback by the sudden change in mood, but he tried not to show it. "Well then, very good ... Mayor Jefton," he replied, this time with a deep, formal version of the Mayoral bow.

"Not yet, Fras Dragon Gold Librarian. There are papers to be signed, I know the legislation."

"Now that you have agreed, the articles will be scribed up for a ceremony this evening. The Frelle Zarvora, OverMayor of the Southeast Alliance and Highliber of Libris, is currently visiting us to take care of some business in person. Because her signature and seal will go straight onto the document, your status as Mayor-Seneschal will be law by the time you climb into your old bed in the palace tonight."

Down below in the Calculor itself the shift change began, with fresh components diffusing in to relieve those who had just completed eight hours of work.

Tarrin glanced down at the tattered old clockwork on his belt, and checked the changeover against it. "Now if you will excuse me, Fras Mayor, I see that the shift is changing. I have another pleasant duty to perform, you see."

"Nothing could be so pleasant as the scribing of my articles of office, at least as far as I am concerned."

"Come now, don't worry. I shall order the work commenced on that as I am escorting you out of here."

"Then please, get me out of here at once."

Lackeys with clipboards bustled along with Tarrin and Jefton as they passed through the corridors of the administrative block on the way to the main reception lobby of Libris. Tarrin gave instructions that would restore a facade of the Mayor-Pretender's former status, then gave him into the care of a herald to arrange further details such as robes and forms of address.

"Just what is that other pleasant duty that you have scheduled for today?" asked Jefton as they stood shaking hands on the vast point-flower mosaic in the lobby.

"Oh something very auspicious, Fras Mayor. The first of the non-felonious components in the Libris Calculor is to be released today."

"So, so, the Highliber Zarvora trusts you a great deal."

"The Highliber would not also be OverMayor if she could not delegate some of her work. I shall see you this evening, Fras."

*****

FUNCTION 9 had just returned to his private cell, and was sitting alone when Tarrin arrived. At thirty five, FUNCTION 9 was not one of the oldest components in the Calculor, yet he was one of the longest serving. As a FUNCTION he had advanced as far as he could, as he was brilliant with mathematical methods. None of the skilled, younger recruits had overtaken his early records for feats of mental arithmetic, and he had even invented methods of improving the workings of the very Calculor in which he was imprisoned.

The clanging of a swagger stick drawn across the bars brought his head up from a book of pre-Greatwinter mathematics. He recognized Tarrin, the Dragon Gold in charge of the Libris Calculor.

"You work diligently in your free time," observed Tarrin.

"Free time is only for the free, Fras Dragon Gold," he replied with bored forbearance. "I have to survive within this rat race of a Calculor, and you keep introducing younger and faster rats."

Tarrin clasped his hands behind his back and studied the component for a moment. FUNCTION 9 was well groomed, and dressed in clothing that paralleled the fashions in the city outside.

These robes he had sewn himself, or so the regulators reported. *Highly intelligent, and definitely not broken in spirit*, Tarrin mused to himself. *Defiant and proud, but not a rebel.*

"May I come in?" Tarrin asked as FUNCTION 9 looked back to his book.

"That depends on whether you have the key," he said without looking up.

FUNCTION 9's head jerked up as he heard the creak of tumblers moving. Tarrin stepped into the cell, leaving the door wide open. His cloak was drawn aside to display a flintlock in his belt.

"Must you insult me as well as keep me prisoner, Fras Dragon Gold?" asked FUNCTION 9.

"How so?"

"By trying to tempt me with that gun. Why would I endanger years of seniority in this place by making a futile attack on your person?"

Tarrin sat down on the bunk and drew his pistol. Reversing it, he reached over and placed it on FUNCTION 9's writing desk.

"Very nice, Fras librarian, but please take it away. Components get shot if guns are found in their possession. You should know, they're your rules."

"But you are not a component, Fras Denkar Newfeld," said Tarrin as he drew a scroll from his sleeve.

Taking the pillow from the cell bunk, he placed the roll of parchment on it. He stood up, bowed, and presented it to the still-seated component. FUNCTION 9 stared back at him steadily, then slowly reached out and picked up the scroll between his thumb and forefinger.

"The Highliber's seal," he observed as he broke the wax. "Hmm. Be it known to all the usual time-serving lackeys and civil servants, and their constable lapdogs, that the guest of the Mayor of Rochester, designated as FUNCTION 9, is a free man, and is henceforth to be known as Fras Denkar Newfeld."

"Not quite the Highliber Zarvora Cybeline's wording."

"Except for the substance. So, is this a joke, then, or am I really free to go?"

Tarrin produced another scroll, which was unsealed. "I have here the Articles of Release from the Calculor. You are the first to have the opportunity to sign them. In fact I only had them drawn up this morning."

FUNCTION 9 unrolled the second scroll and read the Articles carefully. Tarrin ran his swagger stick along the bars again, then tried to balance it on the tip of his finger, without much success.

"Insufferable legal babble," Tarrin said as he noted that FUNCTION 9 was reading the text for the third time. "In short it says that you must agree never to speak of the internal workings of the Calculor to anyone outside Libris under pain of death — unless you have the agreement of the Highliber. You must accept that you were mistakenly imprisoned here, and will consider the matter closed for a sum of three hundred gold royals. In her roles as both OverMayor and Highliber, Frelle Zarvora Cybeline expresses her regrets for your mistaken incarceration."

"Regrets! She keeps me here ten years, the best ten years of my life, then gives me a bag of gold and throws me out on my ear with only a few regrets?"

"What more do you want?"

"Ten years of seniority at Oldenberg University, for a start. I'd be lucky to get work as an accounts clerk after mouldering in here for a decade."

"So you don't accept the Articles of Release?"

The scroll trembled slightly in FUNCTION 9's hands, and he felt the beginnings of tears welling in his eyes. *Fight it down, don't show weakness in front of this ratty little librarian,* he said to himself as he tried to smother gratitude with anger.

"Of course I do!" he exclaimed, snatching a quill from a Nathalia clay grotesque on his writing desk and checking the cut. He bared his teeth in a parody of a smile. "Don't think that I'm not fascinated by the work in this Calculor, mind, I just hate being a component." He scratched out his signature in neat, even loops at the bottom of the Articles.

"One final scroll, now that you are Fras Denkar Newfeld again," said Tarrin. "The Highliber and I had some sympathy for the injustice of your incarceration here. This is an offer of employment that goes some way to restoring your lost seniority."

Denkar read, then slowly looked up. His colour and composure were both gone. "Now this really is some twisted little joke," he said in a clipped whisper. "You want to employ me as a Dragon Green Librarian in the embassy at Kalgoorlie? That's on the other side of the known world! "

"It's a good salary, and they speak the same language as us."

"I prefer this Mayorate, for all that you're done to me. What about work in Libris?"

"Ah now, in Libris we have no vacancies pending, but in Kalgoorlie we could arrange an even higher rank, subject to the usual examinations, of course."

Denkar replaced his quill. "No, thank you. Freedom by itself will do nicely." He picked up his pillow, placed the scroll upon it and handed it back to Tarrin.

Tarrin and Denkar emerged from the cell. The component had already picked the badges of Calculor rank and numbers from his uniform, although patterns of thread traced out what he had been until only minutes before. Several Dragon Red guards challenged Denkar, then saluted in amazement as Tarrin held up the scrolls. Denkar paused by the Regulators' canteen.

"May I?" he asked, gesturing to Tarrin's flintlock.

Tarrin stared back at him for some moments, then reluctantly drew the pistol from his belt and handed it to him butt first. Denkar cocked the striker, then entered the canteen. Several regulators of Red, Green and Blue rank were sitting around a table playing cards and drinking beer. Denkar gripped the gun with both hands and fired at a ceramic jug of black beer on the table. It shattered amid gouts of foam, and the librarians burst back from the table. A moment later nine guns were trained on Denkar's head.

"Fras Tarrin, did he take you hostage?" gasped a Dragon Blue as she wiped the foam from her face with her free hand.

"Lower your guns," replied Tarrin. "Do it! Fras Denkar Newfeld, formerly known as FUNCTION 9, has been released by decree of the Highliber."

There was devastated, incredulous silence. Denkar savoured the moment, then handed the pistol back to Tarrin.

"I'll not be the last component to be released," he warned before turning his back on them and walking from the canteen.

"Why did you do that?" asked Tarrin as he hurried after him.

"To improve their behaviour toward the other components," replied Denkar without breaking stride. "A parting gift to my former comrades in slavery."

"You just escaped death by no more than good luck!" snapped Tarrin. "Why did you really do it?"

"To prove something to myself."

"To prove what?"

Denkar stopped and whirled around so suddenly that Tarrin nearly collided with him. The former FUNCTION's expression was one of unsettling perception.

"There's more going on than just my release from the Calculor, or you would be marching me straight back to my cell after that canteen trick. What is really going on?"

Tarrin stared at the floor. "The Highliber only tells me —"

"Very little at best, and nothing if she can help it. All right then, what is *your* theory?"

"Many of the important components in the early Calculor were like you, ah ..."

"Kidnapped."

Tarrin stepped around him and continued down the corridor with his hands clasped behind his back. Denkar stared after him for a moment, his hands still on his hips, then he shrugged and strode after him.

"We prefer the term conscripted," said Tarrin. "Yes, I do admit that several dozen people were inducted into the Calculor without being felons. We needed your skills, both to run the Calculor and to train the felons. The Battle Calculor is known to the outside world for six years now, and the Libris Calculor has become an open secret, so there is no point in keeping you here either to protect a secret, or for skills that are no longer unique."

"So even the mighty Highliber-Mayor is not so high above the law as to be able to keep innocent components imprisoned — as opposed to criminal components?"

"That's the gist of it."

"Well, Fras Tarrin, I don't believe you, but that's hardly relevant to anything, is it? Meantime, let's get me paid off and outside the walls of Libris before the urge to shoot at a Dragon Librarian seizes me again."

*****

Denkar stepped hesitantly through the gates of the Libris forecourt and into the streets of Rochester. The sky was luridly bright after ten years inside the huge library, and he shaded his eyes as he walked. For the first time he saw the Mirrorsun band, a faint, slightly darker blue band that had appeared across the sky five years earlier. There would be other eyes watching, he was sure of that. He bought a honey pastry with a gold royal and told the astonished vendor to keep the change. At the paraline terminus he booked a passage to Oldenberg, but the pedal train was not due to leave for hours. Tarrin had given him a voucher for the Cafe Marellia, an expensive eatery just across Paraline Square.

I'm meant to go here, Denkar decided. *I could rebel, but why bother? They would get their way eventually.*

As he reached the front door he beckoned to a man standing in the street.

"Did you mean me, Fras?"

"Yes, come in, call your friends who are watching me from a greater distance as well."

"I don't understand, Fras."

"Of course you do. I want all my shadows to have a coffee with me. I'll pay, of course."

With his face still blank the man turned and walked briskly away. Moments later a waiter was at Denkar's side, wax gleaming on his hair and long moustache as if it was dark, textured wood that had just been varnished.

"Lady in reserve bower, Fras," he murmured, his eyebrows arching. "Liking your company, she is."

Denkar was well beyond surprise by now. "Indeed. But I may not be liking *her* company, Fras waiter." He winked and pressed a silver noble into his hand. "Tell me now, is she pretty?"

The waiter smiled knowingly. "Thank you, generous Fras. Beautiful lady, Fras, beautiful lady. Fine, delicate face, good Fras, with bushy black hair untied — and such eyes! Expensive silver orbile combs in hair, hah, from rich husband too busy making money, yes?" He nudged Denkar's arm. "Big eyes like velvet —"

"Stop! Enough. Either she tipped you more than I did, or she really is all of these things. Tell me, though, is she a Dragon Librarian?"

"No uniform, Fras. Who knows?"

"Not a librarian, perhaps. In a way I'm disappointed, but in a way I'm relieved as well. Lead the way, Fras waiter."

They walked among chunky but polished redwood tables and benches, at which a cross-section of the bland, bored upper class of Rochester were seated before their eggshell coffee cups and dainty squares of bread with emu paté. Denkar noted that body-hugging shirts with loose sleeves were the latest in fashion.

The reserve bowers were a row of rooms running down the centre of the cafe, with doors on either side. The waiter gestured to a lattice door, then left.

Denkar rapped at the door, and a resonant, honeyed contralto voice responded "Enter". He pressed the latch down and pushed the door to the candle-lit bower open. Her face was partly shadowed, but there was absolutely no doubt of the lady's identity.

"Highliber!"

"Will you close the door behind you please, Fras Denkar?"

Denkar sat down warily on the leather of the bench seat, the horsehair padding scrunching in the silence like the crackle of kindling in a fire. Finding the Highliber in there was surprise enough, but when Denkar found himself thinking that she really was beautiful he was nothing less than astonished. He had never seen her like this before. Her hair was unbound and bushy, embroidered with a few grey strands and pinned to frame her face. Her face was relaxed and remarkably winsome in the privacy of the bower. He had only ever seen her being rigidly formal at official announcements, or with her features contorted by rage when she had visited the Calculor in a vile temper because of some malfunction. Here she was now, the very wellspring of his enslavement, and he noted with dreamy detachment that no hate was blazing up within him. She was like Tarrin, or the door of his cell: just a thing that had once confined him. But unlike Tarrin, she was a very attractive woman.

"Do you wish me to apologize for your nine years of slavery, Fras Denkar?" she asked after a short, awkward silence.

"No need, Frelle Highliber, I — it was comfortable slavery." Denkar was fascinated to hear himself speak. For all his quite justifiable bitterness he was somehow being pleasant to her.

"But you prefer freedom?" she asked slowly, as if she was surprised as well.

"Yes, but ..."

"But?"

"The years in the Calculor were fascinating. I learned such skills at mathematics as I could have never done at Oldenberg, and I made discoveries in calculating theory, too. Being within the Calculor is not so bad as you may imagine. I had friends in there, I may even meet them again, yourself willing."

She nodded, her eyes never leaving him. Denkar held her gaze for a moment, then looked down, unsettled.

"Interesting, interesting," she said. "And now what are you going to do? Return home, go shopping in the markets, drink in the taverns and chase wenches?"

"Home, well yes, they may even remember me there. As for shopping, I'll need practice at that. I've had my needs attended to for so long that I've forgotten how. I would certainly like a half-litre of black beer: you forbid that to your components."

"Black beer? I am sorry, that must be an old regulation from the earlier, more desperate times. It will be repealed by tomorrow."

Denkar inclined his head. "You're generous. Ah, but as for wenches, I do have a ... ah, request to make to you in that regard."

Zarvora said nothing, but continued to watch him. It seemed to Denkar that she was preparing to pounce and snatch something away. He took a deep breath, then another. Finally he leaned towards her, defiantly looking into her dark, intense eyes. "I had a sweet Dragon Librarian who would visit me in the darkness of the confinement cells."

"Ah yes, the solitary confinement cells. Did you know that they were never once used to punish anyone by solitary confinement for the whole existence of the Calculor? They were rather heavily booked for private dalliance between regulators and components, however."

"Highliber, I never saw her face but she was lovely beyond telling. I intend to stay in Rochester to try to meet her as one free citizen to another."

"Stay in Rochester! So, Tarrin was right. Denkar, I left my offices and some very important business in Libris to meet with you like this. I really need you to go west to Kalgoorlie."

"I want to work in Libris. I'd start as a Dragon White if I had to."

"I am sorry, but it is not possible. Now Kalgoorlie —"

"Highliber, I am serious about staying. Perhaps I could work as an edutor at Rochester University. You see, I do love that Dragon Librarian, even though I've not seen her face and know nothing about her. I'll come back to Rochester whatever you say. I think that she loves me, and she must know what I look like. If I stay in Rochester she will see me one day. She will come to me, I know it."

"She has work elsewhere, Fras Denkar."

"So you do know her!" he exclaimed, his arms laid along the table, his hands open and pleading. "Please, what is her name?"

"Denkar, I have work for you beyond Rochester, too."

"You — you free me, then you bind my life as tightly as if I was still a prisoner?" He rose to his feet, the menu he had been fiddling with crushed in his left hand. "Well, you can have me dragged about with your Black Runners and your authority, but you can never —"

"Denkar! Lower your voice, sit down and stop waving that thing at me, please — and notice that I did say please. Thank you, that's better. Now hold out your hand — please."

Denkar felt a slight crawling of revulsion as she reached out her small, bone-white hands. She removed the crushed menu from his hand and replaced it with her own. He expected her skin to be moist and as cold as porcelain, yet it was very warm and dry, somehow familiar. She leaned towards him until her face was very close.

"I love you too, Fras Denkar, and I am touched by your devotion to me."

There were no words that could have possibly been appropriate to a revelation like that. For a time he sat staring into her huge, green eyes, then he reached out to touch her hair, which was oddly bushy, very much like his own. He closed his eyes as his fingers caressed her face. It really was her, his fingertips told him that there was no doubt at all.

"It *is* you," he whispered. "But your voice, it was much lighter."

"You mean like this?" she chirped.

In spite of the intensity of their emotions, he found himself giggling. "Oh, Highliber."

"Frelle Zarvora, although you can continue to call me Frelle Shadowliber if you like. I prefer Zarvora or Zar."

"But High — Frelle, ah, Zarvora ... why me?"

"Why you, Denkar, my brave and brilliant lover? Come around to my bench and sit beside me, there is much to tell you." Denkar hesitated only for a moment, then shuffled awkwardly around in the cramped space. Zarvora took his hand again. "Firstly, why you? That is not easy, ah ... can you describe the Call for me?"

"The Call?" Denkar blinked, then frowned as if puzzled. "Ah... the Call is said to have begun around the time of Greatwinter itself, two millennia ago. It is an invisible band of allurement that sweeps over the land at random intervals of anything between days and weeks. Ah, it lasts between two and three hours, travels at a slow walking pace, and it blanks out the minds of all animals weighing more than a large cat, luring them away to an unknown fate. The only cities where its touch is never felt are Rochester and Oldenberg, in this little Mayorate of Rochester. Nobody knows the reason for that. Birds and reptiles are unaffected by the Call, and nobody knows the reason for that, either."

Zarvora put her hand to his cheek, then ran her fingers through his hair. Although she was trying to explain some important matters, the heady sensuality of her presence made it hard for Denkar to concentrate. The huge green eyes, the warm, dry tingling touch of her fingers, the musky, feathery scent of her hair... With an effort he brought himself back to what she was saying.

"Birds are immune to the Call, that is the key. Denkar, under a microscope, your hair has the resemblance of long, fine, tendril-like feathers, just as mine does. Early in 1703 I collected hair samples from every component in the Calculor, while in search of those with just such hair. I found only you. Such people as us are very rare, we call ourselves aviads. You have never made a journey beyond the null-zone that covers Rochester and Oldenberg, have you? You have never felt the touch of the Call."

"Yes, that's true."

"And you never will. We aviads are immune to the Call — just let me finish, please. At first I only wanted to have a child that would be an aviad like me —"

"A child!"

"Shush," she hissed softly, holding a finger to his lips. "With my authority and position being what they are, I had to be careful. Although there are other aviad men in a place called — no, but that is too complicated to explain just now. I arranged trysts with you in the darkened isolation cells, as is the way with other components and regulators in the Libris Calculor. I expected that you would be something of an animal after all that confinement, and I was a little afraid, yet you turned out to be quite endearing. You were interesting to talk to, you could make me laugh, and I just liked to be with you." She began to fiddle with a strand of her own hair, twirling it around her index finger. "Denkar ... you were also seeing another regulator at the time, the one with breasts like prize melons, who wore mid-thigh boots."

"Dolorian. I had been on intimate terms with her for years. I was not her only lover but I was her favourite."

"She is a Dragon Blue now, in Beamflash Communications. When I heard that you had broken off with her for fear of hurting my feelings, well, I grew very fond of you indeed. I had won dozens of duels and several wars, but never a heart."

"Highliber — Zarvora — I feel as if I've been kept as a pet. You actually spied on me and Dolorian?"

"No, no, no," she said imploringly, shaking him gently by the shoulders. "I am not such an ogre as to do that. Dolorian spent a fortnight quizzing everyone who crossed her path about the secret lover of yours who was more alluring than her. Nobody knew that it was me, of course, but every Dragon Librarian in Libris soon knew about you rejecting Dolorian. It was even starting to disrupt Calculor operations to a small extent. She actually made an appointment to see *me* about it, and that took courage. I was secretly pleased because I really needed senior staff who were not completely intimidated by me."

"Poor Dolorian, I hated to hurt her feelings."

"Oh come now, no harm done, and I was very sympathetic. I told her that I had been having similar lover problems myself until recently — it was the first time I had had a love life to talk about, and I was just so proud of myself! After she had a nice long cry and smeared makeup all over my uniform's shoulder I gave her leave for a week to go to the Rutherglen Drinkfest to try to forget you. When she got back she found herself promoted out of Calculor and into Beamflash Comms. She had such a workload that she must have had trouble even remembering her own name for the first month."

Denkar closed his eyes and ran his fingers through Zarvora's bushy hair, trying to recapture what she had been to him until a few minutes earlier, trying to regain her as a lover.

"Everything around me has been controlled. I ... don't know what to say."

"Denkar, darling, after a while a great deal of what I did was actually controlled by wanting to be near *you*, if that makes you feel any better. When I had to start spending so much time away in Kalgoorlie I was torn between being separated from you and telling you everything and risking ... risking a bad reaction."

"The mighty Highliber and OverMayor, frightened of one of her own prisoners?"

"Frightened of losing what we had." She pressed her lips together, then looked down at the crumpled menu. She began trying to smooth it out, as if it was an allegory of Denkar's life. "Concerning your time in the Calculor, all that I can do is apologize. I needed raw calculating power very quickly back in 1696, and you were one of the thousands that I enslaved to get it. Several dozen of the best early FUNCTIONS were as blameless as yourself, I admit it."

"And now they stay while I go free. Tarrin lied to me."

"No, they are to be freed, just as he said. Within a year or two they will be released under the same conditions that I offered to you, but I cannot afford to do that all at once. Think of it this way: if a Mayor ordered you to serve in his army would you refuse? You would have to obey orders, do things that you would rather not, and risk death or enslavement each time you come up against the enemy. If you tried to run away you would be shot for desertion. Is that so very different to the Calculor?"

That analogy had actually occurred to Denkar many times during his years of enforced service. He pondered for a time while Zarvora stroked his hand.

"It was courageous of you, setting me free then telling me all this," he concluded.

"Fras Denkar, I want you of your own free will. I am leaving for Kalgoorlie as soon as I sign a few of Mayor Jefton's powers back to him this evening. A special train will be waiting for me at the Rochester terminus, a military galley engine pulling the Mayoral sleeper car." She slid her arms around his neck and placed her forehead against his. "Will you come with me? Be my friend and my lover, as you were while in the Libris Calculor?"

"In secret, Frelle?" he asked, raising an eyebrow.

"In public, Fras, as the OverMayor's consort. For some time now I have actually been telling people that I have a consort. Many are anxious to meet my mysterious husband who has been too busy to bask in the glories of court life. The captain of the galley engine can marry us, and all the official records can be backdated with the Libris Calculor. We can make up some story about you having such terribly secret work to do that I could not even say that you existed until now."

"Life is hell for the upper classes," sighed Denkar, although he was grinning. He turned away to clasp his hands together on the table and shake his head slowly. "Zarvora ... I can't just change from an unknown prisoner into the consort of the most powerful ruler in the known world. Not in a single afternoon."

"Yes you can, I can give you a briefing on the train. I have some notes all ready —"

Denkar suddenly slid into a fit of laughter, slowly doubling over until his forehead thudded against the tabletop. "My pretty Frelle

Shadowliber, you're just appalling! If only you could hear yourself as I hear you."

"But will you — but no ... no." Zarvora sighed and straightened. "I did not get where I am today by deluding myself." She stood up with awkward, uncoordinated haste. "All right then, I did rather think that nine years enslavement could not be brushed aside so easily. Go your way and build your own life, then. If you ever need more money or get into trouble, just go to any beamflash office. Head your message like this:" She wrote *NEWFELD*CYBELINE* on the corner of the menu and tore it off. "It will reach me, rest assured, and unless I am dead, I shall help. My secret and mysterious husband will have to remain just that."

He held out his hand to her. Zarvora offered hers in turn, but instead of the parting kiss that she expected, Denkar pulled her back down to the seat beside him and jangled the brass bell on the table. They stared into each other's eyes in silence for the moments that the waiter took to arrive. He flung the door open theatrically, with his slate poised and a chalk between his teeth, a knowing grin on his face and his eyebrows arching in a rhythmic and vaguely lewd fashion.

"My wife and I would like to order now, if you please," said Denkar smoothly.

*****

Three thousand kilometres to the west a very different conversation was wending its way toward a rather less optimistic conclusion. An intense, distraught man in an emu leather bush jacket and hobnail boots was pacing the floor of a tavern in Northam, a castellany on the edge of the western Calldeath lands. Seated at a nearby table was a Dragon Silver Librarian from distant Libris, the bands of her rank displayed on a large clasp that fastened her ochre travelling cloak.

Although they were speaking animatedly, the other afternoon patrons of the tavern heard nothing. Darien, the Dragon Librarian, was mute and they were fluttering their hands through the words of Portington sign language.

"I am going back to the Southeast Alliance because you have not changed at all in seven years," Darien signed with slow, emphatic symbols, then thumped the table with her fist for emphasis.

"Me? No change?" he signed in reply. "I learn your history, your language, this sign language, everything for you. I learn your ways too, all your cultures and religions."

"But at heart you do not even like to speak Austaric, Ilyire. Your grammar is all over the place, yet your sister can now speak Austaric as well as the Highliber."

"I fix."

"Grammar is just a symptom," she signed with impatient flourishes. "Jealousy and Alspring protectiveness is the disease. All that I had to do was go out for a drink with the Merredin envoy and there you were, smashing up the tavern and beating him senseless."

"You not tell me about official business. Seem like funny business."

"You should have trusted me."

"I not trust *him*!"

The gesture for 'him' was a violent, slicing stroke, and had a sabre been in Ilyire's hand, the movement would have been little different.

"Ilyire, I am leaving. You are violently over-protective and I cannot stand it."

"Wrong. Am restrained."

"No. You will not accept me for what I am. I am an adult, a fully grown woman. Men have slept with me, have made love with me —"

"You tell who, I kill them!" Ilyire bellowed at the top of his voice, forgetting the sign language, and causing several other patrons to spill their drinks in alarm. He held onto a stay-beam beneath a shelf while he fought his temper back under control.

Darien drummed her fingers on the table for what seemed an agonizingly long time to Ilyire. "So that is an example of your new restraint," she signed as Ilyire sheepishly made a gesture of apology.

Several patrons had their hands on their swaggersticks as she stood up and dropped a copper beside her pewter goblet, but Ilyire did not attempt to stop her as she walked out. The vintner sighed with relief as Ilyire himself left a minute later.

"The Constable's Runners can have 'im if he's want to raise hell in the streets," he said to a serving boy.

"Skinny sort of shadowlad, but strong as ye'd never think, Fras," the boy replied. "That stay-beam's splintered where he gripped it."

The vintner whistled as he scratched at the slivers of wood. "Ee, that be kauri, too. Still, a bullet would stop 'im just the same as you or me, and if he carries on like that much longer it's a Runner's bullet he'll be getting, too."

Ilyire did manage to control his behaviour, however. He went to the stables around the corner and got his horse, then set off to the west for the Calldeath lands. He did not ride particularly hard, for he suspected that worse was to come than he had just experienced in the tavern. He was soon to meet his sister, Theresla.

The Calldeath lands were marked by a drystone wall snaking across the hills, though the boundary varied a few kilometres from time to time, so no wall was really effective, even as a warning. Every week or so a Call would sweep over the land like an invisible, drifting net, luring creatures into the Calldeath lands, where the Call never ceased. Any mammal larger than a cat or terrier would wander off and not return. When Ilyire's horse suddenly became less responsive and settled into a steady walking pace, he knew that he had crossed the boundary.

Like Zarvora, Denkar and his sister, Theresla, Ilyire was an aviad. Birds and reptiles were immune to the Call, and 2,000 years in the past, the dying achievement of the Anglaic civilization had been to incorporate genetic material from birds into the human genome. It had been a rough, blind experiment, and had seemed like a failure at the time, but over the centuries occasional aviads arose in the population. True, humans killed them through blind fear — for being immune to the Call gave them too much of an advantage — but by the Year of Greatwinter's Waning 1706 the aviads' numbers had grown to the point where they had established small, secret settlements in the Calldeath lands that encircled the continent.

By sunset Ilyire was ten kilometres into the Calldeath lands and within sight of a wooden stockade of very recent construction. Its angles and colours were starkly geometrical and vivid against the overgrown leafy jumble of the Calldeath countryside, and it drew his eyes as he approached. He did not pay as much attention as he might to an overhang of branches dripping with vines.

The dirkfang cat that waited in the vine-shrouded cover weighed nearly fifteen kilograms and had fangs three centimetres long. Seven hundred generations earlier its ancestors had sat purring upon human laps and eaten canned pilchards in aspic from saucers on newspapers. The evolutionary predilection for cats to grow heavy and develop huge fangs had been boosted more than anyone could have guessed by the procession of large, mindless animals passing through the Calldeath lands on the way to the sea. Weight was required to pull them down, and large fangs to flay them open to die of blood loss. The balance was delicate. Those dirkfangs that grew too heavy were themselves drawn off by the Call. Lately something had altered in the equation, however: some of the animals could fight back.

The cat sprang with precision rather than surprise in mind. It expected to subdue its prey with a few slashes and bites. Ilyire brought up his well-padded arms as it sprang, then twisted from the saddle as it made contact. The dirkfang was thrown clear in a flurry of dust and scrabbling paws, and it regained its feet to be confronted by a human on his knees and very much aware of what was happening. Ilyire slowly drew a flintlock from his belt and cocked the striker. The big cat mewled and began to inch forward on its belly. Ilyire smiled, then uncocked the striker and returned the gun to his belt.

The cat sprang, but Ilyire executed a turn-dodge, snatching at one outstretched paw, whipping the cat off-balance and slamming it to the ground. Claws slashed through leather, cloth and skin as Ilyire used his superior weight to pin down the animal until he could position himself to slam the heel of his hand into the dirkfang's throat.

He stood back, watching the cat writhing and gasping its life away while his own lacerations began to assert themselves with an increasing urgency. The Call-anchor on his horse had dropped when his weight had been removed from the saddle switch, and the grapples were now snagged on a vine-smothered bush. He bent over the dirkfang, seized its head and twisted.

The sun was down by now, and the glow of Mirrorsun was rising above the trees in the east. Tonight it was a glowing red oval in the middle of the band. There was also a faint orange corona. By the ruddy light, Ilyire saw a single aviad emerge from the stockade as he led his Call-enraptured horse toward the gate.

"So, cutting it fine tonight, Fras," said the man, who was in his early fifties. "The cats are out and about here, and they've still not learned to leave us alone."

"Unlucky," said Ilyire, heaving the body of the dirkfang off his saddle. "Cat did not kill me."

Ilyire flung the body into the compound and then dragged his horse into the stables. The older aviad whistled as he examined the dead cat.

"No cuts, Fras. You — you clubbed it down with a swagger stick, yes?"

"No. Bare hands. Very macho. Yes?"

"Yes, well, yes indeed, Fras Ilyire. You will be wanting the pelt and fangs, of course, but —"

"But nothing. Have scratches, have good fight. That's all I want. You keep body."

Ilyire left the stables and entered the stockade's little hall. He removed his torn leathers and unrolled a medician's kit. The air grew sweet with the scent of eucalyptus oil as he began to clean his scratches. The other aviad brought a kettle of hot water over from the grate and poured it into a bowl beside him.

"So so, you are depressed again, Fras."

"Hurt from scratches dulls hurt in heart."

"More fighting with your sister, Theresla?"

"Always fighting with Theresla, that nothing new. This ... something else."

"Another woman, a romantic interest, perchance?"

"Honour holds me silent."

"Now then, I — ah, I hear the others with their horses. They have the counter-Call wagon quite close now. In a day, perhaps two, we can leave the Highliber's precious rockets for the Callbait beyond the boundary."

Ilyire was glad of a change of subject, and seized on the rockets before the talk drifted back to his personal affairs.

"We had rockets in Alspring. War rockets big as two metres and made of brass. What special about ancient rockets?"

"They're big, Fras, that's what makes them special. They be built in three pieces that boost each other higher, and the biggest piece is nine metres long on the four rockets that are on the wagon."

"Nine metres. Big, yes, is big. But how could Highliber shoot, ah, ancient and complex thing?"

"Oh they're simple enough in principle. Just an enormously strong tube filled with explosive. Simple, fantastic things, they are, and the metal seems as strong as ever after 2,000 years in that museum. There were other types of rockets there too, types to use liquid explosives, but Frelle Zarvora wanted nothing to do with them. She said that she would have enough trouble making a solid explosive for such simple rockets as these."

"Black gunpowder is plentiful."

"Ah no, the explosive must be much more powerful."

"More powerful than black gunpowder! That is wonder indeed."

The other aviads were inside the stockade by now, dragging and prodding their Call-bemused horses into the stables and exclaiming at the body of the dirkfang. Soon three men and two women entered the hall. Ilyire recognized Sondian, a councillor from the Macedon settlement in the Southeast Alliance.

"Ilyire, you're back in the west again," Sondian said as he caught sight of the Alspring Ghan by the fire. "Did you kill that dirkfang out there?"

"Was me. Where my sister?"

"Not with us. She's much further in, at the Perth abandon. How did you kill —"

"Who is with her?"

"Nobody."

"Then how you know where she be?"

Sondian's warm welcome rapidly chilled. "She stayed here. She told us of her plans. Then she travelled on alone."

"Where did she sleep? Who slept with her?"

Sondian slowly drew a well worn flintlock and pulled back the striker until there was a soft click. He cradled the gun in both hands as he stood leaning against a kauri pillar.

"Listen and listen carefully, Ilyire the Ghan from Glenellen. You may be twice as strong as a comparable man, faster of reflex and immune to the Call, but remember that we're all aviads here so everything that makes you special is just ordinary. If you want to live among us, you must observe our manners and courtesies."

"Will not have my sister defiled!" Ilyire shouted, flinging down his mug and standing.

Sondian looked at him for a moment, then gently released the striker and tossed his gun to one of the women. At his signal the three other aviad men began to close in on Ilyire.

"Best not to reach for the gun, Fras," said the woman holding Sondian's flintlock.

Ilyire lunged, throwing a punch at Sondian. The Ghan's reflexes were attuned to dealing with humans, and Sondian easily dodged him, seizing his arm and throwing him over his shoulder and onto a chair, which smashed. Ilyire was pinned down at once, and they removed his gun.

"Get him out," said Sondian.

"The stables?" asked one of the men pinning Ilyire's arms.

"Right outside. If he can kill dirkfangs with his bare hands, he should be safe enough."

Ilyire was stood up and marched toward the door, with a man holding each arm. Sondian strode up behind him, and without warning delivered a bone-jarringly hard kick to his backside with a heavy hob-nailed boot. Ilyire cried out and collapsed.

"Get out, crawl," snarled Sondian. "There are too few aviads and too many humans for us to fight among ourselves. I'll beamflash the guards at the counter-Call wagon to offer you no assistance, and to shoot to kill if you come too close."

Ilyire turned his head. "You defiled my sister —"

Sondian backhanded Ilyire across the face, striking him so hard that the Ghan lost his senses for a moment. When he revived Sondian was gripping him by the hair.

"Listen well, you pathetic little worm. Not only did I not touch your strange and demented sister, but I am greatly insulted by the insinuation that I might have. Now take your filthy, twisted, diseased, perverted little mind and get out!"

Ilyire spent the night beside the stockade, huddled by a fire of offcuts left by the carpenters and wainwrights. He kept watch as shapes warily prowled in the distance and spent his time making a crutch and fire-hardened T-spear. In the morning, soon after the aviad men had left with their horses to return to the wagons, he turned his back on the rising sun and limped off into the west.

Sondian watched from the crude gallery of the beamflash scaffold.

"If we're lucky the dirkfang cats may eat him."

"From what I've seen of his sister, *she* may eat him. Did you see her catching mice when she was here, and —"

"Yes, and that's enough. Strange, though, that compared to him she's actually sensible and civilized in her own way. At least she goes to the trouble to hold up a mask to hide her strangeness. Sometimes."

"I suppose that we all do, Fras."

"Yes, yes, yes. Release his horse and leave the anchor pinned, the Call will lure it west along the road. It will pass him quickly, and he may be able to catch it."

"Generous and gracious of you, Fras."

"Well, his sister may be hungry."

Ilyire limped along slowly, now very careful to watch for lurking cats and other predators. Presently he encountered the rocket transport wagons. Musket barrels followed him as he approached, and until he was out of sight. The wagon containing the rockets was the biggest that he had ever seen, but the ancient devices themselves were swathed in ropes and tarpaulins. The counter-Call wagon that pulled it was far more striking. It was long enough to accommodate twelve horses, side by side, on the tray. They were being strapped into their frames as Ilyire went past, and he noticed that they faced backwards to the west where the Call was luring them. Their hoofs drove two articulated treadmills, which in turn drove the wheels through a gearbox. The horses mindlessly strained to walk west, but the engine-wagon travelled east, pulling the wagon loaded with rockets behind it. It was a device that could only ever have been used by aviads in the Calldeath lands, where the Call never ceased.

Some time later Ilyire's own horse caught up with him as it followed the Call west. He was mightily glad to be able to ride again, even though it hurt to sit in the saddle.

*****

Ilyire surveyed the overgrown buildings and towers of the Perth abandon systematically, looking for the standard sign of habitation in abandons. It had been two days, and although he had encountered signs of recent exploration and salvage work, there was no — but there it was, fluttering in the wind from the sea. A flag, the one object that could not have lasted two millennia, and could not have been put there by any other than an aviad.

Theresla was living in what had once been a luxurious serviced home unit. It was now on the new littoral that had extended into the streets of the Perth abandon. Ilyire blew his whistle to announce himself, then dismounted. His horse strained to continue west, and into the water.

"Can't drag you all way back," he said as if in apology, then pulled his saddlebags off and released the reins.

The horse immediately set off for the water, and went splashing in until it could begin swimming. He took out his telescope and followed its progress until its head was lost amid the greenish-grey choppy waves of what seemed to be quite a large bay.

"A cruel experiment," observed a voice behind him, and Ilyire jerked around to discover Theresla watching him.

"Sister!" he exclaimed.

She was staring at him from barely three metres away — a girl-woman half a head shorter than himself, with her hair braided into a bushy pony-tail. She was dressed in the tie-cotton green and red tunic and trews of the other aviads, Ilyire noted with instant disapproval. Her expression was very odd, intense, calculating, almost hungry, and somehow devoid of the mischief and mockery that she always reserved for him.

"What of my books?" she asked.

Ilyire took a package from his saddlebags and tossed it to her. He did not attempt any more friendly form of greeting.

"You don't want them," he said sullenly. "You wanted me away, only."

"Think what you will," she said, turning away and gesturing for him to follow.

Theresla began to walk away, and Ilyire fell in beside her as they made their way amid crumbled buildings smothered with vines. The trees were now higher than most of the ruins, and were loud with the buzzing and clicking of insects in the heat of the day. Miraculously, some of the ancient towers had retained their shape over two millennia, and looked like oblong, sharp-edged hills under their mantles of green vines.

Theresla explained that a dirkfang had been stalking Ilyire as he watched his horse swimming away. They did not always hunt by night. Theresla had sent it off, but instead of seeming grateful Ilyire admonished her.

"Why you living here? This dangerous place."

"I am alone, Ilyire. Surely that should please you."

"You should be safe. Safe from dangers. Safe from desires."

"So what do you suggest?"

"Return to Kalgoorlie. Set up convent. Spread our great Alspring Orthodox Gentheist faith."

Theresla stopped and gestured to the vine-smothered trees and mounds that had once been buildings.

"These have not been disturbed in nineteen centuries," shc said. "Further inland the buildings have been torn apart to build our new fortresses and towns. Here in the Calldeath region the buildings just crumble slowly back into the land. Precious little is left for all the glory of the Anglaic civilization."

"I know all that. Anglaics walk on moon, now trees grow in their roads. So what? Nothing by sinful mortals be built is lasting."

A few minutes later they reached the overgrown pile of masonry that was Theresla's unit. She opened the shutters to the barred windows and skylight, and Ilyire was surprised how light and ventilated her living space was.

"We can learn a lot from what is here, in this undisturbed abandon," she said. "Aviads do not arise among the peoples of the western Mayorates and castellanies, it is something in their genototem. Thus this abandon has not been disturbed since the Call first began to scour the land. What is here is what was here in 2021, in the old dating."

"So. You study abandon before is disturbed?"

"Yes. Now that the Highliber has secretly brought aviad settlers across from the southeast, there will be plundering and disturbance, even with the best of intentions."

"Met some. Bastards."

"You fought with them, I learned of that from my beamflash link," she said, jabbing his chest with her finger. "That was stupid of you. Ilyire, the glories of ancient science are all around you, yet all that fills your mind is sex and suspicion. Look around you, what do you see?"

Ilyire snorted impatiently, then sullenly turned to look out through the heavy mesh and bars protecting the window. Beyond was a wide expanse of water.

"Those things like blocks in water, over west," he said, pointing. "They look to be big beamflash towers."

"But they are too close together to be that," Theresla replied.

"Used water for defence against freebooters?" he suggested.

"According to the old maps of Perth, those towers were once on dry land. The water is higher than it used to be."

He took the map from her and studied it for some time. Theresla leaned against the mesh of the window, extending her senses to probe for the consciousness that lived in the water.

"There is a point empathic activity away out there in that bay, and part of this continual Call comes from there," she said.

"So what?" grunted Ilyire.

She raised her eyes to the skylight. "All right, then. Let's speculate on what took place after the 21st Century. For whatever reason, the world was becoming warmer. Zarvora's studies have come across countless references to the burning of coal by artisans, and other terms that are not yet understood. The consensus was that the sea level would rise, and that water out there is called the sea. Mirrorsun was an attempt to reverse this warming. The machines that created it worked too slowly, though, and it is 2,000 years too late."

"So. Band-in-sky has uses."

"It's trying to restore the world to what it was in earlier centuries."

"Don't understand all this burning of fossils. What for us to learn? If world warmer, what of Greatwinter?"

"I have many answers, Ilyire, but not all the answers," concluded Theresla. "Come with me and look at some of the marvels I have found. It's better than talk. There is a museum not far from here. It was well built, and it has not collapsed under the weight of vines and centuries."

*****

They entered warily, looking for predators that might be lurking inside. The museum was a series of high-ceilinged, spacious hallways, but they were now dark caverns because of the vines smothering the windows. Most of the exhibits were either cumpled piles of corrosion or encrusted with mould and bat droppings. The few surviving exhibits were incomprehensible to Ilyire. There was a musty, feline scent, and the flapping of bat wings high above them. Theresla unclipped a tinder-lock from her belt, lit the fuse to a paper-wrapped charge, then tossed it ahead of her. The blast was a sharp, echoing whiplash, and two tabby shapes frantically scrambled from their lairs and streaked out of the building.

"The dirkfangs can be befriended, but it takes time," she explained. "I discovered those rockets that you saw on the counter-Call transporter in here. Something of their workings was described on that slab of very hard polished rock over to the left."

There were a dozen rockets left in the display amid the crumbling exhibits, all with faded paintwork, and with their nose cones partly cut away to display the complexity of the payloads. Ilyire surveyed them uncomprehendingly.

"Two thousand years old," said Theresla. "Most materials of the old civilization technology are brittle and useless after such a time has passed. Not the rockets. They are made of something more durable."

"And those men came here with their reverse-wagon?"

"To remove four of the rockets, yes. There were two aviad women and the Highliber as well. Zarvora studied the rockets and their plaques for an entire day before deciding upon which ones to remove. She really does intend to make them work again."

"Where did they sleep?"

She stared at him, hands on hips. "Ilyire, you amaze me. Someone comes here with a team of assistants to revive the glories of the old civilization, and all that you can think of is whether or not one of them slept with your sister."

"There! You said it!" Ilyire cried. "You slept with one. It was Sondian, I know it."

"Sondian, a fine man and a good leader, an example for other aviads to —"

"He defiled you, then he beat me. Know his kind. Domination pervert. Power and sex same for him. I hunt him down, I kill him."

"Ilyire I did not unload my virginity on him or anyone else, and I'll thank you to leave Sondian alone. He's the leader of the colony here, and they need his wisdom and leadership."

"I bring his head in bag, I show you. Rent he put in your honour be fix. Where are guns? Want guns. You give me that one you carry."

Theresla drew the flintlock from her belt. Ilyire started eagerly forward, then froze as she cocked the striker and pointed it at his chest. It had a short barrel, but a bore of at least 45 points.

"You have turned yourself into a thing, half-brother, so I am treating you as a thing."

She fired, looking straight into his eyes. Ilyire saw a flash before Theresla vanished behind the cloud of smoke that belched out between them.

*****

Ilyire awoke in the late afternoon, lying alone and exactly where he had fallen. Needles seemed to stab at his chest each time he breathed, and the pain increased when he sat up. His hidden metal breastplate had absorbed the impact of the shot, but not before buckling inwards and breaking two ribs. There was quite an impressive hole in his tunic.

Using his knife he cut the straps of the breastplate away, and the pain lessened at once. He looked at Theresla's footprints in the dust and felt an unfamiliar numbness. She had shot him. There had been death in her eyes and she had shot him. She had not laid his body out in the way prescribed in the scriptures, she had shot him and left him where he had fallen.

"I ... am dead," he said experimentally, and his voice echoed through the ancient gallery.

He looked around. His saddlebags and T-spear were where he had dropped them. Theresla had wanted nothing from him, she had merely removed an annoyance.

"Sondian bestrode you," he hissed slowly and maliciously, but no slash of white-hot rage cut across his heart. "Sondian defiled Theresla!" he shouted at the top of his voice, then mingled demented laughter with the lingering echoes.

Ilyire felt that he stood there for an eternity, robbed of direction and purpose. The light was fading as he finally removed his breastplate and pounded out the dent using a hammer left by Sondian's crew. At the back of his mind something was bothering him, and suddenly he had it: Theresla's expression had been the same when she had shot him as when she had first come up behind him. She had meant to kill him all along.

Taking a stub of wax crayon from his saddlebags Ilyire selected a clear area of wall and began to write. It hurt to reach up, but he was glad of the pain as it seemed to blot out something else that he did not want to face. He stood back to survey the yellow capitals.

ILYIRE ALIVE.
DAMN THERESLA.
NOT WORTHY TO SMELL FART.

On his way out of the Calldeath lands Ilyire noted that the dirkfangs left him alone. He was walking against the perennial Call, and the cats knew to leave any creature alone which could do that.

*****

A procession of burlap-clad figures walked steadily across the red desert landscape of frost-shattered pebbles and sand, in single file and in step, and led by the abbot of Baelsha monastery. In the distance was a cairn of rocks, growing more distinct and larger as they approached. The abbot walked around the cairn as they arrived, then entered the cramped alcove within it that faced away to the south. Once satisfied that all was in order for the monks to go to work on it, he stood back.

The place was soon swept clean, and the heavy cistern bolted to the wall of the shelter was checked. Two of the monks unpacked flatbread and dates wrapped in greasepaper. They carefully stored the food on a rock ledge that served as a pantry. While the abbot watched, the monks unlaced the necks of four goatskins of water and emptied them into the cistern in the gloom of the alcove.

Returning outside again, the abbot gestured to three other monks who had taken no part in the preparation of the alcove. The taller of them began to strip off his clothing of burlap and cotton, and finally his flat wicker hat, so that he stood naked before the abbot in the intense desert sunlight.

A slight shake of the abbot's head sent the other six monks running to make a row behind their now naked companion. They stood to attention with their feet together.

"Re!" barked the abbot, and all bowed from the waist.

The abbot took a small book from the slingbag across his back and beckoned the naked monk to step forward. He handed the book to him, then stepped back. They bowed to each other again.

"Brother Glasken, you are about to embark upon the most important ten days of your life," the abbot said sternly as Glasken stood before him, clutching the book. "This is the culmination of five years of celibacy, abstinence, prayer, fasting, freedom from the vices of the world, and training in the ways of our pure but demanding martial arts. There were many times, Brother Glasken, that I thought you would fall from our regime but you proved me wrong, I am pleased to admit. Here now is your final and greatest test.

"In five days or so, the Call will come, the Call that rolls across the land and sweeps untethered men, women and children out of their lives and south to oblivion. When the seductive touch of the Call reaches into your soul to draw you away, you must resist it with no more than your mind and willpower, as we have taught you. With no tether, sand-anchor, trained Call-terriers, or Call-walls, you will resist its allure. You have nothing to wear, and only straw to sleep beneath in the cold of the desert night. Nothing that you have to hand can be used to tether yourself. Brother Glasken, do you wish to step back from this final test?"

"I do not, your reverence."

"Brother Glasken, you can return with us to Baelsha Monastery. The hamstring tendon in your right leg will be severed, but nothing more will happen to you. You will live out your life as a gardener with us. It would be an honoured existence of prayer and meditation. Do you wish to step back from this final test?"

"I do not, your reverence."

"Brother Glasken, should you resist the Call you will become a full monk of Baelsha, bound by your vows of poverty, chastity and obedience, bound to my authority, bound by death should you ever try to leave. Should it be God's will that the Call prove too strong for you, you will walk out into the desert and die within a few days. Do you wish to step back from this final test?"

"I do not, your reverence."

"Then by your own free will do I bind you to this test. Re!"

They all bowed from the waist again, then the abbot stepped forward with a broad smile and shook Glasken's hand.

"Please, get out of the sun and into the shelter, Brother Glasken," he said genially. "Pray and prepare yourself, but have no fear. Should you fail, you will be in paradise within a few days."

"But if I should resist the Call, your reverence, it would put the rest of my lifetime between me and paradise. You almost make it more attractive to fail."

The abbot put a fatherly arm across the naked monk's shoulder and gestured to the shelter. "I know what you mean, Brother Glasken, but hold the set of your mind very carefully. Should you have a desire to surrender to the Call, why that would be suicide. That would be jumping into hell!"

"Your reverence, I understand. Even after all these five years at Baelsha sometimes a little joke slips past my guard."

"Ah, Brother Glasken, guard against laughter. Remember, all laughter is at the expense of someone, and in this case it is yourself. Should the devil make you chuckle just as the Call arrives, you may have his company for all of eternity."

"Your warning is the staff with which I shall beat him, your reverence."

"God's will be done. Work hard and pass the test, Brother Glasken. You have been my greatest challenge so far."

Four figures trudged away from the cairn, this time in a less formal step. The abbot's head was low as he walked.

"Five years ago he crawled into our vegetable garden from the desert, starving and crazed with thirst," the abbot said to the others. "Could he really have come all the way from the Alspring cities, as he claimed? And if so, what drove him to face the immensity of the desert?"

"A fugitive from justice, your reverence?" said the monk carrying Glasken's clothing and hat.

"Perhaps. Or perhaps he really is what he says he is: a lost philosopher and explorer, who had been charting the extent of the land. A strange and ... a *driven* man is Brother Glasken. I hope with all my heart that he is not taken by the Call. The years that I have dedicated to bringing his lusts and passions under control have seen the greatest challenges I have faced since I took this office."

Glasken watched the monks fading into the heat shimmers at the horizon, gibbering to himself softly.

"Alone at last, and with ten days before they return. Soon there will be others I can talk to freely — aside from myself. Myself! The only civilized company at Baelsha, that's what you are, Johnny Glasken. Ah... I've kept myself sane by talking to myself for five years, but very soon John Glasken will talk to John Glasken no more."

At last he decided that the monks really were gone. He darted into the shelter, as eager and excited as he had been on the morning of his third Christmas.

He reached into the cistern, stretching down until his head was almost submerged. There they were! Dozens of pebbles wrapped in squares of cloth, and ten tightly-tied leather bundles. Glasken fished them out by the handful, gasping with relief as much as for breath.

"Ten little waterskins of rat, cat and bird, thirty squares of cloth, and the thread and thonging that bound them while they travelled within the waterskins. Now, little prayer book, answer my prayers." He eased back the cover boards of the prayer book and peered between the spine and the binding. "A scrap of razor and a needle — everything's here, everything!"

Glasken began to sew the squares of cloth together, his fingers flashing along to leave well-practised stitches behind them. He muttered dementedly as he worked.

"My magic carpet to carry me away from here to the Western Mayorates, to women, wine, revels, seduction, women, money, gambling, bawdy singing, women, more women..."

Once his kilt and a sun-cape were complete, Glasken used the razor to dress some of the straw, which he quickly wove into a wide conical hat. His water pouches seemed depressingly small as he filled them, but he also gorged himself on water, dates and flatbread. Every so often he checked outside, making sure that the abbot had not decided to creep back to check on him.

Using some of the thonging, Glasken strapped several pieces of flatbread and some dates between the hat and his shaven head. He carefully left the book in a corner, open in mid-prayer, then he rumpled the straw as if he had been sleeping in it. Another check outside, and Glasken estimated that the sun had less than an hour to set. He looked out to the west, to where the abbot and other monks had disappeared. He laughed to himself and spoke to the horizon.

"Careful you were to inspect me, Abbot Haleforth, but you never thought that I'd break into *your* rooms and inspect *your* pack, aye, *and* put a needle and razor into that little book that you've been torturing me with for all these years past. I know you packed a telescope, you scabby old fox, I know you're sitting out there squinting back at me. Well then, roast in the sun while I recline and feast in the cool of my stone verandah. Roast, for when you set forth for your monastery at sunset, I'll set forth too, but I'll be going south. Roast, all of ye lazy lackey monks as well, who doubtless wondered which kind and charitable soul had already filled those four goatskins with water when they came into in the kitchen at dawn — aye, and had laced up the necks good and tight. Pah, lock the pantry against hungry monastic prowlers of the night will ye, Abbot Haleforth? Well ye never thought to lock the water cistern as well!"

As the last glow of the sun was fading from the sky, Glasken drank from the cistern until he was almost sick, then set off for the south. He moved at a slow, shambling pace to leave tracks as if he was in the grip of the Call. As he walked he glanced back at the cairn, then to the west where Baelsha was two days walk distant.

"Goodbye, Baelsha," said Glasken with a wave to the faintly glowing horizon. "Give me long enough and I'll bed a wench and drink a pint for each and every one of you, aye, even though you number twice twelve dozen."

Using the stars and Mirrorsun as clock and compass, he continued due south. When the waning moon rose to augment Mirrorsun's orange light he broke into a steady jog-trot across the rocky sand. Often he stumbled, sometimes he fell, but he pressed on in high spirits. Not long after the sun rose he drained two of his precious little water pouches and carefully bound them to his feet with thonging from around his neck. His tough soles were now bleeding from several small gashes, but Glasken padded the makeshift sandals with some of his flatbread.

Brother John Glasken of Baelsha Monastery had managed to travel an incredible 100 kilometres at the end of two nights and one searingly-hot day. Five years of training and discipline had given him quite extraordinary powers of endurance. His routine in the days that followed was to sleep during the hottest part of the day, with his cotton sheet rigged as a sunshade. Glasken was experienced with survival in the desert after his three ordeals a half-decade earlier, but although raw lizards and snakes supplemented his flatbread and dates, his water diminished faster than he had planned. His rate of progress dropped as well, and he was soon making less than 50 kilometres per day.

On the eighth day a pile of whitened bones appeared in his path. By now Glasken was limping heavily, and welcomed any chance to stop. He squatted and examined the skeleton, which had been partly scattered by scavengers. Lying beside the pelvis was a dagger with the Baelsha cross engraved on the blade. A little purse nearby had rotted to reveal six coins, all from the Kalgoorlie Mayorate. Glasken scooped up the dagger and coins, then noticed something long and straight lying half-buried in the sand: a staff!

"Alas, Brother, I mourn for you," he said as he knelt in the sand, his hand on the skull, "and may your soul rest in peace. How did you ever get all these things past that old devil and his watch-monks? Or perhaps you brought these at the expense of food and water-skins. Very foolish, but I appreciate your sacrifice."

Glasken stood up, leaning gratefully on the staff. "I'll buy a candle for you in that underground Christian cathedral at Kalgoorlie, and then I'll drink to your memory with a pretty wench in some tavern. Meantime, I'd best be limping on. By my estimate the Great Western Paraline is still 100 kilometres away, and my water ran out this morning."

*****

The wind train was nothing more than a speck amid the shimmers on the horizon as it came into sight from the platform at the Naretha railside. A small group of people stood watching as it approached, its array of tall, tubular rotors and their framework of masts and rigging distinct above the flat, sleek body. The Railside Master looked at the register in his hand, then at the schedule plate. Away on the wind train, at the forward masthead, a twinkling of light began, and almost at once a bell clanged for attention at the base of the station's beamflash relay tower. The Railside Master strode over, trying to seem neither casual nor anxious. The register board bore the code of Highliber Zarvora.

"That's her, the Highliber is on that train."

All at once the railside's militia ran to take up guard positions, leaving a group of a dozen men in gearjack coveralls and a single traveller standing on the platform.

The rotors of the train had been disengaged, and were spinning freely as it approached. Its brakes were squealing and shuddering. As it came to a stop the gearjacks jumped down and ran with cans of sunflower oil to the oil traps at the axle heads of the coaches, while others crawled beneath the wind engine to attend to the bearing wells. They felt them for overheating first, then topped up the lubricating oil. Fires in badly-maintained traps were not so much possible as likely. Each of the huge steel-rimmed, wood laminate mansel wheels was then inspected for warping and slippage. High above them the riggers adjusted and tuned the ropes, masts and spars that held the spinning rotor tubes vertical.

Two passengers stepped out onto the platform, glad of a chance to be on solid ground for a few minutes. The Railside Master stood nervously with his clipboard, noting that one of the passengers was a tall woman dressed in an inspector's uniform of the Libris Beamflash Network, and with her black, bushy hair clipped back from her face with silver orbile combs. She nodded to him, just a single, curt nod that all was in order and satisfactory as far as she was concerned. The Railside Master threw a quick salute back, then busied himself with his board, writing "Inspected by OverMayor Zarvora. Found to be satisfactory."

As the crew began to load water and supplies aboard, a man detached himself from a group of gangers sheltering from the sun beneath the railside awning. He walked up to the overgear.

"Greetings of the afternoon, honourable Fras Overgear," the tall, tanned man said in a strange amalgam of Alliance and Kargoorlie accents. "I wish to work a passage west, I wish to serve aboard your glorious broad-gauge Great Western Paraline wind train."

The overgear looked him up and down. He was big and strong, with muscles balanced in good proportion. A blanket roll was slung over his shoulder, a dagger and small waterpouch at his belt. He held an ashwood staff that seemed very weathered, and his patched olive trews, tunic and cap were the type that the paraline gangers wore. His sandals looked several sizes too small, however. When he removed his cap for the bow's flourish there was about a fortnight's stubble visible on his scalp.

"Did you arrive on an earlier train's crew, and were you thrown off?" the overgear asked.

"I've not worked on a wind train for years, but I was once a cabin boy and runner, then an apprentice gearjack."

"You're hardly a cabin boy now. We do need extra hands for rotor windlass and gearjack work, but we have no time to spare on training anyone. What can you offer us?"

"Strength to wind the rotors up and down, and to screw down the brakeblocks. I can tell when an oil trap is running hot on the axle head, and when a rim or flange has slipped its seating on the mansel." *Mind you*, thought Glasken, *I only learned all those terms by listening to gearjacks and riggers singing tuning shanties in the Rail's End tavern years ago, but you don't have to know that.* "I've also had training in beamflash towers, so I know the unsecured codes."

The overgear was more impressed that he showed. Too much enthusiasm, and the stranger might expect to be paid as well.

"Aye ... well that's a start. We're short of a relief beamflash monitor ... and you're strong besides. If you could do what you're told and work the gears and handles on order, then take over at the beamflash seat as needed, we might give you passage to Kalgoorlie."

"That's all that I want."

"How did you get out here to Naretha?"

"I've been in the desert to the north for two years, meditating. Now I want to return to Kalgoorlie."

"So, a hermit. And what is your name?"

"John."

"Just John?"

"John Glasken."

The overgear considered. He was experienced at picking fugitives and troublemakers, but this one had no obvious hallmarks of either.

"Well then, Fras John Glasken, you're on approval. Start by loading those boxes beside the warehouse into the supply wagon."

The overgear went over to the Railside Master as Glasken got to work.

"What do you know of him?" he asked.

The Railside Master scratched the back of his neck, then looked across to where Glasken was working. "He arrived about a week ago, wearing rags and crawling along the paraline from the west. He was raving with thirst, and by the look of his stubble his head seemed to have been shaved recently."

"What was his story?"

"Once he had regained his senses he said he was a student of Cordabeldian theology who had gone out into the desert to meditate. He got so engrossed in his meditation that he ran his supplies down too far. He had some coins, and he used them to pay for the food and clothing that we gave him. He even has a couple of Kalgoorlie silver nobles left."

The overgear rubbed his chin as he looked across at Glasken, who was obviously working hard to impress him.

"So you had no trouble with him?"

"Oh no, he's worked well. My gangers have nothing but praise for him, they say he can do the work of ten men — in fact when I did my noon inspection yesterday there were ten men sitting idle and only Glasken working, yet still the rails, baulks and transoms were stacked in good order by the evening. And speaking of evenings, why Fras, you would think that the man had not been to a revel in five years. He led the singing, led the drinking races, and then played jigs, reels, flings and half-skips on my old lutina until the men had danced themselves into collapse."

"What? And he claims to be a religious hermit?"

"The Cordabeldians believe that some sin is permissible as long as penance is done for it. Perhaps this one was building up credit for a few sins to come."

They both laughed. "So, he appears to be good natured and diligent, as well as muscled for honest work. A splendid combination, that, aye and I did sense a hint of education in his speech. I'll keep an eye on him, but he could be a rare good recruit. We had to crew this train in such a hurry that full shifts could not be covered." He bent closer and winked conspiratorially. "Like to know where this broadline engine was engaged?"

"Why, Peterborough — oh no! You don't mean to say that the broad gauge track has reached Morgan."

"No less. It's not official, of course, but were you to have a little celebration once this train has gone ..."

"Why yes, ah ... Mr Brunel's 2132nd birthday anniversary is not for two months, but we could always celebrate it early."

"I'd best return to my work. Long life and broad gauge, good Fras."

"Long life and broad gauge."

The stopover was done in 45 minutes, and Glasken joined the gearjacks as they unscrewed the brake blocks and released the wheels. The overgear waited for the captain to ring through for primary torque, then the brass arrow of the dial slipped forward a notch. At the overgear's signal each gearmate pushed back the clutch lever-rack and engaged the gear boxes to the bank of rotors that spun in the wind. The rotor engines strained forward against the couplings, then the train began to roll west again. There was a ragged cheer from the waving gangers who had come to see Glasken off, all of them looking the worse for the carousing of the night before.

From inside the luxurious Mayoral coach Denkar noted the send-off. "Someone popular seems to have joined us," he remarked to Zarvora.

"The overgear recruited an extra gearjack just now," she replied, without looking up from the ancient text that she was studying.

"He's being farewelled by a lot of men who look as if they have very bad hangovers. He must be quite a drinker."

"If he is a rake and drunkard named Glasken, I have a five year old reward of a thousand gold royals outstanding for him."

Denkar turned from the window. "Who is Glasken?"

"You may know him as FUNCTION 3084, one of the only two men ever to escape from either of my calculors."

"FUNCTION 3084, the big lutina player! Yes, I remember that one. Ah, but from what I remember of him, dearest Frelle, if he were still alive he would surely have been arrested by someone for something else by now. Were that the case, you would soon have been informed."

"True, Fras Den, too true. There is no way that Fras Glasken could have been kept out of trouble for five years unless he has been gelded by the Alspring Ghans or killed."

She put down her book and patted the seat beside her. Denkar walked across the gently-rocking floor and sat down with an arm around her shoulders.

"Now, to continue your briefing on Kalgoorlie sciences," she said. "We in the Alliance are ahead of them in calculor technology, optics, code theory and a few other related areas. They have nothing like Libris, however. It is a treasure house of texts that the Kalgoorlian edutors and engineers have never been able to fully appreciate. They are particularly weak in calculor programming, but then we have had a head start, and have been perfecting our techniques operationally since 1696."

Denkar turned and peered into a microscope which was bolted to a bracket in Zarvora's desk. Beneath the objective, a human hair lay beside one of his own and one of Zarvora's. The latter two certainly had a fluffy, feathery appearance.

"When can I meet some more fellow aviads?"

Zarvora thought for a moment. "There are two other aviads working in the Calldeath lands to the far west, in an abandon known as Perth. They are brother and sister, a pair of Alspring Ghans named Theresla and Ilyire. Theresla is a little unconventional, to say the least, and Ilyire is a very moral and upright Orthodox Gentheist who is coping badly with our civilization and its Liberal Gentheist, Christian and Islamic mixture."

"Alspring Ghans, I have read a little about them in Calculor data stream reports."

"How did you get access to those as an unsecured component?"

"Oh, allow me a few secrets please, Frelle Zar, it shows what a clever component I was. So, there is an isolated civilization in the deserts to the north of the Nullarbor Plain."

"Yes. Those two aviads arrived some six years ago as part of a scientific expedition. They stayed to work with us. Like you and me, they are immune to the Call."

"Are all of them aviads to the north?"

"No, they are as rare there as in the Alliance. A few of their more adventurous traders now bring camel caravans to Maralinga Railside to trade, and samples of their hair show all to be human. We have no political contacts as yet, but they will come in their own good time.

"Theresla has been doing some very good work. She discovered a museum in the Perth abandon, and within it were several large, ancient rockets. Other aviads have plundered the Calldeath abandons in the eastern part of the continent, but here in the west the abandons are untouched. Aviads appear not to arise among the peoples of the west, I do not know why. Whatever the reason, there are things in the half-drowned abandon of Perth that I need to transport to the paraline terminus at Northam. Big, heavy rockets and other things. I have arranged for some aviads from Macedon, a secret community in the eastern Calldeath lands, to come across and do the work. In return, they have a whole, new unoccupied Calldeath area to explore and settle in."

"So there is an organized community of aviads in the southeastern Calldeath region?"

"Oh there are plenty more, Den, but their approach to the constrictions on our world is not in accord with my views. Still, we have a lot of goods and services to exchange, and they perform good work in the Calldeath lands for me. How ... broadminded are you?"

"Broadminded?" The question caught him by surprise, and he peered into the microscope again while he mused. "I'm no John Glasken, and lewdness for its own sake holds nothing for me, but I would tolerate anything harmless in other folk. Scholarship and technology is my interest. Give me a good enough reason and I would do most anything for you, though, Zar."

"I may have to call in your word on that," said Zarvora, looking uncomfortable.

"Ah but, Frelle Zar, give me a *scientific* reason and I would do it willingly besides."

*****

After the vast expanse of the Nullarbor Plain, Denkar welcomed the occasional scatter of trees that soon thickened into an open eucalypt forest as the train slowly rumbled west with a light breeze spinning its rotors. An inspector of customs came aboard at Coonana, but he did no more than exchange pleasantries with the distinguished guest of his Mayor. John Glasken watched with puzzled relief from his hiding place behind the rear-starboard gearbox in the primary rotor engine. The inspector strode past through the access corridor without the slightest attempt at a search for lurking aliens who lacked border papers.

"Someone important aboard," he muttered, still unable to break the habit of talking to himself that had kept him sane for five years.

They rolled into Kalgoorlie two days later, after being delayed by particularly light winds. The sun was down, and the railside was lit up with lanterns of all colours. A brass band played the Rochester Mayoral anthem. On the platform the waiting crowd cheered as the carbide running-lights of the huge wind train came into sight, the vertical blades of its mighty rotors flashing and gleaming as it approached.

Inside the rotor engine the Purser suddenly realized that the pennants of the Highliber and OverMayor of the Southeast Alliance were still furled, just as the cheers of the welcoming crowd and the blaring of the band became audible above the rumbling of the wheels and rotors.

"You, take these!" he cried as the bare-chested and sweating Glasken finished winding down a rotor drum. "Climb the front of the rotor engine and stand by the port railing. Hold these pennants up as we pull into the railside."

"But, Fras Purser, my tunic —"

"DO AS I SAY! Try to look dignified, and whatever you do, don't drop the pennants, and don't fall!"

Glasken had not seen himself in a mirror for over five years, and had no idea of how the ordeal in Baelsha had changed his physique — which had previously been impressive, if slightly chubby. Gasps mingled with the cheers of the crowd as the magnificent, bare-chested pennant bearer at the front of the rotor engine was illuminated by the lanterns and torches of the railside. Sweat glistened on his skin, and the dancing flames highlighted the outlines of his muscles with dark shadows. Glasken began to catch comments as he rolled past the crowd on the platform.

"Look at that figurehead."

"Fanciful carving."

"Nay, he's real, he smiled at me."

"Does gearjack work do *that* for you?"

"I'm joining Great Western."

"He must be a Dragon Librarian."

"He's a Tiger Dragon, I've heard of them."

"Elite guard of the Highliber."

"Wish he'd guard me."

"The Highliber's consort, that's who he is."

Girls in white togettras showered the puzzled Glasken with rose petals and mint leaves meant for Zarvora and Denkar. Glasken slowly realized that most of the waving and cheering was being directed at him. The train came to a smooth stop with the engine facing into the darkness of the marshalling yards beyond the railside. Glasken crawled back through the access hatch with the pennants. The Purser was elsewhere, but his dustcape and slingpack were still there, abandoned beside the flare locker. Glasken was alone.

"I know I agreed to work my passage, but I'm worth a bonus," he mused as he rummaged for the feel of a purse in the slingpack. The purse was large, and contained mixed gold and silver. He reached in for a generous handful, then returned it to the slingpack saying "Blame shoddy accounting for the shortfall, Fras."

Moments later he was on the platform with his packroll under his arm and his tunic improvised into a purse and tied to his belt. Several girls in the crowd recognized him at once as the pennant bearer from the front of the train.

"Fras, Fras, are you a Tiger Dragon?" one of them called breathlessly.

"Sweet Frelle, if I am, I am also not at liberty to tell you," he replied in a deep, educated tone that marked him as something more than a gearjack.

"Fras, are you off duty now, with the Mayor's guards there to protect Frelle Highliber-OverMayor and her consort?" her companion asked.

The Highliber, and on the same train! Glasken got such a fright that his knees nearly buckled, and he did actually drop his rollpack.

"Fras Tiger Dragon, are you all right?" squeaked the first girl.

Glasken was careful to steady himself on her arm as he scooped up his rollpack. The other put her hands against his chest, her eyes wide with concern. The feel of smooth, soft female skin against his after so long nearly made him pass out again.

"Four days without sleep while I worked the beamflash and rotor gears alternately ... it took its toll," he sighed. "We lost some crew in the fighting at — ah, but I cannot speak of that."

"Oh, brave Fras, rest on me."

"And me!"

"Fras, have you eaten, will you drink?" called a portly man wearing a vintner's striped sash. "My tavern is but close by. Come, bring your Frelle lady friends, honour my humble establishment."

Not a hundred paces away Zarvora and Denkar stepped from the train as a fourteen bombard salute began to boom out and fireworks streaked into the sky.

Denkar noticed an olive-skinned man of short but powerful build in bead-point and ray robes. He was approaching at the head of a large retinue that seemed to have at least one member of every race that Denkar knew of, then more besides. A racial mixing bowl, Kalgoorlie was well known to be that. One of the courtiers was leading a tiny pony that was being ridden by twin boys of about a year or two in age dressed in the Rochester pennant colours.

Zarvora squeezed his arm and her indrawn breath hissed between her clenched teeth. "Denkar, I had meant to tell you before you — I am sorry, if I ..."

"What? I can't hear with the noise."

"Shh. Mayor Bouros, my dear friend!" she called.

"OverMayor Zarvora, my fulsome pleasure to greet you again," Bouros declared loudly as he stretched his arms out to embrace Zarvora.

"Mayor Bouros, I have missed your hospitality. This is —"

"Fras Denkar, your consort. Fras! A pleasure."

Denkar, crushed in the Mayor of Kalgoorlie's embrace, wheezed "Delighted". Bouros stood back to regard him.

"Ah yes, reserved, and keen eyes, intelligent eyes. Don't tell me, Frelle, but he is an engineer. No, the mighty Frelle Zarvora Cybeline, Highliber of Libris, Mayor of Rochester and OverMayor of the Southeast Alliance could take none other but an engineer for a consort. Tell me, Fras, what is your field?" he said, putting an arm around Denkar's shoulders.

"I — ah, applied mathematical systems —"

"Mathematics and engineering! The Empress of Sciences and —" Bouros suddenly raised a hand, then put a finger to his lips." Ah, Frelle Zarvora, how could I be so indiscreet? An engineer of systems that ... cannot be spoken of. Fras Denkar, I too am an engineer, but merely of structures, and of fluid dynamics. I am a graduate of the University of Oldenberg."

"I taught there for five years," Denkar exclaimed.

"You taught at my old university?" Bouros said, his voice booming out again. "Frelle Zarvora, your good taste never ceases to amaze me. Ah, but what manner of barbarian am I? You must be desperate to greet your magnificent twin sons yet I stand blocking the path. Dahz!"

"What's this? Are you a widow?" Denkar hissed to Zarvora behind his hand.

Zarvora whispered urgently back in Denkar's ear. "Please, just play along, and say that you like the names. Bouros helped choose them, and he is a fanatical admirer of Brunel."

"Brunel?" whispered Denkar. "Was he your husband?"

Her elbow dug into his ribs. "No, you are my only husband. These are your sons."

"Frelle Zarvora, Fras Denkar, here are your boys, safe and hale," Bouros announced proudly.

Zarvora lifted the toddlers from the pony and the unsteady and bewildered Denkar was glad that he had to kneel to embrace them. "Charles and Isambard, this is your father," Zarvora said gently while Mayor Bouros led the cheering. The twins were still at an age when they greeted all strangers without reservation, and they hugged and kissed Denkar at once.

"Hullo, fine ancient names you have," Denkar managed.

"This daddy?" Isambard asked Zarvora, who nodded.

"Charles and Isambard, fine names for fine boys," said Bouros. "Isambard was my humble suggestion, after Brunel, and Zarvora named Charles after the legendary Babbage. But come now, I have had a welcome prepared for you both for a day past, but the winds saw fit to thwart me."

Bouros led them away to a cable terminus where his private tramcar was waiting. His wife nudged Zarvora as they walked.

"Frelle, that pennant bearer on your train, who was he?" she said slyly, batting her eyelashes.

"Pennant bearer? What pen — oh, one of the Tiger Dragons, I think."

"Such a body, good Frelle. Like Bouros when he was younger, except tall. Ah, such shoulders, such muscles, a chest such as one could not put arms around, oh and as handsome as the devil's temptation. Frelle, I have five beautiful daughters, all of marriagable age. My husband's younger sister is of just such an age, too."

Zarvora blinked in surprise at the string of superlatives.

"I shall have the Tiger Dragon Blue of my guard make enquiries and introductions, gracious Frelle," she replied.

The tramcars worked whether the Call was sweeping over the city or not, and were powered by a wind pulley farm backed up by a water dropwheel station. The Mayoral Palace was situated directly over some old shaftworks, and Bouros proudly showed Denkar an innovation of his own invention. Certain rooms were designed to lower themselves if an operator with a dead-hand switch was affected by the

Call. The room would then drop bodily on cables until it had descended so far into the earth that the Call ceased to operate upon it.

"It's an affront to our dignity as humans to be subject to the whims of the Call, don't you think so?" Bouros remarked to Denkar as they inspected the small rooms.

"Ah well, being free of the Call does have its advantages," Denkar agreed.

*****

"Oh, my head," Glasken said aloud, wincing at the pain of his hangover.

He decided not to speak again. *Where am I?* he wondered. *Big arches, incense, drapes and pictures on the walls, coloured glass in the windows ... It looks like a church. Maybe I'm dead. Feel like I should be. Wonder who the mourners will be ... but this is a bed. Haven't slept in a proper bed since 1701.*

"Fras Tiger Dragon, are you awake?" whispered a light female voice from somewhere under the covers beside him.

"Ah — aye."

An arm and a leg snaked over him, and black hair washed across his face. Almost at once the opiates of arousal began to blunt the ferocity of Glasken's headache. He noticed a gold wirework coronet still tangled in her curly hair.

"I have never, never met a man like you," said the woman, who looked to be in her late twenties. While not actually fat, she had certainly had access to fine food and drink for most of her life. Glasken found the effect quite pleasing after the privations of Baelsha. Her skin was light brown, its natural colour rather than from tanning. "Do you still like me, Johnny, now that it is morning?" she crooned.

"I choose with good taste, be I drunk or not, Frelle."

"But, dear Fras Johnny, would you have chosen me from all those others were I not the sister of the Mayor?"

Glasken's hangover vanished, sucked down into an enormous chasm that had opened up at the bottom of his stomach. He was thankful that he was already lying down, and that she was whispering into his ear and not watching his face go pale. *The sister of the Mayor!* He did not even know her name. He did not even know the Mayor's name if it came to that, although he was fairly sure that the Mayorate was Kalgoorlie. No names, that was serious. A magistrate's daughter back in Rochester had once raked the skin of his arm with her fingernails and set the household's guard dogs after him for forgetting her name as they lay a-bed together. Glasken began to caress the woman's soft curves with his fingertips as he called upon the ingenuity that had saved his life on more than one occasion.

"Tell me of the use of names in ah, Kalgoorlie, Frelle," he murmured in a deep voice that had been made deeper by the singing of the night before. "What form of address should I use for you in public, and before your servants, and what name is your pleasure in private?"

"What names, Johnny? But —"

"Ah now, Frelle, remember that I have never been to this Mayorate before, and I do not want to seem a yokel either in your bed or before your servants. Teach me the manners of love as Kalgoorlie has it, my sweet and silken-skinned Frelle."

The lesson on manners in the Western Mayorates lasted all through the morning, punctuated only by the servants bringing breakfast. Varsellia had to join the Mayoral table at lunch time to help her brother entertain his honoured guests from the east, but she left three serving girls to tend Glasken's needs. They did just that.

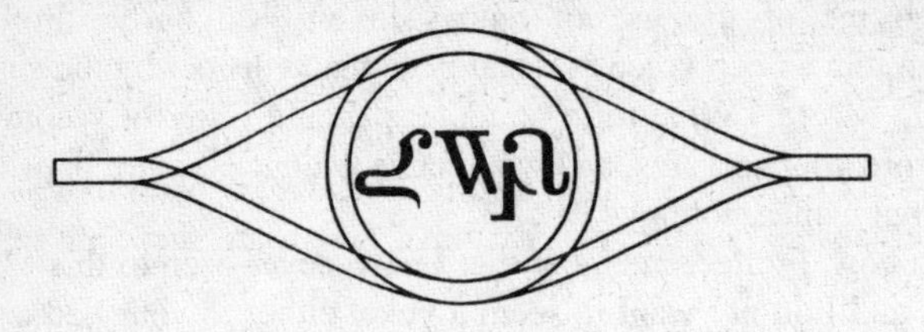

Part 2

THERESLA

As the Glenellen lancers formed up against the Neverland freebooter cavalry, the city's battle calculor made an outline assessment of both the terrain and the enemy. Scribes pushed coloured blocks about on the scenario groundsheet, and runners hurried about with weighting cards that identified the speed, weapons and experience of the various blocks of fighters. Senior components studied tactical cards detailing freebooter behaviour in similar battles of the past. Glenellen's battle calculor was no longer a novelty in the Alspring cities, in fact this was its fourth use in a major battle. Its record was thus far flawless.

Overhand Baragania frowned and tugged hard at his beard as he surveyed the model battlefield on the scenario groundsheet.

"The Neverland freebooters are a weak but difficult enemy," he said to his deputy, Mundaer. "Their ranks are open, and they are lightly armed and armoured, yet they are faster than us." He shrugged and spread his fingers. "They can do us little damage, but we cannot catch them."

"Except in a trap," said Mundaer smugly, straightening his ochre robes.

"They are not being so obliging as to enter our trap."

The Boardmaster was hovering beside them with his cue at the ready. "Would they but come here, to this plain south of the hills, we could let them exhaust their attack parameters on our heavy brigades," he said eagerly. "All the while we would be encircling them with mounted archers disguised as lancers."

"Nobody wants to fall into a trap," replied Baragania simply.

"But it's their move!" exclaimed the Boardmaster, as if impatient with one of the contestants in a game of chess or champions.

"Perhaps so, yet they do not move, so we are stuck with this stand off amid the heat, flies and red dust."

The Boardmaster cursed sharply, then flung a block in the Neverlander colours to the ground and stamped on it.

"Sympathetic magic, Boardmaster?" asked Mundaer mirthlessly. "You're being hopeful."

"But there's no obvious trap, Major-Director Mundaer! Our riders wear lancers' armour and gambesons, and they carry lances while concealing their bows."

"No obvious trap, yet we now have a reputation for fighting with deadly coordination and strange tactics," replied Mundaer. "They're just suspicious, nothing more."

"Still, that does not help us to catch them," added the Overhand.

Mundaer walked around the scenario groundsheet several times while the Overhand and Boardmaster stood watching. Scribes respectfully moved back and forth out of the way as he paced, and he occasionally bent to tap terrain pins and nudge blocks with his riding whip. Moving and reconfiguring the groundsheet was not easy, and the scribes and Boardmaster were as anxious as the Overhand and his deputy to confront the Neverlanders with a decisive battle.

"With respect, Commander, but why not move our trap?" Mundaer said with a flourish of his whip.

"Because here the ground is hilly where the Neverlanders are sheltering. We can't maintain the level of communications that our battle calculor requires. We need to fight on a plain with this sort of enemy."

"But we can make a plain! If we send in a dozen small units of heavies with heliostats to take the hilltops and dig trenchforts, they will have a view of the whole area. The freebooters may attack one individual hilltop with overwhelming numbers, but meantime we could use the cover of the hills to guide in our mounted archers unseen — the battle calculor can give us the optimal path."

"Hills that are really a plain, invisible archers ... this is all very appealing, but it relies totally on the heliostat signals."

"How can they fail, Commander? The sky is cloudless, the air is still, and there is little grass for the freebooters to set fire."

Baragania glanced from the map to the hills, then back to the map. Five weeks of desert skirmishes and discomfort had worn down the resolve of his troops and lancers, but for the Neverland freebooters the parched, dusty landscape was home. There was a subtle danger, of course. The freebooters could swamp one of the hilltop positions and annihilate the troops there in a fast and furious strike, then retreat and claim a victory. A Glenellen position wiped out by freebooters: the emotional impact on the Glenellen Makulad was likely to be far worse than the military significance. Overhand Baragania fingered his neck nervously at the prospect of explaining something like that to his master.

"Major-Director Mundaer, have the battle calculor work out the times for every possible route the mounted archers would need to reach each hill."

"Already done, Commander. Nineteen minutes by my Call anchor-belt's timer."

"As long as that? Too long — but wait. If the mounted archers could be split into two groups and deployed at either end of the cluster of hills, then that time would be halved and they could arrive in time to blunt any attack. Meantime, the rest would arrive as a second wave. Yes, I like that. Tell the calculor translators what we want, then begin the deployment of our men in the hills."

*****

The deployment took five hours, which was not far different from what the battle calculor had predicted. Both the Glenellen officers and their men were eager for a fight, so eager that they were willing to go looking for one.

"There now, a heliostat signal," said Baragania. "Mundaer, what is it?"

"Freebooter movement, Commander. Grid 44 by 79 with a vector of A9 at 40 degrees."

"That threatens our battle calculor!" exclaimed the Boardmaster as he moved his blocks and beheld an instant overview of the battlefield. "They're coming here, through those smooth, shallow gullies." He jabbed at charblack shading on the groundsheet.

"We're dug down behind lancers and archers," said Baragania. "We stay."

But the Neverlanders did not attack the battle calculor. Instead they rode for the line of sight between Baragania's command group and the hills. They appeared to be leading packhorses, and as the Glenellen officers watched, the freebooters cut the packs free and abandoned them. Immediately smoke began to belch from the fallen packs: thick, acrid black smoke.

"Smokepots?" wondered Mundaer, scratching his neck at the base of his helmet. "But they can scarcely hide behind —"

"Regroup, here!" shouted Baragania. "Transmit the message at once!"

"Commander?"

"Do as I say, now!"

Mundaer barked an order to the heliostat operator, and Baragania listened to the click of the mechanism while watching the nearest hilltop through his telescope. Tendrils of smoke began to drift across the field of view.

"What are they waiting for?" he shouted, then he saw a faint twinkle through the smoke. "What was the message?"

"REQUEST CONFIRMATION," replied the observer at the large telescope beside the heliostat mirror.

"Send confirmation!" called Baragania frantically, but heavier billows of smoke were already across the field of view.

"The battle calculor has worked out all six possible scenarios," began Mundaer tentatively, unsure of what was unfolding.

"Damnation to that, we've lost already!" said the Overhand quietly, shaking his head. "Our signal lines are gone and our men are trained to fight only under instruction. Extraordinary! The first blow was a gash above our eyes to blind us with our own blood."

"There!" cried Mundaer, pointing at a dust cloud. "Something in those gullies, look at all that dust! Freebooter cavalry, about six thousand, at least half of their force. They're going to hit the Calculor."

"Break post, go, move! Get the battle calculor moving. Make for the smoke pots first. We'll use their own smoke as cover, and then dash for the nearest hilltop."

The battle calculor and its escort were already in motion when scouts reported that the dust was being raised by a few dozen freebooters trailing ropes and sacking behind their horses and camels. Baragania decided that the nearest hilltop, the one designated by the scribes as Hill Alpha, was still the safest and most strategically important position. He ordered everyone to keep moving. In the distance they could hear trumpets and whistles, and the sounds of a conflict. The smokepots were flaming out as they passed them, and the air was clear to the hill before them.

Abruptly arrows began to pour down from Hill Alpha. The freebooters had captured it behind the screen of smoke. Overhand Baragania ordered a retreat to a rocky outcrop that was within sight of the hills still held by his own men.

"They can't have taken more than one hill," insisted Mundaer, who was struggling to cope with what was happening. "The battle calculor programs proved there was no time."

"Masterful: Hill Alpha," said the Boardmaster. "They took the very hill that could cause us the greatest delay setting up the battle calculor again. What say the heliostats?"

"We're just getting their attention," replied Mundaer. "Green flare, fire when ready."

The arc of green smoke drew heliostat reports from two hilltops, and the twinkling signals began to tell their story. Hill Alpha had been attacked almost as soon as the pall of smoke had gone up, smothered in a suicidal charge by the freebooters who had paid with casualties of at least ten to one to buy their victory. The smoke pots and riders trailing dust-raisers had added to the confusion, but the other eleven hills were secure, as were the two groups of mounted archers.

Mundaer began to regain confidence when he realized that very little real damage had been done to the Glenellen forces, aside from the loss of the men on Hill Alpha. The Overhand Baragania was less optimistic.

"Signal the archers to converge to this outcrop," ordered Baragania. "Then we'll go from hill to hill, collecting our garrisons in greater strength."

"But Commander, that's retreat. Why do it, when we are close to full strength?"

For a moment the Overhand's composure cracked. He seized the Major-Director by his pennant scarf and shook him roughly. "Of all the stupid..." Then, just as quickly, his control returned. "Where are the Neverlanders?"

"On Hill Alpha," replied the confused and uncomprehending officer, "and riding about with dust-raisers and smoke bombs."

"I say that only 10% of Neverlander men are accounted for there."

"There's more than that. The battle calculor estimates that 11.2% of their known forces are all that are required for —"

"Damn you, Major-Director! Can't you see? All those dozens of men with their cumbersome folding desks, cards and abacus frames can better my experience by only one point in a hundred! Gah, the battle calculor can screw itself, I'm done listening to it. If I were you, I'd be thinking about how to explain this to our esteemed monarch, the Makulad of Glenellen, and the inquisition that he is sure to order after this debacle. Now get the archers back here before something else goes wrong for us."

It was not as if it had been a bad decision by the Overhand, it merely hastened the inevitable. The mounted archers of his first group rode to skirt a ridge adjoining Hill Alpha. The ridge could not be adequately scouted for the Glenellen archers, yet they chose to skirt it as the shortest route available to regroup. As they were riding through the neighbouring gorge a cloudburst of arrows descended upon them from the main force of Neverlander freebooters, who had been concealed there. Within minutes there was blind panic among the Glenellen archers. Many fled up the slopes of Hill Alpha, not remembering that it was in freebooter hands. These were slaughtered. Others reached the summits of Hills Beta, Gamma and Delta. The second group of archers made it safely to the outcrop of rock where the Overhand was sheltering.

By late in the afternoon the Neverlanders had brought in more smokepots, and were again disrupting the signals between the hilltop positions and the Glenellen Commander. Scouts and messengers were ridden down and slaughtered by what appeared to be elite freebooter squads assigned specifically to that purpose, yet some Glenellen messengers managed to reach their assigned hills with their messages. By morning, Hills Kappa, Mu, Theta and Lambda had been evacuated and the garrisons consolidated with the main group. It was a feat of desperation that seemed to surprise even the Neverlanders.

"The freebooters are treating this like the Surgeon's Gambit in the champions board game," Baragania told a meeting of his officers and nobles. "Who can tell me what that is?"

A captain from Hill Lambda shook a tassled lance with his unit's colours. "Esteemed Overhand, the enemy's forces are mostly left on the board until the king is ready to fall."

"Right! That is what we are on the sharp edge of here. We need to get our remaining hilltop garrisons back together with us, but I estimate six thousand of the enemy are in the hills in a rapid-strike force. We have been evacuating hills singly, and I think that they will rush to the next garrison that shows signs of movement. They are strong and fast enough to do that. Instead, we shall move all seven remaining garrisons at once. One or two could be trapped and wiped out, but that's better than losing them all one by one."

The Neverland freebooters had another surprise. They were known not to have bombards, but siege rockets were lighter than cannons, and could be transported in racks by camels. They had not even been modelled on the scenario board. Siege rockets were notoriously inaccurate and at extreme range they could barely hit a 100 metre diameter circle, yet the main Glenellen encampment was significantly bigger than this. The first of the rockets plunged down among the Glenellen men and exploded a quarter hour after the meeting. The warhead flung deadly metal shards into humans, horses, and camels.

By the time the consolidation order went out from the Overhand's heliostat there was rebellion in some of the garrisons. They did not want to add their own bodies to a shooting gallery for the Neverlander rocket artillery. At last three garrisons were convinced to rejoin the main force, but two were mauled by the freebooters. Rockets continued to plunge into the main Glenellen encampment, at the rate of one every five minutes.

Overhand Baragania finally decided to cut his losses and return to Glenellen. He had over half of his original force, which was still double the freebooter numbers, and his men were adequately provisioned for the three week journey back. Their morale improved at once, for they would now be out of reach of the siege rockets.

"This is a miracle," declared Baragania as he rode. "This morning I expected to be lying dead in the sand by noon, yet here I am at the head of an orderly retreat of over half my men."

Mundaer was looking back toward the hills. "There! Another puff of smoke. They're using the siege rockets on our four rebel garrisons now."

"Good, it will keep the Neverlanders occupied for a while and it saves us the trouble of executing our own traitors. Boardmaster, what estimate would you give for reaching Glenellen?" he called.

The Boardmaster rode his camel over at once. "No less than two weeks, no more than three, Overhand."

"We shall, of course, be executed for our trouble. The invincible battle calculor has been humbled. There's been four men out of every ten dead, and a great boost to the confidence of the freebooters."

"Why are we returning, then?" asked Mundaer morosely.

"Why? To deliver 10,000 valuable troops to the city for its defence and for the protection of our families from ruin and slavery."

"I can't understand what went wrong with the battle calculor!" exclaimed the Boardmaster.

"Ah, but nothing went wrong. From what I can tell, however, the Neverland freebooters were commanded by someone who knew exactly what a battle calculor can do, and what it cannot. That makes us very vulnerable."

*****

The gardens of the Mayoral Palace of Kalgoorlie had been designed by the grandfather of the current Mayor, specifically with dalliance in mind. There were a true maze of hedges, bushes and hidden alcoves, surrounded by a cloister square fifty metres on a side. Couples not only had privacy, but they could hear others approaching by the crunch of pebbles underfoot. To Glasken, the gardens were partly a discreet and direct route from the main gate to Varsellia's rooms, and partly an excellent venue for the purpose for which they had originally been designed. He had become quite familiar with them since arriving in Kalgoorlie. To Ilyire, the gardens were a place where he could be alone without leaving the city, and he needed to be alone increasingly often. He could easily avoid others within the maze if he stayed alert and moved sufficiently fast.

One clear, bright autumn day in April, Ilyire did not move quite fast enough. Glasken had been slipping away from Varsellia's rooms in the late afternoon, all spruced up for a night of revelling in the market quarter of the city. He almost walked straight into Ilyire in the deserted garden maze, appearing like a phantom amid the tall topiaried hedges. Ilyire had been dozing on a small rectangle of lawn, but he jack-knifed to his feet at once.

"Glasken!" he exclaimed, at first in amazement alone.

Glasken began to ease back at once, holding his swagger stick before him in both hands. Ilyire had a swagger stick as well.

"So, first time I glad to see you," Ilyire added, stepping slowly but confidently toward the bigger man.

Glasken eased back another step, glancing back out of the corner of his eye.

"Can't say I share the feeling," he replied in an oddly casual tone.

Ilyire advanced on Glasken with confident contempt, yet he was unsure of what he actually intended to do. Theresla wanted Glasken recaptured, but Ilyire was no longer dedicated to Theresla's service. Zarvora had a big reward posted for Glasken, yet Ilyire held money in contempt. Ilyire had actually helped a woman abduct Glasken over five years earlier, and had experienced a lot of trouble over the incident. In a very real sense Ilyire resented the fact that Glasken existed at all, and wanted to do no more than humiliate and imprison him. Glasken did not share his indecision about what to do.

Ilyire reached out with a feint, at which Glasken twisted and took the first step of a headlong flight — except that his back leg swung straight up and around in an arc as his arms counter-rotated. Glasken's foot caught Ilyire squarely on the cheek, sending him sprawling, stunned, and with a bone cracked.

The Alspring Ghan recovered fast enough to roll as he hit the path in a shower of polished quartz stones. Glasken swung a blow at his knuckles to make him drop the swagger stick, but missed as he slid in the pebbles himself. Seizing the advantage Ilyire rolled a blow at Glasken's face with his swagger stick, but his old enemy seemed to rotate about a vertical axis as he deflected the blow upwards with his forearm. Ilyire spun with his own momentum, Glasken's knee slammed into his ribs, then his elbow caught Ilyire in the back of the neck.

The Ghan crashed down into a terra cotta drain, senseless for a moment, his swagger stick gone. Glasken stood clear, but did not flee. Barely aware or what had happened, or perhaps unable to accept it, Ilyire lunged up at Glasken. Glasken let himself be caught this time but somehow twisted in his opponent's grip. Ilyire's arm was wrenched around, Glasken's arm and shoulder levering him into another uncontrolled fall. The impact winded him, and again he found himself lying on white quartz pebbles. His arm was twisted behind his back and scarlet waves of pain washed past his eyes. After a moment

Glasken released his very precise grip on a nerve in Ilyire's neck, yet he kept him pinned to the path.

"You dirty, *filthy* wretch," Glasken said smoothly, before he eased his grip and stood clear.

Ilyire was too taken aback to struggle at first, or even to stand up. He just glared at Glasken out of the corner of one eye. He tried to spit at the man who had him pinned to the path, but his head was twisted too far around.

"You wanting to ravish my sister!" Ilyire panted. "I kill you."

Again Glasken jabbed at the nerve, and again Ilyire was racked by such pain that he could barely draw breath.

"I've been into to your treasure cave near the edge of the world," said Glasken as he released the nerve again. "The one with ERVELLE carved at the rim, just beneath the flat rock that conceals it."

"Swine —" Ilyire began, then caught himself. Horror chilled him. He stared at the terra cotta gutter beside the path, suddenly desperate to turn into cold water and flow away to hide.

"Swine? Me?" Glasken was saying. "I discovered a fair princess in the foul clutches of a man from the Alspring cities. A man who sleeps with her bones."

"Thief, I'll kill you for this," whined Ilyire, trying to fan anger through the cold shroud of shame.

"Yes, you probably would kill me if you could. I sleep with the Mayor's sister, and she gives me access to all sorts of interesting documents. I read Frelle Darien's transcript of your account of your first, lone journey to the Edge, and of how you rescued the bones of a girl named EVA NELL. I suppose that the Frelle Dragon Silver could be forgiven for getting a few details wrong in recalling such a long and rambling tale after an hour or so had elapsed. Luck was on your side then, but it's not now. I saw the cave and the name carved at the entrance. The correct name."

"I kill you, I kill you," squealed Ilyire, but there was despair rather than threat in his voice.

"I could kill *you*, Ilyire, merely by pressing this blood vessel here, in your neck, for a minute of so. You are as battered as a battlefield corpse, yet I have not one scratch. Nobody would ever suspect me of being the killer."

Ilyire's breath came now in short, wheezing gasps. "Kill me then. As I live, I live to kill you."

"But only to keep your precious sister from finding out about Ervelle. That's not the vendetta of honour, that's the sting of a guilty conscience. Sleep with a corpse, do you?"

"Not true!"

"Sleep with the bones of Ervelle herself, the most revered legend of the Alspring cities, at that. Poor girl. You despise me for the rogering of such maids as would have me, yet what have *you* been doing to a helpless shade who cannot even scream for help? No woman has ever wanted to scream for help while in my arms, Fras Ilyire. They've screamed and giggled for a few other reasons, though. *I* am a good lover. *You* are a pervert."

"No, no."

"Then what about that bed in the cave? A small, fine skull with a gold headband of eight claws holding a green emerald barely smaller than my thumb. Do you want me to recount what else I found in there?"

Ilyire did not. Glasken told him anyway. The Ghan did not move at first, even to raise his eyes.

"I know what's going on in your mind," Glasken said as he slowly released Ilyire and stood clear. "You're desperate to kill me, rather than just gloat about your superior morals. Don't even think about it, Fras. Have you heard of lawyers?"

Ilyire looked up at Glasken now, but his expression was a study in hopelessness.

"So, you have. I've had to engage a few in my time to keep myself out of the stocks — none too successfully on some occasions. Lawyers can do marvellous things, you know. They can hold sealed letters in trust, to be sent to such people as Abbess Theresla in the event of my death. Kill me, Fras Ilyire, and your private perversions will become exceedingly public. Remember what you used to call me on that journey through the desert with your sister? Camel turd, penis pustule? Imagine what you will be called: bone buggerer, most likely — and the very bones of Ervelle herself."

"No! No, never, I lay close to her bones to guard her, I only wanted to give Ervelle the protection that she never had in life, please, please, believe me, Fras Glasken, Fras John Glasken. I couldn't live if, if ..."

Ilyire was on his knees with his hands clasped in supplication, tears streaming down his face, then he bent down and began to strike his forehead against the pebbles of the path. Glasken unfolded his arms in surprise at the suddenness and extent of Ilyire's collapse. It was not often that he found himself in the position of the despiser, rather than the despised, and he could not carry it off very well. He reached down and seized the devastated man by the arm.

"Stop that, your forehead's bleeding," he said as he hauled Ilyire up. "Come now, up you get and piss off."

"Deserve to die. Here, take knife. Kill me."

"Put it away and —"

Ilyire twisted out of his grip. "Then I kill myself!"

The toe of Glasken's boot flickered out delicately to send the knife spinning high into the air across the garden and out of sight. It stuck in the buttocks of a wooden cherub in the cloisters' gargoyleresque, where it remained undiscovered for a number of months. Glasken stood with his hands on his hips looking down at Ilyire, who was now curled up on the path with his hands over his head, weeping hysterically.

"Up you get now, man of the Alspring cities. I can't leave you like this, so you're coming with me."

After some persuasion Ilyire stood up and wiped at his eyes with his sleeve. "What — where we going?"

"Off to a medician's shop."

Ilyire threw up his hands, then tore at his hair. "No philtre, no medician could help."

"This shop is where souls are healed, Fras Ilyire. It's called the Green Dragon's Tankard."

*****

Fourteen hours later dawn was in the sky above the Mayoral Palace, but the lamps at the street corners were still alight as Glasken and Ilyire finally returned. Mirrorsun was just above the western horizon, spilling its light in between the spires and towers bordering the square, and the nightly shape-changing glow was that of a six-rayed star. Glasken pushed the brake chocks on the stolen costermonger's cart down onto the wheels as they emerged into the square before the palace gates. Ilyire was lying on the tray, singing incoherently with his legs hanging over the frontboard. Glasken had some quiet words to the three girls who had been helping to push the cart, and they departed into the pre-dawn shadows after each leaving a kiss on his cheek. Two of them also kissed Ilyire.

"Frash Glashken, what I like is you help man, heep, ah, into gutter, who is," Ilyire bawled emotionally as the none-too-steady Glasken helped him out of the cart and onto the cobblestones of the square.

"That's *out* of the gutter, Fras Drinking Apprentice."

"Everyone dis-pishes, er ... Ilyire."

"Shame on them."

"Own sister shot me."

"Lucky she missed."

"She didn't."

"Lucky you're tough. Now, where's the palace? Ah, over here."

Ilyire began to sing in ancient Anglaic: "*I belong te Glascow, Dear old Glascow town.*"

"Shush! The guards'll think we're drunk."

"Where's Glascow?"

"Long, long way north. Near Canberra, I think. Who cares? Drunks in Sundew been singing about it for centuries."

"What'r more words?"

"Gah, you won't even remember those when you wake."

Ilyire lurched free of Glasken's supporting arm and stood for a moment with his hands on his new friend's shoulders.

"I telling you, Johnny ... lying with Belgine tonight, ah, like standing on world-Edge, looking at Call-god creatures. Huge new world."

"Rubbish. She's only a small girl."

"Glashkin!" shouted Ilyire, seizing the lapels of Glasken's tunic more for support than aggression.

"Shhh. The palace guards are watching us."

"Did you ever robert my sishter?"

"Roger your sister."

"So you did! Filthy swine, lucky I didn't find out. Would have killed you." Ilyire paused to emit something between a belch and a sob. "What was she like? What was she like?"

"I never did it," said Glasken, fanning the air between them.

"You didn't? Why not?"

"Don't know. I tried."

"Weird girl. Eats mice, poisons suitors, shot me. I've — not felt so ... ah, whatever word is ... since she shot me."

"Protective, probably. That's understandable."

"Where's next tavern?"

"It's nearly dawn, and we're at the palace. You, Ilyire, are going to bed. I'm going to clean myself up and try to cope with the lovely Frelle Varsellia."

"Fine, fine girl. What's she like? What's she like?"

"Stop that! 'Tis dishonourable to tell."

"Fine, plump girl. Like ride on haycart with broken axle, yes?"

Ilyire collapsed to the cobblestones amid wild and gasping peals of laughter, dragging Glasken down with him. Back on their feet again, they meandered toward the main gates, and the six increasingly uneasy guards. Ilyire suddenly lurched to a stop.

"Frash, friend," he said, confronting Glasken again. "You take my treasure in cave ... at the Edge. Just one promise."

"What sort of promise? If it involves your sister —"

"No. Never. But poor, shamed myself cannot go to cave again. Not worthy. Friend, take all treasure, but gather bones of Ervelle. Bury her at Maralinga. Got graveyard there for Ghans. Ghans who die in desert, following Call. Do it, Frash, for me. Please."

"A noble gesture," said Glasken, taking off his cap to Ilyire with an unsteady flourish.

"Is not gesture! You put her soul to rest. Very heroic man needed, to that do. You must! I'm not hero. I'm worse than ... worm."

"I ... dunno, worms have all the fun," said Glasken, elbowing him in the ribs.

Ilyire collapsed again with a cry of pain. Glasken helped him up.

"I'm sorry, Fras Yire. What did I hit? Lovebite?"

"Fras Glasken, Johnny ... big jokings."

"Do you have a map of how to reach the cave?"

"No."

"Can you draw one?"

"No. Navigated by, ah ... innuendo? Intercourse? Intuition! Yes, yes, navigated by intuition. Theresla made maps."

"Well, can you take me there?"

"No, Fras. Shame would kill me."

"Gah, dummart, well how do you expect me to help?" Glasken waved to the guards. "Will ye help him inside?" he called.

"We know you both, Fras Glasken," replied the duty officer. "You take him in. We can't leave our posts."

"Thank God," murmured the gate sergeant.

They watched them struggle past through the entrance, and presently heard the rattle of a pulley lift's mechanism. The six guards relaxed visibly.

"They're the floor domo's responsibility now," the officer said with relief as he noted their entrance in the gate register.

"Thought Fras Ilyire didn't drink," said the sergeant, who was staring at the abandoned cart across the square.

"After three weeks of watching Fras Glasken arrive back here at all hours in unspeakable condition and in bawdy company, I've ceased to be surprised by anything to do with the man," the duty officer replied.

*****

Zarvora was awakened by the sound of distant shouting and smashing crockery. She shook Denkar awake. "Listen!" she hissed.

"Some cook throwing a tantrum," he muttered sleepily, pulling the covers over his head again.

"It doesn't sound like that."

"Zar, I've been up until 4am converting your trajectory equations into binary on punch tape. Unless the palace is on fire, I want to sleep."

Zarvora strained for words in the distant argument.

"Filthy wretch, get out!" shrieked a female voice.

"I'm going, don't shout," pleaded a man.

"I'll shout what I want! You're not a Tiger Dragon, you're a damn gearjack from the wind trains. You lied to me!"

There was a series of percussive smashes and inarticulate cries of rage, then running feet.

"Drunk! Drunk every night!" Something like a very large vase smashed and fragments skidded and tinkled. A cry of fear reached Zarvora. "And when you've not been mounting a tavern bench you've been mounting my serving maids!"

A door slammed, sending booming echoes through the corridors and cloisters of the palace. For some moments there was silence, but this was broken by another smash and a cry of surprise.

"And take your filthy rye whisky with you! Nobody makes a dupe of the Mayor's sister!"

Zarvora raised an eyebrow. "But somebody appears to have done so, nonetheless," she said to Denkar, whose only reply was deep and regular breathing.

She stretched out along the bed, but could not get back to sleep. Outbursts like that were rare in the palace, and one of the parties in the dispute had been Varsellia. She had been shouting about a Tiger Dragon. Zarvora pushed back the covers and stood up, stretching for a lingering moment before stepping into the drench bath.

Wrapping herself in a towel, she went into the next room to check her sleeping sons. She drew the curtains against the sunlight, so that they would not wake early and disturb Denkar.

Although she had arisen to investigate the disturbance, Zarvora was in no hurry. It was indeed prudent to let Varsellia calm down a little before calling by to speak with her. She dressed in her working clothes of grey cotton trews and tunic, then went down to the palace kitchens for breakfast.

"Frelle Varsellia seemed a little excitable this morning," she mentioned to the serving maid who brought the tray of coffee and freshly baked raisin bread.

"The good lady discovered that her lover was not all that he claimed to be," the maid replied.

"He claimed to be a Tiger Dragon, I heard her saying."

"So did most of the palace, Frelle. Aye, he was only a gearjack, but his speech was well formed, as if he might have been an edutor." The maid looked to the floor and blushed a little. "I can tell you, though, that Frelle Varsellia has discarded a rare accomplished lover."

"Do you tell from experience?" asked Zarvora, daintily cutting up a slice of warm bread.

"Fras Johnny was generous with his affection, Frelle."

"Johnny, an ancient name," said Zarvora, before taking a sip of coffee.

"Aye, Frelle, but nothing else was ancient about Johnny Glasken."

Zarvora froze, the slice of raisin bread poised between her teeth. "Glasken? I once had a John Glasken in my, ah, Libris staff."

"As a Tiger Dragon, Frelle Highliber?" asked the maid eagerly.

"No, but he was doing very secret and important work," Zarvora conceded with a wink. "Well now, I must pay my condolences to Frelle Varsellia. Thank you for breakfast."

On her way to Varsellia's rooms Zarvora noticed heavy snoring from the room occupied by Ilyire. The door was ajar, which was unusual for the generally paranoid Ghan. She pushed it open to find him on his back and snoring, sprawled across his bed still fully dressed. His trews and codpiece were on backwards, however, and a fashionable shade of ruddy women's cheek-ochre was smeared over his face and collar. What appeared to be claret stained the ruffles down the front of his orange tunic.

"Ilyire."

Normally the single word should have woken him from any sleep, but this time there was no reaction whatever. She shook his leg, which should have made him leap to his feet with a knife in his hand. Still he did not stir. Finally she took a ray-stipple pitcher of water from the sideboard and poured it over his head. Ilyire spluttered, and his eyes opened.

"Ah, sister ..."

"I am the Highliber, Zarvora."

"Wasser difference? Both yell at me, order me about. Both strange as the devil's codpiece."

"What the hell has been going on? Have you been drinking?"

Ilyire raised his head slightly, then cried out in pain and flopped back onto the pillow, moaning. Zarvora pulled open the towel drawer in the sideboard beside the bed, only to discover that he had vomited into it. She left, returning some minutes later with another pitcher of water, a towel and a glass tumbler containing some white powder.

"Get up, drink this," she said, splashing more water over him.

"Lemmedie."

"Come on, head up and drink this."

"No! No, that's wha' Fras Johnny sayn'all night. Drink this, drink that."

"Drink! This is salts of willow for your headache and soda for your stomach."

Ilyire drank, but threw up almost at once. Zarvora skipped back in alarm from the foul torrent, then forced him to drink pure water until he had ceased to vomit. After that she gave him more of the mixture, and eventually he lay back, panting with exhaustion but reasonably lucid.

"What were you doing last night?" she demanded.

"Please. Not loud."

"Ilyire! If I'd not seen this with my own eyes I would never have believed it. What did you do?"

"Can't remember ... much."

"Well start with the last thing that you can recall."

"Ah ... Belgine, lovely girl. Soft as silk."

"You! I don't believe it."

"She bade me protect, ah, her from cold. How — how could I refuse ... appeal for protection? I'm ... religious man. I'm bound to protect distressed Frelles. Andeltine said 'Save me from cold'."

"Belgine."

"Her too."

"Pah, never mind. What cold?"

"She'd ... taken off her clothes. Flung herself upon me."

"And you did more than keep her warm?"

"I'se embarrassed. No idea what to do — aye, but good teacher, she was."

"Prudent, too," said Zarvora, lifting two generous lengths of sheepgut sheath from his half-open pouch with the tip of her dagger.

"Those sheep ... died fr'a good cause. Johnny Glasken gave 'em to me. They stops the consequential, er, consquasious —"

"Glasken? *The* John Glasken. Alive?"

"Embarrassing. Didn't know any positions. Know a few now, though. Women's thighs ... heavenly. You know that, Highliber?"

Zarvora blinked. "Apart from my own thighs, you appear to be ahead of me by two pairs to nil — at least," she said, again shaking her head. "So, you met John Glasken and spent a night drinking and wenching with him?"

"Fine fella, misjudged him ..." mumbled Ilyire, pulling a sheet over his face.

Zarvora pulled it away again. "And he was staying here, in the palace? As Varsellia's bobble-boy? How long has this been going on?"

"Dunno. Arrived on your wind train, he says. You should know."

"*My* wind train?"

Zarvora could get no more sense from him, but an enquiry to the palace guard revealed that Ilyire had arrived at the gate on a costermonger's cart accompanied by Glasken and three rather dishevelled and tired looking women — who had vanished back into the city. A check with the Constable's Runners turned up a report of three women and a tall, strong looking man pushing someone singing in a foreign language on a stolen cart. A check of the Felonies Register at the Constable's Watchhouse led her to the fruit and vegetable markets south of the paraline railside. She began asking after a girl named Belgine at the nearby taverns, and at the Green Dragon's Tankard she finally met with success. Glasken was staying at the tavern, but was in no condition to see anyone, and apparently had company.

"Has he committed a felony?" asked the tavern master, rubbing his hands anxiously as he stared at the official braiding on Zarvora's tunic.

"No, but he is a man of importance and I want him kept safe," said Zarvora as she opened her hand to display three gold royals on her palm. She tipped them onto the counter. "Report his movements to the Constable's Watchhouse every day, will you? Tell them WATCHBOOK SE379G with each report."

He swept the coins from the beer-seasoned counter and wrote down the reference. "By my life, Frelle, I'll guard him as my own son."

*****

The retreating Glenellen army was within a day of the city and riding as fast as their horses and camels could manage when the freebooters made their challenge. The ground was largely open, but bounded by wide gullies.

"This terrain is close to the optimum for a battle calculor," suggested the Boardmaster as Overhand Baragania, standing in the stirrups of his camel's saddle frame, studied the Neverland freebooter movements ahead of them.

"There will be no use of the battle calculor," replied the Overhand firmly. "Now then, over there: the heavy brigades will chase the freebooters along those gullies and tear their rearguard to shreds, while our mounted archers come across to outflank them."

"The men are not trained for this sort of fighting, Commander," pleaded the Boardmaster. "They would be out of sight, having to make decisions themselves and without the benefit of the battle calculor."

"Precisely. Neither is the enemy expecting it."

They watched the heavy brigades stream into the wave gullies in a wide, leisurely pincer movement. Presently the distant thunder of hooves gave way to battle cries, whistles and the clash of weapons, interspersed with occasional gunshots. The Overhand sent out scouts with heliostats, only to have them run down by small, fast squads of freebooter lancers.

"Again, they hack at our communications," said the Overhand. "They try to keep us blind and deaf."

"Commander, the advantage is still ours, we outnumber them and we're on open ground," Major-Director Mundaer insisted.

"I hope you are right. See there, our archers riding across on their correct vector. Come now, let us move toward the wave gullies ourselves. Keep my pennon high, now. The helioscouts need a focus for their signals."

As they began to move along at a leisurely canter a rider suddenly appeared over the edge of the wave gullies and rode furiously away into the centre of the plain.

"One of the heavies, a deserter, by Dalahrus!" the Boardmaster exclaimed.

"Freebooter squads are after him," said Baragania.

"He seems to be trying to use a hand-heliostat," Mundaer observed through his telescope. "It's impossible on a galloping horse."

As they watched, the lancer glanced again at his pursuers, then reined his horse in. As they closed the gap he began to signal to the direction of the Overhand's pennon. Moments later he was obliterated in a swirl of dust and flashing weapons.

"Brave man, he gave his life for that message," said Mundaer. He hawked and spat into the red sand. "Well, did you get any of it?"

"It was the codes for 'archers' and 'trap'," said the Boardmaster.

"Ah, he was calling for our archers to be sent in to trap them quickly," said Mundaer, turning to the Overhand.

"Not 'archers-trap'," said the Boardmaster. "That's a separate code, it cannot be confused with the others."

"A man with death at his back has a right to confusion."

The Alspring archers had reached the wave gully now, and were vanishing over the edge.

"Three freebooter squads, behind us!" cried the captain of the Overhand's escort. "See there! Cutting us off from the square."

"Make for where the heavies are!" ordered Baragania.

"We outnumber them, Commander, we could turn back and charge," suggested Mundaer.

"That may be what they want. They could be trying to distract us with ciphers. Forward, ignore them unless they attack."

They changed to horses in anticipation of the fighting ahead. As they rode, the squads of freebooter lancers gradually closed in. When the Overhand finally realized that he had to fight and closed with the nearest and weakest group, a reserve squad of Alspring lancers came out of the wave gully, seemingly not needed from the battle. The final conflict was drawn out and savage, and lasted for more than twenty minutes. The Overhand and Boardmaster were taken prisoner, but Major-Director Mundaer died in the fighting. Most of the battle calculor components had been sent on ahead, however, and reached Glenellen safely.

The Neverland freebooters dressed very much alike, but as soon as their leader spoke Baragania knew it had to be the she-demon herself, the one known as Lemorel. She treated him with courtesy, having him mounted on a horse that one of her own lancers led beside her.

"I know about your battle calculor," she said as they approached the nearest wave gully. Baragania looked over the edge, and was speechless with shock.

The gully was a scene of carnage. The heavy brigade had been set upon by Neverlander archers disguised as lancers: exactly the tactic Baragania had used to try to ensnare the Neverlanders in the previous battle. The archers had shot down the horses of the Glenellen vanguard, plugging the gully so that those behind floundered under a rain of arrows. By the time the Alspring archers arrived, the Neverlanders were ready for them.

"Never let your enemy choose the battlefield if you can possibly help it," said Lemorel to Baragania from the shadows beneath her heavy veil and hood.

"I tried not to," replied Baragania with undisguised exasperation. "That was why I retreated from those hills in the north."

"A good move, a brilliant move. I thought I had you, but you slipped away in good order. Was that your battle calculor's advice?"

"Calculor? Pah!" He spat, with a dismissive cut of his hand. "My horse could have advised me better." He patted the horse's neck, then spread his hands and shrugged hopelessly. "No, that was experience guiding me. The battle calculor brought us disaster."

"Calculors can do that when used incorrectly, Overhand. You must not stop thinking while you are using them, or you will surely be lost. Behold," she said with a sweep of her hand. "All lost."

The Commander was again silent at the sight of the gully filled with dead and dying. After a moment he hung his head and closed his eyes.

"And yet the battle calculor worked before," he said slowly, unsure of what fundamental point he was missing.

"Ah yes, but through luck and good leadership as much as the battle calculor itself. The Highliber of Libris designed the original battle calculor as a strategic weapon, not a tactical aid. It brought the entire resources of the Mayorate behind the action over scenarios spanning hundreds of kilometres. Oh it can be used as a tactical aid too, if the enemy has never fought against one before. When used against a force commanded by someone who knows a battle calculor's limitations, well, nobody knows the consequences better than you, just now."

"Annihilated," he breathed.

"Not so. My Neverlanders fight only as much as they have to. Life in the desert is short enough without throwing warriors away in futile combat. I stopped the fighting as soon as your force was broken, and not a minute later. Had your Major-Director not been hell-bent on fighting to the death, you would not have lost a single one of your personal staff. I am recruiting, Overhand Baragania. Consider it."

"You want me to join you?" asked Baragania, looking up at once.

A subtle twist in the skin about her eyes betrayed a smile beneath the veil. *Her eyes!* Baragania had a whole lifetime of knowing people only as the eyes above veils. *A woman, definitely a woman.*

"An uncommon offer from a truly exceptional enemy," he concluded.

"You have a choice. Become a prisoner, and perhaps your family will ransom you. You can also become one of my probationary overhands, but if you do that there is no going back. One desertion, one betrayal, and the consequences will be unimaginably cruel for you. I do not deal in annihilation unless it is liable to be of use to me, and I need clever people like you. I shall have captured all the Alspring cities very soon. After that, there is a world beyond to take. My spy-merchants are out and at work there already. You could grow with me, Overhand Baragania, but think upon it at leisure. I neither want nor expect an answer straight away."

"I shall treat your offer very seriously, my Lady Commander," he said in a level voice.

She put her whip gently but firmly across his chest. "Just Commander, when speaking to me."

As the Glenellen overhand was being led away to join the other captives, one of Lemorel's own Neverlander overhands moved in closer at her gesture.

"Glenellen lies before you," he said with flamboyant enthusiasm. "Take it and there will be rich pickings."

Her riding whip thudded against his chest. It was not a heavy blow, just a caution.

"We are not petty thieves, Genkeric. If you want to have pickings, I can arrange for you to tend a rag and bone cart."

"Commander, I meant only for the men."

"No! You're still thinking like a raggy nomad, a petty thief. Glenellen is a symbol of strength. I want it to be mine, and I don't want its power weakened by looting and pillage. With Glenellen mine, Ringwood will join with me against Alspring itself. I shall no longer be just another freebooter warlord. Go after that Glenellen overhand there, give him a tour of our forces. Be polite to him, be friendly: he may be fighting beside us in the next battle."

Some days later Overhand Genkeric died in a confused, minor skirmish not far from Glenellen's Walls. He was quickly replaced. There were plenty of senior officers available from the ranks of the Glenellen prisoners.

*****

Riots were unusual in Kalgoorlie, as were civil disturbances of any kind. Thus the chanting mob drew a crowd of spectators that was bigger than itself, and so it gained the strength to intimidate further by that very increase in numbers. The overall mob was still not large, it numbered no more than a thousand, yet that was enough to intimidate merchants, vendors and artisans nearby. The leaders carried banners bearing the Gentheist symbol of a wreath of green leaves surrounding a blue circle, and they were chanting a mixture of prayers and slogans. Zarvora could not see the mob beyond the palace walls, but she could distinguish a dominant chant of "No steam!" among all the others as she swung herself up into the saddle of her horse.

"It shames me that you must travel on horseback when a cable tram is available," said Mayor Bouros to Denkar, who was having difficulty with his mount after ten years out of the saddle.

"I understand, a group of riders gives them nothing to focus on," Denkar replied. "They think to attack the escorted, not the escorters."

"Why not send out troops to clear the way?" Zarvora asked.

"They have women and children mixed in among them."

"An old trick of the Gentheists in the Southeast. Human shields. Hurt them and you are branded as a butcher."

"Oh so! That's where a lot of these Gentheists are from, even though they wear the robes of my Kalgoorlie subjects."

"So if they attack us, what then?"

"I received a warning through your own Dragon Librarian and beamflash network, from a Frelle who has no voice. Folk tell her a great deal: they think that just because she cannot talk, she cannot communicate."

"Darien. One of my most trusted diplomats."

"I'm forewarned, so I'm prepared. If there's fighting, stay with the rest of us, and no heroics, if you please."

Zarvora slashed the air with her swagger stick, then rested it back over her shoulder while Denkar experimentally rode his horse around the courtyard. The gates were then pushed open and the forty riders moved out toward the crowd of protesters. The Gentheist leaders held back at first, looking for the carriage or cable tram that was being escorted, but when the gates closed behind the last of the riders without a vehicle appearing, they led a surge toward the rows of horses.

With the exception of Denkar and Zarvora, all of the riders had experience in the cavalry, and when fringes of the crowd began to close in front of them chanting "No steam! No steam!" they brought their swagger sticks to the ready and rode straight for them at a trot. Those in front tried to push back, but those safely behind them continued to advance toward the riders. The leading riders reared their horses, which had been trained to lash out with their hooves. It was the cue for fighting to break out, for the Gentheist leaders had deliberately set up the confrontation with violence as an end. Screams and blood were added to the jostling swirl of bodies. The riders were all dressed in cavalry leather and ringwork, except for the Mayor who also wore his heavy gold chain of office over his armour. Swagger sticks and sabres clashed, but the riders had the advantage in terms of arms, armour and horses. The column made steady progress through the crowd.

The gunshot itself was barely audible, but a rider beside Mayor Bouros flopped forward and began to slide from his saddle. Denkar reached over to hold him up as something whizzed past his head, followed by the bark of a second shot.

"That's two!" shouted the Mayor, lifting a whistle to his lips.

At his signal the riders drew flintlocks and began firing birdshot at those rioters who were half a dozen back from the horses. The rout began almost immediately, while scattered gunshots continued from further back in the crowd. The distant gates of the palace compound suddenly opened again, and a far larger squad of cavalry poured out, cantering straight into the rioters and laying about them with sabres. Barely six minutes from when the first blow had landed, the riot was over. One of the Mayor's officers and nineteen rioters were dead. Three of the dead were children.

The trip to the university was postponed until the afternoon while the Mayor called a Noontime Magistrade in the square before the palace. Two Gentheist priests and five civil leaders had been caught and identified as being among the rioters. All but one were foreign nationals, four from the Southeast Alliance and two from Woomera.

A massive scaffold wagon was wheeled out from the stables, and the collapsible gibbets folded out into place. As a crowd of Kalgoorlie citizens gathered, the bodies of the dead were laid out on stretchers before the gallows. A small group of Gentheists began a chant, but they were immediately surrounded and their leader escorted away to stand with the others on trial. The Mayor ascended the steps of the scaffold wagon and began to read from a scroll.

"My loyal subjects, justice rests with the Mayor through the text of the Mayoral Charter. Through discretion I delegate my authority of justice to the magistrates of this city and Mayorate, but I retain the authority to pass sentence when I have personally witnessed an act of felony. In this case, I saw a crowd led by these men attack cavalry escorting myself, appearing as Mayor and wearing my chain of office. This is treason. During the fighting shots were fired that killed one of my loyal officers. This is murder. When more riders came to rescue us, these members of the crowd laid out here were trampled to death. As you can see, several are women and children, and these were made part of the crowd by the cowardly Gentheist leaders who used them as shields to fight behind. This is also murder."

The square was in silence. A clock in a tower began to ring out the count for noon. A herald with an agenda board climbed the steps and stood beside the Mayor.

"On the charge of treason I find these men guilty, but commute the usual sentence on my discretion. On the charge of murdering my officer, I declare the charge to need further investigation and pass it to the City Constable. On the charge of inciting a riot that led to the deaths of these people before you, I find these men guilty. I have been in contact with their Mayors via beamflash and have obtained orders of extradiem proxian. I sentence them to death. Carry out my order, Constable."

The swift retribution caught both the Kalgoorlie citizens and the Gentheist extremists by surprise. The seven men were wrestled to their gibbets and into their nooses. One by one the platforms beneath their feet fell away, leaving them spinning and dangling. The single late-comer stood wide-eyed and horrified as the Mayor turned to him.

"For incitement to riot within a public gathering I find you guilty, and sentence you to three hundred strokes of the sunrise and fifteen years in the Bonelake Penal Garrison. Carry out the first part of the sentence at once."

The Gentheist died after two hundred strokes, and was left bound to the triangle set up beside the scaffold wagon and its grisly display. The City Constable's report showed that two thirds of the rioters had been from outside the Mayorate, and deportation proceedings for the remaining Gentheist militants were begun at once.

It was not until late afternoon that Mayor Bouros and his two guests finally reached the University and entered the walled research park.

Wind rotors and windmills spun in the dry, warm breeze, and there was the steady rush of water being pumped into reserve tanks to provide back-up power. The smell of burning alcohol and vegetable oil was on the air, mixed in with more exotic chemical scents.

"This is our power field," said the Mayor as they walked between the pumps and rotors. "It drives the cable trams in the city, the water pumps and lifts in the underground shafts, and the bellows in some of the smelters."

"It smells something like a brewery," said Denkar.

"Close. It's a distillery. We make alcohol here for fuel export. The Gentheists maintain that we also have steam engines hidden down in the shafts and burning alcohol, but that's all nonsense, isn't it?" The Mayor arched an eyebrow and — unnervingly — smiled on only one side of his face. "Alcohol burners are maintained at the bottom of the shafts, and they circulate air from the surface by convection. Some of the rising hot air also turns turbines that power small generators in Faraday cages a kilometre down."

"They are convection engines, Denkar," Zarvora said. "They are weak, but have been accepted by all the major religions as not coming under the steam and explosive gas proscribium."

"Not quite, Frelle," said Bouros. "The Gentheists are still arguing among themselves about convection engines."

"They seemed fairly united when they attacked us this morning," Denkar observed.

"Ah no, Fras, that was nothing to do with convection engines. Their spies have gleaned word of the two beautiful triple-expansion high pressure steam engines that also burn alcohol and vegetable oil, and reside at the bottom of my deepest shafts. After all, I have to have a reliable source of power, don't I?"

The Edutor-General of Physics met them as they stepped out of a lift that dropped so far that Denkar's ears were popping constantly with the pressure difference. Vegetable oil lamps gave the shafts the scent of some enormous kitchen, and Denkar was somehow reminded of Libris. They toured several workshops first. These were filled with artisans at benches and desks, which were piled with wire and glassware, and vats of beeswax.

Warm rushing air was everywhere, along with the scent of alcohol and sunflower oil, and the glow of oil lamps. Faraday cages were built into several tunnels, so that no electromagnetic signals leaked out to attract the attention of the orbiting Wanderers — and conversely, so that any electromagnetic thunderbolt from the ancient military satellites would be absorbed before it affected the equipment.

"Mayor Bouros has been experimenting with ancient electrical devices in the same way as I was reconstructing the calculating machines of the old civilization," Zarvora explained. "When I came across here on a diplomatic visit I discovered that he was very advanced in his work. Much of what I thought I would have to pioneer myself in the field of electrical studies was already accomplished. He has a spark-gap or sparkflash transceiver that can send an invisible signal across empty space."

"I have a two hundred metre length of tunnel fully shielded for my electrical experiments," Bouros said proudly. "There's nothing else like it in the known world."

"Well in Oldenburg we had the Loyal Company of Electrical Studies," began Denkar.

"Pah! Faraday cages the size of broom closets and pedal-powered generators no bigger than a tinderbox. This is *real* electricity, just like the ancients had it."

The steam engines were nothing like the soot-belching, wheeled juggernauts of admonitory religious texts. They chuffed and hissed busily and steadily, and their brasswork was polished so that it gleamed with dozens of highlights in the glow of the lamps. There was a dull roar from the burner of the alcohol and oil mix boiler, and an insect-like whirr from the generators spinning beside both engines. Denkar noted two cables in varnished wooden trays, both insulated with poorpaper soaked in beeswax and bound down by woven mesh.

"Come this way now," said the Mayor, putting a thick arm about Denkar's shoulders and gesturing along the mesh-shielded tunnel. "Along here we have the greatest triumphs of my sixteen year rule and patronage of this laboratory. I have prepared demonstrations of an arc-lamp and a type of beamflash signaller called a clickwire that uses shielded copper wire, and electromagnets that produce clicks, and can be used in the same way as beamflash mechanisms. They are not affected by fog or smoke, and wires can travel over the horizon and beyond the line of sight."

"The Loyal Company tried that back in 1681," said Denkar. "Shielded wires were slung between two houses containing Faraday cages, but a currawong landed on one of the wires and disturbed the foil and pitch shielding with its claws. A Wanderer passed overhead as they were testing it, and flash! It became all smoke, flames, melted wire and beeswax."

"Hah! Foil and pitch shielding indeed. We use woven mesh over poorpaper and beeswax down here. Still, that was a noble effort, and one day we may make such things operational. It's only a matter of engineering of course."

"Of course."

"Now then, I also have a sparkflash radio to demonstrate, an electric engine that drives a water pump, and best of all, a model electric tramway. First, however, I have also been working with your lovely Frelle wife on a tiny but clever device that she calls a dual-state electromagnetic relay — DSER to you. It can store the status of something like an abacus bead —"

"Why yes! An electric abacus frame, and you could have dozens of DSERs for each component to use," Denkar exclaimed, suddenly catching on. "And each frame could be connected to the central correlators by a bundle of wires. Why with a few hundred component people you could out-perform the entire Libris Calculor."

"Well ... that is possible, but it was not our approach," said Bouros. "Take a look at this device here."

To Denkar it looked like nothing at all. Layers of polished wooden racks and metal struts were draped with wires and springs, and sounded something like the Calculor of Libris in miniature.

"This is a calculor," said Zarvora. "Although less versatile than my first Calculor, it is faster and more accurate in tasks of pure calculation."

"It is the Highliber's design," the Edutor-General added. "She calls it an Induction-Switch Relay calculor, or ISR calculor. It's powered by electricity from one of the sunflower oil and alcohol fired generators you saw earlier. This one has the equivalent of 256 component-steps per timed cycle. Originally there were four cycles per second, but that has been speeded up somewhat."

"In terms of raw calculating power it is roughly the same as the Islamic calculor in Libris," said Zarvora.

"The calculating power of over 256 people in a machine the size of a haywagon?"

"Ah, but this is a tiny device, Fras Denkar," said Bouros grandly. "Frelle Zarvora has designed a machine of over 4,096 component-steps in capacity. That is more than the great Calculor of Libris itself can boast. All that slows us down is the lack of sufficient artisans to build switches as fast as we can install them, but we are recruiting clockmakers from wherever we can."

"That's just fabulous," Denkar said in awe, running his hand along the frame of the electric calculor. "When does work start on the big machine?"

"We still have 2,000 DSER units to make," began Bouros, but Zarvora waved him silent with a flourish that ended with a finger on her lips.

Taking Denkar by the arm she led him to tall double doors in the rock wall, which the Edutor-General and Bouros hurried ahead to open. Beyond it they passed along a short archway cut in the rock, then into a hall-sized cavern as alive with clattering and clicking as the insistent pounding of hail on a metal roof. The thing itself was a metal lattice of scaffolding draped with wires and cables, and the warm air reeked of beeswax and ozone. The roof gleamed with metal mesh, and a half-dozen people were tending a complex bank of instruments on a raised platform surrounded by a railing.

"Here now is my little wedding present for you two dearest of my dear friends," said Bouros, coming up behind them and putting his arms around their shoulders. "It's a little late — when did you say you were married, Zarvora?"

"I ... two years — no! Three years ago."

"We forgot to date — that is, we keep forgetting *the* date," added Denkar.

"Lucky man," said Bouros, grinning broadly and wagging a finger at him, "having a wife who doesn't bother about silly things like wedding anniversaries. We decided that this calculor can be made partly operational with a mere 2,048 units, so here it is, all ready at half-power."

"My need for calculating power has exceeded even what the Libris machine can offer," said Zarvora. "Unfortunately it has also exceeded my ability to do the development and research to improve it all by myself. I have decided to begin to bring the cream of the FUNCTIONS of the Libris Calculor across to help with the work, and because of my special feelings for you, I wanted you to be first — but you know why that is the case. Would you like to take charge of this machine's development while I continue with other researches?"

Denkar had been following the signs and wires festooned from the steel racks, trying to make some sense of the architecture.

"Where are the correlator registers?" he asked.

"Why that board stretching along the wall there. A dozen regulators plug and unplug the wires according to instructions that arrive from above via that paper tape punch."

"I designed a harpsichord keyboard in a Faraday cage that sends impulses down a kilometre of shielded wire," added Zarvora.

"Why not replace all those plugs on the board with a bank of DSER connections?" asked Denkar.

"Why, because ..." The Mayor scratched his head, then turned to Zarvora. She shrugged and spread her hands. "Look, there is a coffee room with a chalkboard just past that rack to the right. Would you like to repeat what you just said while I scribe up a diagram?"

As they were leaving Zarvora whispered in Denkar's ear. "Tonight we had better think up a plausible date in 1703 for our marriage. I can beamflash a message to Tarrin in secured code and he can enter some forged records in the Libris data store."

"Don't bother him," Denkar whispered back. "All that I have to do is prepare an innocent-looking numeric string to go down the beamflash and straight into the Libris Calculor. We don't need Tarrin."

"You do not understand, Den. We need someone with a password to —"

"No, no, I broke your Calculor's transmission conduit codes back in 1697. I've been able to do whatever I wanted to in your data store for eight years."

Zarvora stopped dead in her tracks. "You what?" she shrieked. Bouros and the Edutor-General stopped and turned. Zarvora waved to them to walk on.

"I can write a numeric string to go down the beamflash network and take over the transmission conduits so that the data that follows is automatically acted upon by the Calculor."

Horror stabbed through Zarvora like the blade of a dagger. "You — you were capable of vandalizing my Libris Calculor for eight years?"

"I confined myself to a few harmless experiments."

"You could have started wars, ruined the economy, destroyed my power and credibility completely, yet, yet ... you did nothing?"

"Zar, darling. I'm not a vandal. The Calculor is an absolutely exquisite piece of work, why should I want to damage it?"

Zarvora's shocked reaction sublimed into warmth and adoration, and she suddenly realized that she was unreservedly trusting someome for the first time in her life.

So this is what it is like to be rescued from a dragon by a handsome kavelar, she thought as she flung her arms around Denkar.

Bouros and the Edutor-General again looked back to where Zarvora and Denkar were standing in the golden lamplight of the tunnel.

"Just look at them, kissing and embracing each other so affectionately," said Bouros.

"It must be a very exciting day for them," agreed the Edutor-General. "Why, getting such a magnificent wedding present as this must melt away the years and make it seem as if they have only just been married."

"Aye, true. Now what could I fashion for my own wife so that our romance would blaze up as fiercely as with those two?"

*****

The wind train journey did not get off to a good start for Glasken. The Eastward K207 had been listed to leave on time until he had booked himself aboard, then the schedule was put back an hour. Glasken cursed, spat on the platform, and made for a nearby tavern. As he sat sipping his ale beneath a vine-smothered pergola he noted that several of the loafers near the station were strutting slowly, rather than just wandering about indolently.

"Black Runners," he said to the serving girl who was removing his empty tankard.

"Indeed, Fras?" she said with polite scepticism.

"Hi, you doubt me," he said, putting an arm around her waist and raising his free hand. "Oi, Black Runners! Ye stand out like tits on a bull!"

Of the dozen people who turned at his shout, two moved with a quite distinct reflex skill.

"Surely they're not all Black Runners, Fras?"

"World's full of 'em," replied Glasken loudly. "Well, time for a stroll down Tumble Street," he said as he stood up.

The girl squeaked with shock and indignation, then ran off. Glasken shouldered his rollpack, twirled his swagger stick and sauntered off toward a tangle of shabby buildings and alleyways nearby. A half hour later he reappeared, a slash across his rollpack and his swagger stick splintered. As he arrived at the platform he stopped to remove a tuft of hair from the toe of his boot.

Darien was on the platform, dressed in a neutral ochre kaftan and blending in with the Kalgoorlie crowd so well that he nearly missed her.

"Frelle Darien, so you're the Dragon dignitary that the Black Runners held the train for," Glasken boomed as he strode through the gate. "I suppose you're on your usual hush-hush work, so I won't bother asking."

Glasken's appalling pun had in fact been accidental, but it was not lost on Darien. She swung a slap at his face, but again Baelsha's training came to his rescue. A quarter-step twist-dodge allowed Darien's hand to sweep harmlessly past his face, and she spun and stumbled with the momentum of her own blow. Without looking back at him she picked herself up and ran from the platform. One of the men who had tried to ambush Glasken in Tumble Street only minutes before came stumbling through the gate holding a bloodied kerchief to his head.

"Oi, she forgot her journey cases," Glasken called to him, tapping the brassbound wooden luggage with his swagger stick. The man glared at Glasken, then pocketed his kerchief and snatched up the journey cases. "I've owed that to you bastards in the Black Runners since 1699," Glasken added, grinning as if hoping for another attack.

The man stalked off, with blood starting to trickle down his face again. Glasken felt a touch at his arm.

"Varsellia!" he exclaimed after staring for a moment.

She held a finger to her lips, then drew Glasken back away from the crowd. The Mayor's sister was dressed as a common goodwife, and ochre sun powder had been heavily applied to her face, giving her the appearance of a much older woman.

"Surely you are not leaving forever?" she said anxiously, without so much as a formal greeting. "I do apologize for throwing you out — though I still think the blame was not all mine."

"Pah, that's nothing, worse has been done to me."

"You are naughty for drinking every night in the taverns."

"And you're guilty of parading me about in front of your petty noble friends as your pet man."

They stood in silence for a moment, contemplating their respective sins and staring down at the red flagstones of the platform.

"So we are both sorry, Fras Reprobate," Varsellia conceded, and Glasken nodded. "Did Ilyire pass on my message?"

"Yes he did, but why are you here, Frelle?"

"To see you off with a sweet memory of Kalgoorlie, lonely boy. I've been watching, I saw you go to Tumble Street and —"

"Oh that! I only went there for some privacy, to beat up a few acquaintances of mine for old times sake. As for the paraline trip, I hope to raise some ... well, venture capital for mercantile dealings."

Her face brightened into a wide smile. "So you're not leaving forever?"

"Weeks, at most."

"Hmm. Mercantile dealings indeed. Well be sure to visit the palace upon your return, Fras Johnny. As the Mayor's sister I can give you some important introductions. Am I forgiven?"

"As long as I am."

When the wind train finally pulled out, it was with a galley engine pushing it until it was clear of the city and able to take better advantage of the light and uncertain breeze.

Near the outskirts of the city the houses were smaller and lower, but still neat little jumbles of red-on-white blocks. Finally they passed through the paraline gate in the immense curve of the city's outer defensive wall, but there were still whole suburbs of nomad tents and shanty dwellings before the train reached the irrigated patchwork of farmland.

"Thae sae Mirrorsun's weakening ther winds," said the Merredinian cook as Glasken bought several jars of ale.

"As long as I'm not pushing pedals in a galley engine, Fras, then I don't care," Glasken replied as he flipped a copper from his change to the man.

"Think thee that Mirrorsun be Deity's disapproving of wind trains, Fras?"

"I think Mirrorsun's the Deity's way of lighting drunks home on moonless nights."

Glasken bought another rollpack and swagger stick at the railside market at Coonana, along with a cap that sported a wicker frame eyeshade and goosefeather painted with one of Mirrorsun's many shapes. He also bought a reel of white ribbon and a handful of lead shot. The wind had begun to pick up by then, and the train made two hundred kilometres per day thereafter. A few kilometres past Naretha Railside he dropped a full bottle of ale through his window into the darkness, and it landed with a clink rather than a smash. It was unlikely that any other refugee from Baelsha would find it before some paraline ganger came by, but Glasken was happier for the gesture.

As the train rolled through Cook Railside on the fourth day of the journey, Glasken was reclining in drink-shrouded contentment, sipping delicately at macadamia mash brandy and watching the treeless expanse of the Nullarbor Plain passing the window. Sensibly, he was chained to the shackle rail on the wall by his waist. He had by now checked the passenger register for unattached women, but there was only one and she was in a private compartment at the back of the train. He thought through various pretexts to meet with her, but there was always the possibility that she was old or unattractive, so he found lethargy the better option.

He was roused as someone walking past stumbled at the open door to his tiny compartment. He caught a flash of green and red needlework woven with gold thread into black fabric very like fine cheesecloth. A woman's robes! She wore a veil of blue gauze that hung from just below her eyes but only reached down to her chin.

"Ta'aal baek, Frelle," he said politely, assuming that she was Islamic, and that a husband, father or other guardian would be close to hand.

"But surely you are not a Southmoor," the woman replied, and Glasken sat up at once.

"No, I'm of the Southeast Alliance, Rochester most recently. John Glasken's the name. Do come in — should you feel my hospitality is honourable."

She stood regarding him for a moment, and he noted what beautiful eyes she had. With the expertise of a practised lecher he also noted that the nipples of her breasts were beginning to stand up under the cloth, and as if to confirm his observation she sinuously slid down into the seat across from him.

"I am Wilpenellia Tienes, from the Capentarian Mayorate of Buchanan."

"I do not know it," he replied easily. "Is it west of Kalgoorlie?"

"No, it's directly north of here."

"Alspring?" exclaimed Glasken with alarm, uncrossing his legs and sitting bolt upright.

"No, not those barbaric nomads!" she exclaimed, throwing her hands up in mock horror. "Carpentaria's Mayorates are far to the north of there. Have you not heard of the Northwest Paraline Authority, and the link through the Great Sandy Desert?"

Glasken had not, but the idea seemed plausible enough.

"So, what faith do you follow there?" he asked.

"Reformed Gentheist, not the Orthodox Gentheist of those Alspring Ghans. I am a scholar, on my way to work on some rare texts at the great library of Rochester, Libris. You look to be a man of learning, have you studied in Libris?"

"In a manner of speaking. You should be impressed by Libris. Why when I worked in there I simply couldn't get out of the place. Just lately I've been settling family matters to the west: an unfortunate death of a distant relative that involved a great deal of wealth."

With these words, Glasken stretched out along his seat like a large and languid cat.

"Ah, a man of means," she said. "And do you like this train travel?"

"With the right sort of company it can become tolerable."

"I hate it, in fact I have a tent that my servants set up every two days or so. There I stay in comfort until the next wind train arrives."

"An eminently civilized method of travel, Frelle. And when is your next stop?"

"Oh, I thought to disembark tonight, possibly at Maralinga Railside. Have you been there?"

"Yes, but years ago. Since then it has grown into a fortified garrison post and beamflash relay, with a nomad market and even a hostelry. The camel patrol station provides maintenance on the paraline from there, and the Call sweeps over it very frequently for some reason. Boring, you might say."

"Boring? Ah, but, Fras Glasken, what glorious peace there is in the desert. Not a sound but the wind, none of the bustle of the towns and cities, nor the rumble and rattle of the trains. Have you ever slept in the desert, Fras?"

She drew breath rapidly, so that her veil outlined the pouting lips beneath. Glasken found the effect unsettlingly erotic.

"I — have been known to. And I do admit that it was rare tranquil."

"So, you have experience in this country ... and I have nothing but my maids and eunuchs for company. Would your timetable allow you to extend your trip by a day or two to watch over my tent and ply me with tales of the Alliance Mayorates?"

Glasken considered, his heart rate accelerating. The woman was forward indeed ... and whatever he did here, it would be to his advantage.

"I might be persuaded," he conceded. "Would you drink to such a thing?"

"Only from a glass tumbler, Fras. We must remain civilized, whatever the beauty and tranquillity of the wilderness we travel."

Glasken jerked the service cord for a new jar of brandy and an extra tumbler, and once the waiter had gone they drank to the Nullarbor Plain and the tranquillity of the desert. Glasken was already ahead by an entire jar, but felt obliged to match her drink for drink. He did not notice the heavily disguised Theresla squeeze something into her mouth while feigning to politely stifle a belch.

Theresla slid over to his bench with a flowing rustle of cloth, and Glasken's arm snaked under hers to seize and fondle her left breast. She immediately lifted her veil a little and planted her lips against his, sliding her tongue into his mouth in a lingering, passionate kiss. The nightwing solution in her mouth — that she was immune to — worked surprisingly quickly on even such a large and powerfully-built man as Glasken.

In an unexpected bonus for Theresla, a Call rolled over the train while it was still a kilometre from the Maralinga Railside. As the train thumped into the safety buffers Theresla already had Glasken on a lead. She dragged him to the stables and appropriated two camels, which she loaded with packs that she had ready aboard the train. Glasken was too large and strong for her to strap into a saddle, so she let him walk south beside the camels on the end of a rope. When the Call stopped for the night she fed him, then manoeuvred him into his saddle frame. The food that she had given him had been mixed with salts of nightwing, and Glasken fell asleep. Theresla led their camels out of the stationary Call zone and further south, toward the Edge.

*****

Glasken awoke with dawn seeping through the fabric of an ochre-coloured tent. His head was muddled with something that was not quite sleep, but he knew at once from the silence that he was somewhere very remote. There was a sweet, pleasant scent on the air, and the ground was strewn with blankets and air-cushions.

"Where's the train?" he said to nobody in particular, and was surprised to be answered.

"Long gone, my bold and passionate lover," a woman's voice purred from the other side of the tent. "Was I right? Was my tent indeed more comfortable than the train?"

Glasken raised his head, to see the veiled face of a kneeling, seemingly naked woman across the other side of the tent. "Wilpenellia?"

"Oh, Fras, but you hold the spirits rare well. Why last night you drank so much as would kill a squad of our finest lancers in Carpentaria. How are your passions this morning?"

Glasken considered. His head was muddled rather than splitting with a hangover, and his lusts seemed as rampant as if he had been abstaining for several days.

"My passions are in perfect working order, Frelle Wilpenellia," he said guardedly, unwilling to concede that he remembered nothing past kissing her aboard the train.

She slowly raised herself to her knees, confirming that she was naked except for the veil. Her skin was faintly honey-brown. Glasken got to his knees as well, noting that he too was naked.

"Frelle, you had best remind me," he said, affecting a suave leer. Then he recognized the smallish yet perfectly formed breasts in the Davantine classic shape. He began shuffling across the blanket toward her, knowing full well that they would never meet.

"Wait!" she said, holding up a hand. "Wait, please, Fras..."

"What is it?"

"Just — a cramp, it will pass, just wait."

This was Theresla, there was no doubt about it at all. That shape, that voice ... the last time any woman had ever asked him to wait, it had been Theresla, and a Call had been close at hand. She could sense it coming, she would wait until it was nearly upon them and say 'Come to me, Johnny Glasken. Come do what you will.'

"Ah, the cramp has passed. Come now, Johnny Glasken, and do what you will."

Glasken slammed down mental shutters developed and nurtured in him by the abbot of Baelsha over many, many celibate years. He squeezed desire from himself like water wrung from a sponge as the Call's front rolled across the tent. Glasken was torn by allurement that he did not think possible clawing at everything that made up his being, yet he remained hunched over with his fists clenched, shivering and gasping for breath. Theresla stared down at him in amazement.

"You resist it," she whispered. "A human resisting the Call, not just collapsing. How?"

Glasken did not reply. There were hours of this to go yet, and he needed all his strength to last that long.

"You resist the Call by yourself, the allure of my charms has nothing to do with it," Theresla continued. "How did this happen? Who spoiled you so?"

Slowly she tilted his head up. His eyes were open, he was aware of her naked body a handspan from his face, yet she no longer allured him. He would not let her allure him.

*****

The trailing edge of the Call passed the tent, and Glasken slumped to the blanket, limp and exhausted.

"That was amazing, Fras Glasken," said Theresla.

"A ... man of talent, Frelle Abbess," panted Glasken. "I should have known you'd drag me back to this very spot for another of your weird experiments. At least this time it was inside a tent."

"Please, have a drink."

"More of your drugs and potions?"

"I'll partake first."

"You probably drink a little every day to become immune, just like your brother."

"Oh take it, damn you!" shouted Theresla, flinging the waterskin across to him. "You have nothing that I want anymore. Your desire for my body once let me reach out beyond the Call itself, but now you are like a cold, empty cave. You fought against the allure of both me and the Call, like a cornered rat against a terrier. Even the Koorees can't stay awake like you did, they just collapse. You're not an aviad either, but — but how did you do that? You must be the only human in the world who can remain even partly aware during a Call."

"I've had lessons."

"From who?"

"Never mind. The technique is exhausting so I prefer to use a tether, like other folk. So, what now? Where are we? I'd like to be about my business, if you please."

"A long way south of the paraline, not far from the Edge itself. The very spot where I conducted my first experiments with you over five years ago. As to what now, we can return to the line and catch a wind train whenever you like."

"I like now," said Glasken, sitting up and rummaging unsuccessfully for his clothing and boots.

"Fras, we are far from anywhere," she said as she lay back and raised a leg enticingly, staring up at the roof of the tent. "If you wish to introduce me to the delights of the flesh, I would be amenable. Virginity is of no more use to me now that you are spoiled."

Glasken gave her a sidelong glance, then frowned and shook his head. With that he caught sight of his clothing in a corner and crawled across to retrive it.

"You'd better let another relieve you of that inexperience, Frelle," he said as he checked that his purse and pockets had not been looted. "No slight on your wonderful charms, of course, but I just have no trust in anything that you say. Not after what you did with me five years ago, and what you just tried to do again."

"Nobody has *ever* denied me what I have sought!" snapped Theresla, abruptly sitting up on the blanket.

Glasken shrugged, pointedly holding his bundle of clothing across his loins. "It has nevertheless happened, Frelle." He reached for his flintlock pistol, then presented it to her butt first. "Here, kill me to prevent the world from learning that a man has rejected your advances — yet it has still happened."

Theresla slumped back on her haunches, her head turned to one side. "Take it away, Fras. I'll leave you alone."

"Time to go, if we are to go," said Glasken. "I'll dress outside."

"Oh do it in here. I would not be embarrassed."

"But I would. I find the acts of clothing and de-clothing to be intensely erotic, Frelle Theresla."

Glasken unlaced the tent flap and stepped outside, looking around as he began to dress. As he suspected, it was the flat, treeless semi-desert of the Nullarbor Plain, and off to one side were the Edge cliffs with the dark blue of the ocean horizon beyond. By its very nature it was almost devoid of landmarks, but nearby was the crude Call-wall that he had built back in 1700 ... and close by was the flat stone covering the hole in the ground that was the entrance to Ilyire's treasure cave.

This is an incredible stroke of luck, he thought to himself. Theresla had brought him to the very place that he had been seeking, the place to which Ilyire would not return.

Theresla emerged from the tent fully dressed. "Apparently Ilyire has a treasure cave somewhere near here," she said as she joined him. "Darien mentioned it in a letter to me."

"I'll wager it's well hidden," replied Glasken, suspecting this to be yet another of her tricks, but trying to be polite.

"We could search for it and share what we find."

"Plunder my friend's treasure? I'd rather not."

"Your friend? Ah, but that's right. I hear that you got him rolling drunk then had him laid a-bed with a couple of hopsicles who pour beer at the Green Dragon's Tankard. So, he's changed too. He used to be such a nuisance to me."

"So you shot him?"

"Fras Glasken, I had first tapped his chest and felt the concealed armour before I took aim. I wanted to shock him, not kill him. Ilyire drinking and wenching, while you — you were once the very incarnation of the verb priapic, but now neither sex nor even wealth tempt you."

"They got me into a lot of trouble, Frelle. They have their attractions, I must say, but I have learned to approach them with a lot more caution."

Glasken walked over to where the camels were tethered and checked the gear and harnesses. "Bloody camels," he muttered. "Even when they are standing up, you feel as if you are falling."

Theresla had already begun to pack away the gear from the tent as he returned, but he stopped dead as she turned to point his own flintlock pistol at him.

Glasken raised his hands. "More nuttery in the name of science, Frelle?" he asked wearily.

"Fras Glasken, I've tried to give you my body, I've tried to give you wealth, but now you are going to get the third gift I have to offer whether you want it or not. Walk toward the Edge, and when you enter that narrow Calldeath region, do whatever you do to resist it."

Theresla put the gun down as Glasken entered and began to fight the weaker permanent Call. Theresla held him by the belt tether and walked beside him, ready to trip him if he suddenly lost control. Glasken was by now very tired, but was still awake and aware as they reached the edge of the cliff. It dropped sheer to rocks pounded by the ocean waves.

"Stop here, Fras Glasken, and look out across the water. Those dark shapes out there, note them well. They are the source of the Call. See there, one broke the surface and blew water into the air. No human has ever seen such a sight as this, and not many aviads have done so either. Remember this, all of it. Down there on the rocks, the bones of animals and people that plunged to their death after being lured here by the Call. The treasure in Ilyire's secret cave came from down there, from such folk who fell just a little short of answering the Call in the truest possible sense. Look a little further out, that great dark thing is one of the Call-creatures' livestock. It is a fanged fish as long as the carriage of a wind train. The Call-creatures are even bigger. Yes, brave Fras, and I know that you are growing very tired. Come back out of the Calldeath strip with me now, and I shall take you back to Maralinga. Do not fear me, either. There will be no more tricks."

*****

The journey back to the paraline took several days. Theresla and Glasken rode together, exchanging stories of the preceding five years, ranging from her explorations in the Calldeath lands to Ilyire's first night on the town. Glasken was reluctant to talk about his time in

Baelsha, but under persistent questioning he eventually outlined some of his training, trials and torments.

"I begin to understand," Theresla said as their camels swayed along together. "The monks taught you to meditate on an object like a mandala, except that it was something that symbolized the Call's greatest hold upon you. That symbol, that mandala-object was almost certainly me."

"Why, yes!" agreed Glasken in surprise. "How did you know that?"

"You, Fras, are highly, perhaps even grotesquely oversexed. I once used that feature to attune myself to voices within the Call. Now, however, you have been trained to use my image as a channel to divert the allure of the Call past you. You know within the deepest recesses of your mind that you will never let yourself have a physical consummation with me, and that is your strength. If you did you would lose that fantastic and unique resistance to the Call. I am probably the only woman throughout the entire world that you cannot allow yourself to mount."

Glasken nodded agreement and sat up a little more erect in the saddle. He knew that he was exceptional in his resistance to the Call, but to be considered unique was something more like an honour. He rode on in silence for a time, thinking through the logic of it.

"The Baelsha monks, the Kooree nomads, all of them merely drop down unconscious at the touch of the Call, but I can remain awake as well. Why is that?"

"As I said before, you're very highly sexed. Your sexual energies are probably so great as to cancel out the Call itself when channelled through my image. In a way it's probably not much different from the way that I held you against the Call without a tether, back in 1700. I was able to hear —"

She suddenly stopped speaking, and sat rubbing her chin and staring ahead with unfocussed eyes.

"What could you hear, Frelle?" asked Glasken after a moment.

"Oh ... I was able to hear Ilyire shouting and cursing from the base of the cliff, where I had left him stranded. Ah, my senses became very acute."

"It was the opposite with me. I was blanked."

"That was in 1700. What about this time?"

"Very different. Your voice sounded distant and echoing. There were other voices as well, but speaking a confused and garbled language. It was like picking a few familiar words out of the background babble of a crowded tavern in a foreign Mayorate. It was somewhat ... familiar, rather like being drunk and hallucinating. I didn't know what to make of it."

"Can you remember any of the words?"

"Ah ... no, they were just a confused dreamlike sound. If you had asked me earlier I might have recalled a few. It was like when you later walked me through that Calldeath strip to the Edge itself. I saw dark, distant shapes in an incomprehendably large lake, but none of it was like anything that I had encountered before, so it had no meaning for me."

Theresla thought about this for many minutes, staring straight ahead. Glasken surreptitiously dropped yet another length of white ribbon weighted at one end by a flintlock leadshot.

"Live long, Fras Glasken," Theresla said at last. "Do not get yourself killed for a very long time."

"Well, the same to you too, Frelle," asked Glasken puzzled, "but what do you really mean by saying that?"

Theresla turned to stare directly at him. "I mean what I mean, Fras. *I* am special, but *you* are extraordinary, and quite possibly unique. At some time in the future I may wish to ..."

"To what?" he asked suspiciously.

"I don't know yet, but whatever it is, it will be harmless. Trust me — No! Whatever you do, don't trust me, not ever."

They both began to laugh.

"Nothing easier to do than that, Frelle Theresla. So what will you do now? Continue your journey east to Libris or wherever?"

"No, I have business in Kalgoorlie. I was returning from the western Calldeath lands anyway when Zarvora sent word that you were alive and in Kalgoorlie, but I only boarded the train after someone dropped word to me that you were boarding. It took the word of Mayor Bouros himself to convince the Great Western Paraline Authority to depart from their precious schedule for even one hour."

"Oh so! Then what about those Tiger Dragons and the Dragon Silver Librarian in disguise at the terminus platform?"

"I've no idea. Tell me."

"Never mind. You said never to trust you."

A white smudge was by now visible on the straight-edge horizon, and Glasken realized that they were within sight of Maralinga. He hurriedly checked a little compass concealed in his hand while pretending to cough.

"How were you deflowered, Fras Glasken, if you don't mind me asking?"

Glasken nearly dropped his compass in surprise, but rccovered well. He glanced across furtively to Theresla, but she had turned away with a fit of giggling.

"Ah now," he said, firmly ignoring her mirth, "when I was fourteen I was quite a good hand with the lutina, with my voice already deep. I used to be hired by the local hicks to serenade their Frelles for them, and one night the girl at the upstairs window thought that I was the one who was meant to be invited in. Not knowing any better, I went inside, then found that she had more in mind than a couple more songs and a goblet of grape juice. I nearly broke and ran in a panic, I mean one of the older lads at our school had thought the navel to be involved when he found himself in similar circumstances. He had never been allowed to hear the end of it."

"What did you do?"

"I put my hands over my eyes and said 'Pretty Frelle, this is my very first time', fully expecting to be laughed out of the house. Instead she said 'How wonderful, my first virgin. I had been wondering if all men were born already deflowered'. We had a wonderful time together. She was an earthy, jolly Frelle."

"And her, ah, I mean what of your client? The one who hired you to play and sing on his behalf?"

"He went off in a fury and sent some bully boys over to lie in wait for me when I left. It was quite a fight, but the bruises were worth it. They also smashed the lutina, but it was not hired in my name, so did I care?"

"That's lovely, Fras Glasken," Theresla laughed as he dropped another stone and white ribbon. "Couples seem to get together in such silly and unsuitable ways, don't they, yet their unions can lead to great merchant houses, mighty alliances of Mayorates, advances in scholarship, anything and everything. Just one awkward, vulnerable moment, one silly remark, one desperate gesture when pride, dignity and self-respect are offered to another in one's trembling hand ..."

"One gently pinched bottom that does not result in a slap?"

Theresla pouted at him, but her eyes narrowed. "You have a way of going straight for the crude basics, Fras, but in a sense it's quite a virtue. Tell me now, if you were a woman, and were you interested in ... initiation, what would you do?"

"Find a man."

"By my age, the alluring men are all taken, and those that are left have been left for a variety of very good reasons."

Glasken thought for a moment on functional requirements. "Theresla, if you're really determined to bed someone for its own sake, then just select a nice Fras who is already taken and get him to a hostelry one afternoon with a couple of jars of the great leveller."

"Fras Glasken! That's ... that's worth further thought. Is there anyone that you would recommend?"

"Men are quite out of my experience ... Ah now, but wait, I should have thought of it earlier! You could try the Libris Calculor in Rochester. Many of the men there have been starved of passion through punishment or whatever. It's a cruel torture, most surely. One Dragon Librarian named Dolorian once allowed me to fondle her through the bars of my cell, then flounced off without allowing what I had assumed was to follow. I — I thought that I would take fire, so hot did I burn. Cruel bitch, it was a hateful thing to do to a man."

"So, the Calculor men are visited by some of their female guards?"

"The regulators, yes."

"The women must have a feeling of control."

"Perhaps, but they make those poor imprisoned sods very happy, whatever the circumstance. You would, especially."

"Interesting advice, but I am not going to Rochester for some weeks."

"Well, if those weeks are fruitless, bear it in mind."

Theresla reached over and gave him a playful push with the end of her riding whip. "What of Varsellia? She was very worried about losing you as her fluffy bit."

" 'Bit of fluff' is the term. That's all patched up now. We're friends again."

"Friends. You have never been in love, Fras Johnny Glasken."

It was a statement rather than a question. He thought about it for a moment.

"You may be right."

"In one of our classic Alspring romances it is written that rakes don't really like women, they like only sex and conquest. You, Fras Johnny, are not a rake, for all your wild behaviour. Your heart is in the right place, even if the rest of you is somewhat, ah, somewhat ..."

"Thank you, Frelle, I get the idea — and you're right. You've pointed out a genuine weakness in me that I must take steps to repair. I must work harder at caring less and turning into a true rake."

"Fras Glasken, think again. Rake? Pah! Some day I am going to enjoy a truly epic fit of hysterics at your expense when you are proved wrong."

*****

With Theresla safely on a wind train that was vanishing into the heat shimmers of the west, Glasken strode over to the stables to equip himself for a second — and this time lone — expedition across the Nullarbor. As he fumbled for gold coins to pay for stores and camels he felt a square of poorpaper at the bottom of his purse. He took it out and unfolded it, then read it aloud.

"Fras Glasken, Theresla is return palace. Highliber tell her. You go paraline Great Western. I fix so Theresla know. Varsellia says call in to squeeze her some time. Or something like that, yes? Your drinker friend, Ilyire."

Glasken smiled and dropped the paper into the coals of the stables' forge, where it ignited with a pop and became smoke and ash. It had been a desperate gamble, but it had paid off. Theresla had taken him where Ilyire could not bring himself to go again, and this time Glasken had been careful to note directions and drop markers as they returned to Maralinga.

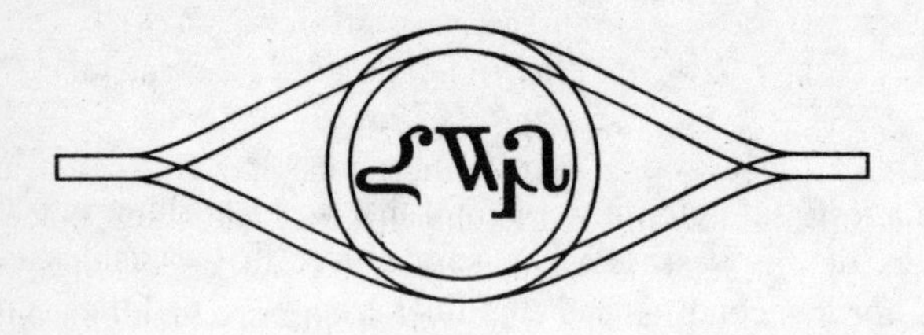

Part 3

JEMLI

Glasken spent a number of weeks on the Nullarbor, and returned to Ilyire's treasure cave at the Edge several times to strip it of everything of value. He re-secreted about three quarters of the treasure in several other caves of his own choosing. He also removed Ervelle's bones and wrapped them in a saddle blanket. Finally, he stood in the cemetery at Maralinga Railside early one morning and saw to it that the bones of Ervelle were buried properly. A hired band played the old Alspring tune, *Ervelle's Farewell*, that he had taught them only the day before, while a Reformed Gentheist lay minister from the beamflash crew — the closest equivalent of the Alspring Orthodox Gentheist religion that Glasken knew of — read a service.

"Ilyire begs forgiveness," Glasken said in Alspring as he sprinkled a handful of pinkish limestone dust into the open grave, "and we'd best not judge him too harshly. Without Ilyire you'd not be here."

The headstone bore Ervelle's name in both Alspring script and Austaric Roman, and well as the dates of her birth and death. The stone had been sent out on a wind train by Ilyire, and was there when Glasken had returned with her bones. Glasken stood watching the hired paraline navvies shovelling limestone rock and sand into the grave, and a plume of dust streamed away from the hole in the hot, blustery wind like a tenuous white soul that was frcc at last. He raised his cap a fraction.

"Glad to be of service, Frelle," he whispered, "and I hope one day in the future to meet some girl as wonderful as you were said to be. Preferably today. Theresla was right, I can't be a real rake: I'm too romantic at heart."

A wind train was due in the afternoon, and Glasken wandered about the railside, looking at the changes that had taken place in the six years since he had last been there. What surprised him most was the scatter of Alspring Ghans who were living in a small encampment to the east of the railside. There were fifteen or twenty of them, and about sixty camels munching on fodder in wooden troughs. Two Kooree men were lounging in the shade of the warehouse, speaking to one of the uniformed railside staff. Glasken could draw his own conclusions easily enough: the Ghans had negotiated some sort of caravan rights across Kooree land, and were now trading with merchants on the wind trains. Coffee would be of great interest to the merchants from the inland. He doubted that any political contacts had as yet been established.

The sight of the Ghans brought memories back to him, and he began to wonder what had happened to the Dragon Silver Librarian who had abducted him from Maralinga all those years ago and taken him north through the deserts and to the edge of the territory of the Alspring Cities. Had Lemorel been somehow responsible for these tenuous trade links that he saw now, or had she been killed within minutes of him escaping her? That had been during a fight with a group of Alspring Ghans, a fight that his former lover had provoked. *Probably not,* Glasken decided. *She'd already shot most of them before I was up on my camel and away.*

Glasken found himself feeling no remorse at all for any of his dealings with Lemorel. He had indeed cheated on her while they had been lovers back at Rochester University, but that hardly justified her setting the Black Runners onto him, having him sent to the Libris Calculor, then subjecting him to enforced celibacy and slave labour — and worst of all, tantalizing him with the quite ravishingly attractive Frelle Dolorian. Had he not escaped via the Battle Calculor at Woodvale, he would still be in Libris, and his love life would be confined to memories and longings. Again, when he had emerged from the desert with Theresla and Ilyire after unspeakable trials and suffering, it was Lemorel who had stolen up behind him and his paramour for the night and clouted him in mid-coitus. Revenge was one thing, vindictive sadism was quite another.

Wandering past the railside's cemetery Glasken noticed that three Ghan merchants were prostrating themselves before Ervelle's grave and wailing softly in unison. He recognized some words: it was a prayer of reconciliation. The ticketmaster came up to him as he stood watching.

"It took them only minutes to discover that grave this morning, Fras. They're been wailing there in rotation ever since."

"They must have heard the tune being played at the burial."

"Just whose bones are they?"

"Ervelle was an exceedingly beautiful young Alspring woman who was mistakenly sentenced to death a very long time ago. She was turned loose into a Call, strapped to a camel. I ... chanced upon the bones, and was already familiar with the legend. The legend is very famous with the Alspring Ghans, as you can see."

"I certainly do. Fras, you may have made Maralinga some sort of shrine or holy place for them. Your name should be on the headstone too."

"Oh no, no, good Fras, my name should definitely not be there. Ervelle is at rest and there's an end of it. I don't want to be part of someone else's legend."

"As you will, Fras. Now, this afternoon's wind train west has no A-class compartments left, according to the beamflash."

"Ach, no! I couldn't sit up in a B-class seat all the way to Kalgoorlie, not after five weeks on a camel."

"Fras, Fras, let me finish. I fully expect that several A-class compartments will be vacated when the train arrives, however. Merchants, especially coffee merchants, come here to trade with the Ghans, Fras, then return east. It always happens."

The wind train was later than expected, and Glasken impatiently paced the platform with his heavy rollpack. He would have loved to have had a drink at the railside refectory, but with a rollpack full of gold he was not about to let himself get drunk. He settled on a bath and shave, luxuriating in cool water from the cisterns for a half hour. The glow of the sunset faded in the west as Mirrorsun rose in the east. Its form this night was a dull bar of reddish light across the band in the sky, and the band was actually visible right across the sky due to earthlight. He was staring up at the sky when he realized that he could hear the rumble of the wind train finally arriving.

Glasken stood back as the front rotor engine rolled past, its brake blocks squealing and its rotors disengaged and spinning free. In the lamplight it looked like some enormous, unwieldy insect. The Alspring Ghans rushed about, shouting their wares to the merchants emerging from the coaches, and the quiet railside rapidly became a bustling night market. Merchants' lackeys unloaded bags of coffee beans and a variety of spices. Glasken was about to push his way through the crowd to one of the carriages when he suddenly noticed Darien stepping down from a carriage.

Dragon Silver Librarian and former friend of Lemorel, he reminded himself — for the memories that had emerged with the proximity of so many Ghans were still fresh in his mind

He eased back into the shadows beside the kiosk and watched while a robed Alspring Ghan went up to her and addressed her after an elaborate flourish. The mute Darien selected a card from a small satchel on her belt and handed it to him. He read, bowed, then gestured toward the camp. Glasken was puzzled, but relieved that she was going away. Only now did he make for the train. The railside's ticket seller met him at the door of the A-class carriage.

"Fras Glasken, you are in luck. The Purser's board shows that several A-class compartments are now free. I have assigned A1 to you, I'll just mark your ticket."

Glasken was pleased with that. He wanted privacy whenever he opened his rollpack, quite apart from the luxury of having a folding bunk to stretch out along, and his own privy and demi-drench.

"Was one of them vacated by a Dragon Silver Librarian?" he asked casually.

"I cannot say, Fras."

"Former lover," Glasken lied easily.

"Ah," sighed the ticket seller. "You shall travel in peace."

The whistle blew for departure, and a check was made that all but the five merchant passengers were back aboard. Glasken held up his ticket to an approaching conductor, but the rotund and splendidly-dressed man brushed past him without a word. He was dabbing essence of hedgerose on his face from a small bottle, and his freshly waxed moustache looked as if it had been carved out of blackwood and oil-polished. *Aye, and in your position I'd not expect anyone to get on at Maralinga either,* Glasken concluded, then wondered why the conductor was wearing a parade uniform in the middle of the Nullarbor Plain.

The train began to roll slowly along the rails, with a smooth and gently rocking motion. Glasken checked his ticket: compartment A1. He noted that compartments A5 up to A2 were vacant, with their doors open, but A1 was shut as he reached it. Glasken assumed that it was something to do with it being reserved for him, and he slid the door aside and stepped in without breaking stride.

A woman in her mid-twenties was reclining on the bench seat. She was very tall, but with a well-curved and attractive figure beneath her plain dretan of sienna cotton. Her face was a pleasant oval, framed by honey-brown hair that was unbound and cascading down to the seat and as far as the floor. She was wearing scuffed clogs on her feet. At the sight of Glasken she shrank back in alarm.

"Oh — I'm in here!" she squeaked in surprise, then snapped in a much deeper voice: "Now you get out!"

Glasken was quite weary, and in no mood to be pushed around. He sat down heavily beside her, footsore from pacing the platform and depressed from the funeral.

"Indeed you are in here, Frelle, but A1 has been assigned to me." He held up the ticket, which had been marked to A1.

"A1 was not booked," she insisted.

"I only boarded the train a minute ago." His eyes flicked from her to her luggage. He noticed a large, battered artisan's toolbag and overnighter in the corner.

"The conductor assigned me to A1," she insisted. "You get out or I'm seeing the conductor."

Glasken began to rub the muscles along the back of his neck. "It's my bet that you're about to see more of him that I ever wish to. Artisans like you can't afford A-class tickets. You crept up here from B or even C. *You* get out and get back to your place. I'm going to report the both of you to the Purser."

A subtle sag of her shoulders showed that his retort had hit home, and that her resolve had collapsed. With her lips pressed together she stood up and hoisted her bag's strap to her shoulder.

"Good Fras, I — I, please, I apologize, I'll go." Her tone was now completely different. "My miserly clockmaker husband gave me only enough for a B-class fare, but just now the conductor said he'd let me ride in a vacant A-class compartment for tonight. Please, good Fras, don't report me. I'm not up to a fine, and they'll impound the tools of my trade if I can't pay. I'd have to sell my hair."

Suddenly Glasken imagined himself in her position, staring down with her hurt, frightened brown eyes. The woman was tall, so she would have had trouble sleeping in even the B-class seats. No doubt the conductor had hastened to make things more comfortable for her in return for a little company during the rest of the journey, now that the coffee merchants were gone.

Just because you're big, everyone assumes it doesn't matter if you're hurt, he thought to himself.

She began to sidle out, giving a deferential little bow at each step. He thrust his foot out to block the doorway.

"Frelle, I've just made a complete beast of myself," he said as he reached for the strap of his rollpack. "I've just hurt you, and I'm very, very sorry. *Don't* say you forgive me, I don't deserve it. You stay here, I'll move to A2. If anyone else gives you trouble, just call me and I'll punch some manners into him."

Glasken stood up, unfolding and straightening to his full two metres. He blinked with surprise to find that even when standing he still had to look up slightly to meet her eyes.

"You — you're leaving? But A1 is booked to you," she said, plainly confused.

"I'm giving myself a lesson in manners, Frelle. Besides, compartments A2 to A5 are still vacant. They're all the same."

"Then you'll not report me to the Purser, good Fras?"

"As I said, no great harm done, pretty Frelle. Nothing that a mere smack on the bottom would not set right."

He grinned wearily at her. She grinned back, yet something subtle was being transformed in her expression. Her face hardly seemed to belong to the same woman as she regarded him coyly over her shoulder.

"So, you'd be liking to smack bottoms, Fras?"

"Only if I be allowed to rub them better again, Frelle," he quipped, finding the words out of his mouth before he was aware of speaking them.

She put her free hand on her hip, then presented the curve of her left buttock to him with a slow, rolling motion.

"Well Fras, I'm waiting," she said, batting her unusually long eyelashes at him.

Glasken did a double take: he had not even been trying to seduce the woman, and furthermore she was also still free to share any of the vacant compartments with the conductor. He reached for her hand.

"Pretty, graceful Frelle, I could never bring myself to smack a bottom as lovely as yours," he declared, then brushed her hand with a kiss. "But you don't have to play up to me. I understand what you have arranged with, ah, your friend out there."

She dropped her bag and slid her arms about him. "Fras, you have just behaved as more of a gentleman to me than any man ever has. Please don't walk out, or I really will be hurt."

Glasken slowly put his arms about her and squeezed gently. "Well then, I can't have you hurt," he whispered. "That would never do."

Her lips hovered close to Glasken's, and after another moment they drew each other into a long, soft kiss. Her skin was slightly moist, and he could feel her heart pattering wildly. At length he edged the door closed with his boot. Now he was very thankful that he had paid the price of a shave and bath back at Maralinga Railside. She slipped off her blackwood clogs, and their eyes were level as they stood together with their foreheads pressed together.

Nearly an hour later Glasken rang for service. The conductor rapped at the door after an unusually long delay.

"A jar of Sundew rosé and two tumblers, if you please," called Glasken without opening the door. "And leave 'em in the shutterbox."

"Very good, Fras," replied the conductor, making a note in his pocketbook. He walked briskly down the narrow corridor as if he was anxious to complete some unpleasant duty and have it out of the way. He reached the galley and sought out the cook. "A jar of Sundew leg-opener for the pair in A1," he snapped.

"So, Fras, your little arrangement for the night has gone awry?"

"That would be bad enough in itself, but ... but I overheard what must have been the most *ridiculous* proposition in the history of the Great Western Paraline Authority."

"Ridiculous or not, if it worked it was well wrought."

"That's what hurts. I had other A-class compartments free, she *knew* that, yet she chose to stay in A1 with him."

"Well Fras, he must be exceptional indeed," said the cook as he placed Glasken's jar and two tumblers on a tray. "If you were of a spiteful nature you might pray for strong winds."

*****

The following morning Glasken and his companion lay together on the narrow bunk in compartment A1, she watching the brightening sky and almost featureless panorama of the Nullarbor Plain through the window of the compartment, and he regarding the shape of the breasts pressing against his chest.

"Are you sure you can breathe under my weight, Fras Johnny?" she asked yet again.

"Stay there, pretty Frelle, please. I can feel you all the better from below," he said as he lay caressing her long and sinuous back.

"I'm ninety kilograms."

"So? I'm fifteen more than that. Frelle Jemli, you're also as svelte as any dancing girl. You just happen to be quite a lot taller." He peered at a passing K-stone and frowned to see the train making good time. "So, your clockmaker husband is in Kalgoorlie already?"

"No, he's back in Rochester doing contract work for Libris, the big library there," she said with unmistakable distaste in her tone. She stretched out with her hands against the bulkhead. "He heard about the demand for clockwork in Kalgoorlie but was not sure about leaving secure employ in Rochester. I said I'd go in his stead, to see what the place was really like. I have some skill in clockwork myself, my father was a clockmaker, you see. The plan is that I work in the west a while and test out the prospects."

"Oh so! You will be alone. Will you be in need of someone to tend the springs of your clockwork."

"Yesss. Will your key will be available for winding, Fras Johnny Glasken?"

Glasken rolled on top of her. "Aye, that it will. You had best send your husband bad reports of the place or he will order you back."

"Pah, then he can sleep alone!" she replied, wriggling against Glasken and holding him more tightly against her. "I'm never going back to Rochester and its strutting Dragon Librarians, or to Rutherglen to be harassed by the Constable's Runners."

"Surely you've not been a felon, Frelle?" asked Glasken, at once nervous about his bag full of gold on the floor.

She put a hand theatrically to her forehead, then flung both arms in the air before squeezing Glasken again. "No, it's a family felony that I need to escape from. I've got a sister as you'd never believe. Brains of the Family, that's what dada always called her, and just because she passed a few exams and brought home damn stupid depressed poets all reading their rubbish to dada, brother and me besides — biggest audience they ever got, if you ask me. I've hated poets ever since then. You're not a poet, are you, Fras?"

"Not damn likely, although I'm known to play the lutina and sing when I've a half-litre in me."

"Ah, that's a relief."

"How come you to be a clockmaker?"

"Ach, dada made me an apprentice at fourteen and saved the money to send Brains of the Family to median level at school. 'What about me then?' I asked? 'Oh no,' says the teachers to dada, 'she's too slow, look at her.' *Of course* I looked slow, I was two metres tall when I was in 5th grade, but I was only eleven! What the fykart did they expect? I *looked* eighteen, but I wasn't eighteen and stupid, I was eleven and bright."

"Dummart bastards," Glasken sighed. "I was big for my age too, and I got the same treatment. So, you got pushed into the workshop?"

"Pah, not without a struggle. I studied harder, I knew what dada would do so I minded my lessons while I could still have 'em. As soon as I was the minimum age, Bang! Straight into shop, grinding lenses and cutting gearwheels. Ah, Fras, but I studied and studied by myself after that, and I made a little money washing folks' windows and the like. In '96, when time for medians came round, I booked myself in and paid the fee myself too. They said I needed four years more formal school but I said get away, it's my money. I got my median certificate too, that I did, but only just — and only *one year* after my older sister who's got four years of age on me. Anyone impressed? Pah! Do you think dada cared for anyone but Brains of the Family older sister and heir-to-business brother? Not bloody likely! Everyone said 'Poor big, silly girl, she was lucky to pass.' Damn right I was lucky to only just pass, I was only sixteen!"

"Fine work indeed," said Glasken. "That's three years ahead of me, age-wise."

"Unfair, Fras, it was unfair. It really — now there's a thought. Where's the privy in A-class?"

Glasken rolled to one side and pointed to what she had assumed to be a wardrobe. "All self-contained luxury in here, Frelle Jemli."

She rummaged for something in her bag, then sidled through the narrow door of the privy. Within her now open bag Glasken could see several books. Suddenly he sat up on the bunk with a start. It was not so much the title, *Encyclopedia of Mechanical Physics*, that had alarmed him, as the embossed red letters declaring *Libris Reading Room Reference: Do Not Remove.*

Jemli emerged and washed her hands in the demi-drench with a little bar of scented soap.

"You would not be a Dragon Librarian travelling incognito?" asked Glasken nervously. "Would you?"

"Librarian! Absolutely not, Fras. Why do you ask?"

"That book I can see in your bag."

"Oh that?" she said dismissively. "I stole it."

"From the *Libris Reading Room*?"

"Aye. It wasn't easy, the place is fearsomely well guarded, but I needed it."

"But, but, but — it was *Libris*! Readers in there get shot for even picking their noses before touching the books, you know? One fart and it's twenty years on a chain gang if you wake the duty librarian at the Reference Desk, and *you* stole a *book*?"

"I stole eleven books from there, Fras. They're in my bag."

"Gak —" Glasken choked, and was speechless for a moment." But why? You can't sell them, no fence would be game to touch them. It's safer to rob a Constable's Watchhouse."

"I needed them, and there's an end to it! I had no money to buy transcript sheets, and no time to spend copying out what I needed for my subjects."

"Subjects? For advancement in your Guild, you mean?"

"The Guild? Pox take the Guild, though none of its members could get it up long enough to catch the pox. It's Rochester University I was in. I've done the subjects of Physics, Mathematics, Logic, Chemistric, Philosophy, Accounting, Contract Law, and Applied Merchantile Morality at Rochester one year at a time while studying by night and grinding lenses and tending the books of my doddering husband's business by day. Took me eight years, even with stolen books to use at home at my leisure — and I used the term leisure loosely, Fras."

"Extraordinary. And after all that effort you gave it up to come to Kalgoorlie before doing the final year?"

"Oh no, when this chance for Kalgoorlie came, why I thought to myself: damn husband and damn lenswork and damn stupid little gearwheels, *I'm* transferring my subject credits to Kalgoorlie University, and once I get the money together I'm enrolling and doing my four finals, one at a time. I'll graduate in four years, Fras, and after that it's divorce and into the beamflash service for me. Tower captain, I'll be that in 25 years, you mark my words. I like beamflash towers, they're like me and you, Fras: damn hell tall and damn hell proud of it!"

"Uh, let's go back a way. Divorce?"

"Aye, my father wanted me provided for once he was dead, so thinking that I'd not a brain to keep my head from floating away he made over a little of his money to one of his smelly old artisan friends with a trust provision to ration an allowance to me — *if* I married the old fart. I had no damn choice, did I now, what with the legal system being what it is for women on their own who are not Dragon Librarians. Hah, but once in Kalgoorlie I can't be extradited, and by law my husband can't touch my own savings. He thinks he has me because if I leave him he gets my share of dada's will. Pah, I'm willing to lose it to get rid of him. Easy money is easily lost. After all, the rest of the money went to another trust to clear my sister's name, but the lawyers soon cleaned that one out for nothing in return."

Glasken was intrigued yet repelled by Jemli's constant reference to her sister. He lay back against the compartment wall and asked: "This sister of yours, what had she done?"

"Ach, she kept shooting folk. Her poet boyfriend suicided because ... ah, I don't know, he couldn't get a poem to come out right or something."

"He could have tried farting," Glasken said with a wicked, sidelong grin.

"Hi there, that's a ripper," she laughed, doubling over on the edge of the bunk. "Fras Glassy, I'm impressed, you're a sweet man."

"Glassy, now that's a good name for me, lots of rakish class and dash. You're a clever one with words."

"You're having away with me."

"Nay, I've already had you."

She rumpled his hair, then kissed him. "Glassy! Naughty boy. So anyway, where was I?"

"Dead poet."

"Ah yes, so what does Brains of the Family do to make herself feel better? She shoots out her number two boyfriend and shoots out the Magistrate's Champion besides. Could you imagine? I mean fancy doing a thing like that? Now then, the poor churl had another girlfriend — I mean it's hardly a surprise if you know what I mean — and the girl wasn't all that impressed with having him shot out, so she sent someone over to take a shot at older sister. Damn loon missed and shot out our brother instead. Come now, Glassy, I know you're not listening, you can't be hearing all this and not be on the floor with laughter by now."

"Pretty Frelle Jemli, you've got to be making this up. Girls like that just don't exist."

"Pah, it's all true, and it gets worse. I can give you names to check in Civil Records and Registers. Won't though: swore I'd never speak older sister's name again. So, there I was one night in shop's parlour, reading *Vineyard Frolics* and minding my own business when Bang! Suddenly little brother is bleeding his life out all over me and dada throwing up into the clockwork timer of the UnderMayor's spare Call-belt. And how does older sister help out? She's straight around to the Magistrate for a legal Vendetta Script, paid for with money she borrowed from me, then it's away to her — now let's get this right ... number two boyfriend's number one girlfriend's family estate — and shoots out eight people! Honestly, do you think life got a bit hard for us in Rutherglen after that? I'm telling you, people didn't want to know us! At least I had no distractions from boys trying to court me while I studied at home for my median exams. I mean with a sister like that, who'd dare?"

The idea of being without a lover was deeply offensive to Glasken. He put his arms protectively around her, and hugged her with genuine heartfelt sympathy.

"You've got no idea how relieved I was when she got a position in Libris, Fras Glassy. I ran out and bought the bloody paraline ticket out of my own purse, I'm telling you. I was so happy that she was going, I even asked her to write. Wish I hadn't. Two years went by and she writes back that she's having a great time, she's got a boyfriend and she's just shot a few more people. I wrote back and told her not to write any more. When husband moved me to Rochester I told dada that I'd never speak to him again if he let older sister know I was there in Rochester with her. Finally she shot one churl too many and had to run for it, and I've not heard of her since. Apparently dada died on the spot when he learned that she could be cashed in for six hundred royals at any Constable's Watchhouse in the Southeast Alliance. I wasn't even there to see him out and I'm sad about that — even though the old bastard never gave me a break. Lawyers got most of the shop's worth, as I told you. I'd been in Rochester three years with husband by then, grinding lenses, cutting metal plate for gearwheels and stealing library books for studies. And do you think the old fykart made provision to have himself buried, oh no, so who has to pay but me?"

"You must have been at Rochester about when I was," Glasken commented, his knees drawn up and his chin resting pensively on them.

"Aye, that I probably was."

"Didn't you, ah, try to seek a bit of excitement, try to get away from your husband: taverns, dances, fairs, the like?"

"Glassy, dalliance is hard to come by when you're a Frelle who is two hundred and one centimetres tall, poor, trying to study in what spare time as comes to hand, speaking as roughly as I be, and constantly in the company of guildsmen who know each other's business better than their own. Oh, Glassy, there were a few boys for me here and there, but they only wanted me for the novelty of my height, I'd nothing else to offer. One tumble, and that was it: they'd see me coming and away they'd be. That hurt more than anything else, I think. After a while, I didn't bother."

"I wish you'd met me then — but perhaps it's as well you didn't. I was a bit of a monster in those days."

"Monster, pah! I knew all about monsters, I had one for a sister. There was her to avoid in Rochester, too. I tried to stay out of the way in the shop or behind curtains in the stall in the market, but I'd often see her mincing about with her Dragon Librarian friends, with their fancy uniforms, expensive flintlocks and Dragon Colour armbands of rank, all looking so pure and superior that you'd think they pissed rosewater. My husband once said, 'Lookey there now, be that your sister over yon?' when we were about in the market, and I said 'Keep your fykart voice down!' and shot into the Red Wagon to stay out of sight and sink a half-litre to cool off temper — Fras? What's the matter? You're crying."

She put out a hand and stroked his head gently. Glasken immediately snaked his arms around her and held her tightly, his chin resting over her shoulder.

"Please don't say any more, Frelle."

"But, Fras —"

"You're just beautiful, beautiful all the way through, the most beautiful woman I've ever met." He pulled back a little and rested his forehead against hers, gazing into her chocolate-brown eyes.

Jemli rubbed his back lightly, feeling both confused and nervous. Glasken was no less confused. *What am I doing?* he wondered. *I have the Mayor of Kalgoorlie's sister waiting for me when I return, yet my heart is slipping away to a clockmaker's wife with hardly a copper to spare. Damn you, Theresla, you must have cursed me to fall in love. I'll get you for it some day.*

"I'm sorry if I shot off my mouth a bit there, Glassy, but I've had nobody to tell all that to for eight years, and once it started, out it all came. I thought you'd not want to see a churlene like me again for all your pleasant talk, so it didn't really matter if you got an earful."

"Ach, I've always liked the East Highlands accent and I love hearing you talk. I come from Sundew, can you tell it from listening to me, or has Rochester warped my speech too much?"

Jemli wiped his eyes with her hair, and Glasken swung his legs over the edge of the bunk to sit beside her. They sat together naked for some time, with their heads together and their backs to the passing monotony of the Nullarbor. On impulse, Jemli gathered up her cascade of brown hair and draped it over his back.

"I've always wanted to do that with someone, but nobody's been special enough until now," she said with her arm around his shoulders.

"Your hair is exquisite."

"It's nice enough, but it's also three months of University fees if the trade in Kalgoorlie is not up to promise. Long hair is a blessing, it's like a purse that nobody would think to steal. Just snip, snip, then —"

"Never!" exclaimed Glasken angrily. "Don't say it, don't even think it!" He put his hands over his ears.

Jemli shrank away, alarmed. He caressed her cheek for a moment to reassure her, then reached down and picked up his rollpack He undid the laces and rummaged within it for a moment. To Jemli's astonishment he pulled out a handful of Alspring gold coins and dropped them into her open bag over the stolen Libris books.

"Here's gold. Don't work, don't cut hair, finish fykart degree in one year, and tell me when more's needed," he said in a parody of Jemli's Eastern Highlands accent.

"Fras! That *is* gold. Any one of those coins would keep me in food and rent for over a month."

"I'll upgrade your ticket too, should you wish to ride in here with me for the rest of the way."

"Oh, Fras, you don't have to do that. You —"

"Jemli, please, just shut up for a moment and let me make a fool of myself." He cupped her jaw in his hands and looked into her eyes. "I love you, Jemli, you're wonderful — No! Don't reply now, just think on it for a time. I don't want to hear some hasty reply that's said because it's the thing to say, rather than felt. Now, will you stay in here?"

"Stay? Glassy, even without such fittings as you it's heaven in here. I've been able to stretch out for the first time in days. You really were the ride of my life, too, you know. If you really want me, I love — sorry, ah, your company."

"I too want your company, and most desperately."

"Then I stay here." She draped her hair over his back again. "Now I want to hear of you, Glassy. Who are you?"

He was sitting back, feeling very much at ease ... yet his ease dissipated as he thought about his past. *Well, she seems shockproof*, he thought to himself, *so the truth should do.*

"A graduate of Rochester University who raised hell in taverns while you were risking your life to steal books. Shame on me."

"Oh, Fras, you silly boy."

"Jemli, so you want to know about me? I tell you I've travelled in discomforts such as your wildest dreams would never conjure. It's wonderful to have you here with me, in style, in comfort."

"Are you sure? I'm not used to getting anything for free."

"Frelle! Please, don't insult me, I don't want to hire you as a whore. We may have gotten our hands upon each other's undercottons a trifle easily, but really, Frelle, you're just so beautiful, like both of my mothers in one."

"Two mothers?"

"Long story, don't ask. And will you keep company with me in Kalgoorlie?"

"Fras Glassy, you're too good to be true. There's either something wrong with you or you're married."

"Jemli, you're also too good to be true, and you *are* married."

"Oh, Fras, do you really mean that? If you do, my heart is as big as the rest of me, and a very easy target for one such as tall as you."

Glasken swallowed and walked two fingers along the edge of the bunk, then took a deep breath.

"I ... may have a few nights occupied from time to time, business contacts of a female kind, you see. In the Mayoral Palace. Do you mind? Would you be jealous?"

"*Me* be jealous? Hah! What have we just been up to, and me a married woman and all. Business contacts, eh? They're to be cultivated, for sure." She reached down and hefted his rollpack. "I'd say 4,000 royals worth of gold are in there."

"Incredible! You're almost exactly right."

"I'm in metals, it's my trade to know. Is it honestly come by?"

"Believe it or not, it's all mine, and with the law's blessing."

"Now that's a relief. What's to be done with it all?"

"Ah, a bit of a revel, I suppose. Nay, a really, really big revel, more likely."

"Taverns are big in Kalgoorlie just now, and well priced too. I read it in the *Real Estate Fancier's Monthly* in Libris' Reading Room before I left Rochester. What about buying a tavern? You've more than enough."

"A tavern!" exclaimed Glasken, as if he had discovered a gold royal on the floor. "I never thought of that. I rather fancy myself owning a tavern, now that you mention it ... Let's look over the prospects in Kalgoorlie, then discuss it over dinner at the Bullfrog's Rest."

"Done, I'd love that. Then you can have a really big revel with me for free." Suddenly she was silent.

"What's the matter?"

"What's love feel like, Fras Glassy?" she said, leaning her head against his. "I've not ever had a chance to find out."

"How do you feel now?"

"Fevered and trembling all over, and melting inside, as if I was pleasantly unwell, and as if I could brush my fingertips down your cheek forever — and like I'd break fykart sister's neck if she so much as dared to step into the same Mayorate as you were in!"

"They're the right symptoms, and I'm feeling them too, Frelle Jemmy. Do you like the name Jemmy?"

"Darling Fras, call me Jemmy lots and lots and lots of times over. I love you too, I really do, I really know it — but remember, I'm supposed to be hearing all about you just now! Tell me about yourself, my Glassy."

"Me? Ah then, where to start? Drinking and wenching through Rochester University?"

"Depressing. I missed out."

"What about a maniac girlfriend?"

"Worse. Reminds me of older sister."

"Slavery in Libris?"

"Sounds like my marriage."

"Since I escaped from Libris I've been redeemable for a thousand royals with any Constable in the Southeast Alliance. Still love me?"

"Even more. You've a better price on your head than my sister has."

"What about getting shot at while serving in the army at the Battle of Woodvale, desertion from aforesaid army, going on sale at the Balranald slave markets and being bought by a Southmoor caravan master for nine gold royals equivalent — Ach, I was so humiliated by that."

"Aye, I'd hate to be a slave too."

"Slavery be damned, I'm worth more than nine royals!" He grinned, though slightly embarrassed by the memory. "Next came escaping the Southmoor caravan and crawling three quarters dead through the hot, red deserts until I came to an outpost of the mighty inland cities of Alspring."

"Ah yes, now this is sounding to be a tale better than my own drab life so far. Pray go on, my Glassy darling."

*****

By Coonana the Nullarbor Plain had given way to open eucalypt forest that was interspersed with patches of grassland and dotted with waterholes. Nomads were visible from the wind train, some with camel caravans, others in painted wagons drawn by mules. The town itself was a major interchange for the wind trains, one of the places where east and west-bound trains were able to pass on the paraline. Jemli marvelled at the colourful pageant beyond the wind train as it slowly rumbled into the railside.

"Kalgoorlie is much warmer, drier and windier than Rochester," Glasken explained. "Coonana is a foretaste."

"What are all those colourfully-dressed people?"

"The locals and nomads have a market whenever two trains meet here. The trains stay together for only a few hours, but a lot of money changes hands. It is said that the latest fashions always arise among the stalls of Coonana before they are seen on the streets of Kalgoorlie."

Jemli stared longingly through the window as Glasken stood behind her, thoughtfully running a finger along the drab brown cloth on her back.

"We should visit the market, you know, and dress you in Kalgoorlie style."

"Oh, Glassy, I couldn't. How could I pay?"
"Use the gold in your bag."

Glasken had spent time in the market when travelling east five weeks before. For sheer variety and diversity of colour it was unmatched along the paraline. It was the place where fashions were workshopped and experimented with, and where exotica was to be found. The paraline railsides such as Maralinga and Naretha were exotic and isolated, but Coonana was the cultural beachhead of the Western Mayorates.

Glasken shouldered his rollpack as they prepared to leave, but Jemli decided to leave her artisan bag with the Purser. They visited the sugar fruit stalls, then bought small bags of nuts and pastries for the remaining journey. Jemli discovered the metalwork stalls next, some of whose products had travelled as far as the Libris Calculor, to be incorporated in the mechanisms in Zarvora's study.

"Fras Glasken, fancy meeting you here!"

Glasken closed his eyes before he even began turning. He recognized Theresla's voice all too well.

"The day's fortune to you, Frelle. Travelling east, I hope?"

"Oh yes, I regret. I'm on the eastbound train on the siding beside yours."

He opened his eyes to see her smiling broadly. She was dressed in the current style of mirror-inlaid cheesecloth dyed dark blue, with a lyrebird picked out in highlight beads. The cut of the cleavage did not suit her, for her breasts were not especially big.

"And what should I expect in the Alliance, Fras?" she asked, with hands on hips. "Was it cold and drab, as usual? Kalgoorlie was wonderful in the autumn festival. *I* seduced a man!"

"Poor devil," replied Glasken, folding his arms and arching his eyebrows.

"It was for scientific purposes. I think he enjoyed it ... and I did too." She gave him a little push, and giggled.

"Is he still alive?" he asked with exaggerated sarcasm.

Glasken suddenly remembered Jemli, and quickly glanced around. She was watching from beside a metalwork stall with large, unblinking and worried eyes, her hands clasped together. He hurried back to her, reluctantly beckoning Theresla to follow.

"Frelle Theresla, this is my ..." He took a deep breath and gathered Jemli close against him. "My ... very special friend, Jemli."

Theresla noted the plain brown dretan and blackwood clogs then looked up at Jemli's very nervous face. Theresla was not a short woman, but her forehead barely came up to Jemli's chin.

"My word, you beautiful, magnificent Frelle!" she exclaimed, with her hands again on her hips. She turned to Glasken. "Fras Glasken, stop looking so worried. I told you never to trust what I say."

"Frelle Theresla is an edutor, a woman of science, and, ah, quite a lot more besides," Glasken babbled desperately.

"So this is why you went back to the Alliance, Fras Glasken. What a lovely, lovely figure you have, Frelle."

"Why, why thank you, Frelle Theresla," stammered Jemli, still nervous and overawed.

"Frelle Jemli has a husband —"

"And you stole her away? You wicked man! No surprise. If I was a man I'd steal her too. Well, come on, Frelle Jemli, you're in luck," she said, linking arms with her. "I've just come from the clothing run, and I can't wait to show you where everything is. We'll soon have you out of those Rochester drabs and into Kalgoorlie fashions."

"I don't want to impose," said Jemli.

"Just behave yourself, Frelle Abbess," added Glasken.

"Off to the vintner's tent with you, Fras Glasken," replied Theresla, snapping her fingers and pointing. "We don't need you. Come along, Jemli, I'm sure we are about to become the closest of friends."

Glasken stood staring after them, then suddenly realized that he was gnawing the butt of his swagger stick.

An hour later Theresla returned to join him beneath the awning of the vintner's tent. Jemli was still at the clothing run, as most of her purchases had to be altered or custom-sewn.

"Fras Glasken, who is now my adopted brother, I have something important to tell you," Theresla said seriously.

"Frelle Theresla," he replied, a little taken aback, "I'm honoured to become your brother." He leaned across to touch foreheads with her, then snapped his fingers for the serving maid and called "Chilled half-jars, Mergeline white!"

They poured the little jars into each other's goblets, and toasted Theresla's future.

"So what is this something important?" he asked.

Theresla looked up from swirling her goblet. "I have learned that there is a bay south of Rochester where some of the Call-creatures have been in dissent with the others for a long time," she explained. "I am going there, to live near them. I hope to develop new techniques in communication, but just what we communicate with each other is anyone's guess. They are so, so different to us. Ah, but the weather will be bleak after a lifetime of warm deserts. We must endure some discomforts for Science, is that not so, Fras?"

Glasken allowed himself a smile. "Your dalliance in Kalgoorlie ... did it weaken your psychic ears?"

Theresla looked away across the crowded market. "Thanks indeed for your concern, Fras. Well ... yes, but it changed me in other ways beside. We always need to change, especially when we think we are perfect. You taught me that."

She flipped a copper coin into the air. It spun back over her shoulder and landed with a splash in Glasken's tankard.

"Nice shot," he said without moving.

"Pure chance," she said, turning back. "Now, how did you really meet Jemli?"

"On the wind train. It was pure chance."

"Well look after her. You never will get another chance like that."

Glasken reached slowly for her hand. After several false starts he said: "Thank you for leading me to Ilyire's treasure cave."

Theresla snatched her hand back, turned red, then white, then red again. "Consider your face slapped," she said, then took his hand again and kissed it, adding ruefully: "Fras Brother, I would trust you with my life after hearing that."

"Frelle Sister, I've already trusted you with my life."

*****

On the streets of Glenellen there was apprehension as the first day of the month of Gimleyat was about to begin. As the horizon brightened with the dawn the vendors in the market were already doing a heavy trade in foodstuffs, particularly food that could be stored for a lengthy time. Nuts, dates, sultanas, dried mutton, candied apricots and figs, salted whitefish, rice and seedflour commanded outrageous prices from customers who were nonetheless relieved to buy any supplies at all. The vendors of cloths, perfumes, utensiles and Call anchor-belts sat idle at their respective stalls, watching the nearby bedlam over their red cotton veils as the sunlight spilled across the horizon, painting the towers and cliffs an almost fluorescent red.

"So, the great day is here," said Emzilae, the nomad cloth merchant. "The mighty Commander Lemorel rides into the city at the second hour past dawn."

Heczet the vendor of Call anchor-belts reached over and set a clockwork release to one hour. "One hour, then I pack my stall and go home to hide. There will be looting."

"Looting? How so?" asked Emzilae, brushing at a moth with his emu feather whisk.

"The Commander's nomad army of Neverlanders," drawled Zeter from his perfume stand. "They're barbarians, they've never seen a city before. They don't understand money, they just take whatever they want."

"One hour," declared Heczet again. "Then I pack my stall and hide it. When I watch the parade enter the city gates I will be wearing rags and have a pox-badge around my neck."

"Ah, but the city will be full of beggars when the Commander enters," said Emzilae. "I saw it happen at Gossluff, Tempe and Ayer. The same thing, every time. It will happen in mighty Alspring too, when the Commander conquers their armies."

Emzilae stood up, stretched, then clapped his hands. A youth with a whispy, pubescent beard scuttled around from the back of the stall. He was unveiled, the sign of an apprentice who has as yet no means or skill to guard a sanctum of his own.

"Master?"

"It's time, Da. I want twelve dozen camels, twenty handlers with their own weapons, and six strong eunuchs to pack and carry, all to be here in two hours."

"Aye, Master."

When the boy had disappeared into the bustle of the market Zeter sauntered across to Emzilae's stall and fingered a bolt of deep blue cloth.

"A-he, fine Northmoor cotton," said Emzilae. "A fine, fine bargain at —"

"You have only enough to pack two camels."

"Alas, such cloth is in short supply, my friend."

"So, a pack-beast for Da and another camel for you to ride as well, others for the handlers and eunuchs, and that leaves 114 excess camels."

"A-he, they are needed to carry dried fish, candied fruits, roasted almonds, spiced walnuts, and the like."

Zeter jerked a thumb at the mêlée across at the food stalls, then gestured to the blue cloth between them. "Just now you would be lucky to trade a whole bolt of this cloth for a single dried fish."

"A-he, but within two hours I will be able to buy that same fish for a copper or two. Nomads know the cities better than you think, my worthy perfumier." He gestured to his chest, his fingers spread. "This nomad has seen the Commander enter half a dozen cities in triumph. Her warriors are highly disciplined, and to show that nobody should dare attack her she never has more than a hundred of her personal guard with her."

Now Heczet walked over to the stall. "But only yesterday you were describing scenes of bloody horror in Gossluff. Youths cut down in the street for sport, girls stripped and raped in their very sanctum-rooms, looting and burning, followed by starvation for those who survived. What of all that? You were standing on a fish barrel, shouting it to all who would listen."

"And listen they did. Just look at the boom in foodstuffs across the way."

Zeter suddenly straightened, his hands on his hips. "Oh so, then what is to come may not be as it seems?"

"A-he, such suspicion."

"So what happened in Gossluff?" asked Zeter.

Emzilae's face split in a wide, knowing grin. "Why, the Commander entered at the head of a few dozen lancers and rode through the boulevard to the Palace of the Makulad. She was met there by the Makulad and his College of Elders, who surrendered the city to her. Without dismounting she drew a flintlock pistol and shot the Makulad dead through the heart, then killed his son with the second barrel. The rest of his family and some of the Elders were led off into slavery, but that was the worst of it: two killings, no looting, rape, murder or any such thing."

"By the noontime heat!" exclaimed Zeter. "So who rules Gossluff now?"

"An exiled pretender, whose family lost power in that city centuries ago. The Commander said that she was re-installing him as the rightful Makulad. The same will happen here, too. Later this morning the fugitive Prince Alextoyne will ride through the gates at the right hand of the Commander, and when she has shot your Makulad he will ascend to the throne. There will be new taxes to fund her wars —"

"Prince Alextoyne?" exclaimed Heczet. "The descendant of Makulad Moyzenko, who lost the throne for love of the beautiful Ervelle?"

"None other. A popular choice?"

"An inspired choice. This is like a fairytale coming true, the Golden Age of three hundred years ago being restored ... but what of your place in all this, Emzilae, nomad cloth merchant? Just why did you preach rape and pillage, while now you smile and pour balm on the wounds of our defeat?"

Emzilae smiled enigmatically, looking across to the struggling crowds fighting over the dwindling stocks of food.

"You have no broader vision, friends. In two hours those fools will realize that the Commander is no threat to them, other than her war tax. Those who have spent their savings upon food will want money for the tax, especially since those with no money must provide cloth, weapons or even sons for the Commander's army." Emzilae patted the coin bags of his float. "When they come streaming back with their bags of dates, rice and dried meat, I shall be here to buy, and what I buy I shall take to Alspring to sell at twenty times its value when the Commander lays siege to the city."

Heczet and Zeter stood back, incredulous.

"But such a rich caravan, you will have. Surely freebooters would fall upon you without a ruinously large escort."

"My friend, no freebooter would dare touch me. I am under the protection of the Commander."

"She uses you?"

"But of course. I spread fear, and then she enters and shows mercy. The mood of the people becomes one of great relief that they have been granted their lives and property. They are inclined to fear her because of her reputation, and so behave themselves, and yet she has another fully functioning city to support her wars. A pillaged city is of no lasting value to a conquerer, you see."

"So the great Lemorel is not such a demon after all," said Heczet, rubbing his beard.

Emzilae frowned. "Demon she can be, rest assured. There is a nameless town, a place of five thousand souls not far from Olgadowns. It was a proud, fortified place, and they resisted her for five weeks. I passed through the place two months after the fall, and it was a horror such as I could never describe. Not a man, woman, child or beast was spared, and the surviving officers were tortured to death before the rulers of Ayer, Olgadowns and Tempe as a warning. Every item of pottery was smashed, everything that would burn was torched, then the town was left just like that, as an example to others. Bones lie in the streets still, and the houses are all burned-out shells. Commander Lemorel has an evil temper when resisted."

Zeter was wringing his hands nervously, glancing to the crowd then back to his own stall. "I, ah, should make a presentation to the Commander, a blend of my rarest fragrances in a phial of Carpentarian porcelain. I will say that it is to refresh her after the heat and dust of her ride."

"A-he, she will like that," said Emzilae with a shallow nod. He inclined his head toward Heczet. "I also happen to know that she is a great judge of fine lenses and clockwork."

"She is? Truly she is?" exclaimed Heczet. "Then I shall buy a fine chronograph and sextant set. Morgyo has one to sell at a very low price, what with the silly panic about the city being looted."

Later that morning Lemorel Milderellen rode into the city on a war camel at the head of ninety lancers. As Emzilae had predicted, she shot the Makulad dead, dispersed the women of his family into slavery in various convents, and had the men and boys gelded before being taken away to the slave markets. Prince Alextoyne was made the new Makulad of Glenellen, and for his gift of perfume Zeter was made Royal Hospitalier in the palace. Heczet's gift had him appointed official agent of Glenellen to supply Lemorel's army, a position which brought him wealth, property, a royal title, but eventually the attention of loyalist assassins as well.

Emzilae did indeed spend the afternoon buying food stores at the market at less than a fiftieth of what had been charged in the morning, being ever careful to undercut the local vendors who were charging even more ruinous rates. The city was almost back to normal now, except that Ghan nomad guards were in charge of the palace, and Ghan wardens were stationed at every watchhouse in the city.

Servants thronged about Emzilae's stall, laden with sacks of food to be sold for coins to pay the war tax, while camels carried sacks away to the pens just outside the gates of the city. Emzilae supervised, sometimes bargaining, sometimes carrying sacks, and even driving camels through the crowds. The people wore an odd mixture of beggars' rags, disguises and fine robes, and most were in a festive mood. The red stone and mud houses and towers were now decked out with nomad pennons and colours, while veiled women waved coyly from balconies, often throwing flowers to passing nomads in the local gesture of flirtation.

Emzilae found Glenellen a beautiful and pleasing place, and was tempted to make the city the centre of his operations. As he rode about with his sacks of food he noted some of the more attractively placed houses as possible future residences, paying special attention to those with well established gardens showing green over the red walls.

The merchant was packing away his stall in the evening when a eunuch came past with a cartload of flour sacks.

"We can't take any more, even for a single copper," barked Emzilae's boy immediately.

The merchant caught snatches of pleading, words concerning menfolk of a great house all dead in battle, great and noble ladies cowering unprotected in the sanctum halls of their mansion. Emzilae peered out at the unveiled eunuch. His clothing was rich and bright, and his speech was the unmistakable mixture of flawless grammar and deliberate, deferential mistakes that marked a servant of the nobility.

"Da, hold a moment," cried Emzilae. "I may be able to help."

*****

The mansion that Emzilae was led to was substantial, and had obviously attracted a hefty rate of tax from Lemorel's assessors. Emzilae admired the alternating statuettes of red and white marble, all inset with eyes and nipples of black opal. He was shown to a banqueting cloister, misted cool by water sprays and encrusted by live ivy and vines. The food was excellent, and skilled musicians played while demurely veiled girls with their midriffs enticingly bare swayed through the local dances. The mistress of the house sat beside him, seeing to his every need, and slowly pouring out the tale of the family's misfortune. The features of her face were quite distinct beneath her fine veil of blue gauze.

"So because my husband and our two sons died in the decisive battle before the city walls, we have been punished more severely than most others. Our rate of war tax is ruinous, more than the worth of our house. My daughters have not been brought up to domestic service, yet I scarcely have the coin to set them up in a convent."

"Such fine, high-spirited girls, they would not be happy in such a place anyway," sighed Emzilae.

The girls giggled and squirmed, and Emzilae noted that they were pulling the cloth of their trouselles tight to show off the curves of their legs. He turned to Mistress Cycantia.

"They are lucky to have such a loyal and devoted mother as you."

"Alas, sir, loyalty and devotion will not pay the war tax that has been imposed upon us. We are lucky, I do admit it. Why, just this morning I thought that by now my head would be severed from my shoulders, and that my daughters would be the ravished playthings of the Commander's nomad lancers. We had the phials of banegold in our hands, ready for death, but then we saw that the Commander's men were nothing like the reputation that went before them."

"Rumours, stupid rumours. What do you want of me, then?"

"You travel widely, you must know of families where a bride is needed."

"With the wars, madame, there is no shortage of girls for such young men as survive, even as third and fourth invel-spouses. Even I have three invel-wives, although my first spouse is long dead."

"Then ... what can I do? Can we beg for crusts, must my daughters be whores?"

"My dear lady, all of my little wealth could barely pay a sliver of your war tax, and you would not be the first such family to be brought low by the conquests of the Commander."

"Then take one of my daughters as your mistress, you seem as civil a man as I have met."

"Oh, great lady, I —"

She clapped her hands, and at once the musicians and servants slipped away, drawing curtains across the doors as they went. The three teenage girls sat with their backs to them, then one turned, stood, and slipped the half-blouse halter from her shoulders to reveal well-formed, youthful breasts. Next her trouselles dropped to the floor, and last of all went her veil. She stood naked to face him for a moment, her face a study in brave determination coloured by unhappiness, then she slowly turned to walk from the room as a second girl stood.

"Stop!" said Emzilae. "Young ladies, please, cover your courageous sister. Ah, I understand what you want of me now, A-he, yes, but I do not want you humiliated before me."

"But sir, the humiliation will be greater for those of them who do not go with you," protested Mistress Cycantia.

"We shall see about that. Young ladies, leave us alone now."

When they had gone Mistress Cycantia put a hand on his.

"A civilized gesture, sir, but —"

"Think nothing of it. Besides, my taste does not run to girls."

"Ah, sir!" she replied with a bat of her hand, blushing red above her veil. "I do apologize."

"A-he, not that either. Da is my apprentice, not my catamite."

Mistress Cycantia' eyebrows came together in a puzzled frown above her veil, then Emzilae stroked her hand gently.

"Madame, I am a bold, hardworking man, used to taking great risks. I am of lowly birth, but I have a little influence with the Commander Lemorel because of my services to her. I shall do what I can for your family. You may have to give up most of your servants, your girls may have to learn some domestic skills, but perhaps the Commander will let you keep this house."

Mistress Cycantia suddenly lost her composure and burst into tears, prostrating herself before him. The nomad merchant gently took her by the shoulders and raised her so that they knelt before each other.

"Sir, sir, whatever you want —"

"A-he, no. What I want and what I allow myself to have are very different." He ran his fingers along her temples and into her greying but still dark hair. "You are a loyal mother, drowned in tragedy, yet fighting for her family in the face of catastrophe. I do this for you, madame, to save your lovely face from being lined with yet more sorrow."

"Sir! You must be joking. I'm forty one, both my face and my figure is fully lined with a lifetime of candied dates and apricots."

"Good lady, we Neverland nomads are more refined than we are given credit for. As I said, I have influence with the Commander. She will listen to me if I petition her to be made sanctum keeper of this house. Would you accept that?"

"Merciful, generous sir, yes, yes."

At that very moment Lemorel was in the palace issuing proclamations. Henceforth, any Neverlander who married a widow in Glenellen would exempt her house from any punitive war tax, but all property would devolve into his possession. She had done it at Gossluff, but Emzilae had been unprepared that time.

Emzilae hurried to the palace as the rising glow of Mirrorsun illuminated the vanquished city. He registered himself as the sanctum keeper of the Cycantia family with Lemorel's assessors, while much more wealthy and senior Ghans stared longingly at their splendid mansion with his pennon already tied to the gate. Emzilae slept in the traditional place for the sanctum keeper on his first night: before the doors to the women's sanctum. Strictly following tradition, he was curled up on a mat with a single cushion beneath his head, his sabre drawn and in his hand. He was determined to behave with propriety and win the hearts of the family, rather than forcing a dishonourable union with Mistress Cycantia or any of her daughters. If Lemorel ever lost power, he would still remain the hero who rescued them and treated them with respect in their darkest of times. If Mistress Cycantia married him of her own free will, he would remain part of the nobility forever.

The following morning the house scribe came to enquire after Emzilae's lineage as a eunuch rubbed the stiffness of his night on the floor away. Emzilae just happened to have his totemscript in the same bag as his accounts and notes of credit and loadage. His totemscript contained a lot of truth, with centuries-old links to certain noble houses in cities where the records would later be found to be burned. The framework of truth would support the embroidery of lies — he had been bribing scribes long enough to know that.

Mistress Cycantia joined him for mid-morning coffee, just as he finished briefing Da on what business was to be conducted in the afternoon. The house scribe was with her.

"Sir, there is a name that puzzles me amid your many Neverland families and tribal tentbonds," she said as they sat cross-legged on camel hair cushions either side of the low table.

"Alas, the folk of my family are all obscure Neverlanders, madame," he said with a circular wave of his hands.

"Gimlec Stadouri, at fifteen removes."

"Ah yes, but he was not a Neverlander. Some feud in his home city drove him into exile with my people."

"Sir, are you descended from Stadouri?"

"Of course, it has been in my totemscript for over four centuries."

"But he was from a noble family in Ayer, although his line was cut short at the time of his exile," marvelled the house scribe. "Now it seems that his blood flows on amid the nomads. Neverlander you might be, but a thread of Alspring nobility winds through your family vine. Some of this script is beyond checking, but —"

"But there is no need," cried Mistress Cycantia. "Emzilae's nobility shines through his actions last night. Welcome back to the Alspring cities, Emzilae of the house of Stadouri."

"Oh, mistress, it is but a thread, and I am but a merchant."

"You stood by this house, sir, and now this house stands beside you." She regarded him through her eyelashes. "A bond of marriage might not restore your ancestor's family title, but you could become the head of a new house-line."

Emzilae considered, then raised his coffee cup to her.

"A bond of marriage could give me far better than that," he said softly to her.

Mistress Cycantia reddened, smiled knowingly, then hastily waved the house-scribe from the room.

To Mistress Cycantia, Emzilae's very profitable act of compassion was not at all dampened later that day, when she discovered that the streets of Glenellen were alive with Ghan officers and merchants all falling over themselves to do what her newly betrothed had just done. Indeed some noble widows of the city were forcing the Ghan invaders to actually bid for the right to save them from the war tax. To Mistress Cycantia her hero Emzilae could do no wrong, however: he had been wise enough to prefer her to any of her daughters.

1,200 kilometres to the southwest, in compartment A1 of a Great Western wind train, Glasken's rather more altruistic compassion had brought him no more than the devoted love of a very poor woman whose husband was still very much alive, yet that union would eventually shape the destiny of the entire continent.

*****

As with all her other conquests, Lemorel ruled by inspiring fear-ravaged anticipation followed by relief in the people that she conquered. Life went on as before in Glenellen as long as nobody challenged her rule, but the punishments were severe for resistance. When an offender was caught, the whole family was punished, giving households the incentive to become unofficial extensions of the Neverlander wardenry and to keep rebellious members in check. With Glenellen in her hands, only the capital, Alspring, remained against her. Unknown to all of them, however, Glenellen itself had been her ultimate prize.

With the proclamations done, she secured the palace and had the Seneschal summoned. He was a tall and dignified man, wearing a heavy red mask below his eyes as a mark of his duty to protect the palace. Lemorel paced before him, her riding whip held behind her back. It seemed to him that she was steeling herself to do something that was bound to be distressing, yet he could not imagine what it would be.

"There is a device in this palace," she said at last, while continuing to pace with restless, driven strides. Unknown to them all, she was anticipating the greatest moment of her life to be close. "It is a device made up of some two hundred people with abacus frames and known as a calculor. Where is it?"

"In the great median tower, on the tenth level, your — ah, Majesty."

"My title is Frelle Commander."

"Thank you, Frelle Commander."

"Now take me to the calculor."

The calculor hall was on two separate floors in the tower, and the components worked in very cramped conditions. Nikalan was one of ten FUNCTIONS at the front of the hall, and the machine was whirring and clacking through a calibration task as Lemorel entered. She recognized him at once, but she wore a blue veil and so would be unknown to him.

"System halt!" shouted the Chief Regulator, and the tasks being performed tapered away into silence as an orderly shutdown was performed.

"A fascinating design," said Lemorel as she picked her way through the maze of wires and struts. "Components sitting at desk-frames stacked atop each other five high. That means much faster transmission speeds, and faster calculation times for the same number of components."

"My own innovation, Frelle Commander," said an Elder who had been standing beside the Chief Regulator. "There were areas of the original design that were too concerned with neat layout and too dismissive of efficiency."

Lemorel regarded him coldly, yet her veil hid her expression. "There was a man who designed this for you. Where is he?"

"That man is myself, Frelle Commander," replied the Elder.

"I shall not ask again. A prisoner was brought here from the Fostoria Oasis seven years ago. His name may have been FUNCTION 3073 or it may have been Nikalan Vittasner. Bring him to me!"

Interpreting Lemorel's tone as anger with Nikalan, the Chief Regulator decided to gain favour by presenting the long-escaped fugitive to Lemorel in person. He took the keys from the System Warden and strode over to a complex of desks where he unlocked a shackle on a thin, white leg from the second row up. He reached into the desk, dragged Nikalan down by one arm, then marched him to where Lemorel was standing. He forced him to his knees, then pushed him in the back with his foot, to prostrate the component before her. Looking up for Lemorel's approval, he saw a twin flash as her double-barreled flintlock discharged. For the first time in her life she had lost control so badly that she had fired both barrels together.

"Nikalan, my poor, shattered Nikalan," she crooned as she knelt and held him in her arms. "This is Lemorel, Lemorel here with you again."

"Lemorel? Will take me back to Libris and the Calculor?"

Lemorel looked into the vacant eyes, her control again slipping away, like a greased rope within her grasp. He knew her, but she was not enough. Only as part of a bigger machine could she ever be what he could love. With a great effort she caught herself.

She had conquered over a million people for this moment, yet her long-sought holy grail was no more than a handful of shattered pieces. As she knelt with him she suddenly saw her new self for the first time. She was larger than life now, she was vast and powerful. Nikalan was no more than the scrap of smoking fusecord that had unleashed the power of a mighty bombard. By the time she stood up again, Nikalan had become nothing to her.

"The Libris Calculor is very far away, Fras Nikalan, but give me time," she said in a bland tone." I shall take you back to it, I promise."

She helped him to his feet and gestured to the Seneschal, who came trotting over quickly.

"Take Fras Nikalan Vittasner and have him bathed by the concubines and eunuchs of the former Makulad. By the time he is clean and dry I want the palace tailors to have a suit of the Makulad's robes altered to his fit, then see that he dines better than any other in the palace. He is to be veiled as protected by my sanctum."

"But, Frelle Commander, what about Prince Alextoyne?"

"Have him serve at Fras Nikalan's meal. Nikalan is to be put in the Makulad's bed tonight, and the new Makulad is to stay in the guest rooms."

"Yes, Frelle Commander."

"Seneschal, I owe what I am today to this man. Allow him to be harmed, and I will do some thing so pointlessly hideous that you will die as much from disbelief as pain. I am insane, Fras Seneschal, never forget that! Nikalan, go with this man."

"But my shift is not over."

"This is a promotion. You are System Controller now, and you must rest before beginning your new duties."

When they had gone Lemorel gave the body of the Chief Regulator a vicious kick, then seized the Elder who had built the calculor. She held him by the hair and made him stare at the corpse, which had been decapitated above the eyes.

"Clean that up before the components get upset," she snarled.

"At once, Frelle Commander, at once."

"And another thing. If I *ever* hear *anyone* refer to you as more than a lackey who helped Nikalan to build this calculor, I shall have you killed in exactly the same way."

With a kick to his buttocks she sent him sprawling, then walked from the calculor hall without another word.

Lemorel was forced to undergo purification and penance for shooting a man in the head, an act proscribed under the Orthodox Gentheist religion of the Alspring cities and Neverlander nomads. The head was seen as the link between the Deity and the human soul, and as such was held sacred. One could be poisoned, shot through the heart, even decapitated, but the head itself could not be harmed.

The sacrilege was tempered, however, by the romance of the circumstances in the eyes of her followers. It was as if she had found her long-lost lover, but he was dead — and she had shot his murderer. A great commander was expected to be passionate, so in a sense the incident had worked in her favour.

Within a week she was again with her army, leading them east to Alspring's chequerboard walls of red and white stone blocks. This was the last of the great cities of the inland region, and her Council of Overhands was anxious to know what would happen after Alspring had fallen.

Lemorel had made each of her Council of Overhands a member of her personal sanctum. She gathered them in her circular tent of red ochre and yellow stippling, and as the tent flap was drawn she slipped the ties of her veil, then let her outer robes fall to the ground. The effect was startling for the Ghan men, both the Neverlanders and those of the Alspring cities. Straight hair cut sharply at shoulder level, painted red lips, and eyes traced out in ebony liner. Her skin was powdered a slight shade pink, rather than the tusk-white of Ghan erotica, and she wore black riding trousers and a black shirt unbuttoned to display her cleavage as did no other Ghan woman. Two double-barrelled Morelacs and two daggers were at her belt. Seductress and daughter, child and warrior, nun and fiend, protector and protected: to them Lemorel was all these in one. Although she was entrancing, they could not see her as one of their own women. They could not get a hold on her by any familiar values.

"A drive south, to hit and conquer the fat, soft lands of Woomera and the Southeast Alliance," she told the gathering as they sat cross-legged before her. There was no muttering, but an uneasy shifting and rustling of the men in their varied but colourful styles of robes, head windings and veils.

"But, Commander, where will the time be to enjoy what we have conquered?" asked Baragania. "Even the Neverlander nomads among us are hungry to enjoy the newly-won lands and riches."

"Then you can enjoy them under infidel rule," she said in a carefully understated voice.

All of them knew her ways of speech by now. When a thing was so because it was beyond her control, she always said it softly. When Baragania did not reply, she took a small white cylinder from her sleeve. She slipped the string from its rim, and it unwound into a long streamer of paper tape, all punched with little holes.

"This is a message taken by my spies from one of the Woomera Confederation's beamflash tower machines. The former Abbess of the great convent in Glenellen has just married the consort of the OverMayor of the Southeast Alliance, to become their invel-spouse. The ceremony was at Kalgoorlie."

Again she was silent, and she paced before them while they muttered among themselves and speculated about consequences of such a union.

"Do you know what that means?" she suddenly shouted, flinging the streamer of tape at the cross-legged half-circle of men. "It means that OverMayor Zarvora can claim associative rule in Glenellen. Since the Abbess' father died she is the heir to his seat as an Elder, and the OverMayor can claim the right to restore her as a member of the College of Elders." Lemorel paused again to let her words be discussed and assimilated. "I have no intention of restoring any part of the rule of the previous Makulad's dynasty, or that of his College of Elders, so the OverMayor has the excuse she needs to attack."

"Commander, the rights of the Abbess Theresla are forfeit because she deserted the protection of her sanctum keeper, the Marshal of the Convent of —" began Baragania.

"Wrong!" shouted Lemorel. "Under the convention of the Forgiveness of Ervelle, one of your most respected laws, any woman who deserts her sanctum keeper under the protection of a male member of her family, and in order to marry for love, and into a union that is above her station is — come on, someone tell me now, who can tell me?"

"Is blameless under the eyes of the Deity and the rule of law," came the quavering voice of an aged overhand from Ayer.

Lemorel stood with her hands on her hips, triumph in every angle of her posture. "Theresla has opened the way for the southern Liberal Gentheist infidels to stream north to here. Her invel-sister, the OverMayor is already preparing to gather Kalgoorlie into her mighty web of alliances, why else would the wedding have been held in Kalgoorlie? The OverMayor wants nothing less than rule of the entire continent."

There was another pause, but this time the muttering and hand-waving of the overhands was bright with marvel at Lemorel's breadth of vision and foresight.

"I have no particular liking for a bloody conquest of the Southeast Alliance. It was my home, my dear parents and brother are buried there. My surviving sister dwells in contentment there with her devoted husband, and doubtless there are many children clinging to her robes and looking to her for protection by now. *I* do not want to attack my home, but I have no choice. The safety of my new home and you, my people, comes first. The Deity cries out for it. The Deity is even slowing the winds that drive their wind trains as a sign of disapproval. What other sign do you want? Mirrorsun torn asunder?"

*****

The Rochester OverMagistrate banged his staff for order, and laid it in the rack across his desk. He took his seat, then the Constable of the Court picked up the staff and banged it once more for the court to be seated. The OverMagistrate picked up his highlight scroll and adjusted his spectacles. Tarrin sat glumly on the back bench as the representative for the accused.

"Case of the morning: the Family of FUNCTION 22 against the Mayorate of Rochester, in the matter of false imprisonment for nine years in a device known as the Libris Calculor."

"Are the assailants present?" called the Constable after banging the staff on the floor twice. A man and two women stood up.

"Fal Levey, attorney for the assailant, present."

"Pakul ak-Temros, Rochester Association for Human Rights and joint assailant, present."

"Gemile Levey, joint assailant and wife of the imprisoned, Endarian Levey."

"Objection, Fras Overlord," exclaimed the man beside Tarrin. "The legal name for this man is FUNCTION 22, and this is a court of law."

"Endarian is my husband and not a designation, you Librarian bastard!" screamed Gemile Levey. "He was christened Endarian James Levey and if you think —"

"Order! Order!" bellowed the Constable, pounding the floor with the OverMagistrate's staff until there was silence.

"Frelle Levey, another ourburst like that and I shall have you expelled from the court until such time as you are called as a witness," admonished the OverMagistrate. "As to the objection, overruled! This court is sitting to determine the legality of FUNCTION — ah, Fras Endarian Levey's incarceration, and the name FUNCTION 22 is a product of that incarceration. Henceforth the prisoner will be referred to as Fras Endarian James Levey, which may be abbreviated to Fras Levey. Constable, proceed."

"Are the defendants present?" called the Constable.

Tarrin and his attorney stood.

"Tarrin Dargetty, Dragon Gold Librarian, the Mayoral Library of Libris in the Mayorate of Rochester. I am representing the Mayorate on behalf of the Mayor and Highliber."

"Holward Derris, attorney for the defendant, being the Mayorate of Rochester."

"The court will be seated," the Constable concluded.

"Fras Assailant, you have the floor," said the OverMagistrate as he shuffled through his poorpaper briefing notes.

"He's not sympathetic," whispered Holward as Tarrin sat preparing himself for the ordeal ahead. "My objection should never have been overruled, the law is the word of the Mayor in decree until challenged and —"

"Order!" warned the Constable.

"Fras Overlord, I wish to call my first witness," said the attorney for the assailants. "Fras Tarrin Dargetty."

*****

Tarrin and his attorney ordered emu steak and kidney pies for lunch as they sat in the taproom of the Drunken Wizard. Both were nursing a fist-shot of macadamia whisky.

"He should be free by now," grumbled Holward.

"Didn't even want to be free," muttered Tarrin. "Told me as much. Has an ... understanding with MULTIPLIER 417 — lovely woman."

"His wife's been sleeping with her attorney, the Scribe of the Court told me."

"Then why free FUNCTION 22, ah, what's his name again?"

"Fras Levey." Holward stared into his fist-shot whisky. "The attorney has now created a precedent by freeing a component who does not want to be freed. That means he can mount a class action to free all components who are not held in the Calculor against a specific felony or who have served out their original sentences. That will be a major professional victory, as well as giving him a major share of the damages that the OverMagistrate awards. Drink up, here come our pies."

Two large pies were placed before them, but Tarrin seemed not to notice.

Holward smiled up at the serving wench. "Thanks, Frelle, oh, and two dogheads of ale at your convenience."

"We're doomed," said Tarrin morosely.

"Oh no, not at all. A class action will take some time to assemble, and will apply only to Alliance citizens who were not felons. That means all Southmoors are excluded until the Emir signs an extradition treaty, and that's not happened in two centuries. The felons still serving their original sentences are also excluded."

"But the felons who have served out their original terms are not excluded, and if they go, then the heart of the Calculor will be cut out. Our most experienced components are those most likely to be released."

"Ah, but how many of those are of military service age? Even though it's peace time you can still have a goodly number for two years of military service — fighting for the Mayor and Mayorate by working in the Calculor. Now should you be able to convince the Frelle Mayor and Highliber to start a Class A war, you would have the right to demand five years of military service from everyone, felon or nay."

"A Class A war is an invasion of the Alliance," said Tarrin, shaking his head. "There are no states left that could manage that. The Alliance has become too powerful."

"Well, whatever, but as you can see, there is no cause to give up hope. The Calculor may grow a little lean, but it is by no means broken."

"The Highliber will be furious nevertheless."

Holward began to cut into his pie. "Fras Tarrin, the problem is that the Highliber's power is being eroded by her own innovations. For example the Mayors are learning to move troops by galley train and use the beamflash towers in their politics. They have their own calculor teams, as they call them." He washed down his pie with a mouthful of newly-arrived ale.

"I know what you mean, and it's another reason to drag us through the courts," said Tarrin as he at last took a bite from his pie. "The Libris Calculor is the greatest source of trained components in all of the known world. I have heard rumours that the Human Rights people are being funded by a secret group of Mayors, all of whom are anxious to build up their own calculors with experienced people."

"But surely the Highliber will not take that without a fight? What does she think about all this, what are her plans to fight the releases?"

"She says that she needs the Calculor, and she has instructed me to fight the releases all the way. Other than that, nothing. She spends most of her time in Kalgoorlie, and sends her programming instructions and data over the beamflash tower network. I feel used, abandoned, Fras. The Calculor is in decline, and nobody seems to care but me."

*****

Orion's tavern was in the railside quarter of Kalgoorlie. Denkar wandered about the rooftop beer garden as he waited Orion's arrival, sweltering in the white mask of an auditor. The shady rooftop garden was cultivated from both local and rare, imported plants, all strange and subtle. Golden tongue shrubs attracted swarms of bees, which provided a soothing yet busy background as mixed and complex as that of the city streets below. Denkar assumed that there were hives close by, then remembered that the big tavern was famous for its mead. Ferns grew in stone tubs amid the bushes in whitish limestone soil, and their fronds were soft and lurid green in the shade of the garden's follystones. Beneath these were subtle, spidery plants with flowers about the size of a small pea, but with no leaves. Bending closer Denkar noted that each of the flowers was fringed with a frill of red tendrils, and that each of them ended in a sticky drop of fluid. One of the flowers had a tiny insect struggling in its sticky tendrils.

"A sundew," announced a voice behind him.

"Yes, yes, a carnivorous species," said Denkar, neither turning nor getting up. "I've seen them only in illustrations, until now."

"Where I was born they grow wild. The previous landlord planted this garden, and I had some exotica imported."

"Subtle, yet very pretty," said Denkar, turning to take in the whole garden as he straightened.

"Thank you, but enough of the garden. Welcome to the Bullfrog's Rest, home of the finest mead and chardontal white in Kalgoorlie. This rooftop garden is built on a single slab of abandonstone, the biggest outside the Kalgoorlie Mayoral Palace. The back wall is designed to tip it safely into the storage sheds at the rear if a bad enough earthquake hits us." He gave a formal bow. "I'm Jack Orion, and I'll not be so crass as to ask your name while you are wearing the mask of the auditor."

"I'm nothing to fear, Fras Orion. All that I want to do is verify a few details about your property, in order to track down felons elsewhere in our expanding network of Mayorate alliances. Let's get down to business."

They bowed again, shook hands, exchanged script cards, and rattled through the Business Morality Oath together. Lackeys came running with wickerwork chairs and deep cellar mead. Denkar sat back with a clipboard against his knee and began to scribble with a charblack stylus as they talked.

"So, Fras Orion, you bought this property a mere six weeks ago?" he asked once the small talk was over.

"That I did," replied Orion, gazing at the bees at work in the golden tongues. "A fine investment — nay, more than an investment, a real home. After living all of my life in the deserts of Kalgoorlie, such a city as this is heaven on earth."

"You seem rich, for someone so young."

"I come from a good family."

"A rich family too, perhaps. You paid for this estate with gold bars, according to my contracts register in Rochester."

"So? Is not gold an accepted standard?"

"Of course. I see that you also have a fine collection of Alspring gold coin, as well as personal and harness jewelry."

"Ah, so you have heard of it too. It's been the pride of my family for generations. Would you like to see some of the choicest pieces?"

"Later. Undoubtedly, but later. Now then, some weeks ago a diligent clerk in the Rochester treasury noticed an increase in unregistered gold bars in the inter-Mayorate repository. Fearing that they were adulterated, he had them examined. It was quite a desirable sort of adulteration, as it happened. The gold in those bars turned out to be of an even finer grade than either the Alliance Standard or the Kalgoorlie Benchmark."

"Is this not a cause to celebrate?"

"Indeed, but on inspection of the standards and sample stables by the Calculor, the gold turned out to be identical to that of the gold coins originating in the Alspring Cities."

"Ah ha, I know what you are going to say, but rest assured that I have not been robbed, Fras Auditor. Not one gold coin, not a single ring of my Alspring collection is missing."

Denkar leaned back, holding his clipboard out at arms length. He looked up at his host's face again and nodded to himself. Orion gently brushed away a bee that had alighted on the rim of his polished silver goblet, then he took a sip of mead. Denkar finally held up a sketch.

"Oh, very good!" exclaimed Orion. "Such an excellent likeness of me — although is my expression really quite so sombre today? May I keep it?"

"Of course. Here, take it."

Denkar leaned forward and handed the sketch to his host. After a moment the man's eyes bulged as if he were being strangled.

"By your expression, Fras Orion, I gather that you have seen the caption at the base."

His host began to read again, but aloud this time. The words were slow and deliberate: "COPY OF CALCULOR COMPONENT FILE SKETCH / COMPONENT NUMBER 3084, FUNCTION.

FEBRUARY 1700 GW. DRAWN BY THE HAND OF WILBUR TENTERFORTH, PERSONNEL LACKEY, GRADE 2."

"I have a very poor way with art, Fras Glasken. I must confess that I merely added your month's growth of beard."

Glasken slowly raised a hand, but Denkar just settled back in his chair and chuckled as he removed his auditor's mask.

"Please do not signal your hidden lackey to shoot me, Fras Glasken, it is all so unnecessary. All that I want is an honest talk with you, and the answers to a few questions. You will not be returned to the Calculor, it no longer has such an appetite for components as when you knew it. I am Denkar Newfeld."

Glasken's hand froze for a moment, then he lowered it slowly to his lap.

"If it is about the gold —" Glasken began, but Denkar shook his head and reached for his goblet of mead. He took a mouthful before replying.

"It seems that we have something in common, Fras Glasken," he said, rummaging in his sleeves. He held up a strip of punched tape. "You and your friend, Nikalan, were the first components to escape from the Calculor, while I am the first component ever to be legally discharged from its service."

"You do seem a little familiar, Fras," said Glasken, looking at him more closely now. "Ah ... a senior FUNCTION, were you not?"

"I was FUNCTION 9 for 9 years, 2 months, 3 weeks, 6 days, 14 hours and approximately 12 minutes."

"And they let you go?"

"They did just that."

Glasken frowned doubtfully. "In my limited experience in the Calculor's ranks, Fras, the better that you performed, the more they wanted to keep you in the Calculor."

"In mine, too. Nevertheless, one day, eight months ago on February the 17th, I was visited in my cell by Fras Tarrin Dargetty, as you know, one of the very Dragon Gold Librarians who run Libris. He informed me that I had been granted my freedom."

Glasken clasped his hands together and stared intently at Denkar. "What was demanded from you in return?"

"Nothing. But I was offered work, which I accepted."

"Did you agree willingly?"

"Does the Emir of Cowra believe in Islam? Do sheep have wool? Does the Call lure people away? Before the colours of the setting sun of that day were inspiring the membership of the Rochester and District Watercolour Painters' Society, I was on a train going west in the company of a most beautiful woman. What do you make of that?"

"Sounds to me like you managed to roger some highly placed Dragon Librarian, Fras, and please her mightily at that."

Denkar gazed at him steadily, his eyes unblinking.

"Fras Glasken, you have a grubby mind ... yet the world is a rather grubby place so it probably works to your advantage. Now, to business: services are required of you."

"Really? What manner of services?"

"Not onerous services, and none much past the end of this year. It involves the chemistry of explosives, and some calculor work — as a regulator, not a component. It is ... like weapons development work, let us say. Now, you are still an escaped felon with a half-century of sentence to serve."

"That's no worry, Kalgoorlie has no extradition agreement with the Southeast Alliance," said Glasken smugly.

"As of last night, wrong."

Glasken's smugness evaporated. "That's a worry."

"However, last night the Highliber and OverMayor Zarvora signed a provisional pardon for you."

"A pardon? The devil she did!" exclaimed Glasken, then his eyes narrowed. "Where's my copy?"

"Uh uh, it will be given to you and registered with the Constables' Presidium once you sign her contract to do a little work. The Highliber needs experts in the chemistric of explosives who also understand the workings and programming of a calculor. You will be paid in money, and at the end of the contract you will be granted a full pardon."

"Can I have that in the contract?" asked Glasken eagerly.

"I ... don't see why not."

They were interrupted by the domo lackey, who had arrived to announce lunch. Glasken handed the charcoal portrait to the lackey as he stood up, then thought the better of it and snatched the sketch back. He escorted Denkar down to a dining room on the top residential floor of the tavern. It was hung with green and blue ventilation drapes and cooled by convection fans. Denkar looked out through the doors of a small balcony with a view facing east over the city.

"A nice place to breakfast and watch the sunrise," he remarked.

"I'm never out of bed for sunrise," chuckled Glasken.

Just then an oval-faced, delicately pretty woman standing slightly taller than even Glasken himself glided in to join them. Her cotton robe was cobalt blue, sewn with sparkling highlight beads and tied at the waist with a flouncework silk belt woven with gilt thread. To Denkar it looked as if she was wearing a reflection of the the morning sky and its stars in a blue lake, with a wisp of glowing cloud at the waist and crowned by a sunburst of hair that was pinned back with silver orbiles. The honey-brown tresses reached down sheer past her knees.

Indeed, why bother to be up and about at dawn when sunrise is already in bed with you, Denkar thought to himself.

"Jemli, this is Fras Denkar," said Glasken. "He has an offer of employ for me to work for the Mayorate."

"Excellent Fras, it is my delight to meet you," she said demurely in a deep, mellow contralto, which sounded like the local upper class Austaric speech on a faint but distinct foundation of some east highlands accent.

"Beautiful Frelle, I am delighted as much to lay eyes on you as to meet you," replied Denkar, bowing. "On behalf of the Highliber Zarvora —"

"What? Highliber? A Dragon Librarian? You brought a librarian in here!" she snapped at Glasken, who had clapped a hand over his face, groaned "Oh no!" and begun to turn away. Denkar backed across the room as Jemli bore down on him.

"I've come over two thousand kilometres in the most fykart uncomfortable wind train in the known world to get away from librarians and now he brings one into the house, and if you think you're going to recruit him as a Dragon Librarian it'll be over my dead body. I'll have you know we're doing very well in taverns and imports, thank you very much —" Denkar came to rest against the wall and Jemli seized him by the lapels. "— and let me tell you that I'd rather see Glassy go off to war than work in a fykart library and what's more I'd rather go off to war *myself* than let him work in a fykart library, so you go back to that Highliber of yours and you tell her she can take her fykart contract of employment and —"

"Jemli!" shouted Glasken. "Put him down, and leave him alone. He's not a librarian."

"He's not?"

"It's chemistric and analysis work he's offering me: developing better gunpowder for rockets and bombards, that sort of thing. The

Highliber is doing experiments for the Kalgoorlie Mayor, and needs folk with skills other than librarianship to help her."

Jemli lowered Denkar to the floor and began to smooth down his lapels.

"Excellent Fras, I do apologize," she said with her eyes closed, as she concentrated on reassembling the scattered fragments of what she had learned so far in the Sharpentians Academy of Elocution and Deportment.

"Think nothing of it, Frelle," the severely rattled Denkar replied.

Lunch was in a newly vogue style known as 'oasis lavish', although the conversation was nervy and strained. When the meal was over Glasken showed off his small collection of Alspring jewelry, then they went to the master parlour. By now it was mid-afternoon, and Jemli left them for lectures at the university. When she bent down to favour Denkar with a touch of their foreheads on her way out, he had an impression of being within a scented waterfall of brown hair. *All is apparently forgiven*, he decided.

"Impressive lady you have there, Fras Glasken," Denkar remarked when she was gone, although there was still a quaver in his voice.

"Just like that, six hundred and ninety one silver nobles worth of elocution lessons blown sky-high," muttered Glasken, staring into his goblet. Then he smirked. "You should have seen the look on your face."

Denkar failed to see anything funny about the incident, but tried not to show it. "Where did you meet her?"

"It started as a bit of a fling on a wind train crossing the Nullarbor, but I soon grew very fond of her. She's a qualified clockwork and lensmaker, and she was on her way here to sound out the prospects for work before her husband upped stakes to come over from Rochester. I kept in contact with her after we arrived."

"I'm not surprised."

Something indefinable had by now permeated across from Denkar to Glasken, and the proprietor of the Bullfrog's Rest found himself trusting his guest a little. He leaned forward, dropping his voice to a confidential tone. "We'd been sleeping together on the night before I was due to buy the Bullfrog's Rest, so when I went out to sign the papers she tagged along as — well, she's quite presentable and charming until someone says 'librarian' in front of her, if you know what I mean."

"Strong men go running for cover with their hands held to their ears?"

"That's the idea. Her sister was a Dragon Librarian, and a real maniac by all accounts. Kept on shooting boyfriends and such like, then leaving Jemli to clean up the mess."

"How did she ever manage to get a boyfriend in the first place?"

"Who knows? You'd have to be a real fool not to pick her for a lunatic and run screaming. Jemmy won't even mention her name, would you believe it?" He changed tone, mimicking Jemli's accent. " 'I'm tired of not being able to choose for myself, that what I am, and I couldn't choose my husband and I couldn't choose my sister but I'm away from both of them now and I'm not havin' her find out where I am or she'll be straight around to dump dead boyfriends on my doorstep and trying to get her hands on *your* undercotts, Glassy, and I'm just not having it because I saw you first and there's an end of it!' "

Glasken paused for a moment and pressed his fingertips into his eyelids.

"Shee-mesh, but I'm getting good at sounding like her, am I not? I'm going to have to be careful of that. Anyway, there we all were in the Bullfrog's Rest — in this very room, actually — with the scripts and articles of possession ready to sign when the vendor's lawyer handed me the accounts book. I flicked through it and thought, yea, that's an accounts book with accounts written up in it, and I handed it to Jemli to put in her bag. She must have thought I meant her to check it over, because that's what she used to do for her husband, and her father before him. Before I'd finished my half litre — and I'm not a slow drinker — she's gone through most of the entries in her head and uncovered six hundred Kalgoorlie royals worth of outstanding debts and anomalies. Well, you never heard anything like what followed!"

"I just did, most likely."

"My right ear was ringing for days afterwards. 'What are you doin' here tryin' to rob my Glassy?' and 'I've found more botched entries in here than a whorehouse gets on old folks' day and you take that quill and strike six hundred royals right off the price or I'm straight away to the City Constable's Accountant with this book and I'm tellin' him —'. Get the idea?"

"Vividly."

"Willie Junstaker was the vendor, and he got such a fright that he dropped the price by 1000 royals. I got the whole place for 2900! I mean, Willie wasn't all that much of a felon, he just didn't keep books very carefully. Well, after that I took Jemli straight back to the hostelry where she was staying, bundled her gear together and moved her into the Bullfrog's Rest with me. I'm not stupid. I give her 5% clear for managing the books. I probably should give her more, but I'm a mean sort of bastard. Oh, and Willie bought a tavern in Coolgardie with the money from the sale, and even *he* sends his books over on the wind train every week for her to look over — for a percentage. He's not stupid either."

"And her husband?"

"Hah. She's written to him that the clockwork and lens business over here is barely adequate to support her, that she's struggling to cope, and that he should stay where he is. I certainly hope he stays in Rochester, I'd be ruined if I didn't have Jemmy to mind the books — quite apart from all her other virtues."

"But, Fras Glasken, how can you stand her outbursts? It must be like having a market full of costermongers take turns to shout in your face all day."

"Actually, she's never lost her temper with me, and she always practises what she learns in elocution classes whenever we're talking. Most of what I hear from her is slow, beautifully-enunciated Austaric with an upper-class Kalgoorlie accent. I tell you what, though, if you want a real laugh sometime, come down to the markets with us one Saturday morning and listen to what happens when some poor loon of a vendor gets on the wrong side of her."

Denkar took a sip from his goblet. "Speaking of your lady associates, Fras, could we get onto the less pleasant subject of Frelle Lemorel Milderellen? In particular, I would like to learn more about your departure from Maralinga with her about six years ago."

"Ouch. Well now, I was engaged in an amorous grapple with a young lady in the stables," Glasken said, unconsciously rubbing the back of his head. "Without warning, I was clubbed down from behind. The girl that I had been, ah, preoccupied with, gave me no warning, but I suppose she was hardly in a position to do so."

"A Dragon Orange named Weldiline Rostoros confessed to aiding Lemorel Milderellen to abduct you."

"Duplicitous wench."

"She was sent to the Libris Calculor, where she is to this day. Pray continue."

"I awoke to find myself bound into the saddle of a camel, with Lemorel leading myself and some pack camels north. She said that she wanted to use me to learn about Alspring language and living. She intended to set my fellow component, Nikalan Vittasner, free from whichever Alspring noble was holding him in slavery. I stayed with her for six weeks as we moved north, and I taught her some basics of Alspring speech, and even the commonest techniques for survival in the desert. Finally I saw my chance to escape. We had reached the outlying fringes of Alspring influence, and encountered a Neverland Ghan trading caravan. The sight of a man held subservient to a woman was repugnant to the Ghans, and there was a rather heated argument. By the time I'd finally managed to slip free and make a dash for it on a camel, she'd shot five of the merchants and was too busy reloading to look to me."

"Did you see her again after that?"

"No. I fled southwest, but my camel had few provisions in its saddlebags and the country was an absolute nightmare. The camel died after a week, or perhaps it was two. I struggled on, living off the land as a Kooree nomad would do. Then a Kooree tribe took me in and fed me when I was near to collapse. I seemed to get along well with them, except that their women showed no special interest in me. Mostlike their ideas of what was handsome did not include my own best features. I lost track of time and distance, and they even tried to teach me their secret of resisting the Call, without much success as it turned out. At first that was not a problem, as the Call only sweeps over that part of the country every few months, but eventually it was the Call that took me from them. The Kooree nomads don't have sand anchors, you see, and the timer mechanism on the one that I wore was well beyond repair. One minute I was walking along with the tribe, the next I was in a steep, blind gully, and the Call had passed on. The tribe was nowhere to be seen."

Glasken thought of the thirst, and drained his goblet at once. He rang for the floor lackey and a new jar.

"The Call is known to attack one's willpower through the erotic weaknesses in the mind," said Denkar.

"Whatever the truth is, I was not able to resist as the nomads had tried to train me. I found myself alone in the desert and fit to die. I tried to dig for roots and water frogs, but I had no tools and I was too weak. All that I can remember is wandering into a garden irrigated by enclosed pottery channels, then strong hands picking me up and carrying me to a cool, wonderful building. It was a monastery, but what monks they were! A Christian sect of martial arts fanatics, no less. Five long years I spent with them! No smoking, no drinking, no sex. Prayer was mixed in with toiling in the irrigated fields and training in multitudes of ways to kill people that you would not dream possible. There was also a death penalty for attempting to leave."

Glasken thought of Baelsha and drained his goblet again.

"Yet here you are," prompted Denkar.

"Indeed. After a short time I learned that it was futile to oppose them, and I became quite a good novice and apostate. I was finally sent into the wilderness to meditate, but I missed the comforts of civilization. I had worked out where the monastery was from maps in their library, and it turned out to be within several days hard pace from the Great Western Paraline. I fled, reached the paraline, and found a railside where I waited for a wind train and talked my way onto the crew. I worked my passage to Kalgoorlie, and hence to here."

"And the Alspring gold?"

"I had a little cache hidden away. I recovered it and used it to buy what you see around you."

"I'm surprised. I would have expected you to have spent it all on the greatest revel of the century, but instead you bought this tavern."

"I *was* tempted, Fras Newfeld, but revels have gotten me into any amount of trouble in the past, and I have grown wary of them."

Glasken leaned forward to fill Denkar's goblet again. He drained the rest of the jar without bothering with his own.

"Wise of you, Fras Glasken. Now, I in turn have a little story for your consideration. Until several months ago I worked in the Libris Calculor to the best of my skill, and I even introduced a few design enhancements that improved its performance. Suddenly I was freed, but asked to come west and work for the Highliber as a Dragon Librarian."

"Oh fykart, so you really are one of the Dragons. Don't let Jemli know that."

"Absolutely not. So, I went west and performed certain tasks involving a new type of calculor."

Glasken shuddered, picked up the jar again, and discovered that it was empty. He rang for another two jars. "I hope you were easy on the components."

"The components are always bright, tireless and uncomplaining, rest assured. Then ... enter a certain Frelle Theresla, Dragon Gold, Edutor of the Chair of Call Theory at the University of Rochester, Personal Advisor to the Highliber Zarvora — and weirdo."

"We've met — ah, but you know that," said Glasken, seeming to shrink a little into his chair. "Does she still eat grilled mice on toast?"

"When there is toast available, quite probably. I was approached by her one morning at the Kalgoorlie Mayoral Palace. We had coffee in her rooms, during which she made her intentions toward me very plain. She is quite attractive and fascinating of course."

"Of course." Glasken allowed himself a smile. "I've actually become friends with her lately, in a brotherly sort of way."

"Nevertheless, I pointed out that my wife, Frelle Zarvora, was very dear to me, and that it would hardly be fair to cheat upon her."

"Very generous of — Hell and Greatwinter! You're the *Highliber's* consort?" exclaimed Glasken, jolting bolt upright and spilling his newly-arrived drink.

"Correct. At any rate, I went off to work at the University, where I am developing ... but never mind that. I rolled home fourteen hours later, reeking of sweat and burned beeswax insulation, covered in grease and soot, and near-blinded by a migraine, only to be confronted by Zarvora and Theresla. Theresla had asked Zarvora for permission to become my invel-spouse. Zarvora had agreed to give up her right to invel-husbands if I would wed Theresla."

Glasken thought for a moment. Liberal Gentheism allowed multiple spouses, but only to one partner or the other. Zarvora would have given up her right to other husbands so that Theresla could marry into their partnership.

"Should I ask?" Glasken said with a shrug.

"Oh I agreed to it. I was almost surprised that they bothered to consult me. Zarvora might make some peculiar decisions, but she always seems to know what she is doing. Two weeks later we had a full Mayoral wedding: Theresla in white, Zarvora and I in gold."

"New-star-in-the-morning-sky symbolism. Very traditional."

"So was everything else. Service by the Gentheist bishop, Mayor Bouros to present the invel-bride while his wife and sister cried their eyes out, public holiday, choirs, massed bands, and a stupendous feast."

"But where was Zarvora when, ah ..?"

"Away at the University observatory with a dozen or so astronomers, watching the occultation of some particularly bright star by the Mirrorsun band. In a way I wish she'd stayed. Theresla and I spent the night with such pursuits as you have thorough familiarity with, I'm sure. I awoke to find that she had just popped out to fetch breakfast. I looked out of the window to see her climbing out of the palace garden's lake, all smeared in mutton fat and lampblack but otherwise naked. She had a green crayfish between her teeth."

Glasken closed his eyes and exhaled. A clock began to ring out the hour somewhere close by with cool, pure chimes.

"So, your night of, ah — look, did you actually roger her? That is, in the classic sense?"

"Well yes, as a matter of fact. There was one odd thing about it, though."

"Only one?"

"One in particular. Although she was consummate at little social niceties and the general banter that preceeds the act of seduction, she was ..."

"Was something of a virgin?"

Denkar smiled broadly. "I've never encountered any degree of virginity other than 100% or nil, Fras John, but yes, Frelle Theresla did appear to be of the former status."

"So what did she do to you?"

"Why, nothing. She threw me the claws of the crayfish and said that it was my treat for being a good lover. It seemed unwise to refuse, given the circumstances, so I rang for a servant who took them away to the kitchens to be cooked. My new invel-spouse ate the tail meat raw. After that, well, she and my wife had some sort of, ah ..."

"Roster?"

"Not quite the word that is used in an extended Gentheist marriage, but it will do. Generally Theresla would come to me clothed in black silk and finely perfumed, and we would spend the night quite sleeplessly."

"Such strange partners are not to my taste."

"It was not particularly exotic, she was an inexperienced lover. Although fierce and passionate, what we did was all very conventional. She got along very well with my twin sons, she seems to have a way with children and animals."

"She dangled her virginity before me four times," said Glasken, shaking his head. "On the first three occasions she snatched it away just as I tried to accept. On the fourth, I ran screaming. Two months ago I met her at the Coonana markets, and she was on her way east. We had reached our siblingish sort of arrangement by then."

"True, she only stayed for a week after the wedding, thank the Deity for that. By the end of seven days I needed a technician standing beside me to slap me awake every so often as I worked at the University, and I was pissing pure coffee."

"Did she harm you?"

Denkar gazed off into the gardens. There was a wry expression on his face. "No. Our nights together were undeniably pleasant, yet I must admit to having been worried about where it was all leading. Her behaviour was strange in some ways, but perfectly civilized in others. She likes raw mice marinated in red wine — gutted, but not boned or skinned. It upset the palace cooks somewhat, you understand. I'll be seeing her again soon. The Highliber wants me to go east and seek her out over some business that I cannot discuss with you."

Denkar drained his goblet and placed it upside down on the tabletop in the Kalgoorlie gesture for farewell.

"I am sincerely delighted by this meeting with you," Glasken said as they stood up together. "Do pass on my regards to her, and those of Jemli — she and Jemli have met, you see."

Denkar winced at the mention of Jemli. "You have changed since you were 3084," he said as he shook Glasken's hand. "Perhaps the Koorees taught you something, or perhaps it was your time with the monks, perhaps even Jemli's influence. Thank you for your hospitality, and may your tavern thrive."

"May your components be sober, and your books free of worms and silverfish, Fras Librarian. You will always have a welcome here."

"As you will with us. Will you accept Zarvora's contract work?"

Glasken rubbed his chin doubtfully. "Is it real work? Safe, technical work?"

"Yes."

"No standing naked on the edge of the world while some Alspring virgin nutter waves her shrubbery at me without delivering the goods?"

"Not unless you like that sort of thing."

"I wish that you had kept silent."

"Ah, but I could not, Fras Glasken. Your gold bars had raised suspicions in the administration before I came upon the case. I merely did some investigations and got to you first. As for the future, well the Highliber may have you questioned about the Alspring roads and towns, but I doubt it. Alspring merchants have established trade contacts, and I doubt that you could add anything to what they have told us. As for your felonies, well if Mayors and overhands can get away with sending thousands to their death, then why can't John

Glasken be pardoned for striking the Rector of Villiers College on the head with a bag of gold?"

They shook hands, and slightly unsteady by now, made their way out into the street. Denkar mounted his horse and gestured to his escort to set off.

"I shall consider the offer, Fras Denkar," said Glasken.

"Do more than that, Fras Johnny. I was a respectable edutor in Oldenberg University, but that did not save me from nine years in the Calculor. When the formal offer arrives from the Highliber today, I advise you to accept. Otherwise she will take you on her own terms. This way you will be free, you will be paid, and your property will remain yours."

"How long will my services be required?"

"Less than a year, perhaps only a few months. I must catch up with my escort now. Fortune be with you, Fras."

"Fortune be with you too, Fras Denkar."

When Glasken returned inside he was met by an excited lackey. "Fras Orion, a message has arrived for you, a message from the Highliber herself!"

"Gah, start calling me Glasken again," he replied.

*****

To say that Glasken was apprehensive as a palace lackey showed him into Zarvora's meeting parlour would be an understatement of the most epic proportions.

"Fras Glasken, welcome," she said genially. "The very man I wanted to see — but I suppose all the girls say that to you?"

A joke from the Highliber seemed almost a contradiction in terms. Glasken tried to force a grin.

"A graduate in Chemistric, with experience in the Libris Calculor, Fras Glasken, you are a rare combination and I need that exact combination just now. How would you like some months of contract work translating explosives experiments into calculor input? I might offer twenty gold royals per month."

"Twenty five," croaked Glasken in a desultory attempt to seem awkward.

"Done! Oh, and here's your pardon for hitting the Rector of your old university college with that bag of coins. There are still 56 years of your sentence outstanding on that conviction, and until now you were still liable for rearrest. I'm surprised that you did not change your name more often."

"Glasken is a common name, Frelle Highliber, and Kalgoorlie has no extradition treaty with the Alliance. I decided to change to Orion only when I needed to open an office in Rochester."

"Hmmm, you can change it back to Glasken Enterprises now. So ... you own a tavern, and have an importing business."

"I want to settle down and become established, Frelle. There's been too much running in my life, I need to feel wanted."

"Wanted. Well as of now you are no longer wanted in every constable's watchhouse in the Southeast Alliance, but doubtless you can live with that. I was impressed with that trick you used to escape my Battle Calculor: persuading the Libris Calculor to release you by tampering with the transmission codes. Do not try to feed any such creative data strings to the new calculor at the University, will you?"

"I am your loyal, obedient and dedicated employee," declared Glasken with a bow.

*****

Denkar did not journey all the way from Kalgoorlie to Rochester, but left his galley train at the Bendigo abandon. After disguising himself as a Gentheist pilgrim, he began a journey south, on foot.

The Calldeath lands south of Rochester had been colonized by refugee aviads for a century, although less formal groups had lived there for much longer. Macedon was a town of about two thousand aviads, and had been built behind abandonstone walls on the slope of a lop-sided mountain. It was surrounded by extensive farmlands, and its principal buildings were the university and technologium, although the factory quarter was growing rapidly.

Denkar noted everything with voracious fascination as the deputy Mayor, Guidolov, took him on a tour.

"We have very small numbers here, Fras Denkar, so naturally we use devices to save labour wherever we can. In this building here, for example, we have a steam engine fired by alcohol and crop tailings to mill grain for bread."

Denkar looked the building over, approving the clean, compact efficiency of the mill compared to those of humans. "You have no problem with the religious aversion to steam power?"

"Fras, when you consider that every person in here would be executed by human society merely for being immune to the Call, is it any wonder that we have no respect for other laws of that society? We are a pious and religious community, and we follow the Gentheist principle that we should use no more than we can grow, and that all should be in balance. Other than that, development is as we see fit."

"What else is run by steam?"

"Water is pumped for irrigation, wood is cut in the sawmill, and there is a small mobile engine driven by steam traction that pulls carts along our roads throughout the farm grid."

"Amazing. And you say there are other towns like this?"

The deputy Mayor beamed with pride. "There are five more over a thousand, and another twenty settlements bigger than a hundred. We estimate twelve thousand aviads live in the Calldeath lands fringing the Southeast Alliance, and we have explorers extending our influence to the tribes to the north. You know about the exploration and colonies in the far west, I presume."

"Yes, and I know that the Highliber transported two hundred of your people to the west in return for two of your steam engines and the labour to get her rockets out of that museum in the abandon of Perth."

"The Highliber has been of great use to us. We modified our town charter to base the Council on a library structure, and are planning a beamflash network. Even better, we may still find a Calldeath sanctuary in the west."

"Calldeath sanctuary?"

"Don't you know what that is?"

"No."

"Just as Rochester and Oldenberg are in null zones where the Call never sweeps through, so we hope to find an area within the Calldeath lands that does not have a permanent Call over it."

"But why should we aviads need that?"

"For our children. Even aviad children are lured by the Call until they reach puberty. That means we can either keep them here as vegetables for their first twelve years, or we have to live in human lands in secret to bring up our children."

"So there is no real alternative to the latter?"

The deputy Mayor shrugged with resignation. "Unless we find a Calldeath sanctuary, that's all we can do."

Later that day they took a ride on the steam tractors to the edge of an abandon that was being mined for building materials. There was a crew of ten using a steam crane and a steam crusher, and their output was that of a crew of one hundred humans.

They are building a whole new world, reflected Denkar proudly, *and I am one of them.*

"And further down that path?" he asked, pointing south along a partly restored road.

"It leads to the salt water, the ocean, the sea, whatever name you like to use for it. That road in particular leads to a bay called Phillip Bay, which is about thirty kilometres across. Beyond that is limitless water known as the Bass Ocean."

The idea of virtually unlimited water both perplexed and allured Denkar. "Have you ever seen the Call creatures?" he asked.

The deputy Mayor shook his head casually, and did not seem interested. "There is no clear and close vantage to watch from. We have watched animals and humans walk into the water and keep going out until they vanish. Sometimes their bodies are washed back ashore, dead. Occasionally we have seen dark fins and a splash as the victims go under."

"You never try to follow them out with boats?"

"Oh no, Fras, never. It was tried at the Gambier abandon in 1617, and the two boats used just seemed to disappear in a swirl of spray. Smashed planks bearing the marks of huge teeth were later washed ashore. Fifteen of our best edutors and warriors died in that tragedy, and we have always been too few in number to waste lives like that. Thus we have a total ban on venturing into the salt water. One aviad is living on the shores of the bay at present, though."

"Would she be a rather eccentric woman named Theresla? My invel-spouse?"

"Yes, and she had your genototem release signed by Pandoral, the Gentheist Bishop of Kalgoorlie, and the Highliber herself, of course. Remarkable, truly remarkable. The dirkfang cats don't attack her, one was even seen to sit on her lap and purr."

"They probably think she's another cat. This genototem release, what — oh never mind, I have a lot more questions to ask Theresla. Could I be taken to meet her?"

"Your pardon, Fras, but I have nobody to spare at present. If you could wait a week ..."

"A week! I'll find my own way tomorrow."

"That will not be possible, Fras. There are too few of us aviads. We cannot allow a single life to be risked in travelling the Calldeath lands alone."

"But you let Theresla go by herself."

"Theresla is different. The cats do not attack her, and she knows how to look after herself. I have the full Libris profile on you, Fras Denkar: you have been free for only a few months after spending the previous nine years working in the Libris Calculor — 'practically as a prisoner', as the Highliber put it. You don't have the skills to travel the Calldeath wilderness alone, and you will not be permitted to risk your life. You are a gifted mathematician, you must be protected."

They returned to the town, where the sentries were told that Denkar was not permitted beyond the walls. Other than that, he had freedom to go wherever he wished. He occupied his first few hours wandering about studying the town and its society. The architecture was not on a grand scale, except for one auditorium in the university that could accommodate a thousand people. The houses were a mixture of terraces with woodlace trim, decorator-artline bungalows, and functionalist revival cottages. At the centre of the town, beside the university, was a little square shaded by gum trees. There was a scatter of cafes under canvas awnings in the dappled light. The incongruity of a cobbled square with outdoor cafes serving coffee and seedcakes in the middle of the Calldeath lands was not lost on Denkar. Student couples strolled hand in hand in the weak winter sunshine, or sat at tables gazing into each others' eyes, their cups and plates forgotten. Three youths sat at another table, gesturing first at the faint band of Mirrorsun in the blue sky, and then at a diagram that one of them had chalked on the wooden tabletop. It could easily have been Rochester or Oldenberg.

Denkar ordered a jar of beer beneath the awning of a small tavern, noting that the currency was in Rochestrian royals, nobles and coppers. Very soon he was surrounded by curious edutors and students. He had worked in the Calculor of Libris, after all. They were operating a primitive calculor in the university, but it was made up of only sixty components and only ran twice a week in five hour sessions. A lot of their design problems had already been overcome by Zarvora many years earlier, and he was fairly free with his advice. He did not have the heart to tell them about the new machine in Kalgoorlie.

The senior edutor of Physic took him to the university and showed him a Faraday cage ten metres by ten metres, which housed an electrical laboratory. Denkar quickly recognized the equipment for a sparkflash transceiver, a simplified version of the Kalgoorlie design.

After an afternoon of being quizzed and questioned on calculor theory and architecture, Denkar made his way to the modest abandonstone cloister-plan house where Guidolov, his wife, Nayene, and their family lived. For all his frustration at being held there, Denkar certainly felt better for a meal — of roast emu steaks in orange sauce on a bed of rice and nuts, with a large bowl of Rochester salad in the centre of the table. Their two teenage daughters were well educated and friendly, having been brought up at a villa near Oldenberg. Their other three daughters were still at the same villa. The two teenagers had some odd conspiracy of nudges, giggles and snickers that their parents either frowned at or tried to ignore. Nayene had the figure of comfortably approaching middle-age, and was wearing a low cut Northmoor print in a style that was currently all the rage in Kalgoorlie.

"A Kalgoorlie import, Frelle?" asked Denkar.

"Why thank you, Fras, but no, the pattern was sent along the beamflash in a numerical string. All that I did was select the cloth to suit it, and adjust some seams to suit my own figure's conditions."

"Tailored to perfection, Frelle," replied the weary Denkar, his manner friendly and gracious, but automatic.

"Now then, Fras, you have no silly qualms about genototem hospitality?" asked Guidolov genially. The two girls giggled.

"Fras Deputy Mayor, your hospitality is my rule."

"Splendid! Come now, young Frelles, off to your rooms and into your coding exercises — now! You will excuse us?"

Nayene took Denkar by the arm and led him from the table to his own room. It was a generously large room, tastefully furnished with a double bed at the centre. He turned to see that Nayene had dropped her robes to stand before him wearing only kid-leather lounge boots.

Denkar nearly choked on his own gasp of shock, took a step back and fell over onto the bed. Nayene followed eagerly, and climbed onto him at once, pinning him to the softness of the bedcover.

"See there, your genototem release has been pinned above the bed and inspected by Bishop Pandoral herself," she said brightly. "We allow no lewdness in such intimate and sensitive matters, Fras Denkar, we are a very pious community."

Suddenly the precise meaning of genototem hospitality dawned upon Denkar. He spread his arms in disbelief as he lay there. Nayene took it as a gesture of welcome. She slid her arms beneath him and squeezed, then began to unfasten the ties of his robes, trews and codpiece.

"Forgive me if my manner of seduction is a little clumsy, esteemed and charming Fras, but Macedon is still an isolated little place in the wilderness, for all its machines and researches." She sighed, her head against his chest. "Five daughters, Fras Denkar, but not a single son. I have great hopes for you, though. Your genototem trace is very promising."

It was all very logical, he realized as they climbed between the cool and scented sheets of the wide bed. A small population trying hard to expand, yet constantly in danger of inbreeding. Thus there was this scheme of systematic mixing of bloodlines, 'genototem hospitality'. If only Glasken had been an aviad, he thought to himself as Nayene began to playfully nibble at his ear.

*****

Denkar's escape from Macedon went horribly wrong on the second day. He had thought the huge lizard to be a log until it charged out at him from the collapsed and overgrown ruins in the abandon. Partly by reflex, mostly by panic, he fired both barrels of his Morelac 50 point into its mouth. Quite by luck, one of the lead balls tore through the great reptile's brain. He moved onto open ground, and kept his improvised lance — of a dagger bound to the end of a pole — across his knees as he sat reloading the pistol.

He was about to leave when Theresla seemed to materialize from the bushes at the edge of the clearing. She was panting heavily as she gazed intently at him for a moment, then she looked down at the body of the huge goanna. In spite of her emu-leather bush jacket and laceup boots, she still looked svelte and shapely.

"Denkar, you're here alone," she said in a disapproving tone. "Why did the Mayor of Macedon let you come here without an escort?"

"How about something like 'Welcome, Fras Invel-spouse'?" he replied.

She halted a few paces away and regarded him with hands on hips. "Take it as said," she said impatiently. "Why did they allow you come here alone?"

Denkar remained seated. He was somewhat annoyed at his blunt reception. "They didn't. I was to wait with them for a week while some men could be freed from digging an irrigation canal, and soon that week stretched beyond a fortnight. In the meantime their edutors were anxious to get me involved in the development of their calculor, and as for my sleeping arrangements!"

"Ah yes, Macedon and its genototem hospitality. They have always been concerned about inbreeding. Does the deputy Mayor and his wife still want a son?"

"Yes, and the delightful Vivenia and her medician husband managed to have me stay on two nights because she was still childless after five years of marriage. Do you want details of the other twelve nights?"

"No, I can well imagine."

"Why didn't Zarvora warn me? Why didn't you warn me, if it comes to that?"

"We decided that you would probably have enough to worry about on this trip without wondering about your reception at Macedon."

"Very considerate of you."

"Remember that you have to return via Macedon too."

"No! I'm married to you and I'm married to Zarvora. There's an end of it. I'll find my own way back."

Now Theresla came over to him, kissed him and took his hand in hers.

"Denkar, it was not all delay to make use of your brain and body. The cats and big lizards in this part of the Calldeath lands have learned that people walking in groups are not subject to the Call, and are liable to fight back. Walk alone and you are in danger. Now that you're here, however, welcome. My home is on the other side of that hill, and it has a fine view of the bay."

Someone in the early Twenty First Century had built a very solid dwelling, even to the point of using steel beams and interlocking terra cotta tiles for the roof. It still provided shelter with a view after two thousand years, and Theresla had cleaned out the accumulated creepers and nests. Denkar was surprised at how clean and orderly the place was, given her behaviour in human society.

"Vermin accumulate after a time," she explained. "Every month I seal the doors and windows and light a fire on the ground floor, using the branches of certain specific trees and bushes. I also move my bed around. I am nomadic within my own house, you see."

He glanced about approvingly. The lines, space and lighting were well evident, even after two millennia. "And a pleasant house it is too."

"A house built of greed, Fras Invel-spouse. There is evidence that only four people lived here, yet it could accommodate thirty."

"Thirty! But a mere four would spend their lives merely maintaining it."

"No, they had machines to do that, there is evidence for that. There are piles of overgrown rust and similar oxides that were once their vehicles, there is a tiled cistern that they appeared to use for swimming, and there may even be a flying machine behind the house. The building that sheltered it has collapsed and been overgrown by blackberry tangles." She went to the wide window and stood proudly framing herself against the scenery. "I checked the area around here fairly carefully when I first arrived, and I stopped counting after a thousand similar dwellings. There are more under the water too."

They had a meal of nuts, rasins and wild oranges on a balcony overlooking the bay. Denkar lay on a pile of cushions and rugs that doubled as Theresla's bedding, nervously stroking a purring dirkfang cat that had taken a liking to him and had installed itself on his lap. Theresla explained about her explorations and researches. Her estimate was that the Melbourne abandon had once housed three million people, more than a third of the known population of the continent.

"That seems fanciful," he said, rubbing at his temples for a moment. "No public infrastructure could support so many people in such a small area. The place should be covered in paralines and beamflash towers, and that is clearly not the case."

Therela lay down on the rugs and cushions beside him and held up a complex lump of corrosion about the size of her hand.

"Remember that they could use electrical devices like this might have been, and that they had personal carriages driven by steam and turbine cycle engines."

"Three million people with their own steam tractors!"

"Yes, and this city was no exception, either. It is hardly a surprise that so many of the surviving books speak of the air being rank with fumes. There is hardly any evidence of books, however. No bookcases in the houses, no neighbourhood libraries, only one huge library in the central city area. I've checked it, but those books that survived the mould, insects, rats and mice for two millennia have been taken by other aviads. It seems to have been more of a museum for books than a working library as we know them. I don't know what to make of this city, Denkar: such a huge, advanced yet illiterate society."

"Not so illiterate as you may think."

"How so?" she asked, lying up against him with an arm draped over his chest.

He ran his fingers idly through her hair, straining to assemble complex thoughts into common language. "I've done some experiments on that electric calculor that Zarvora and Bouros built at Kalgoorlie. I took a thousand words from a romantic novel and keyed them into what I have called the volatile memory, to be stored as positions of switches held either open or closed by electromagnetic relays. After an hour I came back and read the entire text back."

"As on paper tape with punched holes?"

"No, I designed a row of one hundred thin wheels on a common axle, each with the letters of the alphabet, numerals and common punctuation painted on the rims. They are spun by gears connected to the calculor to present a line of text at a frame window, just like a line of text in a book or scroll. I read my thousand words of text back with no errors at all. Next I tried moving some words from one place to another, like letters in a printing press. That worked equally well."

"An expensive way to store a page of words."

"Indeed, but with a hundred years of development one may reduce such devices to the size of a small room and store thousands of whole books within them. There is just one vulnerability, however. When I switched off the electrical current to the calculor, the switches were all reset to a zero representation. My page was lost."

Denkar gingerly lifted the dirkfang cat and Theresla's arm aside, then sat up to pour out some more of the soupy yet flavoursome tea that Theresla had brewed out of locally collected herbs. The ceramic pot was a priceless Anglaic artefact that she had found somewhere, as were the matching cups. His head was still pounding from being denied coffee for more than a day, and he attempted to use a Southmoor breathing technique that Ettenbar, the new System Controller of the main Kalgoorlie calculor, had taught him. The afternoon was becoming overcast, and a light wind had made the water of the bay choppy.

Theresla sipped quietly at her tea, her mind turning over possibilities. "You are saying that the Anglaic publishers put all their books into their electric calculors," she said at last, "and that when the supply of electricity stopped, the books were all lost."

"There is more to it than that, but —"

"A stupid idea, even their engineers must have been humble enough to accept that even the best machines have failures. Still, I have met a lot of stupid engineers since I came south from the Alspring cities — present company excepted, darling Fras. It would explain why books were already rare even before Greatwinter. Zarvora has told me of a legend that people actually mined a huge library in the Canberra abandon for books to burn."

Denkar put his finger to her lips. "As I was trying to say, I think there was more to it than that. In another experiment I channelled my thousand words of magnetically held text onto a reel of paper tape."

"Pointless. You can read the symbols represented by the punched holes without a calculor."

"Yes, but the calculor can read it too, and present it back in a much more readable form than punched-hole code. Just imagine a vast library of paper tape reels connected to as many as a hundred calculors. If these calculors were connected by wires to a device in a house like this, then those living here could read whatever they wanted in that library without ever having to open a book or even walk out of the door."

Theresla was impressed by the idea. "Cumbersome ... but it makes sense."

"It did until the anarchic wars of Greatwinter. Some Mayorates must have built the Wanderers in order to cripple the electric libraries of their rivals."

"So their governments were based on libraries too, just as ours are now?"

"Undoubtedly. With the calculors gone, the books and documents were just too hard to read directly from paper tape. Chaos and anarchy followed. Without books their ideas and sciences quickly became distorted and went into decline. There must have been other factors as well, but that would account for the lack of books. Just think: the furnaces of three million steam cars in a city such as this would produce a lot of heat, and perhaps the combined steam cars of the whole world really were heating up the world and poisoning its air.

What I cannot accept is that all steam engines are anathema in the eyes of the Deity, as most major religions claim."

Denkar rubbed at his temples again, and Theresla sat up and began to knead the muscles of his neck and back. He lay out along the Northmoor rug that lay incongruously bright on the cold, grey slab of the balcony, and Theresla straddled him, pressing and rubbing until the joints of his spine crackled. He relaxed, and was aware that at least some of the pain was ebbing away. He also became aware that his tunic had ridden up, and that pubic hair was rubbing rhythmically against the small of his back.

"I would not be a gentleman if I did not offer to turn over," he said as he lay with his eyes closed.

"The offer is appreciated, Fras Invel-spouse."

Denkar rolled over. Theresla was looking down at him with unmistakable longing. She descended upon him with the rippling motion of warm softness that she had practised during their first nights together in Kalgoorlie, and for quite some time Denkar gave no thought to where he was.

"Your genototem hospitality duties don't seem to have damaged you unduly," Theresla remarked as they lay together in a sweaty tangle of limbs.

"Have *you* been involved with the genetotem hospitality?" he asked.

"No, it's only sanctioned for those who want to breed, and if I am to breed, I want it to be with you. As for men beyond Macedon, no. I have a charming, safe man available and you are he. There are too many weirdos around — what are you laughing at?"

"Nothing important."

"Would you prefer to be on top of me?"

"No, I prefer it down here. Like Fras Glasken says, you can run your hands over more of your lady, and she has to share in the work."

Theresla sat upright at once, still astride him. "Glasken! You know him? Did you discuss me? Did he say lewd things about me? Did he boast about rejecting me when we were in the desert together?"

"Please, please, we both spoke as gentlemen, more or less. I think that he probably likes you a little, but after your strange experiments with him he is too suspicious of you to let his guard down again. We spoke mostly in generalities."

The answer seemed to satisfy Theresla. She relaxed a little. "I never thought you'd meet. Ah, but he has become strange indeed.

Twice in the desert, back in 1700, he was almost beside himself to leap astride me and go where no man had gone before, yet in the wind train last March he was ... restrained, disciplined or whatever. I know that out of all women, he refuses dalliance with me alone. What does he think of me now? What did he say? Did he say I was thin and horrid? He used to like plump and raunchy women until he met that enchanting Frelle Jemli."

"Jemli? Enchanting? I've never been so badly frightened by any Frelle. As to your questions, Glasken and I never got down to detail. He said nothing about your appearence, and I never even told him that I call you Mousebreath."

"Denkar, I now never eat mice when I know I am to be with you. Remember my parting words to you in Kalgoorlie: I can't change unless you complain to me."

"Yes, I know. Not to worry, now."

Theresla lay down along Denkar and rubbed her cheek against his, then they began kissing. The dirkfang cat reluctantly moved aside, then was forced to leave the rug altogether by a sudden flurry of activity. It sat on a balcony for some time, indolently watching what its mistress was doing with her guest, and gradually drifting off to sleep again.

Some time later the sun set amid a scatter of clouds with a slash of Mirrorsun band across its disk. Theresla and Denkar lay in each other's arms beneath a blanket, already settled down for the night.

"Glasken does not know what he missed," remarked Denkar as Theresla nibbled idly at his ear, suddenly reminding him of Nayene.

"You are civilized, but Glasken ... I sensed in him a level of sheer sensual desire as I have encountered in no other before or since. He really is a fascinating specimen — in many, many ways. You see, the Call itself has its roots in sensuality and desire, and I found that by balancing his desire for me against the Call itself I could set up what Zarvora and Bouros call a tuned circuit and touch the thoughts of the Call creatures. There is a place on the Nullarbor Plain where the Calldeath region is only some tens of metres wide, and cliffs plunge straight down into the ocean. On one occasion six years ago I used Glasken to study the Call creatures for two full hours. I learned more in that time than any human or aviad has for the past two thousand years, but when I tried to repeat the process a few months ago, he had been spoiled. Some peculiar monastery of Christian martial artists had thrashed self-discipline into him, and some of it appears to have stuck.

Denkar, the man might be educated and intelligent, but he was still an animal, rampant and magnificent. Now he is a little more human, and that has robbed him of something."

"He might well say the same of you."

Theresla smirked. "Denkar, in my last experiment with him, when he was resisting the Call at the Edge by himself, he could 'hear' the thoughts of the Call-creatures within his head, just as I had five years before when I had used him to make my tuned circuit. He described what he sensed without realizing what he had just done. I didn't tell him, and he still doesn't know. I'm still not sure how I could make use of him, though." She wrapped and entangled her limbs even more tightly with his. "But don't be jealous — I have devised other means to study the Call."

Denkar wriggled slightly beside her. "Are you doing your experiments now?"

"Hah! Very clever, but no, you are my friend and invel-spouse, not my experiment. This is for pleasure, and for the love of your company."

The following morning Theresla took her visitor down to the new foreshore, where a chill, steady wind was driving heavy waves onto a jumble of sand, rubble and ruined buildings. They had taken a small telescope with them.

"Be careful of any concealment like those walls over to the left," she advised him. "Large, amphibious carnivores that the ancients called sealions keep up a sort of patrol here. They are clumsy but powerful, and the cetezoid Call creatures use them as we use guard dogs."

Denkar was peering out to sea through the telescope. "I see a dark body from time to time, and sometimes a jet of water."

"They are the dolphins that have this bay as their territory. They generate what is known as the Rochester South Callsweep. They have some sympathy for us land animals, and they have little time for the sealions."

"They lure thousands to their death, yet they have sympathy for us?"

"Be greatful, Fras Denkar. They deliberately start their Callsweep at Elmore instead of further north. That is why Rochester and Oldenberg never feel the Call."

He looked around at her, astonished. "By heaven — the great mystery of two thousand years, yet you toss it to me as casually as a bone to a dog?"

"Your explanation of why books were in decline before Greatwinter was no less wondrous to me, my clever and resourceful lover."

"So you can communicate with these, ah, dolphins?"

"I have learned to, yes. One needs a very non-human attitude, but it can be done by someone like me." She snapped her teeth at him, but he did not even flinch. "I have studied the dolphins near the Perth abandon as well, and the situation with them is the same. They are forced to cast the Call by other, larger creatures: they are called cetezoids, and they appeared in the oceans about the time of Greatwinter. The dolphins are treated like tenant shepherds or peasants, and the Bay Dolphins as I call them, resent it. At the edge of the Nullarbor Plain the cetezoids themselves make the Call, and my Bay Dolphins think that it is a special place where they give birth."

"What do the Bay Dolphins think of us aviads?"

"They are fascinated, they want to know more. The problem is that the sealions and large fish of the bay are beyond their control. It is dangerous even for me to swim around here, but I can look after myself. See that large, dark lump in the seaweed across there? Watch."

Theresla made a series of hissing, sibilant sounds and Denkar thought that he heard something pattering through the bushes. Presently a small, tabby form emerged from some nearby cover, crawling with its belly against the ground, stalking towards the dark shape in the seaweed, then the cat sprang and sank its long fangs into the blubber of the sealion's back. There was a roar that sounded more like outrage than pain, and the cat bounded away as the sealion reared up. With a surly glance at the two aviads it turned to shuffle away toward the water.

"It was stalking us," Theresla explained.

"And the cats obey you?"

"Well ... I'm their leader, one might say."

They walked down to the water's edge. Denkar splashed his hand in it and tasted the salt. He shivered in the stiff wind.

"Are we going to meet your Bay Dolphins?"

"Not today. They don't know you yet, and thanks to you I have essence of man about my legs. They are easy to confuse with new sounds, scents and tastes. They are both curious and worried by anything at all new. Anyway their speech is all clicks, whistles, touches and postures."

"But when you, ah, experimented with Glasken you said that their speech was by thought exchange."

"So it was, and that is why we use an older, physical dolphin language here. We cannot be overheard. The cetezoids do not approve of such fraternization."

"Cetezoids. Where does the word come from?"

"It was a thought-form that I learned in my first and only successful attempt to eavesdrop at the Edge, the Nullarbor cliffs. It seems to be their name for themselves, and oddly enough it seems to be an old human word. Whatever the case, the Bay Dolphins have taught me that and a lot more. Over the next few days I shall gradually introduce you to them, but meantime I have some well-preserved buildings and devices to show you, about two kilometres north of here."

Denkar stayed with her for three weeks. On the day that he was to leave, a trained emu came padding through the bush, a message harness with Macedon colours strapped to its back. Theresla caressed the bird as she removed the container and handed it to Denkar.

"In some local code," he said simply, and handed the unfolded paper back to her.

"Well now, congratulations," she said brightly. "Vivenia is pregnant, and so are two of your other liaisons in Macedon."

"That leaves eleven to worry about," he said with no real enthusiasm. "I mean, they were most charming and civilized women and I was treated wonderfully, but really! Who do they think I am, John Glasken?"

"He would be admirable for the task, but unfortunately he is not an aviad. His hair shows him to be unquestionably human. When put under the microscope, it has none of the feathery texture of my beautiful messenger and friend here." She stroked the emu yet again, then set it loose to forage. "Concerning the eleven Macedon ladies wanting more of your company, you may have to think again. According to this list a full lineage and genototemic trace has now been done, and sixty one additional couples in Macedon are anxious to get you into their guest rooms with the Frelle of the household for the night. Getting Vivenia with child appears to have impressed them rather considerably."

"Seventy two — No! I'm not a stud ram, I'm the senior calculor engineer and programmer for the Alliance and Kalgoorlie. I'm the OverMayor's consort —" He broke off as Theresla began laughing. "Theresla, please, this really is a joke."

"Actually, you are right," said Theresla, regaining composure. "You have business to attend in Rochester, and anyway Zarvora is missing you and your boys want to know where dada is — hence this note. According to the agreement between me, Zarvora and the Mayor of Macedon, you were meant to be detained no more than three days on either of your visits. Still, it would not be diplomatic to make too much of a fuss over their hospitality. We need them as much as they need us."

"Are there any childless couples in that list?"

"Now *that* is very clever of you ... yes, only two. I shall have a few stern words with the Mayor when I take you back, then we shall ask Bishop Pandoral to sanction only the two childless couples to extend their hospitality to you."

"I've met the bishop: such a gentle and charming woman."

"Oh I agree, I stay at her house whenever I visit Macedon and we get along very well. We are both religious leaders, you know. She is separated from her husband, and her son gets into a lot of trouble, but they are not our concern for now. Will you still leave today?"

"Yes." He put his arm around her shoulders. "There is a lot to do in Rochester and Kalgoorlie. The problems in Libris, the programming for Zarvora's explosives and rockets, the work with Mayor Bouros on improved calculor electricals, not to mention briefing Zarvora on your work here. What are you going to do next?"

"Talk with my dolphin friends, build on their trust, study the books that you brought. *Teaching Biology in the Primary School* looks to be promising." She suddenly bared her teeth. "Besides, it is three weeks since I had a raw mouse!"

Denkar left for Rochester after two days at Macedon. This was the least attractive part of the trip, for he would be forced to view the Libris Calculor as one of its masters rather than a component, and even participate in legal debates against releasing an increasing number of components. The electric calculor was a far more humane device.

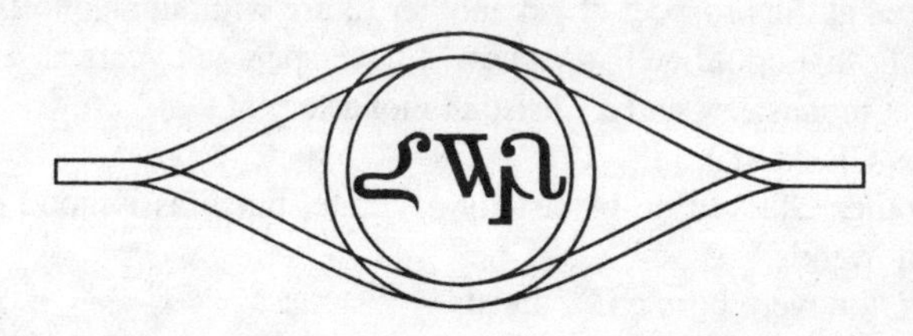

Part 4

ZARVORA

Glasken entered the control room of the Kalgoorlie calculor and received two surprises. Firstly, it was no more than a medium sized room cluttered with the familiar half-harpsichord input keyboards, some very functional paper tape engines for output, and a wall full of gearwheel registers. Only a half dozen operators were on duty, chatting easily and drinking the bitter local coffee sweetened with banksia honey. The second surprise was the System Controller.

"Fras — ah, Fras ... Fras FUNCTION 795?" stammered Glasken from the doorway. "No, 797, that was it."

The System Controller left his work desk and came across to greet him. "Ah, Fras FUNCTION 3084, it is indeed a pleasure to meet with you again, and praise be to Allah that your life was spared over these years past. But your name: you are Fras John Balmak Glasken now, the great Frelle Highliber sent me a personal communication that you would be arriving to work here. She said you were a great and talented Fras who was experienced in both chemistric of explosives and matters of the calculor."

"Yes, but FUNCTION — no, please, what is your real name?"

"Ettenbar Alroymeril, good Fras. Ettenbar to my friends, especially old friends like you. Ha ha, Fras Glasken, I have not yet given up my hope of converting you to the path of Islam, or have you already forgotten?"

Glasken immediately thought of his years in Baelsha and shuddered at the prospect of yet another future without alcohol.

"Well, that could be harder now. I have spent six years as a novice in a strict monastery, and a Christian monastery at that."

"Fras Glasken! You!"

"Brother Glasken, to be strictly accurate, but Fras is good enough between friends."

"But you were born a Gentheist."

"Correct, but I was raised as a Christian, and that was sufficient for Baelsha."

"Well then, Fras, what are you doing here?"

"My last and most difficult test, Fras Ettenbar. I must spend a year abroad in the world, alone while I fight the temptations of the devil. Greed, the drink, and the lovely form of the female body combined with the enchanting female face anticipating the feel of female skin against my own while —"

"No, no, Fras Glasken, please, I understand. Do not torture yourself to demonstrate your great faith to me."

Glasken dropped his pack to the floor, then stretched the stiffness out of his shoulders as he looked around.

"So where's this calculor, then? In the basement?"

"Not so, Fras, it lies a full kilometre below us in ancient tunnels."

"A kilometre! Poor devils, I say. I may be free, but I'll always feel sympathy for the components."

"Ah, but these are happy components, Fras. Their work is faster than that of the Libris machine, even though they do not have the same FUNCTION versatility as in Libris."

Glasken stared at him intently. "Is there something that I am meant to guess about it?"

"No, Fras, but there are certain matters about its architecture that I may not divulge to you." Ettenbar took him by the arm and whispered conspiratorially in his ear. "It only has one processor, but it makes no errors at all."

"The devil you say! Only one processor! Hi then, are there any pretty components or regulators within it?"

"For shame, Fras, and from you who aspire to the clergy!"

Glasken quickly settled into his duties of converting chemical test data into optimization curve programs for use in the underground calculor. He, like everyone else on the project, assumed that the Highliber was designing new weaponry for the Mayor of Kalgoorlie. He was surprised at the power of the explosives, as well as their instability, and after nearly blowing his foot off with a single drop of liquid he decided to leave the mixing of glycerine and concentrated acids to whoever else was foolish enough to volunteer.

The rocketry tests were done on the dry bed of Lake Cowan to the south, generally with rockets no more than a metre in length. There were several impressive explosions, and several more rocket flights where the little missiles flew right out of sight and could not be found again. All the while Glasken carefully invested in the property market of Kalgoorlie, maintained his liaison with Jemli, and even paid an occasional visit to the Mayor's sister. Life was becoming comfortable and prosperous, yet there were some habits that never left him. He trained at the martial arts exercises he had learnt at Baelsha for two hours every day without fail, and the sight of a monk of any denomination or creed would make him duck for cover instantly. Whenever Calls swept over Kalgoorlie he would practise balancing the allure against his self-discipline. The Kooree nomads could collapse themselves at the touch of the Call, the Baelsha monks could meditate through its allure, and the aviads were immune to it, yet in all of the world Glasken was the only human who could maintain even limited movement and control when the Call swept over him. It was an ability he had no intention of abandoning.

One morning Glasken was on the rooftop garden of the Bullfrog's Rest, going through his exercises while Jemli sat watching as she braided her hair. Ilyire called in to visit, and after sitting with Jemli for a time, he began to attempt some of Glasken's moves.

"The spinning back-kick is a very advanced move, Fras," Glasken explained as Ilyire went crashing into a potted thorn fern. "But if you promise to practise every day I could teach you some more basic moves to build upon."

"Basics. Is good idea. Always wishing to protect better."

"Pah, you and that protection ethic — put your feet a shoulders' width apart, thusly."

"Protection good. World is full of evil."

"Bend your knees, keep the same height as you step, it improves your balance. Yes, Ilyire, the world is full of evil, but you cannot be everywhere at once to keep every Frelle and child safe."

"Must never stop trying, Fras. Deity expects it."

"You should teach your fighting arts to us women, Glassy," called Jemli past the large hairpin between her teeth.

"Pah, silly talk," replied Ilyire. "Instead Baelsha should build sister-convent for to protect Frelles."

"Nay, Baelsha is Christian," said Glasken. "They don't have your Orthodox Gentheist protection ..." Glasken's voice trailed away as he stood staring at Jemli. "Was that a serious suggestion, Jemmy?"

"Aye, I suppose. I've been thinking it for some time ... but you'd never teach me."

"How would you know that? You never asked! Why not? Why not indeed? Downstairs with you, and into trouselles and a loose blouse."

"Me, Glassy?"

"You, Jemmy. Ilyire would look stupid in trouselles."

"Well then, all right. I'll not be a minute to change."

Ilyire put a hand on Glasken's shoulder when she had gone.

"Is bold and humane idea, Fras. Some may damn you, but you become Gentheist saint, also maybe."

"Never mind about that. Do you have any idea of how many women we may meet if we started a self-defence academy for exclusively female students? Ah, Jemli, what did I ever do without you and your ideas?"

*****

Lemorel's strategy with the city of Alspring was tailored to suit the siege conditions that were being played out there. The city had sealed itself tightly, with stores laid in and well trained warriors all armed with the finest weapons available. It was a difficult situation for her. In one sense Lemorel was sweeping all before her, but in another she was vulnerable. Time was not on her side, and she had little but conquest to offer her followers. If the conquests stopped, disillusion might set in.

True to her style, she had thought strategically. A year earlier she had arranged the purchase of five bombards from Inglewood, a Mayorate so remote to her followers that none even knew that it existed. The barrels were shipped in cases marked as coffee to the paraline railside of Maralinga, then trekked by eight-camel sling across the deserts to a stronghold where they were mounted on gun carriages. Using contract artisans in several cities, including Alspring itself, she had ordered a large supply of precisely wrought bombard balls, but until now the bombards themselves had only been used in test firings. The other cities had sent their armies out to meet her, as her forces always seemed weaker than was the case. Thus the finely made bombards were of no special advantage. Until now.

It was not enough to lay siege to Alspring, she had to defeat the city quickly. The walls were far thicker and better defended than those of any other city in the area. They were encrusted with bombards, and these could belch copious grapeshot to shred any infantry or cavalry sent against it. Alspring was to be her great test. Against it many other conquerers had been tested and found wanting. Lemorel had to defeat Alspring, or her aura with the Neverland nomads would begin to fade.

The first volley of shots caught the Alspring defenders totally by surprise. They were fired from twice the range of the bombards on the walls, and they smashed among the red and gold domes and spires of the palace. After that a pattern set in, with a shot every two minutes that was sure to land with mathematical precision. Only the palace and one section of wall was being targeted, and the bombardment continued through the night. Presently the palace was a shambles, while the famous chequerboard pattern city walls were ragged and crumbling along the southwest face.

As it became harder for the defenders to mount their own bombards on the southwest wall, the Neverlanders moved in conventional bombards and began pounding the wall at close range. Casualties were heavy among the bombard crews on both sides, but the wall slowly crumbled and fell under the sustained battering. Within the city the word was spreading: Commander Lemorel was only interested in their Grand Makulad, she always spared the common people when she conquered a city. This was the opposite message to that which her spies and agents had spread in Glenellen, but then this was a full siege. The evidence was the smashed towers and domes of the palace, and the untouched temples, houses and shops of everyone else. Siege engines began to appear in the distance, but the ground before the walls was trenched, mined and littered with obstacles. All defending forces were concentrated near the disintegrating part of the wall in preparation for the attack to come.

"We shall lure them into our city like a mouse into the jaws of a cat!" the infuriated Grand Makulad of Alspring ranted to his Elders, senior officers and other advisors. "She shattered my palace, she smashed my treasures. I want her in the stocks, stripped naked with a waterfall of pig dung and offal pouring over her. We shall fight street by street, sponging up their lives in the ruins until her army is bled dry, then my elite Palace Lancers will ride out and crush those cowards that dared not venture inside."

It was a fine, fighting speech, but the audience went its way in small groups, all animated with anxious discussion. Commander Lemorel showed mercy when a city surrendered in the face of overwhelming odds. Commander Lemorel was unspeakably cruel in the face of pointless resistance.

A gunshot echoed through the rubble-strewn corridors and halls of the palace. Someone shrieked inarticulately, then another shot barked out.

"Muskets!" exclaimed the Overhand of Artillery. He and his adjunct rushed back into the Grand Makulad's throne room to find the monarch shot dead before his throne. Nearby was the Overhand of the Palace Lancers, lying dead with two flintlocks beside him. A scroll was tucked into the sash around his waist. The Overhand of Artillery read the words aloud:

"Commander Lemorel wants no life but that of the Grand Makulad. In the Name of the Deity I offer it to her, with mine, for the protection of the women and children of Alspring."

By now other Overhands, Elders and advisors had rushed in, along with the throne room guards.

"Where the hell were you and your men?" the Overhand of Artillery demanded of the guards' captain.

"We were ordered from the room," he replied in a strong monotone.

"Ordered? By whom?"

"The Overhand of Lancers."

"But you answer only to the Grand Makulad."

"He gave his consent to it, sir."

"His consent. I see. And you left the Grand Makulad with a man armed with two loaded pistols?"

"The pistols are the symbols of his protection for the Grand Makulad, sir."

"Once again, I see. All right, then. As the senior overhand I am the Grand Interim for now. Sub-Overhand Dalin, you can command the Palace Lancers. Stay with me, the rest of you, out!"

When they were gone the Overhand indicated the barrel of one of the flintlocks on the floor with the toe of his boot.

"What is that sticking to the barrel?" he asked.

"A white down-feather, sir."

"Yes. Do you think that he discharged that gun into the backside of a chicken and then forgot to clean it, or might someone else have fired it into a feather pillow to muffle the blast?"

"Sir?"

"Look there, a jagged, messy hole in his forehead and the back of his head blown out, yet there are no powder burns around his face. Could he have shot himself from a mere handspan away?"

A Neverlander artillery shot whistled down in the distance, to land with a muffled boom followed by a clatter of heavy masonry.

"A conspiracy, sir?"

"Very probably. My guess is that somewhere nearby a cushion is being burned, and that two guards are frantically reloading their muskets. There were four shots, Dalin, but these two flintlocks were fired into a cushion after the Overhand and Grand Makulad were already dead. I thought at the time that I'd heard muskets, not pistols."

The Overhand went to the fretwork shutters and pushed one open. Beyond the palace the city remained undamaged. Suddenly a bombard shot whistled in and they both recoiled and threw themselves to the lavish carpet as it impacted close by.

They picked themselves up and dusted plaster off their robes.

"The conspirators were right, Dalin," said the Overhand, "whatever the morality of what they did. Run up the orange and white pennants for a truce and assemble a delegation to meet with Commander Lemorel. You will lead it, and you will surrender the city on my behalf."

"Me, sir? A mere Sub-Overhand? Surely Commander Lemorel would be insulted if any less in stature than yourself were to go?"

"I want to remain here and ensure that some hothead does not seize command and resume the siege. If Commander Lemorel is insulted, I offer my life in atonement. Unlike a few of the hypocrites about this place, I really am willing to spend my life to protect the innocent of this city. See to it."

"Yes, sir, Overhand and Grand Interim."

The Overhand turned away to gaze through the window over the city as Dalin began to walk away.

"And Dalin!"

"Sir?"

"Discreetly arrange a tragic accident for the throne room captain and those six guards if you manage to survive the next couple of hours."

"Sir. As good as done."

*****

True to her reputation, Lemorel taxed the city heavily in terms of wealth, weapons, livestock and recruits, but there were no atrocities that could not be attributed to criminals taking advantage of the disruption. She was now the undisputed ruler of the entire centre of the vast continent.

As an exercise in logistics, she soon launched what she termed a thunderbolt strike to the north, at the Carpentarian cities. Rather than following tradition, with all supplies carried on the attack camels, the lancers were instead backed up by armed supply caravans that stood well back from the fighting. Several Carpentarian patrols were wiped out or captured, then a regional city was captured within four days. The shock caused the other cities to seal themselves into siege law, leaving the countryside, roads, farms and canals in the hands of Lemorel's invaders. Each city was isolated, then led to believe that all the others had fallen. Mere brigades of lancers gathered groups of tens of thousands of Carpentarian peasants near the besieged cities, giving the impression of enormous armies. Surrenders were generally swift, and within three months every city was under Lemorel's administration. A population of 900,000, which was not even registered on the Libris Calculor's data cards, had been subdued at the cost of 860 lives.

*****

To the south of Alspring was a gap in a rocky ridge known as Call funnel, where a mercy wall had been built to save people in the grip of the Call from wandering away south into the desert. At the centre of the curved mercy wall was a stone speakers' platform which was used in religious orations, reedpipe concerts, military reviews, high-profile public executions, and even some circus performances. It was known as the Red Stage, both for the executions held there, and for the blood-red stone from which it had been fashioned.

Lemorel strode the Red Stage alone, wearing robes of red ochre that were tied and bound to make her look as small and sharp as possible. She had selected her attire to seem both small and in need of protection, yet hard, sharp and unkillable, like a sabre ant. The veil below her eyes was of such a thin gauze that her face was quite distinct to those standing close by, but it allowed her voice to carry further than the more mundane type. The 9,000 in her audience were the elite lancers and officers of her army, the group that would carry out whatever orders she gave.

She started the oration by congratulating them on conquering all of the Alspring cities in the five years since she had led her first band of Neverlander freebooters into battle, then she went on to rant against the OverMayor in the distant south who was plotting against them. They were cheering spontaneously by the time she told them that they were all united as Alspring Ghans now, led by the Neverlanders. She reminded them that talk of other groupings was treason. To become an officer was to become a Neverlander, and to become a Neverlander was the highest honour of all.

"I once told you that the centre would tremble at your name, and now it is true. I once told you that you would rule the cities that treated you with contempt, and now it is true. I once told you that whole nations would surrender at the mere dust of your approach, and now it is true."

It was several minutes before the cheering, shouting and discharge of muskets had subsided. Lemorel was patient, she was happy to see them as exuberant as they wished to be. They had just won an exhausting race, but they were about to be told that they had to run several times further.

"Now you are mighty. Now you are rich. Now each of you has many invel-wives to protect and you are all blessed in the sight of the Deity."

She paused for emphasis. Her entire appeal to them had been based on headlong and unstoppable expansion, and not one expected that they would be told to go home and tend their new-found prosperity in peace.

"Now I tell you that every overhand will soon be a prince. Every officer will be an overhand. Every lancer will be rich enough to live in a mansion and own a hundred camels. This very day I have had word from my envoys that some cities and states of the eastern continent are begging to be our clients so that together we may subdue the sprawling lands beyond the red and rocky deserts, land where the water never dries up and the grass is green all the year. Neverlanders, nomad lancers that are my mighty and invincible right hand, this day I shall begin to muster an army of a quarter of a million to sweep south —"

The sheer scope of the adventure raised such euphoria that the rest of her oration was lost in deafening cheers and commotion.

*****

Lemorel was true to her word. That afternoon she met with Overhand-in-Chief Baragania and the four logistics overhands who managed the care, feeding, supply and transport of her troops. Scribes had already produced renderings of the routes south from the caravan maps, and details of states beyond the deserts had been culled from maps smuggled north in bags of coffee.

"This is all soft, undefended land," she explained in a hoarse voice as her fingers brushed across the names of states that few of them had known the existence of until recently. "They rely on the desert to keep them safe, yet the desert can be as fickle and unfaithful as a Rochestrian suitor. This land can be crossed by an army of lancers, men able to live in the saddle, carrying all that they need to survive on a minimal number of spare camels. Our spearhead will be the riders on camels, but horses will soon be provided by the Southmoors. Large herds are being moved to the northwest of the Balranald Emirate, by secret agreement. We shall get them here, north of the Barrier Grasslands."

"And cities, great lady? Soft, rich cities like the great explorer Kharek promised to us?" asked a logistics overhand.

"Rich, lazy cities. Cities with no experience of our type of war."

"But they have powerful machines and deadly weapons, Commander Lemorel," Baragania warned.

"Machines that are easily bypassed, or even turned to our own use. We shall use their wind trains and beamflash towers, just as we have built a superior calculor. As for their weapons, we have bought many already, and there are more to be taken. No, our main weapons are camels that carry water and supplies for our army as it crosses the desert, and our long and secret preparations before every strike."

With a nod of heads the logistics overhands indicated that they were satisfied by her explanation, and the discussion moved on to specific invasion scenarios, as modelled by the Glenellen Calculor. The figures were encouraging, and the group became optimistic, then eager.

When finally they had gone, Lemorel sat alone with Baragania, who was one of the very few that she treated as anything like a peer.

"How is Nikalan?" he asked as Lemorel rolled up her maps.

"Improving, but still little more than a shell," she said after a moment, as if she had been struggling to recall a distant memory. "Some of the finest physicians that we have available agree that he has been allowed to do nothing but work on both the Glenellen calculor and battle calculor for far too long. When Nikalan was wandering free with —" She exhaled, then inhaled again. "— with Glasken through the deserts to the Fostoria oasis, he was forced to live a varied existence and his mind was slowly healing. He had lost a great love, and the trauma had unhinged his mind. When allowed to do nothing else but calculor design and mathematics, his mind retreated again into a smooth, pure shell and he slipped further away from our world."

Baragania watched her closely, noting that she now spoke more openly about Nikalan. *Perhaps her own heart is healing itself?* he wondered.

"And how are you, Commander?" he asked. "You came to our lands to rescue him, you conquered us during the course of that rescue, then you found that he had slipped into dementia. This is the day of your greatest triumph, but are you happy?"

"I am happy," she said after a pause to think the question through. "Years ago, when I was about twelve years old, I broke a plate that belonged to my little brother. It had a glazed painting of a freebooter rabbit on it. It was also his favourite, and he was inconsolable for days. My younger sister, Jemli, was very good with her hands, and she glued it back together again. He ate from it, and the glue dissolved when it was washed. Jemli then had a clay base moulded and fired to fit the fragments, then glued it into that. It was heavy and cumbersome, but Jimkree used the rabbit plate for at least five years more, until he grew too old for such things. Nikalan is the same." Lemorel giggled. "Could you imagine it, but one physician attending him employed a harlot who is especially good with very aged clients, and she actually coaxed a response from him. No less than three times, I have been assured. She calls him a sweet little boy, even though he is about thirty five. He can again cut his own bread and pour juice for himself ... yes, the repairs to his mind are proceeding apace."

"Nikalan is not a plate, he is a man."

She dropped her gaze, then looked up at him again. There was still a measure of pain in her eyes. "I know, but can you suggest anything better? Baragania, he was the goal that set me on the road, but now that I have him I find that the road is more important. Nikalan was like a finely bred racing camel: superbly suited to a very specific course, but hopeless for use elsewhere. I bumped him once, and like my brother's plate he fell to the ground and shattered. Just lately I finally admitted to myself that had it not been me, it would have been someone else."

"But what drives you now, Commander? Why, in the moment of your greatest triumph are you not at the celebration of your own victory?"

"Why, you ask? Because the OverMayor of the Southeast Alliance is a fool. She built her entire power base on a calculor and some long, frail networks of paralines and beamflash towers. If I cut her precious infrastructures at strategic points, I can seize two thirds of the continent in less than a year. It is like when I spied upon you and your Glenellen Calculor, many battles ago. You were so very vulnerable, I simply could not wait to engage you, lest someone else realized how very easily you could be defeated.

"Besides, there is more to it than just going on to the next campaign. My agents have already organized joint operations with the Southmoors, and have infiltrated the beamflash and paraline networks. I have even been chipping away at the mightly Libris Calculor itself by financing civil actions to free its components. In fundamentalist Gentheist circles my people have been dropping hints about steam power being used in Kalgoorlie. Baragania, what does all this suggest to you?"

Baragania had no idea, but months of campaigning with Lemorel had taught him to think as she did when the occasion required it. "The war with the Southeast and Woomera has already begun, but in a subtle way," he speculated.

"Precisely, superbly observed and reasoned, my friend. The war has begun. Every single Ghan who travels to Maralinga is a trusted agent. Those same agents have been negotiating right-of-way across Kooree lands for my armies as well. Add all of that activity together, and it becomes a highly noticeable operation. All that it will take to draw attention to itself is a blunder or two, an accident, or even a traitor's word. We must move now. If we wait for a day longer than is needed, we may be noticed — and if we do not take our enemies by surprise, they will be far too strong for us."

*****

The first of Zarvora's operational rockets left Kalgoorlie amid a noisy festival in honour of the glory of technology. The first stage was firmly bolted to a flatbed truck and painted a bright green with red bands. Two galley engines pulled the flatbed and its attendant cars, while another five carried relief crews and all the support equipment that would be needed. It had been arranged that Denkar would stay in Kalgoorlie and provide calculor backup over the beamflash line as Zarvora required it.

"Why Woomera?" Denkar asked yet again as they stood on the platform of the railside, shouting to each other above the cheering and the massed bands.

"I am not even sure myself," Zarvora replied. "It is to do with angles and orbits and tampering with forces that mere mortals like us have not commanded for two millennia. The ancients also used the Woomera site to launch rockets into space, so they may have known something about the location that we cannot even guess at. More than that I cannot say, even to you."

"Why not?"

"Because I would sound insane. Or dangerous. Or reckless. Or even all three. Would it help if I asked you to trust me?"

Further down the platform Glasken was saying goodbye to Jemli, who was by now his business partner and assistant manager.

"If the Golden Jar comes up, begin the bidding at a thousand royals."

"But we have more than that."

"Don't go a copper over 1400 without asking me."

"But you will be in Woomera, darling Glassy."

"Well use the beamflash."

"The beamflash? It's a royal per thousand words!"

"A royal, be buggered. Hey there, sonny, catch."

"Glassy! That was a gold royal."

"You don't make royals by skimping on coppers. You're too much of an accountant, Jemmy, and besides, I know a few matters about this deal that I can threaten to bring out into the open if I really have to. If it goes over 1400, beamflash me. All right?"

"All right, but what about that 2000 extra that you have with the bank?"

"That's to pay your final year studies at Kalgoorlie."

"What? That's a hundred *times* the University's fee. What are you really to do with it?"

Brace yourself, the elocution is cracking, she's not far from going over the edge, Gasken thought to himself. He was glad of the deafening music from the nearby bands.

"Well ... perchance I have to pay a churl to set up an adultery case against your husband."

"That'll be the day. He hasn't had it up in years, and anyway, why bother?"

"Perchance I'm jealous!"

"*You're* jealous of *him*? A doddering fykart who only managed to get his leg over me five times in eight years of marriage, yet you're not jealous of Ilyire spending a week of August with me while you went off to the desert with the Highliber and her bloody rockets and fuel that explodes if you so much as look at it?"

"I wanted it be Ilyire rather than some riff-raff I don't know —"

"Oh, so *you* put him up to it! I was wondering why you were so calm when I tried to confess everything. Here was I all worked up for an abject confession and to plead for you not to leave me because I'd been cheating —"

"Unfaithful."

"Unfaithful, and — will you stop that!"

"Jemli, what the hell was all that fuss about in the first place? I'd told you before I left that I didn't care what you did or who you did it with as long as you exercised a bit of discretion and minded our business reputation. When I got back —"

"When you got back my heart was being torn apart inside of me, but you were only interested in correcting my grammar when I tried to tell you that Ilyire had rogered —"

"Seduced."

"DAMN HELL, Glassy, will you stop that!" she shouted, stamping her foot on the platform. "I felt so guilty when I saw what a sight you were then thought upon what I'd been up to when it had been happening. To think that you'd suggested it to Ilyire in the first place! Why? That's what I want to know. Why? And don't give me that rubbish about fear of some churl with the pox bedding me because you know as well as I do that I'm far too discriminating to be in danger from that."

Glasken grasped at the interruption before he had an answer framed.

"Why, you say? Well it's not so very hard to explain," he babbled as he frantically worked through feelings that had originally been more impulsive than logical. "I actually didn't want to lose you either, that was it, and I knew that Ilyire would not try to take you away from me, whereas someone else might. I really did it to occupy you with someone safe while I was away. Jemmy, I only wanted to keep you."

Jemli thought about his words for a moment. Glasken saw the softening suddenly wash across her features, then she surged forward into his arms, smothering him with hair.

"Oh, Glassy, Glassy, darling, silly Fras. As long as I have a special place in your heart I shall never, never exile you from mine. Silly boy, foolish Glassy."

Glasken sighed with relief as he stroked the back of her head. *Sometimes the truth has a lot going for it*, he thought to himself.

"I ... I think a bit of the Alspring Ghan protection fettish has rubbed off on me, too," he confided into her ear as they embraced. "I like to think of you being safe, snug and well contented for while I endure danger —"

Jemli snapped back like a carriage spring from a broken brace.

"What? Danger he says! You come back with half an ear blown off and three hundred stitches in your back after a wagonload of that abominable unstable rocket fuel exploded because some horse farted too hard — *and* you threw yourself over not just any damn librarian but the Highliber herself."

"Jemmy, the fuel cores were smouldering. I —"

"The others with her were killed!"

"Well ... yes, I —"

"And you expect me to be happy and contented just because you'd set me up with one of your churl friends? Not bloody likely! Would you like to know what was going on back here while you were lying out there in the desert bleeding all over the Highliber?"

"Not re—"

"*Your* friend, Ilyire, and I went through some very mechanical and unsatisfactory actions, then sat on opposite sides of the bed for an hour feeling as guilty as sin and thoroughly miserable."

"You were guilty about being unfaithful to *me*? I never heard anything so ridiculous."

"If I want to feel guilty then I'll feel guilty! For the rest of your time away, Ilyire slept on a mat on the floor with a sword in his hand. He said it made him feel happier, it's some sort of Alspring custom. I just lay in the bed staring up at that damn tasteless Davantine ceiling mural, and I'm telling you I was *not* happy and I was *not* contented!"

"Jemli, dearest —"

"Glassy, I've never been so mortified and embarrassed in all of my life — except for my wedding night — so if *that's* an example of you making things pleasant for me while you're away I'll be looking after myself from now on, thank you very much."

"So what are you going to to? Have the ceiling mural painted over?" asked Glasken, throwing his hands up in the air.

"I — that's not such a bad idea, you know. As a matter of fact, *I* met the Mayor's sister at the University Foundation Day Festival. She's invited me —"

"You what? Varsellia? Don't believe a word she says — or her servants, especially that maid with the curly blonde hair —"

"Gembeline."

"That's her — ach!"

"*I've* got an invitation to live in the palace, for however long you are away. I get along very well with Frelle Varsellia. She's going to teach me to use makeup in the Kalgoorlie style, and belly dancing too: you'll need a medician standing by when I dance for you, Glassy. In return I've promised to show her something of your fighting techniques, and I've been giving her a little help with an accounting sys—"

"So *that's* how Varsellia got a distinction for her last accounting dissertation at the University. Wait a minute, the Foundation Festival was way back in September. Have you two known each other for all of this mmph —"

Jemli put a hand behind Glasken's head and pressed their lips together in a lingering, passionate kiss. Suddenly all the heat of the exchange was gone, and they were wallowing in the mutual affection that their argument had forced out into the open. They stood with their foreheads pressed together as the whistles were blown to warn that the navvies in the galley engines were ready at their pedals.

"Beautiful Frelle Jemli Cogsworth, will you marry me once I'm able to arrange for someone to roll aside Urteg Cogsworth, who has no better claim to fame than being your husband?"

She undulated her body against his, as much for the pleasure of his words as the feel of him. "Jemli Glasken, a beautiful, silvery, shivery name, like a highland waterfall in winter. Yes, my handsome and brave darling, yes, yes, yes. Marry me and make my name so very beautiful. Now look after yourself, what with all those dangerous rockets. What will I do if my handsome lover is killed?"

"Well I've willed you all my money, you could buy another," he said brightly, gesturing in the air with one hand like a Southmoor slave market auctioneer.

"No, I'll never do it, so come back and save me from a future of loneliness."

A relief team of pedal navvies filing aboard the rear galley engine began to hoot and whistle.

"I will be back, though, no matter what," he whispered.

She kissed the ragged remains of his left ear, then he stepped back aboard the carriage while still reaching out to caress her face.

"Don't they look the sweetest pair of lovers you have ever seen?" remarked Denkar, gazing at them from three carriages away.

"I have heard that she has a tongue like a machine-crossbow," replied Zarvora doubtfully.

"But apparently she never flays Glasken with it."

"Strange, that. All through his life he has left a trail of women with the breath knocked out of them and their robes about their ears, not to mention men with severe hangovers, yet look at him now. Perhaps that explosion knocked some sense into his head."

"Without him you'd be dead, like those five engineers."

"I know, and that is hard for me to come to terms with."

The train moved out of the railside slowly and smoothly amid showers of petals and streamers, but the noise died away rapidly once they were into the suburbs of the great inland city. Ettenbar was with Zarvora in the Mayoral coach, finalizing arrangements for returning data to the electric calculor via beamflash.

"These galley engines are an expensive way to move freight, Frelle Highliber," he said as he watched the houses give way to fields and grazing cattle on group-tethers.

"The rocket has to be launched from a precise place at a precise time, little worrier. Expense is no object."

"I could help better if I understood, exalted Frelle."

"Only I understand, Ettenbar, and even I wonder if I really understand."

"If I understood, exalted Frelle, I would give my life to ensure that your results were satisfactory."

"And that is one of the reasons why I am telling you nothing. If you do not know what results I hope to get, you cannot bend the actual results to please me."

Ettenbar laughed and waggled his finger. "Very cunning, exalted Frelle, but shame upon your suspicious nature."

She pulled at a green tassle that hung from the ceiling, then spread diagrams of a launching gantry on the folding table. Moments later there was a scream and a slap just outside the door, then Glasken entered rubbing his cheek.

"I swear, the train lurched just as I walked past her —"

"I am not interested, just sit down and listen," said Zarvora. "In a week we should be in Woomera, and from there the rocket stages and support equipment will be taken by mule cart to where the launching gantry has been assembled. For all of the unloading and mule cart ride, the rockets will be your responsibility. Guard them as you would guard your life, guard them as you would guard your testicles —"

"— for the latter will surely be forfeit if there is any sort of accident," said Glasken in a parody of her tone and accent.

"Fras Glasken, I think that we are beyond threats of that sort by now. I would have said please if you had let me finish."

"Your pardon, Frelle. Where will you be?"

"I am to ride ahead and ensure that the gantry and other equipment is in place for the rocket's arrival. I shall be in charge of its assembly, arming and launching."

"That's a relief, Frelle."

*****

It was long after sunset, and the plains to the northwest of Woomera were illuminated by the glow of that part of the Mirrorsun band opposite the daylight sun. This time the Mirrorsun glow was from sixteen bright points arranged in a square of twelve enclosing a square of four. It was a most intriguing spectacle, yet this night's display, like all those before it, had no real explanation. Many edutors had written many erudite papers on the changing Mirrorsun configurations, but all remained pure speculation.

Lamps outlined a stucture that rose from the dimly illuminated plain like a huge weapon, and yet for all its size it seemed insignificant against the vastness of Mirrorsun in the sky above. Lanterns glowed and moved amid shadowed woodwork structures, an indication of several dozen people hard at work on some very large project. A green flare arched up into the sky and began to fall.

The ancient rocket ignited with a howling roar, and it shot up through the framework of the launching gantry like a thunderbolt out of a giant crossbow. It flew free from the apex rails and the glow of the brilliant gleam of its exhaust jet quickly dwindled as it ascended, leaving dark, dispersing exhausts to occlude the stars. Zarvora and her engineers and technicians watched together, raising their telescopes as the glow grew more distant. When the rocket was barely a speck in the sky, the first stage burned out and separated and the second stage ignited. Presently the rocket was nothing more than a thinning line of glowing but fading smoke. There was a slight break as the second stage burned out and the third ignited.

"It looks good, but it is out of our hands," said Zarvora to the sky.

She turned to the horizon, but did not use her telescope. The Rangemaster continued to watch its progress through his own device, calling the reports out as he was given them.

"Fourth stage ignition reported from the downrange telescopes. The rocket is reported as little more than a moving star. It's too high to track reliably."

Zarvora explosively released the breath that she had been holding. "Give the order 'Transmit', to the four beamflash towers," she ordered, and added more softly: "Let us draw attention to ourselves."

The Rangemaster gestured to the nearby beamflash crew, who ignited a flare in their transmission rig and began to send out the enigmatic order.

"With respect, Highliber, but whose attention do we wish to draw?"

"I do not know, Fras Rangemaster, but should my little 'beacon' electric devices in those beamflash towers begin to smoke and melt, we shall have been successful."

"And the rocket, Highliber?"

"A complex and desperate gamble, Fras Rangemaster, and if it fails we shall return here in a month or so and try again with a second rocket." She lifted her telescope to her eyes again, and focussed toward the southern horizon. "Ah there, a signal from beamflash tower South," she said as she gazed through her telescope.

" 'TRANSMITTER COILS BURNED THROUGH HOUSING AND MELTED.' "

"Highliber, beamflash West —"

"Is reporting the same thing?"

"Yes."

"Then a Wanderer is interested in what we are doing. Let us hope that it is also ... enthusiastic. Too enthusiastic."

*****

High above the atmosphere the fifth stage of the rocket flew smoothly along its trajectory. When its fuel had been exhausted a fuse had burned through a tether and released a timer that ticked out the seconds. Hundreds of kilometres away in space, the ancient orbital fortress detected radio emissions on the ground and shot EMP bursts down until all four sources had been silenced. There had been more than one source, there might be more remaining, its AI command module decided. It remained on alert.

The timer in the rocket's payload engaged the first setting, and a circuit closed. DIT DIT — DIT DIT. The circuit opened again. The transmission had taken less than two seconds. The orbital fortress had not fired, but it tracked the fifth stage as it moved along its ballistic curve. It had transmitted for a moment, and the fortress' control logic had tagged it as suspicious. DIT DIT — DIT DIT — DIT DIT, the signal commenced again, and the fortress spat a pulse adequate to silence it. A fuse burst, the timer ticked on, then the little radio transmitter began again with a new, heavier fuse.

The fortress spat another EMP, but the coils of the transmitter in the rocket were built to withstand a moderate pulse and the DIT DIT continued. Again the fortress fired at the tiny fifth stage, this time a sustained pulse. The circuit finally melted under the load and was silent, yet the fortress continued to follow it with its beam of electromagnetic energy. Zarvora's rocket drew the beam across the limitless backdrop of space ... until it slashed across the band of the nanotech shield that orbited thousands of kilometres further out. Circuits melted and died in their trillions, and the ribbon was cut right through. Each tiny slap of Mirrorsun's fabric was a separate, versatile machine, with a small amount of on-board intelligence and powered by solar radiation. The sum of all the parts was sentient.

The AI command of the fortress traced through paths of logic not run for millennia, then reached a conclusion. A radio source travelling above the atmosphere had resisted EMP attack for an unusual period. It might still be live. A railgun swung around and received its programming, then spat a cloud of alloy spheres on an intercepting trajectory with the fifth stage. Seconds ticked into minutes. Zarvora's rocket was pulverized under a hail of metal that then plunged into the upper atmosphere and streaked into trails of glowing ions.

The orbital fortress moved on and vanished beneath the horizon as the metal fragments of the rocket fell into the atmosphere to burn as well. The fortress noted the disruption in the Mirrorsun band, but continued to ignore the glow from its electrical activity, as it always had: nothing like it was in the ancient mission parameters, and it had not shown any sign of hostility. Each of the old weapons platforms classified Mirrorsun as an unidentifiable but harmless natural phenomenon.

On the ground there were cheers in the Woomera observatory as the monitors observed the first signs of the rent in the band. The Rangemaster congratulated Zarvora on ending Greatwinter's second coming.

"You reached out and slew the gods themselves," he declared grandly, for he had been in the amateur theatre at Woomera University.

Zarvora was pensive as she looked through the eyepiece of her telescope. "Slew it, Fras Rangemaster? I wonder. Perchance I merely annoyed it a great deal."

The Rangemaster put his hands on his hips. "But you cut the band."

"It may recover. The question is one of whether it takes centuries, decades, or merely years."

"So you will launch the second rocket?"

"I shall keep it ready."

Zarvora inspected the initial accounts and measurements of the flight, then handed them to Darien to take back to the beamflash tower in Woomera to transmit west to Kalgoorlie. The hard-copy accounts would follow on the paraline, but they were only for verification, and the archives.

Even as they went about their business, the band's collective consciousness was enhancing itself into a neural network to deal with the rent in its body. Over the days that followed meteor damage lines formed out of chains of nanocells, then whiplashed across the gap to join the two ends and draw them back together. By that time the gap was thousands of kilometres across, but six weeks after the breach the band was whole again. The network now turned its attention to the cause of the trauma that had cost it so dearly in energy and resources. Slowly, ominously, the band began to restructure itself.

Zarvora observed the activity with initial dismay, then she noted that the band was putting itself through strange and unprecedented configurations. It was seeming to experiment with localized concaves in its greater curve, and the localized concaves were focussed on the Wanderers. Zarvora new that she had failed in her attempt to cripple Mirrorsun for at least a few decades, but she dared to hope that something even better might come from her ambitious and desperate project. She decided that it might be worth attempting to antagonize Mirrorsun just a little more.

*****

Glasken had learned to travel light during his journeys since graduating from the University of Rochester in 1699. Thus when called upon to travel with the Highliber's train, he packed a change of clothing, his undercottons, a swagger stick and cheap Gilmey 40 bore, his seal, and some money. He reasoned from past experience that if he was to be robbed, swindled or otherwise set upon there was little point in taking anything of value.

"What I find is that possessions travel better than I do," he explained to Ettenbar as he poured wax into the seal countersinks of a wooden crate and pressed his seal and code down hard. Within were detailed notes and calibrated circuits that had been damaged by the electromagnetic pulses from space.

"Perhaps bags and trunks do not have enraged husbands, fathers and constable's runners in pursuit of them," Ettenbar suggested.

"Very funny. Throw me that strap, now. There, all sealed for the customs bald heads at Coonana to see."

"And what is your design of a barrel and sickle framed by leaves, worthy Fras?" asked Ettenbar as he helped.

"The Kalgoorlie Guild of Master Vintners."

"I did not know that you are a master vintner."

"I'm not. That cost me 500 gold royals."

"You bought it? But, Fras, that is dishonesty."

"Not at all, I look upon it as patronage. Besides, I may not be a master of the Guild, but I *employ* two masters to tend my investments."

"Fras, your logic is convoluted indeed."

Glasken paid for the freight at the paraline depot and returned to the railside hostelry with Ettenbar. For Glasken it had been a quiet trip — it was free of people attempting to abduct, murder, torture, enslave or imprison him. His work in translating trajectory data into calculor input statements for the beamflash had been complex but undemanding, and nothing had happened to the rockets while they were under his control. Much to his surprise the Highliber had granted him the temporary rank of a Dragon Blue Librarian. He did not mention it in his beamflash mail and letters to Jemli.

"Another rocket due in a week," he said to Ettenbar as he snapped his fingers for a waiter in the refectory. "Two weeks more and the third rocket arrives, and then I'm free to drink, sing, and get my face slapped by non-librarians. Ah the waiter. Um, plistebi grep enfola, bieratel, salavou kremti, eti — Gah, how does one say 'Islamic menu' in Woomeran?"

"Viadatem Islam, good Fras," responded the waiter.

"Why the hell didn't you say you spoke Austaric? Lucky for you my Frelle isn't here. Now, a pie, beer and salad for me, and your Islamic menu for my friend here."

The waiter scribbled down the order on his slate and hurried away.

"Well, Fras, I suspect that my own days tending the calculors of the Highliber are over as well," Ettenbar confided as they sat waiting. "Now that this glorious project with the rockets is close to completion, my intent is to return to the Southmoor province of my birth and design a calculor for the university."

"So what about women?"

"Ah ha ha, Fras, you think that I am all working and no passions, but you are wrong. I have been in discreet contact with my family and

... there is talk of an arrangement with a girl that would be a highly suitable match."

"An arranged marriage?"

"A suitable marriage."

"You're mad."

"Fras, Fras, my friend. How can I explain? For many months now I have had the benefit of watching your life and dealings, and nothing could make me long for the tranquility and morality of Southmoor country life more than your example. I have some knowledge of matters theological, Fras Glasken. I can sense that you have had religious discipline in the years since you escaped Libris, and that your monastery story may be in part true, but you have certainly deviated from the path marked out for you."

"That's the story of my life, failing people's expectations."

"Ah now, I did not say failure. You are on a different path, but that does not make you any the worse."

"Look here, my pie and your menu. Where's my beer? Gah, different waiter! Speak Austaric? Thought not. Bieratelissi?"

"Numeren 4 eti 12, da ke," said Ettenbar to the waiter.

"Bloody hell, Ettenbar, why didn't you say you spoke Woomeran?" exclaimed Glasken.

"I thought you wished to make good the chance to practise, Fras."

"Dummart. One day I'll be *your* boss, then we'll see some smart work."

"Ah, whatever else you are, Fras Glasken, you are never boring as company. When the third rocket has gone its way, and we have gone ours, I shall miss you."

"Just as well, most folk seem to hit me without any trouble."

"Ah ha ha, you have the jokings again, but I am serious."

*****

A week later the second rocket had arrived from the paraline terminus, and had been mounted on the railings of the launching frame. This was to be a daytime launch, for reasons determined by Zarvora's calculations of the Wanderers' orbits. The time for the passing of the orbital fortress approached, and the Rangemaster monitored a little windmill attached to a friction axle.

"The wind seldom drops below 15 kilometres per hour, Frelle Highliber," he reported as they made ready.

"The ramp should be safe at that speed."

"But it's gusty wind, 'untidy' wind as the paraline engine drivers would say."

"So what is your opinion?"

"If a gust was to catch the rocket while it was just emerging from the tower and still moving slowly it could alter its course very slightly."

Zarvora weighed up several factors, political as well as technical.

"Set for a launch in four minutes, by my authority," she finally ordered.

A technician set the timer at the base of the rocket, then ran for his bunker 100 metres away. The mechanism clicked, the wind gusted ... the wind gusted just as the igniter flared, distorting the launch tower very slightly. The second rocket rammed itself into the slightly distorted rails, and the watchers saw the top of the ramp shatter in a plume of rocket exhaust and smashed wood. The force snapped the rocket between the first and second stages, and the burning first stage slammed at full thrust into the desert with a boom that shook the observers in their bunker. The upper stages did not fire, but crashed to the ground in a lesser cloud of dust.

Zarvora climbed into the remains of the ramp as soon as it was declared safe. It quickly became clear how lucky they had been. The supporting structure was nearly intact, with only the upper framework and guide rails wrecked. The technicians and engineers estimated a fortnight to make the repairs.

"The upper stages of the rocket are badly dented and twisted," the Rangemaster reported as Zarvora descended to the ground. "They'll have to be taken apart, de-fueled, and beaten back into shape. The armourers and mechanics estimate that as taking no less than four months."

"But meantime there is a third rocket on the way from Kalgoorlie. Damn and damn hell, this was my fault. I should have had tests done for wind distortion. We only have four rockets, we cannot afford to waste any."

A far-off movement caught Zarvora's attention, and she glanced around to where a boundary rider had appeared in the distance, driving his horse as hard as he could over the red sand and broken stone. *Nobody rides like that without there being a crisis of the very worst kind*, she said to herself.

The rider called to the guards as he reached the shelter tower, and they pointed to the launching gantry. As he rode up to her, Zarvora could see that one of his arms hung limp, and was soaked in blood.

"Hostile lancers and musketeers on camels and horses, Frelle Highliber," he wheezed, sitting upright only with difficulty.

"Warriors? Out here?"

"Aye, and making right for the towers and ramp. They must have noticed the explosion. I was shot as I rode from them."

"A patrol from Woomera," ventured the Rangemaster. "A mistake."

"There were hundreds, thousands."

"And to the northeast of here?" responded Zarvora. "Unlikely — wait! How were they dressed? Were they swathed in robes of red, vermillion and orange?"

"Aye, Frelle Highliber."

"Alspring Ghans! Come all the way across the desert like Ilyire's expedition of seven years ago. How many attacked your patrol?"

"A squad of some dozens, Frelle Highliber. They tried to ride us into a pincer-trap, but their camels were too slow for our horses. Even so, they shoot well, and only I have survived out of five. We may have accounted for three of them," he added with pride.

"And they broke off the pursuit?"

"Aye, when we were in sight of the towers. They might have thought that this is a fort."

Zarvora ascended a few steps and peered to the northeast. There were camel lancers in scattered groups, and a central knot of perhaps fifty. Behind them was a vast dust pall from a far larger force.

"The Ghans are said to strike hard and rapidly," she said, shading her eyes against the glare as she leaned away from the timber rails. "I can see them scouting this place ... and I am afraid it is obvious how vulnerable we are here. Yes, they will atttack before the main force arrives. They have surprised us, and they will want to take advantage of that. Ilyire told me that their commanders value surprise highly as a tactic."

"We have sixty lancers here, and nine Tiger Dragons," said the Woomeran marshal. "We should be able to stop a mere eight or nine dozen Ghans, no matter how fierce they may be as warriors."

"There's as many as ten thousand Ghans behind 'em," the rider insisted.

"Pah!"

"Ten thousand, Fras. Probably more."

"Pure fancy," said the marshal dismissively. What do you think, Frelle Highliber?"

"How far away is the main column?" she asked the rider.

"Ten kilometres, no more."

"Assume the worst." She stepped down from her vantage point, and there was a look of grim determination on her face. "Glaetin, take two lancers and escort this man to Woomera, take him to the Overhand."

"Frelle Highliber, he bleeds freely —"

"Well patch him as you ride, but move! Now! A lot more will bleed otherwise. Marrocal, douse the gantry with spirits, then set fire to it. I shall set fire to the papers, drawings and tables in the bunker. Rangemaster, set the timers on the upper stages of the rocket. Make sure that they ignite and wreck themselves. Understand?"

"Aye, Highliber."

"After that, ride for Woomera as hard as you can. Captain Alkem, take the sixty lancers and the Tiger Dragons and set up a rearguard when I ride to the south quadrant tower. Make it seem as if you are defending this burning gantry."

"But, Highliber, we could outpace them if we all left for Woomera right away."

"Fool! Obey orders! I need ten minutes in the beamflash tower to alert the network and clear all wind trains from the paraline. If they capture a wind train they will move like a bushfire, they will shatter our undefended outposts, be in Kalgoorlie within a week, and Peterborough even sooner. Ten minutes, by your anchor timer. After that, ride for Woomera."

Three minutes later Zarvora was pounding up the steps of the wooden beamflash tower, glancing north to where the lancers were riding to intercept an ememy marked only by a cloud of dust. She burst into the beamflash gallery and pushed the transmitter from his seat.

POLL: PRIORITY DRAGON BLACK she keyed. Seconds passed, then the reply came.

ACKNOWLEDGED: BEGIN TRANSMISSION

SATURATION TRANSMISSION: ALL BEAMFLASH LINES: INVASION FROM ALSPRING NATIONS TO THE NORTH OF WOOMERA. ESTIMATE AT LEAST TEN THOUSAND LANCERS, UNKNOWN AUXILIARIES, TEN KILOMETRES

NORTH OF OUTPOST HARTLAK. CLEAR ALL WIND AND GALLEY TRAINS FROM THE PARALINE FROM NARETHA TO WOOMERA, PETERBOROUGH AND BROCKNIL: ALL RAILSIDES MOVE TO FULL WAR ALERT: BURN ALL BUILDINGS AND EQUIPMENT THAT CANNOT BE MOVED WITHIN THE FORTIFIED WALLS: FIRE ON ANY WIND TRAIN THAT DOES NOT ANSWER CODE IN REFERENCE 2T-3GK: BE ALERT FOR OTHER INVASION COLUMNS COMING OUT OF THE NORTH ANYWHERE FROM NARETHA TO BROCKNIL: ACKNOWLEDGE THAT TRANSMISSION HAS BEEN PASSED ON.

There was an unnerving delay of nearly a minute, followed by a twinkling of light in the tower to the south. ACKNOWLEDGED: AWAITING FURTHER ORDERS

Zarvora turned to the beamflash tower's captain and pointed to the north.

"What has been going on over there? Did our lancers hold the invaders back?"

"They're still fighting, Frelle, but they seem to be in trouble."

"In trouble!" exclaimed Zarvora, astounded. "But they're our finest lancers, part of my personal guard."

"It's what I see, Frelle Highliber."

Zarvora thought for a moment, then clicked BURN YOUR TOWER AND EVACUATE TO WOOMERA. She did not wait for an acknowledgement, but seized a lamp and smashed it down on the floor beside the bench.

"Evacuate to Woomera, now!" she barked, then ignited a flare with its fire-strip and flung in into the spilled oil as the crew began to clatter down the steps. For a moment she hesitated, glancing north to where the savage battle between the two groups of elite lancers was raging. Her anchor timer read eight minutes, two minutes more would ensure her safety, yet ...

"Cowardice is punishable by death," she reminded herself, then she took a gabriel rocket from the flare box.

The flames were blazing up around her as she swiveled the launching tube around to point north. She thrust the wick into the flames, then dropped the smoking rocket into the tube and ran for the stairs. As she reached the ground the rocket shrieked away, howling its message to retreat over the red sand and frost-shattered rock. The tower captain was holding her horse ready. As she mounted she pointed south.

"Every man for himself, Captain, and every woman too," she cried as she dug her heels into the horse's flanks.

His reply was lost in the detonation of the flarebox high above. The tower's gallery disintegrated, flinging smoking debris around them. They travelled at a gallop at first, then Zarvora eased back to a canter and glanced back to the north.

"Why are they not retreating, I see only a half dozen —"

She caught herself, horrified by the truth: her elite lancers had been all but wiped out by the time her rocket had shouted its orders. Other riders were streaming across the plain, Ghan lancers on horses from other squads. The tower captain drew a flintlock.

"No!" shouted Zarvora. "Give me your loaded guns."

He drew alongside and handed them over to her, then drew his sabre and rode alongside her. The horses were beginning to tire, and a squad of a dozen Ghans was slowly closing with them. Zarvora turned in the saddle and fired with a smooth sweep of her arm. A Ghan lancer threw up his arms and fell from his mount. She flung the gun away and drew another from her belt. This time she hit a horse and it sprawled amid the red sand and sharp stones, flinging its rider down. The next shot missed. Zarvora dropped the third gun and drew her fourth. Turn, sweep, fire — the head of the leading lancer exploded as the heavy lead ball found its mark. The remaining nine suddenly lost their resolution, and slackened pace a fraction.

In the distance to the south Zarvora noticed that the beamflash relay tower was on fire, trailing a plume of dark smoke into the light wind. Their pursuers began to fire their muskets, and a shot tugged at Zarvora's robes as she reached for her last gun, a stubby Westock half-inch. More riders were closing from behind to join the Ghans — then the pursuers broke into a confused, wheeling, shouting gaggle as the newcomers hacked into them with their sabres.

"The last of our own lancers," shouted the tower captain.

"Then turn, here's enough of fleeing."

The wild scramble that followed lasted no more than a minute, but six Ghans and the beamflash captain lay dead before Zarvora and the three surviving lancers from her personal guard set off for the south again.

"Wild, savage warriors," shouted the man beside her. "We were evenly matched, but we barely held our own. A second squad hit us just as your rocket came over."

They rallied with more surviving lancers at the burning relay tower, then set off for Woomera again, reaching the fortified capital in the late afternoon. The towers of the city rose against the blue sky with the darker blue of the Mirrorsun band arched across like a mighty sash. The Mirrorsun glow itself was the metal in the sash glowing washed-out gold in the daylight sky. The band had drifted into an eccentric orbit as it strove to repair the damage from the Wanderer's beam, and the glow was easily visible late every afternoon.

"I changed the very heavens, yet look at me now," Zarvora muttered under her breath as she rode for the West Gate of the city.

Zarvora's lackey was shouting messages from the beamflash network to her even as she dismounted from her exhausted, trembling horse.

"Force of two thousand on the Great Western Paraline at Warrion, laying siege. Another force reported at Hawker, but no numbers as yet. Yuntall Railside under siege by a force of over five thousand —"

"Yuntall! But that's on the Barrier Paraline to Brocknil."

"It's confirmed, Highliber. Wirramina reports two or three thousand Ghan lancers crossing the Great Western Paraline and moving south, but not attacking."

"A pincer movement. They will meet at the south of Lake Tyers, cutting Woomera off from the Southeastern Alliance. They move fast, and to our most vulnerable points. How do they do it? Did that escapee Vittasner build them another battle calculor? Take me to the paraline depot, now."

The City Overhand of Woomera caught up with Zarvora at the depot, just as she was trying to find a galley engine and crew.

"The Ghans are burning the scrub between our beamflash towers to blind us," he said as he followed her about. "Soon all links with east and west will be gone."

"The beamflash network has done its job already," Zarvora assured him. "Your fortified towns have been warned and secured. Most could withstand a limited siege from a few thousand attackers."

"But Hawker is under attack by ten thousand, perhaps twelve."

Zarvora stared at him in astonishment. "As many as that!"

"And they have bombards. I've requisitioned a galley train to relieve: four hundred troops and a dozen bombards of our own."

"That does not seem enough, but how can we know? Can I travel there with the train?"

"If you wish, Frelle OverMayor, but to be anywhere outside a fortified town or city is dangerous."

That night, as the galley train reached the southern tip of Lake Tyers, Zarvora ordered it stopped. She had a horse unloaded in the darkness, then ordered the captain to proceed without her. As the train moved out over the trestle bridge she sat alone on her horse, watching the wagons dwindle into the distance by the light of Mirrorsun. The Calldeath lands were quite deep here, and were only a quarter-hour ride from this part of the paraline. She set off slowly across the bed of the dry lake.

Suddenly there was a faint flash of light to her left, followed by the sound of a distant blast. The bridge had been mined. *Of course the bridge had been mined!* Zarvora rode on, and after another twenty minutes a faint tingling feeling warned her that she was entering the Calldeath regions. Her horse grew eager to go south, and for a time she let it have its head. Now she was safe from human attack, and she could follow the Calldeath strip all the way to Peterborough.

As she rode, a name kept echoing through her mind. *Lemorel, Lemorel, Lemorel.* Several coded despatches referred to Commander Lemorel, the leader of the Alspring Ghan invaders. Lemorel was most certainly not a Ghan name. Lemorel Milderellen had abducted John Glasken and gone in search of the Alspring cities a half-decade earlier. Lemorel had also been one of her most trusted and promising young Dragon Librarians. No wonder the Ghans knew exactly where to strike in order to do the most damage.

*****

The whirring and swishing sound of the Libris Calculor room began to take on a regular rhythm as the diagnostic program ran its course. There were no anomalies, the Libris Calculor was in perfect order. MULTIPLIER 8 and PORT 3A cleared their frames, and MULTIPLIER 17 sat back from his frame as he tapped the floor pedal with his foot and sent his last calculation away to the local node. The sound of the huge machine began to fade, as if they were leaving a shift and walking away down a corridor.

"Tis running down, PORT," said MULTIPLIER 17, but the components nearby only turned to glare at him. A regulator walked up, rested her cane on his shoulder and held a finger to her lips.

The noise faded further, until there was nothing but the swish of polling signals being sent at five second intervals. Input had ceased, there was no more work being entered. The System Herald stood up and banged the floor with his blackwood rod.

"System Hold!" he called clearly and firmly. The polling signals stopped, and there was silence. Four thousand pairs of eyes were upon him. "Components attend! Shift terminated. Announcement to follow."

Buzzing conversation welled up throughout the Calculor. The Regulator beside MULTIPLIER 17 sat down and began sobbing softly. He put an arm over her shoulders, and she put her head on his chest and began to soak his tunic with tears. He scarcely felt any happier himself.

"Some damn major reconfiguration, I'll bet," said MULTIPLIER 8 to PORT 3A.

"Don't be a dummart," he replied. "They're going to shut down the Calculor."

They sat in silence for a moment. "They can't do that," said MULTIPLIER 8. "What about all our work? Who's to do it?"

"Contract labour, perchance? Perchance the Mayorate itself is no more, perchance the Southmoors have crushed the Mayoral armies, and are advancing on the capital."

"None of that's in the beamflash traffic. Things is quiet, and prosperous — except that inflation on the royal is up to 3.2% per year. That's because there's peace and everyone's going to Rutherglen and Sundew to buy wine, or they're sending our gold north to buy Northmoor carpets for their houses, or putting Confederation glass panes in the windows."

"Then this is it, then ... the end of the machine."

"No, it's a new configuration."

As he spoke there was a deep clack at the back of the Calculor Hall. The heavy curtains that divided the Hall began to be drawn back along the wires. As they bunched up at the back of the hall, the double doors between them opened. A lackey entered carrying a scroll bound with a black ribbon and sealed with black wax. It was a decree from Tarrin, and the System Controller appeared following behind him. He was going to read it in person.

When Tarrin reached the rostrum the System Herald banged his rod for attention in spite of the near-complete silence. "Attend the System Controller!"

"My fellow souls in this great machine, the Calculor of Libris," he began, breaking the seal on the scroll. "I have here a decree from Mayor-Seneschal Jefton, in his capacity as the ruler of Rochester. It reads thus: 'Be it known to all magistrates, servants and officers of the Mayor, and citizens of the dominions of Rochester, the machine known as the Calculor of Libris is hereby declared to be decommissioned. All components who were formerly felons are hereby granted a Mayoral pardon. All components who might have been pressed into the Calculor's service although not felons will be granted their freedom, fifty gold royals and full restoration of their property. Your service in the Calculor of Libris has changed the very world itself. Accept my thanks.' "

He lowered the scroll and surveyed the Calculor Hall. There was no movement amid the ranks of faces focussed on him. He raised his voice again.

"There will, of course, be administrative assistance for those components who have difficulty in readjusting to life outside Libris. All Dragon Librarians who are acting as regulators will be re-deployed to other duties with no loss of rank. Please go to your cells and pack your possessions. The doors will no longer be locked, and the regulators will begin to process you for your discharge. Components of the Libris Calculor, on behalf of the entire Libris staff, goodbye and good luck."

He stepped down from the podium and began to walk back along the corridor through the centre of the Calculor. A component stood up as he passed.

"Fras Controller, what will replace us?" the component pleaded, his hands open and extended. "Please, Fras Controller ... this —"

"This is our home," called PORT 3A from nearby. "This is our Mayorate, our world. You can't take it away from us."

There was a rumble of assent that rippled out across the Calculor. Tarrin shrugged hopelessly as he looked from component to component.

"There are smaller calculors, and even mechanical devices. These have taken over much of the work of beamflash decoding and records control."

"We won't go!" shouted the component in front of him, and his shout was echoed by both the walls and scores of other components.

"There's stores down in the vaults to last months," cried the regulator who had been sitting beside MULTIPLIER 17, "we can stay here."

"This is none of my doing. I fought hard and long for the Calculor. The Mayor will have us removed if we don't go."

"We can arm the components!" cried a regulator. "Twelve thousand components is a fearsome army!"

"Aye, and most of us as has been felons," bellowed a gruff voice. "We can shoot, hit an' stab wi' the best of 'em."

Tarrin looked about him, bemused. "But most of you must want to go!"

"Those who want to go are welcome to go," PORT 3A shouted out across the ranks of the components. "We choose to stay!"

The cheering that erupted was deafening, and components and regulators closest to the doors ran off to tell the off-duty components what was happening. Tarrin was surrounded by angry, shouting components, and was unable to move from where he stood.

Beyond the gates of Libris, the delegates and supporters of the Rochester and Southeast Alliance Human Rights Association waited in vain to welcome the newly-liberated components of the Libris Calculor. When an hour passed with no result they demanded to send in a delegation, refusing to believe that the components had barricaded themselves inside, and that the regulators and guards had joined them. The delegation was beaten up and ejected. The candles in their party globes began to burn out, then it began to rain. The letters in the banners that they carried began to run, and were soon illegible.

The siege of Libris lasted only a few hours, during which the Libris Calculor was again made operational. A message arrived under the OverMayor's personal code, and it declared the entire Southeast Alliance to be in a state of general mobilization. Civil rights were now subject to the provisions of martial law, and the Calculor was most definitely not to be disbanded. Tarrin was carried shoulder high from the Calculor Hall by the components, all grateful for his long series of court battles to keep them where they were.

*****

John Glasken emerged from the beamflash public office after three hours, too exhausted with the strain of arguing with the clerks and lackeys to feel rage. Ettenbar joined him at once and they strode off down the road.

"Morgan! They shipped that bloody third rocket to Morgan and the only reason that it didn't get as far as the marshalling yards in Rochester is that the gauge of the rails changes from broad to narrow at Morgan and they did not have a suitable flatbed available with narrow bogies! Misrouted beamflash message, that's what the Controller of the Morgan Paraline Shunting Yards said. The beamflash system really is letting standards slip, I've never known it to be as bad as this."

"The Highliber will not be pleased!"

"The Highliber will scream so loud that she won't need to beamflash. Fools and incompetents, they're all around me — present company excepted. I'm going to get that rocket back to Woomera on time if I have to strap a saddle to it and ride with it in person."

"A trifle extreme, Fras."

"And then there's the Golden Cup."

"There is a problem with your taverns, Fras 3084?" Ettenbar ventured.

"STOP CALLING ME THAT!" Glasken shouted, but his voice was already hoarse.

"Ah, yes, and I am sorry, Fras Johnny. Under stress I tend to revert to the serenity and discipline of the Libris Calculor."

"Bavani offered the Golden Cup to Jemli for 1,800 royals. She beat him down a couple of hundred, but he made her hold the 1,400 I'd authorized in a bank trust while her messages chased me along the paralines and beamflash network for authority to spend the extra. In the meantime the Mayor's Arms came up for 1,400, could you believe it? Damnable Bavani bought it with *my* bank trust as credibility, then called off the deal for the Golden Cup at 1,600 and paid a fine of fifty royals — *and* refinanced the Mayor's Arms with a mortgage. Bastard, but I'll get him. I've told Jemli to buy stock in the bombard works and munitions factory. I know Bavani, and he knows that I know people in high places. He'll think a war is coming, then panic, sell his taverns, and bury the gold in some desert cave."

"So, heavy dealings with the beamflash, my friend? Yet you prevailed over it?"

"That I did, and now I'm going to have a drink, then catch the next wind train to the Morgan Railside. I booked our tickets through my, ah, remote account with the Rochester Reserve Bank — ah, but what did we ever do before Beamflash Funds Transfer?"

"You paid out of your own money?"

"It was quicker than raising an appropriation. I'll get it back."

"Fras Johnny, but I have the price of the fares on my person."

"You do? Well, what about a silver noble to buy us drinks at that tavern across the street?"

"I regret, good Fras —"

"Ah yes, Islam forbids alcohol to you, what a horror. Still you can't miss what you've never had. Tell you what: give me the price of a rice pie each, and I'll buy myself a half-litre of black ale."

"My friend, it brings me such joy to see you in good spirits again."

"Steady there, I'll not be declared happy until the rocket is back."

The tavern was packed with patrons, and after another long and infuriating wait Glasken emerged with their pies and his tankard. They sat on a pile of roofing shingles and began to eat.

"Lot of worried folk in there," said Glasken between mouthfuls. "Something about a IW10 code. Everyone was saying it was an IW10 code. Come to think of it, there was mention of it in the beamflash office as well."

Ettenbar turned to him at once, eyes wide. "That is Invasion War alert at level 10."

Glasken frowned, put down his pie and took up the tankard of black ale. "War, eh? There's always a war somewhere, I bet it's the Southmoors at Finley. It's as inevitable as the Call. Or maybe some castellian's sent his gamekeepers to shoot at his neighbours again — hope it's not one of my old man's neighbours. The last thing I want on my doorstep is refugee parents." He took a thoughtful swallow of ale.

"Fras Johnny, level 10 is a very large war, with an invasion force of above fifty thousand."

"Fifty thousand!" Froth sprayed over the edge of Glasken's tankard. "There's never even *been* an army that big."

"It is fortunate indeed that you invested in munitions, Fras," said Ettenbar, staring into the distance.

"Very funny — hey, but you're right. Remind me to send a big present to your arranged wedding. Etten, what's wrong? The Call got to you?"

Glasken followed his gaze. Ettenbar was looking down the street, to where a lone rider was slowly approaching on a lame horse. It was a tall woman, with her hair roughly bound back, and wearing a ragged wayfarer's cloak. Soiled bandages covered her left arm, and dark splotches of blood showed through. As she drew near they could see that she had bound a sabre into her injured hand, and there were fang-marks in her boots and the flanks of her horse.

"Highliber!" shouted Ettenbar, dropping his rice pie and running out into the street. Glasken followed, tankard in hand.

Zarvora reined in her horse and looked down at them, but her eyes seemed unable to focus. "Beamflash tower," she managed in a slurred whisper.

Having stopped, the horse was unable to walk any further. Glasken called for a stabler as he helped Zarvora from the saddle. She could hardly stand, but after a sip of his ale she regained her senses.

"Beamflash, take me there."

"Frelle Highliber, you need the attention of a medician first," began Ettenbar.

"Take me to the nearest tower at once," she replied emphatically, a contralto tone returning to her voice.

That was enough for Glasken. "Aye Frelle," he said as he lifted her in his arms and began to walk toward the beamflash tower. He was surprised at how light she seemed, just as Ilyire had been when he had carried the drunken Alspring Ghan into the Kalgoorlie palace. Ettenbar followed, and behind him was a small crowd who were muttering about it being the Highliber.

"Highliber, do not be afraid," said Ettenbar reassuringly. "We are your loyal servants, two FUNCTIONS of the Dexter Register."

"Calculor FUNCTIONS? I can hardly believe it," she mumbled.

"He's raving, Frelle, it's only us, Glasken and Ettenbar," added Glasken, but she had already floated off into unconsciousness.

At the beamflash tower Glasken suddenly found himself given far more deference than had been forthcoming for the previous three hours. Ettenbar went immediately to the deputy captain of the tower, and they were then ushered straight into the counterweight-lift and raised to the beamflash gallery itself. Glasken was still holding Zarvora in his arms. Again he marvelled at what a light, bird-like body she had. The tower captain met them as they stepped out into the gallery, and Zarvora was revived by Ettenbar splashing water on her face. After sipping a little of the water she was able to speak.

"My galley train, mined — it was on the Lake Tyers bridge. I have travelled two hundred kilometres through enemy-held country, skirting the Calldeath lands. Alspring Ghans pursued me, dirkfang cats came out of the Calldeath lands and attacked too. What news is there? Two days since ... heard news."

"Hawker has just fallen," said the captain, assuming that Glasken and Ettenbar had a high security clearance. "Before the signal was lost there was word that Wirrinya was under heavy attack, and unlikely to last another day. There was a fierce attack on the walled capital of Woomera itself, but grapeshot from the bombards drove the Ghans back. The Great Western Paraline's railsides received a destruct order from Kalgoorlie last night, and the rails have been blown up and the rolling stock burned as far west as Naretha."

"Then the desert will do Kalgoorlie's fighting for now. That is good. What else?"

"The Barrier Paraline has been taken from Nackara to Cockburn, and they appear to have captured at least two galley trains and several wind engines. The citadel at Brocknil has held, but the city proper and the railside have fallen to the Ghans. There is also a possibility that the Southmoors have some manner of alliance with the Alspring Ghans."

"The Southmoors! What evidence is there for that?" Zarvora asked, alarm flashing across her face.

"The Darlington beamflash tower was destroyed by Southmoor bombards yesterday. All contact with the Central Confederation has been lost," the tower captain said grimly, then continued to read reports of the devastatingly fast and effective invasion.

In the background, Glasken and Ettenbar listened to the litany of disaster with near incredulity.

"The Ghans attempted to cut off Peterborough, but for once it seems that their lines were over-extended. The Peterborough Mayoral Musketeers Cavalry stopped them in a battle ten kilometres to the east."

"Good to hear that someone is a match for them."

"There is one more piece of good news, Highliber. A suicide squad of about fifty Ghans penetrated all the way to Morgan. They blew up a section of paraline track and detonated another charge against the wall of the beamflash tower. Luckily they had used too little powder, and the tower is still standing and in operation. The paraline track that they blasted turned out to be a shunting line, so traffic is still getting through. The town militia killed them after a bloody shootout."

The news seemed to revive Zarvora. She sat up just as a medician emerged from the lift, and as her hand was being unwrapped she accepted a honeycake from one of the beamflash crew.

"Without help they could not have moved so fast and far in three days," she said to the tower captain. "There must have been advance parties sent out, all coordinated to act at the same time. There must also have been help from within our own system. How many galley engines are there here at Peterborough?"

"Two, Frelle Highliber. Three others were ordered north on the second day of the fighting, and were captured on the line near Hawker."

She removed two of the four pistols from her belt and handed them to Ettenbar. He began cleaning and reloading them at once.

"Set the gangers destroying track to the north and east of the town. Put as much rolling stock behind the two galley engines as they can pull at low speed, and load the train with all the non-combatants that it will carry: women, children and wounded. I shall take it south to Burra, and destroy the line at several points behind it. Tell the Mayor to seal the town and prepare for a long siege. Begin rationing at once. Assemble all sheep and horses that cannot be fed out of stores and send them overland to Morgan. They must not fall into the hands of the Alspring Ghans."

The tower captain nodded at each of Zarvora's instructions, but his manner had no sense of urgency. "OverMayor and Highliber, all that would be unwise. The townsfolk look to you for leadership. Your place is here, defending the edge of your dominions against the invaders."

Zarvora waved his objections aside with her bandaged hand. "That would see me isolated, Fras Captain, for this town is surely to be besieged by the invaders."

"So you will leave us, Frelle Highliber?"

"Yes. Now obey my orders."

In spite of his misgivings, Glasken decided that being close to the Highliber represented his best chance of survival. He and Ettenbar remained in the beamflash gallery as Zarvora's orders were being sent out, then they were themselves sent to make sure that all was in order with the galley train and to pass on Zarvora's instructions in person. By the time they had reached the streets the town had erupted into bedlam, with the truth about the invasion finally public knowledge. Prices increased tenfold within minutes, women and children were hurried along toward the hastily-assembled train by grim-faced men, and agitators were shouting to the crowds that Rochester and the Highliber had abandoned them. The train was standing ready, with the galley engines *Firefly* and *Iron Duke* coupled to pull it. The crowd around it was unruly, a mixture of weeping women, hysterical children and uncertain men being harangued by yet more agitators.

"Good old Glasken, you've chosen another winner," Glasken said aloud as they left the cabin of the lead galley engine after delivering their message.

"Friend Johnny, this is no time to think upon horse racing," replied Ettenbar.

"Ettenbar — look here, have you been in a war before?"

"Why, no."

"I have, and it was not like this. There's something odd about the hostility in Peterborough. A few hours ago people were worried about whatever was happening with this rumoured war, but they were still loyal. Not a whisper of discontent. Nothing. I should know, I stood farting and complaining with them in the queue at the beamflash office, and I jostled with them to call my order in the tavern. Suddenly there's all these men shouting the same message against the Highliber and Rochester. This isn't spontaneous, this is organized."

They arrived back at the beamflash tower, and the clerk in the office rang a message for Zarvora to come down. Glasken and Ettenbar stood waiting nervously while she descended in the pulley lift. She emerged limping but looking better than when they had left. They walked along the streets to the jeers of those who recognized her.

"Run from the Ghans, ya coward!" bawled someone in a hoarse voice, and something flew through the lamplit gloom and splattered on her ragged cloak.

"Stay an' fight, ya bitch!" This time the voice was female, and from a balcony. "Us women belong here, with our men."

"We'd rather welcome the Ghans than fight 'em. Death to the Highliber!"

Glasken and Ettenbar flanked her as they made their way through the thickening crowd.

"Pay no attention, Frelle Exalted Highliber," said Ettenbar, marching proudly erect with a scattershot gun at his shoulder.

"Aye, Frelle Highliber," agreed Glasken. "Folk have been calling me a coward all my life, but did I ever care? Stand back, ye buggers!"

"Interesting how they can call abuse so well in Austaric, although this is a Woomeran town," remarked Zarvora.

"Some of the riff-raff are bilingual," Glasken assured her. "Look to me for an example. Anyway, this is a central paraline interchange from three major points."

"I know mobs, and this one seems better organized than the Great Western Paraline Authority. I shall not forget it."

Zarvora went straight to the lead coach after pushing through the angry, restless crowd at the railside. People began banging on the outside of the coach, while within were shrieking children and their wailing mothers.

"Go to the *Firefly* and tell the captain to wait," she said to Glasken and Ettenbar. They were glad to obey, and immediately made their way forward.

"If this train starts to leave there'll be a riot," Glasken said as Captain Wilsart of the *Firefly*, the lead galley engine, held out a hand and helped him through the forward access hatch.

"Do you have the Highliber's orders?"

"She said to wait. What a nightmare. Who's behind this trouble?"

"Whoever 'tis, the Highliber can count on the Great Western Paraline Authority," replied Captain Wilsart calmly.

Glasken looked out of the driver's window slit, and noted that the track ahead of the train was relatively free of people. A small knot of men with muskets stood on the baulks and transomes, and one of them had a sledge hammer and bolt-wrench over his shoulder. Glasken turned at a commotion behind them. Zarvora was climbing up into the driver's cabin, filthy with grease and dirt, and panting heavily.

"Highliber! Did the crowd beat you?" gasped Ettenbar.

She shook her head. "No, I crawled from the lead carriage under the *Iron Duke*, then entered this engine by the floor access hatch. At my word, prepare to leave. Give your crew and navvies the alert, Captain."

"But what of the *Iron Duke*?" asked the captain of the *Firefly*.

"I uncoupled it as I crawled here. I also unpinned the safety catches on its brakes and jammed them."

"Very good, Highliber," he said as he unclamped the brake lever and engaged the Ready signal.

"Who are those men on the tracks up ahead?" exclaimed Zarvora. "One of them is removing rail bolts!"

Captain Wilsart seized Glasken's shoulders. "Glasken, go down to the forward gunner, tell him to fire the grapeshot barrel at anyone who fires on us when we begin moving. Quickly!" He turned to the driver. "At my word ... Forward!"

The *Firefly* moved smoothly away, with little more noise than the rumble of its wheels on the rails as a warning to those ahead on the track. Some members of the crowd cheered, thinking that the galley engine was abandoning the carriage with the Highliber still in it. One of the gangers looked up to see the galley engine approaching and shouted a warning to his companions. He raised his musket and fired at the driver's window. The bullet glanced off the heavy armoured glass, then the forward gunner replied with grapeshot. The blast annihilated the group of men, and a moment later the *Firefly* jolted over shattered flesh and weapons. The loosened rail held as the galley engine passed over it, then they were clear.

It was not until the exchange of shots that those in the crowd realized that anything was wrong. A peppering of fire lashed out at the departing *Firefly* as people fled or flung themselves behind cover. The leading agitators stormed aboard the *Iron Duke*, but the crew were all loyal Great Western Paraline employees and they feigned confusion. By the time the forward bombard had been unclamped and run out, the *Firefly* had disappeared around a bend and behind a wall.

"The town has been filled with hired churls and churlenes from the independent castellanies, probably in the pay of the Alspring Ghans," Zarvora said grimly to Captain Wilsart. "The entire beamflash tower crew was with them. I could tell by the pattern of clicks from their instruments that they were sending out orders contrary to what I was saying."

"But what will —"

Across the rooftops the gallery at the top of the beamflash tower exploded in a ball of lurid flame. Glasken gasped in horror, but the gunner beside him did not even turn to look. Zarvora climbed down from the access walkway to join them.

"The town walls are ahead there, gunner," she said as the *Firefly* rattled over a set of points. "If the gates are shut you will get but one shot at them, and that must hit the transverse beam or we are all dead."

"Not te worry, Frelle Highliber," he replied. "Just tell me what speed we do."

"Twenty five of your speed units."

"They be miles per hour, Highliber. Good enough for Brunel, good enough for us. Now then, closed the gates be, and twenty five, ye say. Thet's a three nick elevation, and a true of 4.5, and now ..."

On the town wall, two of the militia watched the galley engine approaching with more than purely military interest. In spite of the darkness they were sufficiently expert to be able to identify it from little more than the sound that it made on the paraline's rails, and the outline of its shape from its own running lights.

"There be a GWG Class galley engine of five segment configuration," said musketeer first class Mansorial.

"*Firefly*, that be the *Firefly*, GWG-409/5," replied his companion, Prengian.

"No sighting on a number, we can't claim a confirmed sighting without a sighting of the number."

"No carriages or wagons, now that's worth a note."

"Leave the gates closed, we can hold up a lantern to the number as they wait. Have you got the sightings book?"

A rocket flew straight and true from the *Firefly*'s forward tube, striking the gates a little below the transverse bar and exploding. Instead of breaking, the bar was blown clear of its clamps, and came down just as the *Firefly* was butting through the splintered gates.

"*Firefly* shot out the gate!" cried Mansorial in disbelief.

"I'm a-notin' it in the book," Prengian called back excitedly.

The great wooden beam crushed the rear roof of the galley engine's last segment as it butted through the heavy swinging gates, and the *Firefly* slowed as it dragged the bar clear of the gates. Amid the cries of injured navvies Glasken worked alongside Ettenbar, Captain Wilsart and Zarvora to cut through the tangle of bar, fabric and ashwood frame with hatchets. They wondered that the militia on the wall did not open fire.

"Do we call this sighting an accident or an incident?" asked Prengian.

"Accidents is unintentional, incidents is intended in part."

"Looks to be elements of both here. An incident what results in an accident."

"We should put it to the next meeting of the Peterborough Train Spotters Brotherhood," said Mansorial excitedly. "Good Lord, now look at that! They're convertin' it, they're detachin' the last segment right there on the track."

"You're right!" exclaimed Prengian. "GWG-409/5 has become GWG-409/4. Does this merit a new entry in the book, or is it part of the incident report?"

At last the crew were able to push the bar and wreckage onto the paraline. The rear of the engine was so severely mangled that its wheels were jammed, but galley engines were built from articulated modules. At Captain Wilsart's word the rear section of the *Firefly* was evacuated and unclamped, and the galley engine rumbled forward as if it had been freed from a leash.

"Ah, Prengian," said Mansorial tentatively, as if remembering something important.

"Aye?"

"GWG-409/4, *Firefly*, has just shot out the gate we're a-guardin'."

"Aye, but as GWG-409/5."

"Shouldn't we have fired on it?"

"Ach, that would never do. It's a Great Western Paraline Authority engine, GWG Class! The Peterborough Train Spotters Brotherhood would have us expelled before a single day was past for a-doin' that."

"But the Gate Captain will have us shot for not doin' so when he gets across here."

"Aye, you're right. Let's put a shot or two from the bombardiette into the wreckage of that segment on the paraline."

The little bombard had a flintlock striker instead of a fuse. Mansorial withdrew the safety pin, aligned the sights with the dark mass on the line and squeezed the trigger. A half-kilogram shot was spat from the barrel. It struck the canvas and ashwood wall and smashed into the rocket locker for the rear tube. The damaged segment was blasted apart as the warheads exploded, ripping the mixed-gauge paraline asunder, and in the process rendering the paraline impassable for at least an hour.

"Gah fykart, what do we put in our spotter's book now?" gasped Mansorial.

" 'Rear segment was fired upon by gate defences' ", Prengian replied confidently. "We need not mention it was us as did the firin'."

By this time the *Firefly* was lost in the darkness of the overcast night.

"Five crew dead and fifteen injured," Ettenbar reported to the *Firefly*'s captain as they passed the tiny railside of Gumbowie. "Twenty seven pedal mechanisms are smashed, and a quarter of the roof destroyed. The rear grapeshot bombard and rocket launcher are gone too, with the rear of the engine."

"What about rockets?' asked Zarvora.

"The main store was at the rear."

"What? You mean they went with the wreckage?"

"Yes, Highliber," said Captain Wilsart. "It was felt by the designers that rockets would be in less danger from a collision if kept at the rear."

"How many rockets are left at the front?"

"Three, Frelle Highliber."

The *Firefly* rolled swiftly along through the night. Zarvora had the spare crew relocate the bow rocket launcher and bombard on the roof, so that they could be fired in all directions. They also chopped whatever was just scrap and wreckage from the rear of the engine to reduce their weight. At last there was no more to do. Zarvora, Glasken, Ettenbar and Captain Wilsart retired to the driver's cabin where they sat cleaning and loading their muskets and pistols in the lamplight.

"Soon we should fire a rocket into the tracks behind us," said Zarvora. "We must cut the track where we can."

"Good work, Frelle Highliber," replied Captain Wilsart easily, "but there be better ways."

"Better ways? And you are not upset?"

"As OverMayor you authorized extension of the broad gauge all the way to Rochester, Frelle, and you named your son after Brunel. You can do no wrong."

The answer was not what Zarvora had expected.

"What is it about you Great Western Paraline people?" she said, sitting back with her arms dangling beside her. "Why this fanatical loyalty to some pre-Greatwinter engineer who we know practically nothing about, and his 7 foot paraline gauge?"

"Because it's the best, Frelle. We always ask what Brunel would have done. Oh and by the by, it's 7 foot and one quarter inch."

Zarvora smiled at the correction. "Was Brunel a general too? If he left any writings on battle tactics I ought to look at them."

"He were a man of peace and building, Frelle. Our motto at Great Western Paraline is: Look To Functional Requirements, and your functional requirement is to tear up as much track as can. One rocket would take out a mere rail or two, and take a ten-minute to fix. I'll show you a scheme to do better."

Zarvora sat thinking and resting for some minutes, while the *Firefly*'s captain began to sketch a mechanism at the back of the galley engine's logbook. He handed the logbook to her, and she held it up to a pinlamp.

"Have you ever thought of becoming a Dragon Librarian, Fras Captain?" she asked as she realized what he was proposing.

"Nay, Highliber. Train work is the only real work. No offence, mind. Libraries have their place and someone has to mind books and such like, but I count meself lucky that it's not me."

Zarvora had killed everyone in the Peterborough beamflash tower before she had even lit the fuse to the charge that blew its gallery apart. Thus the final set of messages sent out across the beamflash network was as she intended them to be, and in particular there had been no false orders sent south to Burra and Eudunda. Burra was actually a fortress of the old Spalding castellany, and was well equipped for a siege. It had not been targetted by the infiltrators, and the local governor decided to fight alongside the Southeast Alliance while contact with Woomera was cut off.

The *Firefly* rolled into Burra without further incident. The governor and a small group of dignitaries were at the railside to greet Zarvora and receive their orders.

"Send an unmanned wind engine north," Zarvora instructed the Burra governor. "Attach a baulkdrop truck, and put mines with timers on the sliprails. Set them to drop right on the paraline every ten kilometres — or whatever the distance is in Great Western measure. Set the timers to explode after one minute, and set a large mine to explode in the engine after the last drop is made."

The injured from the *Firefly* were taken into the fort, and mechanics swarmed through the damaged section repairing and replacing mangled pedals and rigging up canvas streamlining. Before the work was complete the crewless wind engine began its journey north, pulling its truck laden with mines. Zarvora was in the beamflash gallery of the Eudunda-facing tower when there was a flash of light to the north, followed by a distant boom.

"That's the first mine dropped," said a beamflash receiver, peering through the telescope facing north. "I can still see the rear running-light of the wind engine. You know, Highliber, that flash of the Peterborough gallery blowing up gave me quite a start. Had spots before my eyes for a good quarter hour."

"They want war by infrastructure, I shall give them war by infrastructure," Zarvora said grimly.

The receiver continued to stare through his telescope's eyepiece. "I can see the glow of Peterborough clearly, and streaks like signal rockets above it. All sorts of colours. A big party to welcome the invaders, it looks to be. Now that wind engine — Argh!"

The flash of light had even caught Zarvora's unaided eyes, and as she pushed the dazzled receiver to one side of the telescope the boom reached the tower gallery.

"Fires, burning trees. Damn timer for the main charge must have gone off early — but wait! Burning carriages, all smashed and tangled, at least a dozen of them. They must have sent a galley train in pursuit of us from Peterborough. Our uncrewed wind engine slammed straight into it."

The receiver massaged his eyes. "A good job, too," he said, "and by a brave Great Western machine."

Twenty minutes later they were travelling south again, with the *Firefly* repaired and a full, fresh crew at the pedals. Glasken was unimpressed by the cold wind in the cabin from the open side windows.

"Can't you have this thing glassed in like the South and Eastern Standard's wind engines?" he asked as he sat shivering beside Captain Wilsart.

"Ah no, Fras. The feel of the wind gives you the mind of the land and weather. I mean, those SES ruffins would take a wind's strength from the gauge on the roof. Can ye imagine that?"

"Seems reasonable to me."

"But, Fras, it's quality of wind that ye want. Is it a steady wind, or is it blustery? What of direction, is the direction changing from minute to minute? How cold is it?"

"Well the wind is damnable cold tonight! I thought your galley engine is independent of the wind's direction."

"Why yes, Fras, but the *Firefly* presents a profile to a headwind, and even more of a profile to a vectored wind. The gears that you select and the pace of the crew depends on the wind — taken with the gradient of the track and the all-upload of the train as well. In a galley engine we must be optimal in our selection of the gearing between the pedals and the drive wheels to balance speed and torque while at the same time not wearying the navvies who push the pedals. As captain, one must become part of the train, Fras, you must feel the wind as the train does. Now Mr Brunel —"

Zarvora interrupted. "This Brunel engineer, he is pre-Greatwinter, yet you know a great deal about him."

"Aye, Frelle, he died 2,080 year ago next September, and those damnable traitors in the Britanical government destroyed the last of the 7' track in 1892 of the old calendar."

"That is right. In a place known as Britanica, I have read about that in one of your paraline verse epics." Her eyes narrowed for a moment. "Now how long ago would that have been?"

"2,047 years, Frelle Highliber."

Zarvora sat upright. "But that is exactly ... Do you know the date that the Call began?"

"2021 of the old calendar, Frelle. 1,918 years ago."

"Correct, all correct. Did you get it from my published papers in the 1702 *Astronomical Transactions*?"

"Nay, just from good bookkeeping and logs, Frelle. Mr Brunel specified that good records must be kept. Some of our paraline epics and sagas help too, for when disorderly Mayors made wars and burned our archives over the centuries, our epics were used to keep the records alive and preserved. Drop into our Kalgoorlie offices sometime, and you can check entries and dates in our archives. We also have there the original pre-Greatwinter model diorama of Pangbourne Station in 1885. It's 36 feet long, and in 4 millimetre to the foot. Nearly all our knowledge of the original Great Western trackwork comes from that model."

Zarvora closed her eyes and lay back. Glasken mixed some of his Naracoorte brandy with some water and held it to her lips. She sipped, coughed, then sipped again. Captain Wilsart went aft to check on the navvies, and Ettenbar had by now fallen asleep.

"Glasken, John Glasken," Zarvora murmured.

"Aye, Frelle?"

She regarded him quizzically in the dim light from the navigation board pinlamps. A long thin scratch across his forehead was beaded with drops of dried blood.

"I have made harsh use of you, Fras Glasken, yet you stayed with me when you could have turned me over to the mob. As for the fuel wagon back in August, well I would be dead without your heroics. What guides you, Fras?"

The question caught Glasken off-guard. He sat hunched over, wringing his hands with the cold in the weak light.

"I'd not stopped to think, Frelle Highliber. I suppose I've been in the stocks for more felonies than I can think of, but ... well, I may be a bastard, but I'm not a traitor. I mean, you're the Highliber and the Alliance is my home — even though I've got some rather nice investments in Kalgoorlie."

Zarvora lay back against the ashwood and canvas wall of the galley engine and thought about what he had said. She stayed that way for several minutes while the train rolled along the tracks to the rhythmic clatter of wheels on rails and the shanty-cycle of the navvies who provided its power.

"These Ghans, they seem to know where to hit us to do most damage," she said at last. "Our strength is in infrastructure, and that is exactly where they are striking hardest. Do you know why that is, Glasken?"

"They've studied us, I suppose."

"No, it is more than that. They are being led by Lemorel Milderellen."

Glasken sat up at once with a loud gasp. "Frelle Highliber! She — I mean I — surely you don't think that *I'm* working with her?"

"Not any more. An evil, difficult war has broken out, Glasken. I did not forsee it. I was caught out, but I managed to escape to rally my armies. The trouble is that there will be no quick and convincing victories through my innovations and ingenious engines, just a lot of desperate men shooting muskets at each other in fields where sheep and emus ought to be grazing. Still, what is the alternative?"

Glasken began to reply, then seemed to think better of it. He hunched over again, almost collapsing in the gloom.

Zarvora had been watching him carefully. "What were you going to say, Fras Glasken?"

He raised his head again and looked directly at her. "I have lived among the Alspring Ghans, at one of their outposts in the desert. They're not monsters."

"So it should not matter that they conquer and rule us? I ... would love to agree. I have friends who are Southmoors, too, and I suppose I could live under their rule, yet still I have fought many wars against the Southmoor cities and states. As for the war with Tandara, why they were neighbours."

"So what are you trying to tell me, Frelle?"

"There is more to this than just a stupid struggle for power, Glasken — on my side, at least. I sometimes feel as if I am trapped in a pit and trying to build a ladder to escape, yet my fellow prisoners keep trying to snatch the wood away to stoke their fires. It annoys me intensely, it makes me very angry. Frelle Milderellen of all people should know better."

Zarvora said no more, but slowly pulled herself up by the cabin railing and stood beside Captain Wilsart, who had returned from his inspection by now. They stood talking, looking out into the darkness ahead of the galley engine. Glasken rewound his Call anchor then joined them a moment later.

"The *Firefly* is travelling at its top endurance cruise speed," the captain commented, a strangely dispassionate inflexion in his voice.

"You are worried about the Ghans or their agents tearing up the tracks or laying mines," said Zarvora.

"Were I a Ghan, that I'd be doing."

"But it's not a Ghan leading the Ghans, Fras. Their leader knows the value of trackwork and captured rolling stock for the transport of her own troops. I'll wager that they cut only the track near Burra or Eudunda, or even mount an attack on the bridge across the river at Morgan. They need transport between towns more than we do, so out here, between towns, we should be safe."

Glasken moved across to the open side window and stood in silence, reassured yet shivering with more than the chill of the night air. In a way he had told the Highliber only part of the truth. The full truth had come to him only as he spoke. He had actually gone to her aid because she was female. Theresla was right: he liked women in general, rather than just sex. He had to admit that if it had been, say, Mayor Jefton in Zarvora's place, he might have been able to rationalize an excuse to run. He looked across at Zarvora, standing beside Captain Wilsart in the gloom. Zarvora: inhumanly strong, unnaturally light, but still a woman. Now she was being civil to him, she actually seemed to respect him. Glasken had to admit to feeling pride and loyalty.

"Pride and loyalty can get you killed," he murmured to himself, but the words seemed insufficient to stoke his fears.

It seemed to him then as if he was flying through the air that was rushing past him from the side window, as if he was a bird flying through the night. Birds had real power and freedom, birds were unaffected by the Call. He closed his eyes and spread his arms for a moment, as if they were wings. Suddenly fingers like talons sank into his left shoulder, and he whirled around with a gasp.

"One day we may give you real wings, Fras Glasken, yes?" said Zarvora pleasantly.

"Wings, Frelle Highliber?" he asked awkwardly, feeling a little foolish.

"Wings, Fras Glasken. But you will have to fight for them. Now, one last small matter to clean up and I need your help to do it. Come back here, away from the driver." She led him down to the now unmanned gunner's chamber. "There are spies within my great system of paralines and beamflash towers, yet I have my own agents as well. Using them, and carrier pigeons, I can get messages through to Kalgoorlie. At Morgan I shall be sending a message back with a lot of coded instructions, and some of those may concern you. You are on intimate terms with an artisan from the Southeast named Jemli Cogsworth."

"Ah yes, a fine —"

"— tall figure of a woman and the only time that you are not dreaming about pressing down on her soft and silken breasts is when you are dreaming about those breasts pressing down on you, excepting of course when you are getting your hands upon the Mayor's sister."

"No, no, Varsellia and I are just business —"

"Fras Glasken, I have been reading transcripts of garbage like that in my security reports until I am sick of the sight of them. I do wish that you would come up with some new expressions during the boar's hour drinks with Ilyire and your other churl associates."

Even in the dim lamplight it was clear that Glasken had lost all of his recently regained colour by now, and although his mouth hung open he was unable to find any appropriate words.

"I can find no records of Jemli using beamflash transmission, except on your business," Zarvora continued.

"That's right, she thinks the charge per word is too high."

"All of her communications with her husband in Rochester are by letter, and those letters have all been checked. They are banal, and generally carry bad reports about the working conditions and cost of living in Kalgoorlie."

"She is not anxious for him to join her."

"Meantime she runs your merchantile interests rather well."

"Ah now, she has a rare talent for that."

"She has made friends with Varsellia, and is living in the Mayoral Palace itself just now."

"They probably talk about me all the time."

"You flatter yourself. Has she ever asked you about the calculor's programming, or my rocket fuel development, or the electrical experiments in the old mineshafts of Kalgoorlie?"

"Only in terms of how long I would be away, whether I was in bed with other women, and if I was would it change things between us. Oh, those metal and coil switches. She once asked if the market for them was liable to trail off in the near future."

"Did she! Was that all? Did she ask you for figures? What did you tell her?"

"I had just asked her to be assistant manager of the newly renamed Glasken Enterprises and Imports. I was offering her ten gold royals a month to forget clockmaking and work for me full time. I was more than fair, and I also offered her —"

"— a 20% partnership and seneschal status if your growth index exceeded 15% in the first year. I read the papers that you lodged. Anything else? Any dealings with my staff, edutors, or other associates?"

"She once said that she fancied Ilyire, but I mistook her meaning at the time."

"Ahhh, yes."

"What? What do you know?"

"Librarians know everything."

"I see. Well as I once said to her, better him than some riff-raff churl with the pox. Ah, but I trust Jemli as I trust no other woman, Frelle Zarvora, in the counting room as well as in bed. She has a strategic outlook, and an excellent head for figures."

"She ought to. Her maiden name is Milderellen and her sister is Lemorel."

Zarvora shot out a hand and caught Glasken as he reeled and fell from his seat. Some minutes and quite a lot of brandy later he was feeling better. Zarvora held his face into the windstream from the driver's side window. As they sat back Zarvora held up a folded square of poorpaper.

"After I intercepted and read this, I decided that the worst of my suspicions were correct, and that Jemli was a spy for Lemorel who was trying to wheedle her way into places where she could do damage at the highest of levels. I actually drew up and signed the order for Jemli's death, Fras Glasken, but now your words have convinced me that she is no spy. Your words saved her life."

Zarvora took Jemli's death notice from her jacket and dipped it down the funnel of a pin-lamp. It burned quickly, flaring up bright in the dark of the cabin. Glasken sat watching, barely comprehending.

"Do you feel happy to be a hero, Fras Glasken?"

"I'm happy that you spared her."

"I am happy too. I did not want to have a pregnant woman killed."

"Ah Highliber, your wisdom and mercy — Pregnant? Jemli?"

"Five months."

"Five?" Glasken held up his fingers and began to count. "January, December, November, October, September —oi, then I'm the father!"

"Congratulations, Fras. I am glad to see you so pleased."

Glasken suddenly realized that he was embracing Zarvora. He hastily released her and backed off a step, then she handed the square of poorpaper to him.

"It is a beamflash message. It has been chasing you around the beamflash network for some days. It was sent to Woomera, then on to Peterborough, then on to Morgan which you gave as your next destination. I just happened to notice it in the routing buffer while I was in the Peterborough beamflash gallery. I had just killed the entire beamflash crew, so I was not under any restrictions."

Glasken unfolded the poorpaper, fumbling with both haste and confusion. "It must be important if she used the beamflash — ah but of course! 'You are going to be a father ... hope you are happy ... Varsellia asked to be your invel-spouse, so of course I said yes —' Gak!" Glasken handed the message back to Zarvora. "I can't go on.You read it and tell me."

"I *have* read it, remember? Jemli uses such pretty, endearing phrases, I must remember a few for next time I write to Denkar. Do not worry, Fras, it is just our age. This is the time of life when people like us try to fit spouses and children into our life's work."

Glasken shook his head, then gazed through the gunsight at the blackness ahead. "Varsellia's pregnant too, I just know that's in there as well. You tell me, I can't bear to look."

She reached out and took the message from him.

"Actually, there is nothing said about that. Regarding the rest of it, Varsellia wants to wear silver rather than white at your Mayoral invel-wedding, and with you and Jemli wearing red ochre waistcoats over gold robes with snowdrops and bluebells in your hair to give a prettier representation of coloured clouds in a morning sky blending up into stars. Of course you will have to marry Jemli first, and Varsellia would like to leave her invel-wedding with you until after the baby is born because otherwise the cut of Jemli's red-ochre waistcoat would not match —"

"Oh shut up," said Glasken with his face in his hands, not thinking of who he was speaking to.

"— with a diagonal cobalt blue silk sash and orange starburst to symbolize Mirrorsun. Wonderful. Why did I ever let that herald talk me into plain gold for Theresla's invel-wedding?"

Glasken dropped his hands and stared at her. His face was a study in baffled amazement. "I don't understand you, Frelle. You joke about a woman whose death-order was in your pocket until just moments ago."

She smiled and touched his arm. "Fras Glasken, I had to turn Jemli into a thing before I could have her killed. Now I need to turn her back into a person. Turning people into things is dangerous, Fras. I thought of the Calculor components as things for many years, then discovered that I loved one of them. That shook my nerve very badly. I can no longer kill and imprison as easily as before. The trouble is that it still has to be done, and that others around me have no such problems. Specifically, Lemorel will scream hellfire when she finds out about you and Jemli. If she ever conquers Kalgoorlie ..."

Glasken raised his hands. "That's enough, I'll fight in your army. Are you looking for musketeers with battle calculor experience?"

"Now that you mention it, I did transmit the order for a general mobilization while in Peterborough's beamflash gallery after I killed the beamflash crew there, so ... your equivalent rank was approximately captain just before you deserted back in 1700. I'll write you a recommendation now, take it to any recruiting stand." She scribbled out a few lines on the back of the beamflash message with the quill from the logbook desk, then handed it to him. "Just how do you manage to do it, Fras Glasken? All those women and all that trouble. It seems to me like a very unproductive way to lead a life. Besides, I must admit that I look at you and feel nothing at all."

"I'm relieved, Frelle Zarvora — no! I mean, er ..."

"I am relieved too, Fras, and I take no offence. Actually I was very grateful when you shielded me just before that fuel wagon blew up some months ago. Did I ever thank you for that?"

"If it was in the first week afterward, Frelle, I was in no condition to remember."

Zarvora reached up, put a hand either side of his neck and kissed him on the forehead. It was almost over before he realized what she had done. Her fingers and lips were warm and dry in the cold air of the galley engine's cabin, and there was a feathery scent about her hair. For many minutes afterwards his skin seemed to glow warm where her fingers and lips had been.

"I thank you now, Fras. My kiss is little enough, but it puts you in a very exclusive club, should you want to boast about it."

Glasken shook his head, as if struggling out of a dream.

"I seldom boast any more, Frelle Zarvora. It gets me into too much trouble."

"Very wise of you. Now then, I am sending some coded despatches to Kalgoorlie soon. Lives will probably be lost so that they may be transmitted, and part of the journey may be by pigeon, so there is no room for rambling. Give me two or three words for Jemli and Varsellia, if you please?"

"PLEASED, YES, LOVE x 2," he said without hesitation.

"Sweet of you, Fras Glasken. Get some rest now. The horrors of his night may not be over yet."

*****

Morgan was on full war alert when they arrived there at 3am. Several suspected Ghan agents and agitators had been lynched from the paraline signal towers, and the bodies swung in the slipstream as the *Firefly* rolled into the railside. Zarvora went straight to the beamflash tower, and established a link to Tarrin at Rochester. Her hope had been to bring the Libris Calculor straight into the war, but the process was slower than she had planned. The Calculor itself had been saved by the siege of its own components, but civil lawsuits had released many components and forced a number of inefficient internal work practices to be implemented. At Zarvora's word Tarrin immediately began to restore the vast machine to what it had once been, but that process was proving disruptive in itself.

Without the Libris Calculor it was difficult to route military trains through the system optimally, and new, secure beamflash codes could not be generated fast enough. Resource and stores inventory cards and punched tapes were beyond access, except through the Libris Calculor, yet Tarrin had taken some initiatives of value. The strategic resources and garrisons communications throughout the Southeast Alliance were temporarily transmitted in unsecured beamflash codes to the War Assembly of Mayors. His reasoning was that it was better to risk disclosure to the enemy than not to use the resources at all. Zarvora was relieved, for it was not far different from what she would have done.

Beamflash reports confirmed a pattern that she had already suspected. The invaders were isolating the cities and towns while using the countryside to the maximum advantage. She would have done the same. She acted at once to neutralize the Ghan strategy. Her orders were to destroy all bridges and several paraline links in isolated stretches of track that could not easily be supplied for repairs. Beamflash towers were to be defended most strongly of all. Supplies that could not be carried into towns were to be destroyed, and cattle in farms threatened by the Ghans were to be shot or turned loose to be taken by the next Call.

The third experimental rocket was located in the marshalling yards, and Zarvora immediately ordered that a narrow gauge coach be demolished down to the base frame and adapted to take the rocket on to Rochester. Glasken and Ettenbar joined in the work, along with Captain Wilsart of the *Firefly*.

"Nothing I like better than smashing up narrer gauge rolling stock," Captain Wilsart laughed as he swung his axe in the lamplight.

"Well mind the base, we want that left usable," called Glasken. He was already supervising a team of carpenters who were rigging a cradle for the cumbersome first stage.

"What's this rocket for anyway?" Captain Wilsart asked.

"If I knew I'd be shot for telling you."

"Ach, but if it's a rocket, it must be of use in the war. We could use the *Firefly* to haul it."

"The engine works and cranes are here in this yard, so the rocket will be transferred here," Glasken insisted. "Ettenbar, have the men clear that wood from the mixed gauge line. Captain, have the *Firefly* haul the rocket out of the marshalling yards and bring it alongside this wagon."

Another half hour passed, and the eastern sky began to brighten. Glasken saw the *Firefly* moving through the yards across sets of points and heard the muffled shanty of the navvies as they pushed the pedals. Captain Wilsart was down on the tracks, throwing the switches in person, while he communicated with his driver via signals from his shutter lantern.

The *Firefly* was turned on the turntable, and finally began to rumble towards them. Glasken saw Captain Wilsart suddenly work the lantern frantically, then drop it and dash along the tracks in the path of the train. As he knelt between the tracks and began striking at something a shot rang out from a nearby carriage, then another. The captain slumped as Glasken aimed for the window where the gunflashes had been and fired at the varnished canvas just below the window shutter. He was rewarded with a thin scream, then he ran for where Captain Wilsart was crawling from the tracks. The *Firefly* approached, its brakes beginning to squeal and its gears grinding as someone within tried to engage reverse gearing.

Glasken was too late. The *Firefly*'s forewheel passed over Captain Wilsart, nearly cutting him in two before the huge machine shuddered to a stop.

Glasken came running up with two of the carpenters as the crew of the galley engine jumped to the ground. The captain was still pinned beneath a wheel.

"Easy with him," said Glasken as they tried to make the man more comfortable by piling stone ballast beneath his body. Captain Wilsart was breathing, but there was nothing that anyone could do for him.

"Mine, between tracks," he whispered. "Jammed dagger ... into release ..."

Glasken looked between the tracks and noted the dark lump just behind the forewheels. In the distance the last of the Ghan raiding party was being hunted down by a squad of Zarvora's Tiger Dragons. Glasken swore softly to himself, then as sunlight began to spill into the marshalling yards, he crawled beneath the engine and examined the mine. Gingerly he peeled the covering cloth back from the spring-loaded trigger transfixed by Captain Wilsart's dagger. The design was Rochestrian. He reached in and unscrewed the detonator, then returned to the bloodied figure of Captain Wilsart. Zarvora and Ettenbar had arrived, and Glasken held up the detonator.

"How is he?" asked Zarvora, although Captain Wilsart's fate was beyond question. Glasken drew a finger across his throat and shrugged.

"Captain, your galley engine and crew are safe," Zarvora said softly to him. "So is my rocket. I shall never forget what you did for the Alliance and for me."

Captain Wilsart coughed blood, which dribbled down his chin and onto his collar. He reached up and patted the rim of the traction wheel that was pinning his crushed pelvis to the rail.

"Glad it wasn't one o' those damned narrer gauge engines as done it," he declared with his last breath.

Zarvora sat back, Captain Wilsart's blood on her hands, and soaking the knees of her trousers. "Just what is it about Brunel's broad gauge and this Great Western Paraline?" she asked yet again.

Only silence was her reply.

*****

Lemorel had known from the start that the invasion of the Woomera Confederation and the Southeast Alliance would be an order of magnitude more difficult than all of her previous campaigns, yet her army was larger than ever before, and she was striking across desert, across the very country that her enemies had relied upon for a shield. Her spies and agents had also prepared her targets well.

The Woomera Confederation was in her hands within nine days. The city of Woomera itself was besieged, along with a few fortified beamflash towers, but nearly every big town had fallen in the surprise of the first onslaught. The beamflash towers along the paraline had fallen to her men and bombards, but the price had been high. The towers were equipped with even-newer Inglewood bombards than Lemorel's, and they had a much better range. Maralinga was the westernmost point of her conquests, yet it had fallen to guile instead of assault. A hundred Ghans posing as coffee merchants had infiltrated that place, and had seized it at the command of a coded message passed along the beamflash network itself.

The broad gauge paraline was almost undamaged from the Lake Tyers bridge to Maralinga, and Lemorel used it to fortify Maralinga against invasion from Kalgoorlie. The deserts and the Nullarbor Plain combined to channel everything that passed between east and west along the paraline. Kalgoorlie was powerless to ship troops further east than Fisher, and as far as the beamflash grid was concerned, the west was blinded to the progress of the war.

It did not go all Lemorel's way, however. Even faced with torture and death the majority of Great Western Paraline Authority were nothing less than obstructive. The Ghans were finally reduced to pulling trucks of supplies along the paraline to Maralinga using camels and horses. A scant thirty kilometres further west, the wind and galley trains were running along newly repaired track, supplying a military barricade that would require the full weight of the Ghan army to breach, and providing materials to repair beamflash towers that had been incapacitated out of precaution. Out in the deserts, the Kooree tribes were unhappy about the Ghan raiding parties dashing across their land, and were quick to fight back. There could be no Ghan invasion of the west for a long time.

Zarvora had expected that the invaders would attack Morgan and Renmark, but Lemorel had another surprise for her. Over the following fortnight she moved directly east across the Barrier Grasslands, sending squads of lancers ahead to spread havoc, then meet up with Southmoor emissaries and lancers at the Lachlan River. She was there in person for the formal diplomatic meeting, which also had a representative from the Central Confederation.

After two days of talks, a sheaf of agreements had been signed. The Central Confederation would be allowed to remain neutral while the Southmoors and Alspring Ghans fought the Southeast Alliance. In return for the dry and sprawling Balranald Emirate, the Southmoors would be given all the Alliance Mayorates as far west as Rochester, and Ghan troops and lancers would advance no further than the Murrumbidgee River. The Southmoors would strike at the eastern border while the Ghans hit Mildura, Wentworth, Robinvale, and all the western paraline and beamflash links.

Unfortunately for Lemorel, Zarvora was not above pre-emptive strikes either. In March, and against the advice of her War Assembly of Mayors, she launched a massive assault across the eastern border, striking deep into Southmoor artisan centres, smashing bridges and physically removing paraline rails on such a scale that Southmoor transport was reduced to a tenth of its normal capacity. She had timed the strike with beamflash network reports of unseasonally heavy rains arriving from the west. The Southmoor prohibition on beamflash communication had worked gravely against them, and they had been unable to coordinate their defence with the Ghans. Meantime the Ghan offensive in the west had been brought to a miserable, shivering halt, as they were unused to fighting in cold, continuous, torrential rain.

By April, Zarvora had earned some respite, and was fighting back in ways that the Ghans found bewildering. Her own lancers were no less experienced than the Ghans', but the invaders were unused to fighting in such cold, lushly vegetated, wet country. When the Ghans struck deep into enemy territory to frighten the cities into siege mode, the Alliance lancers would strike at their supply depots and harass them until they were forced to return to their own lines. Ghan victories became hard-won, bloody and transitory, rather than glorious, quick and decisive. Try as she might, Lemorel could not cut either the beamflash or paraline links any further east than Morgan.

For all her successes, Zarvora remained objective about her weaknesses. Her ever-rebellious western castellanies had gone over to Lemorel without a fight, and the Southmoors were slowly beating her troops back out of their lands in the east. In mid-April the city of Woomera fell, and Lemorel shocked even her own overhands by burning the stubbornly defiant capital of the Woomera Confederation to a warren of smoking shells without allowing any inhabitants to escape. The end of the siege freed seventy thousand Ghan troops and siege engineers, and she determined to bring them to bear against Robinvale, a key beamflash link whose capture would isolate a third of Zarvora's territory.

*****

Meanwhile there were numerous inconclusive strikes and probes for weaknesses. At Dareton a hastily trained line of musketeers faced and broke a charge by five brigades of Ghan lancers. A pin bearing crossed muskets was pressed into Zarvora's wall map to denote the battle, while a scribe added crossed sabres to a map in Lemorel's distant command tent. Within the Libris Calculor, a large vector was added at Dareton for the 105th Calculor Musketeers, and it was assigned several parameters of movement.

*****

The sun was setting on the Dareton battlefield, and the sky above was clear with the promise of a chilly night. Beside a burned-out farmhouse in the red mud of Dareton the exhausted captain of the 105th Calculor Musketeers leaned against a fence post and drained a mouthful of sour wine from a jug, then dropped it into the ashes. Two partly plucked chickens dangled from his forage belt, and he was wearing the grubby jacket of a Great Western Paraline conductor and boots looted from a dead Ghan lancer. His corporal-adjunct sat on a nearby wool bale, patiently reloading their muskets.

"Captain Glasken, I still say that it is immoral to loot —"

"For the last time, you rambling Southmoor ricebrain, there's a difference between foraging and looting. Why oh why did I ever accept you as my adjunct? Look, this is for the good of the Alliance war effort."

"You stole that conductor's jacket at Morgan. That did not assist the Alliance war effort."

"That's different, I don't like conductors. A conductor once had lewd designs on my Frelle Jemli. Anyway, it's my size."

"What about all the Frasses of all the Frelles that *you* have ever had lewd designs upon?"

"Ach, they're free to try to steal my jacket if they like. What a nightmare, did you ever see so many lancers trying to kill you?"

"Until Peterborough, Fras Captain, nobody has ever tried to kill me. You have been in many battles, however."

"Only at Woodvale, and that was as part of the first battle calculor. Today was something far beyond! Standing at the centre of a line of a thousand musketeers while five brigades charged us, and there couldn't have been a dry pair of Alliance trews on the whole battlefield. Can't even remember what I said."

"You said 'Wait for my whistle ye —', well, you called their parentage into question, Fras Captain."

"Why not? Mine certainly is. At least we're alive."

"Six hundred and twenty dead or gravely wounded, Fras, and us with barely a scratch. We are certainly favoured in the eyes of Allah."

"Speak for yourself, look at my neck — and the piece out of my helmet. Cost me sixty five silver nobles at Loxton. Hullo, there's the trumpet. One long, two short, long, two short. That's ... regroup and report to the railside."

Glasken took his musket back and shouldered it as they tramped back across the broken ground to the rally pennant. In the western sky the Mirrorsun band had partly eclipsed the new moon. It was much thinner than before, except for three dish-like thickenings spaced about 40 degrees apart across the sky.

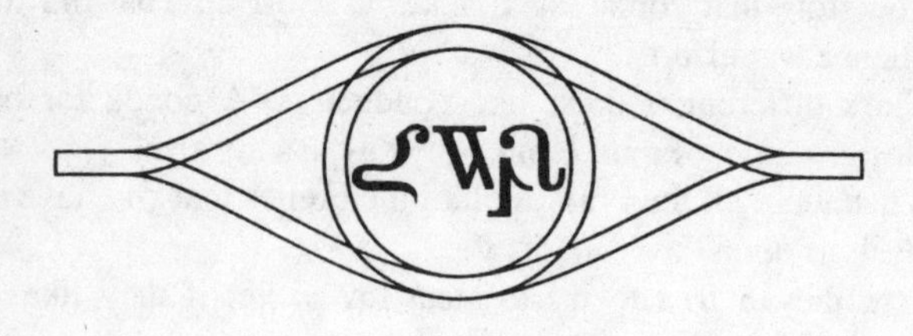

Part 5

DOLORIAN

Theresla was uncomfortable at being in such a large city as Rochester after such a long time in the company of creatures so very different to both humans and aviads. Zarvora's study in Libris was somewhat unsettling in itself, with its shelves of mechanical creatures and complex mechanisms interspersed with books and reels of punched tape. Theresla stretched out in the lounge chair opposite where Zarvora was working, and rested her chin on her hands. She closed her eyes for a long time, and seemed almost asleep. Zarvora was desperate for information from her, for any advantage over the Alspring invaders that she might be able to provide, yet she knew better than to try to pressure her invel-sister. She tapped at the keys of the gutted half-harpsichord that was her console to the Libris Calculor, and studied the logistical and military reports that appeared in code on her racks of gearwheels.

"The sea creatures have a complex society," Theresla suddenly said without opening her eyes. "It is far more advanced than ours in many ways, yet it is still driven by politics and factions. There are groupings of like-minded thinkers, as with our Mayorates, along with power struggles, factions and even duels. At least I think that they are duels. What they do is beyond both our Austaric language and my own vocabulary in their language."

"Will they help us?" Zarvora asked, turning away from her gearwheels.

"What 'us'? To them, we are all creatures of the land, creatures with puny mental control but an alarmingly powerful grasp of physical processes. They remember when humans used to hunt them, when they nearly drove them to extinction."

"But some of us are not human."

"Very true, and aviads are immune to the Call as well. They understand war, dear Frelle. You want them to intervene in a war between their old enemy and a species that they have no control over. They would cheerfully wish both of us a quick trip to hell — or 'the Chasm', as they call it."

"You do not have to tell them why you want transport to the Western Mayorates."

Theresla opened her eyes and sat up. "Oh, but I cannot lie to them, Frelle, that is the problem. I have to open myself totally to communicate at all. Any guile would stand out like a fire in a beamflash tower. Even this conversation will be available to them next time I return to the water."

Zarvora stood up stiffly, then took a few steps as she stretched.

Theresla watched her warily. "Are you considering shooting me?" she began.

"Do not insult me, Frelle Theresla. I don't cut down a tree to get an apple."

"Perhaps not, but many would be stupid enough to do so."

Theresla stood up and embraced Zarvora without another word, and Zarvora was in turn grateful for the affection.

"I am fighting a war against the very stupid just now, and they are very strong," whispered Zarvora with her chin resting over Theresla's shoulder.

"Frelle Invel-sister, I'm not being difficult. I would help if I could. The dolphins of Phillip Bay are my friends and would do almost anything I asked. Once we go beyond the Bay, however, the rules are quite different."

There was nothing in the exchange that Zarvora had not expected, yet she had been living in hope.

"What of Macedon? Will they allow aviads to come and fight with us, to sabotage Ghan positions when the Call sweeps over the battlefields?"

"The mayor and his council are not sympathetic to anything that might endanger their lineage and the genototem strength that they have cultivated so carefully."

"So they prefer to play husband-swapping in safety while Rochester is blown to pieces."

"They were never trustworthy allies, we both know that."

"They might find that the Ghans are less liberal about the movement of citizens than I am. They might find themselves denied access to the estates where they rear their children until they are immune to the Call."

Zarvora stooped to wind her mechanical orrery, then stood watching the planets move.

"Frelle friend, I agree," said Theresla. "It is despicable. That is why I tell them nothing about my null zone scheme."

"What is that?"

"I have been negotiating with the Bay Dolphins for a null zone within the Calldeath lands, probably over Macedon. If the invasion of Alspring Ghans renders the human lands too hostile, the aviads can retreat to total isolation."

Zarvora turned to the window, which looked across the rooftops of Libris, and beyond across Rochester. There was nothing about this view of the city that suggested the impending danger from the north.

"Well now, that is good for aviads in general. Why have you told them nothing?"

"To give them an incentive to support you, not that it did any good. Believe me, Frelle, if there is any way that I can help you, I shall do it. Macedon will too, if it is not likely to deplete their small population. Accept their apologies and do not bite. If we can help, we shall."

*****

Zarvora pondered the maps and charts that hung on the walls and littered the floors of a Libris lecture hall that had been converted into her command headquarters. Vardel Griss, who was now her Overhand-in-Chief was concentrating on the Great Western Paraline link to Kalgoorlie. Tarrin was monitoring a punched tape mechanism.

"Our spies tell us that several kilometres of track have been torn up just west of Maralinga, but nowhere else," said Griss as she gestured to a map with her swagger stick. "If we could coordinate an attack from the west, it would force the Ghans to put some of their strength into a second front, give us a chance to regroup and advance."

"Not a hope," said Zarvora.

"But Highliber —"

"Tarrin, explain the problem."

"The problem is one of strategy," Tarrin began. "The Western armies would depend on the paraline to move their troops across the Nullarbor. The Ghans are more mobile on their camels and horses, and the paraline is impossible to defend along its entire length. A few hundred Ghans could tie down ten thousand Kalgoorlians by a series of quick strikes on the paraline. The desert would make slow travelling for an army using the road, and that army would be fighting heat, distance, and supply lines under constant attack by raiders appearing out of the desert."

"Our spies also tell us that the Ghans are particularly weak and over-stretched in the west," said Griss.

"It could be a ruse, a feint. The Ghans pretend to be weak, we advance, we get shredded by a hidden force. We are holding them in the west. We can't afford to let them begin advancing there."

Griss glared at him, but was unable to fault what he had said. That was indeed a Ghan tactic. She turned back to the map. "You talk as if we have already been defeated, Fras."

"Strategically, yes, we have," replied Tarrin in a flat detached voice. "Lemorel knows our strengths too well, and has hit us precisely where it hurts most. Tactically we have some breathing space and a few advantages however."

"Name one," replied Griss, hanging her head and frowning.

"The Southmoors will not sanction beamflash communications, so Lemorel's commands move slowly compared to ours in some regions. Then again, our paraline grid and galley trains are far more efficient than those on enemy territory for moving troops."

"But their cavalry is far more mobile and versatile," insisted Griss, as if she wanted to be told otherwise.

"But not invincible. They sent five brigades against us at Dareton, but our musketeers broke their charge with discipline and steady shooting."

"And they've learned from that! A Ghan overhand was shot by Lemorel herself for what happened at Dareton. Now they will probably fight with mobile brigades that choose their own ground for each battle. Down at Rutherglen the Southmoors fight in the mud with trenches, stake-pits, snipers and bayonet charges. We can move resources faster, but our resources are limited."

With the exchange played out, they turned to Zarvora, who was staring at an overall map of the southeast.

"Tarrin is right, up to a point," she said slowly. "We have the ability to move faster as long as we can choose the battlefield. Thus we shall do just that. From the paraline at Robinvale we shall strike at Balranald, the weakest Emirate among the Southmoors."

"Weak? What about the hundred and fifty thousand Ghan cavalry that are hitting us along the entire length of our border with Balranald?" asked Griss.

"Ah no, Balranald's political ties with the other Southmoors have always been weak," Tarrin pointed out off-handedly.

Zarvora agreed. "If I were the Emir of Cowra, faced with an unreliable client in the northwest and a strong invader and ally in the same area, I would probably hand over everything north of the line between Balranald and the Central Confederation's border. We know that the Emir of Balranald has declared the city closed, which is fairly unusual considering that we are nowhere near the place. He fears his Ghan allies."

"Seize the land between the Confederation and Balranald, and the Ghans would be cut off from the Southmoors — unless they invaded the Central Confederation," added Tarrin.

Now Griss began to catch on. "But the Confederation has a strong beamflash grid, as well as cavalry that's used to plains-country fighting."

"Yes, and a lot of Balranald territory is still controlled by its Emir," said Tarrin, tapping at that part of the map with his swagger stick. "If he was to support us and his subjects closed ranks against the Ghans, we could hold that strip indefinitely."

"But if we lose that strip, a wedge will be driven right through our heartlands," Zarvora warned. "They will be setting up their bombards on the shores of the Rochester lake moat itself within a week of our first defeat along that strip."

*****

The Mirrorsun band around the Earth had been transformed into a thin cable anchoring three immense concave dishes — pale red disks that shone with dull and metallic light as they traversed the night sky and faded into the blue of day. Zarvora watched the band changing on each night that was clear. She was sure that her first and only successful rocket had been responsible for the change, and she had a good idea of what was soon to happen. It might allow an entirely new technology onto the battlefields of the southeast, and even before the invasion she had begun to rail-freight electrical devices from Kalgoorlie to Rochester. Mirrorsun was going to hit back at the Wanderer battle satellites.

With no warning at all, the elements of the Mirrorsun dishes rotated in unison and at precisely programmed angles, each showing a reflective facet to the sun. An area a quarter of the face of the moon punched the sun's radiation back in a beam that focussed on an orbital fortress that had just cleared a land mass and was over the Pacific ocean. It had not been attacked in millennia and its self-repairing and maintaining extensions had evolved vulnerabilities into its structure and systems. Cooling vanes melted, pipes ruptured, internal circuits fried, and the fortress detonated in a flash that lit up the Earth beneath it.

An ancient comsat in geosynchronous orbit was next. A flickering change in direction of trillions of facets, three searing cones of heat, and within moments it too was gone.

So far no alarm had gone out. High above the north pole another orbital fortress blazed brightly like a tiny, intense sun in Mirrorsun's beam, then exploded into an expanding sphere of debris and ionized gas. Within a moment the facets had switched to above the south pole, where another fortress was passing the axis of rotation of the Earth. Its solar collectors melted and disintegrated first, then coolant burst through heat-weakened walls, internal systems failed, and the fortress burst silently into thousands of shining fragments that winked out as the beam snapped off again.

By now the two other comsats on the far side of the earth had tried to poll the third but received no reply. A malfunction was the first conclusion, but when they tried to poll the now-annihilated fortresses and received no reply, their alarms shrieked through space to the four surviving orbital fortresses. The AIs of the satellites conferred briefly before the immense mirrors of Mirrorsun focussed on the two comsats in turn. The conclusion was an attack from the Earth's surface, an attack from an immense laser projector.

The fourth fortress was scanning the surface when it became a bead of brilliance drawn across the night face of the Earth. Its AI fought to turn its weapons on bearings that were already melting. As it exploded the fifth fortress' AI was analysing the configuration of the Mirrorsun band, and it came to the correct conclusion. An EMP pulse slashed across one Mirrorsun dish, but although it left a thin black line in its wake, it did not sever the fabric. The default setting of the nanotech units was now 'lock'. The mirror focussed more slowly, but the beam was now full on the fifth fortress. Its solar panels began to degrade and fail, and the AI switched to battery backup. More pulses tore across the three dishes, leaving a tracery of black scars. Huge areas of the mirror dishes went dead, and their combined beam weakened.

The sixth orbiter now joined the fight, its AI also having analysed the mirror's orientation correctly. Not being under attack, the fortress played the full fury of its EMP cannons on the mirror, analysing the command structure in Mirrorsun's fabric by the pattern of failures on its surface. The fifth fortress broke off the attack, realizing that it was being aided. It began to rotate itself with an internal gyroscope, trying to spread the heat dispersal over more of its surface.

Further out in space the cable that had seemed only an anchor for the three dishes had been far from passive. Like an immense particle accelerator it pumped a cluster of nanotech units up to 400 miles per second and spat them out into space. The sixth fortress was warned by its doppler radar of the approach of the particles and it spun a cannister to pump a shield of particles to protect its flank. The nanotech units burst and sparkled in the cloud, yet they kept coming in an endless stream. Particle reserves fell to 50%, 40%, 30%. The AI realized that the stream was not self-directing, and it concluded that it could protect itself very simply. A moment later its ion rockets fired precious reserves of propellant. Mirrorsun deployed a beam of focussed sunlight that was a quarter of its former intensity. The fortress furled the arrays and began to rotate. Its AI noted that heat dispersal was tolerable, and that 90% of the solar cells had survived.

Far across the face of the earth the AI fifth fortress began to cycle through damage assessment routines. Its solar arrays were gone, its external sensors fused and blinded, the EMP weapons were jammed and their batteries almost drained. It still had control of its engines, however, and it could use its reserves of fuel to reach the orbit of the band and self-destruct. Its AI was still comparing optimal trajectories when a cloud of nanotech particles slammed into its outer armour, vaporizing themselves as they flayed it open to the backup cloud only milliseconds behind.

The sixth fortress nudged itself into a new orbit as another cloud of particles hurtled toward it. They continued along their now harmless trajectory — then exploded! Debris intersected its orbit, raking the skin of the last fortress, tearing away the armouring of one of the solar arrays and damaging one ion engine. Another cloud approached, and the orbital fortress pumped more shield particles out as it changed orbits again. The nanotech units exploded but were absorbed by the cloud. The AI ran through an analysis: the resources of the Mirrorsun band were infinite, while its own fuel and defences would not last beyond that day. It fired its two remaining engines.

Mirrorsun noted that the fortress was moving to a higher orbit, and it adjusted the stream of nanotech units to intercept the new trajectory. The fortress slipped behind the earth, then climbed to meet the disk, slowly and under constant attack. Hours later it passed through the band, flaying it with EMP bursts and particle clouds, tearing at its fabric until it was reduced to orbiting nanotech rags. As the fortress began the fall from apogee its AI noted that it would now pass through the top layers of the atmosphere on the descent to perigee. The hail of nanotech units continued, exploding into its protective particle clouds, but it no longer changed orbits. Its fuel was spent. Hours later the toughened cylinder plunged through the atmosphere, skipped back into space briefly, then dropped to earth, pulverizing itself in the Andes.

Slowly the band began to assemble itself again. A third of its fabric was dead, but reserves were already being pumped up from the moon's surface.

*****

"Strange lights in the sky," Glasken observed as he lay back on his ground cloth. "Something's changed with Mirrorsun, too. It looks ... tarnished and ragged."

"There are no Wanderers, Fras Glasken, that is another point," said Ettenbar from where he too lay looking upward.

"What? Ach, you're looking in the wrong place."

"No, Fras, I was once a shepherd. I know the sky very well indeed, and I know all the Wanderers' names. *Theten* should be overhead at this moment."

Glasken snorted. "So what if they're gone? In a few hours we'll all be dead, as likely as not. What word of the Southmoors?"

"The Call of this morning scattered them worse than us. Their timers were set to a longer interval than ours, so we were less affected."

"We'd not have been affected at all without this prohibition on Call warnings in our beamflash traffic."

"Ah but that is vital to allow the people of Balranald to ally themselves with us, who use beamflash communication."

"I've never worked out why Islam prohibits warnings for the Call."

"No, no, Islam prohibits nothing specifically to do with the Call. We merely recognize that the Call is an unknown to be treated with respect until such time as it is understood, that is where the prohibition on artificial Call warnings originates. Were the Call to be found to come from a mundane source, why the Southmoors would construct the finest beamflash grid in the world because our mathematics and lensware is the finest —"

"That's unlikely to be before dawn tomorrow, I gather?"

"Regrettably, no."

Early the next morning they marched to a point where the highway neared a wide river. Rochester's small, shallow-draft battle galleys had penetrated all the way to the customs chain at Haytown, and the only bridge between Balranald and the Confederation had been demolished. Ghans lancers had appeared on the northern banks and fired at the galleys, but the boats were armoured against small-arms fire, and their own grapeshot bombards soon scattered the lancers and drove them back. By 8am the access to the border was secure, but heliostat messages told them that an attack was coming at Ravensworth Junction. Southmoor mounted musketeers had ridden sixty kilometres through the night, along the back roads from Wanganella. They were now beginning to dig in.

Overhand Gratian of the Alliance forces called a hurried conference of his captains to brief them on what was to come. The officers were grimy and haggard, but still well disciplined as they gathered around him in the drizzle that had ended a brief period of sunlight. They were hard-pressed, but not defeated.

"The only viable bridge between Balranald and Haytown is here at Ravensworth," the Overhand began, "and if the enemy can rebuild it the Ghans will pour across to join the Southmoors. They have a couple of dozen medium bombards on the banks, and those could sink our battle galleys. We have to take the bridgehead and defend it. Captains Fitzen, Alluwanna, Kearley, Glasken, Ling-zo and Richards will lead their companies in the attack on specific points in Ravensworth, then strike north toward the bridge. Intelligence reports that their line of trenches is about 500 metres from the river, and that's to our advantage. If we dig in there we can use bombards against their bridge repair crews."

"A question, sir."

"Glasken?"

"Won't we be in range of their bombards?"

"As a matter of fact, yes, and our battle calculor at Balranald estimates that no more aid will be available in the foreseeable future. Everything the Alliance has in this sector will have to be thrown into an offensive north from Deniliquin against the Southmoor reinforcements. We here are facing very bad times."

"But if the floodwaters subside they can rig up a pontoon bridge out of range of our bombards, and there's 150,000 of them."

"Correct, Captain Glasken, but this is war. Nothing's certain."

*****

The Alliance attack began about an hour past noon. Alliance bombards concentrated on smashing the higher buildings of the town to deny the Southmoors an overview, while the infantry began an advance in open order across scrubby pasture. At Glasken's whistle company Jay started forward with Dunoonan holding the regimental colours and Ettenbar playing the regimental march on his zurna. Heavy, sustained fire burst from the distant buildings of the town, and men began to cry out and drop before they had gone a dozen paces. To the right a line of two dozen knelt, aimed and fired a ragged volley at the houses before rejoining the march. Another line knelt, fired and stood, but the respite was transitory. Dunoonan staggered for a moment with the standard, then limped on, and the butt of Glasken's musket shattered along one edge as a ball caught it. Something tugged at Glasken's sleeve, something that stung his arm. Even as he was wincing, the back of Sergeant Condolonas' head burst with a sharp wet thud from a ball that had entered by his left eye. Glasken was splattered with warm, wet flesh, and his mesmerized determination to continue the lumbering charge was suddenly broken.

"South-20, all to cover, charge!" he shouted, then broke into a run. Moments later they were pinned down behind an earth wall by sporadic but accurate fire from the outlying houses of the town. Glasken lay panting on his back with his eyes tightly shut, aware that blood was trickling down his sleeve, and that it was probably his. Now his arm began to sting severely. He opened his eyes to see Ettenbar beside him, trying to tighten the reed of his battle zurna.

"Damn hell, Ettenbar, couldn't you play something they liked?" snapped the horrified and exasperated Glasken, at last looking down at his own blood-soaked sleeve.

"*Campbell's Farewell to the Red Rock* is the esteemed —"

"That's *Campbell's* Retreat *from the Red Castle*! What the hell do you mean playing something about a retreat during a charge?"

"With all deference to your rank, Fras Captain, but it is *Campbell's Farewell* —"

"It's *Campbell's Retreat*, you stupid little Southmoor bastard! It's an old Scottish tune. I was born in Sundew, I grew up in Sundew, and my people moved there from wherever Scotland was two thousand years ago. I spent the first eighteen years of my life wearing kilts, eating porridge, playing the bagpipes and learning bloody highland dancing even though there weren't any highlands within two hundred kilometres of the place, and I say it's *Campbell's Retreat*!"

"Is regiment's tune," insisted Ettenbar sullenly.

Glasken realized that sixteen dozen pairs of eyes and ears were following the argument with interest. He stared back, his mind full of jagged, jangling confusion. *I know what they're thinking*, he told himself. *Every one of them is thinking 'If these two loons keep arguing about some obscure piece of musicology I might live an extra few minutes.'*

"Well?" he asked them.

"*Campbell's Farewell to the Red Castle,*" chorused the men. Glasken flopped on his back again, unable to face them. They had all just faced death and many more would be dead within seconds of his next order to charge.

"Is not retreat!" muttered Ettenbar, still fiddling with the reed on his zurna.

"Gah, shaddup! Go poll the men."

Of the 250 men who had started across the field, 195 had reached the shelter of the earth wall.

"And nine men can go no further due to injured legs, Captain," Ettenbar reported.

Glasken thought for a moment, then unfolded his tower scope and peered at the houses. "Two hundred at most," he muttered.

"But Fras, the rate of fire was far above that."

"They probably have three guns each, and they're elite musketeers, no doubt of it. There's a whole swag of tricks like that for over-extended forces. Have spare guns to hand, shoot straight, load fast, but ... yes, but I've got a whole swag of tricks too. Get those nine wounded together, over there, to the left. Give them a dozen spare pistols each from the other men. Tell the sergeants and lieutenants that all the rest are to drop their forage packs and carry only sabres. They're to scrape the mud from their boots, too."

"But, Captain, this is unheard of, the men need their packs."

"There's fifty back on that field who still have their packs but don't need 'em any more. Do as I say."

Glasken gave his officers and sergeants a short and unconventional briefing.

"... and when the final command to *really* charge comes, it will be this white kerchief pulled from my jacket, waved twice and flung down. Everyone's to watch me for that, then it's straight over the top without a yell and run like the whirley-clappers for the Southmoor cover. Total silence, understand? The bastards won't expect that, they'll think their eyes are playing them false because their ears don't hear a charge. We'll be over that ground before they get more than two volleys into us, then it's sabres as has the advantage. Lieutenant Jendrik, if I'm dropped and away, they're yours."

The group started to break up, and Glasken pretended not to notice for a moment.

"Oi, I've not finished," he called so that all of the musketeers could hear. "Any of you caught fighting over prisoners and its fifty lashes each. Anyone starts looting before I've had first pick, ten lashes. Make sure all your gear is marked so you can find it when you come back and not be arguing, there'll be too much to do what with digging in. Now get ready."

Bloody pathetic bravado, Glasken thought to himself. *Anyone who's not stupid will see right through it. On the other hand, we must all be pretty damn stupid to be out here in the mud getting shot to pieces, so who knows?*

Some minutes later the Southmoors heard Glasken's whistle, and a scatter of shots flashed atop the earth wall to their left. The dark shapes of heads appeared all along the wall, and the Southmoors opened fire at once. The heads withdrew, then there was more whistling and cursing, and the battle zurna player struck up *Campbell's Farewell to the Red Castle* again but the tune was cut short. "Rebellion," several Southmoors muttered. Again a few Alliance musketeer heads appeared. Another volley, the heads fell back, then more figures silently swarmed over the bank and came running across the field at an unnaturally great pace.

Glasken had guessed well. There were three muskets to each Southmoor. One more hasty volley tore into the Alliance men, then the Southmoor fire became irregular as some tried to reload and others drew their flintlock pistols and delivered a less coordinated volley. There had been no time to dig stake trenches, and Glasken's unencumbered company raced through the ravaged vegetable gardens with unexpected speed and agility, ducking, dodging and scattering the cowering poultry.

Glasken's reflexes took over as he burst in among the Southmoors with his sabre and demiblade whirling, his flesh-wound forgotten, slicing and punch-chopping with a half-decade of Baelsha training behind every movement. In fact now that the fighting was hand-to-hand, the versatile and battle-hardened men of the 105th were all at a distinct advantage, even though they were outnumbered and two dozen more had been sliced from their ranks by Southmoor fire. Jay company of the 105th took their sector of the town after forty minutes more of bloody, desperate fighting, then went to the assistance of the others. Overhand Gratian was impressed, and he assigned some hundreds more men to Glasken, then left him to dig in and make sure that the bridge stayed down. Balranald was in need of as many musketeers and officers as Gratian could take there.

The Southmoors had been no less overextended than the Alliance forces. The elite musketeers had been rushed in to defend the town against a more numerous but less experienced enemy. Glasken's mind had begun to move in slightly more strategic channels during the course of the war, and he treated his Southmoor prisoners accordingly. While his officers called for all prisoners to be shot, Glasken ordered them stripped to their trews, then had their right hands struck one hard blow each with an axe handle before turning them loose to return to the Southmoor lines.

"A merciful gift, that of life," said Ettenbar.

"Nothing of the kind. They're weaponless and with broken fingers to boot, so they'll tax their own army's support but help them not at all. A pity if any were lutanists or pipers, though."

He noticed that Ettenbar had removed the reed from his battle zurna, and was corking it into a bamboo tube. Glasken broke a twig from the peach tree above him.

"Oi there, Corporal Ettenbar, hold out you hand."

"Yes, Fras Cap— Ach!" he cried as the blow landed and he snatched his hand back. "Dummart b— Allah forgive me."

*****

Zarvora had begun to operate her transmitter even before the fifth and sixth orbital fortresses had been destroyed. She had watched the rapid changes and damage in the Mirrorsun band, then noted that one of the Wanderer satellites had become a dispersing cloud of fragments. She concluded at once that all the Wanderers had been destroyed, and in a way this was reasonable. The fortresses were by then too preoccupied with Mirrorsun to bother with her weak signals on the ground.

She sat at a bench in a darkened room with an array of batteries powering the coils of her tuned circuit while she tapped at her modified beamflash key. Tarrin stared at a tiny air gap through a lens, frowning in the darkness.

"I don't recognize the pattern that you are sending," he said as the hour chimed out from a distant clocktower. "What is this thing meant to do?"

"Flash at you."

Tarrin sighed and squinted at the gap. "I see sparks now." His eyes widened. "UNDERSTOOD AND ACKNOWLEDGED is the message, in standard calibration code."

"There! It works!"

She stood up, wringing her hands together so hard that her knuckles crackled.

"Requisition a galley engine, I must go to Oldenberg and take all of this machinery with me."

"But it would fill two trucks or more, Frelle Highliber."

"Yes. Yes. It filled three when I had it shipped over from Kalgoorlie, just before the invasion. Do it! Now!"

When he had gone Zarvora began to work the key again. As soon as she had noticed the rapid, ominously purposeful changes in the Mirrorsun band, she had sent a message to Denkar through her agents and carrier birds. He was to watch the skies, and if the Wanderers vanished he was to connect a sparkflash transceiver to an unprotected external antenna and await her signal. Now the gamble had paid off.

INSTANTANEOUS COMMUNICATION WITHOUT BEAM-FLASH she typed. REPLY. SPEAK TO ME. I LOVE YOU. TELL ME SOMETHING ABOUT KALGOORLIE.

The sparks began to crackle faintly beneath the eyepiece of the receiver.

I LOVE YOU TOO. THE TWINS SAY HULLO MOTHER. THE SUN IS SETTING AND THE SKY IS CLEAR.

Zarvora tapped a reply.

THE SUN IS HOURS DOWN IN ROCHESTER. SUMMON MAYOR BOUROS TO YOUR RECEIVER. WE HAVE A LOT TO DISCUSS ABOUT THIS WAR. FIRSTLY I WANT CONTACT NAMES FOR THE LOYAL COMPANY OF ELECTRICAL STUDIES OF OLDENBERG YOU ONCE TOLD ME ABOUT.

It was midnight before Zarvora was interrupted by Tarrin, who had finally managed to find the galley engine and three trucks. Reluctantly Zarvora powered the spark gap transceiver down and began to supervise as it was disassembled and packed for transport to Oldenberg.

Down in the system console room of the Libris Calculor she found that Dolorian was visiting the place to discuss some problem with beamflash protocols.

"Frelle Dolorian, just the Frelle Dragon Librarian that I want. Contact your communications deputy up in the beamflash tower. Leave whoever it is in charge. Rouse a lackey to go searching for the six other people on this list here. You are all to be packed and ready to leave for Oldenberg in two hours. Meet me at the paraline terminus on the military platform."

"I — *military*, Frelle Highliber?"

"You have just joined my army with the rank of lieutenant. Your target shooting score in the Libris duelling gallery is ninth highest ranking out of all, so do not pretend that you cannot tell one end of a gun from the other."

"Target work yes, but, but I have no other training."

"You have the key beamflash codes and Calculor protocols memorized. Because of your former association with Lemorel Milderellen you have also been so thoroughly scrutinized by the Black Runners that your security rating is within a point or two of mine. I shall explain the rest on the train. Now move!"

*****

Parsimar Wolen was roused from his bed by the Oldenberg Constable's Runners, who had broken down the door when he had pulled the bed covers over his head and tried to ignore their knocking. With his wife screaming that he was 73, innocent and suffering from arthritis he was bundled into a pony gig still wearing only his nightshirt. As he looked back through the bars of the gig's rear door he noticed that a heavy guard was being put around his shop, and a military transport wagon was standing by.

At the assembly hall of Oldenberg University Parsimar realized that all nine of the members of the Oldenberg Loyal Company of Electrical Studies had been arrested and were huddling together in their nightshirts. He was marched to the group and turned loose by his escort.

"Jarel, what's happened?" he asked as they stood shivering together.

"Don't rightly know, Fras Parsimar. Boteken thinks that electrical studies has been declared a heresy, an' that we're to be burned at the stake."

"Heresy's only punishable by exile, and besides, burnin' at the stake was struck off the books in 1640."

"We'll all be shot, then, I told you we should have made ourselves a secret society instead of a Loyal Company."

"Looks like the nightshirt party we had when you turned 70, 'cept that it's winter and I'm freezing. Ah, Sergeant?"

"Yes, Fras?"

"Might — might I have a blanket, please?"

"Certainly, Fras, and slippers too?"

"What? Ah, yes, thank you."

"The coffee and bread rolls will not be long, we seem to have caught the University refectory by surprise. I'll not be a moment."

The Runner marched off smartly, leaving the two elderly guildsmen staring after him.

"He were actually civil to us," said Jarel incredulously.

"Doesn't sound like we're felons," Parsimar concluded. "Looky there! It's the OverMayor herself."

Zarvora had the hall cleared of the Runners. Soon only the nine men of the Guild remained, and she gathered them around her.

"I apologize for dragging you from your beds, but I have desperate need your services, and martial law is in force. These are the plans for a sparkflash radio transceiver, and out in the marshalling yards three paraline wagons are standing by with a disassembled working model. I want you to have seven more transceivers built, and I want them small enough to fit onto four horse-drawn military wagons each. I want them operational, and their operators trained, within a fortnight."

The Guildsmen gasped, then chattered for a moment.

"But, Frelle OverMayor, the blight of the Wanderers —" began Parsimar.

"The Wanderers have been destroyed. It was due to one of my own experiments, I am not too modest to admit. "

"Three cheers for the OverMayor," shouted Parsimar in a thin, reedy voice.

When the last of the wheezing cheers had died away, Jarel raised his hand. "The cost will be great, Frelle OverMayor. No less than 500 gold royals."

"You can have five hundred thousand gold royals if you need them. You have unlimited resources, Fras, understand? Unlimited. The Rochester Home Guard has sealed the city, the artisans of the paraline workshops, the Guild of Watchmakers and Call Timers, and the University workshops and laboratories are being roused at this very minute. Two hundred artisans, mechanics, engineers and lackeys are on their way from Libris in Rochester to assist you with the work and organization. Now who is Fras Parsimar Wolen, your current Guildmaster?"

"I, I —"

"Delighted to meet you," she said, shaking his hand. "You are hereby appointed Overseer, reporting directly to me. If anyone deliberately obstructs you, then tell me and I shall have them shot. And

I mean anyone! The City Constable, the City Librarian, the City UnderMayor, anyone."

Parsimar was already dizzy with what was flooding past him. Listening to the OverMayor was like trying to drink from a waterfall.

"But, Frelle OverMayor, I'm 73 —"

"And I am 38. Now these drawings are an overview of the sparkflash, and I want to spend the morning reassembling the unit from Libris here, in this hall, to familiarize you with the design."

"I need my pills and tonics," Boteken interjected.

"The University's Faculty of Medicians will suspend all teaching and research work to tend your health while you work. *Nothing* is as important as having those seven transceivers completed as soon as possible. Now then, here is Frelle Dolorian just arrived. She will be in charge of training."

Dolorian entered, carrying a sheaf of files under each arm. She was wearing a borrowed jacket, which she had unsuccessfully tried to button over her breasts. The effect was quite arresting.

Parsimar goggled, then hastily tilted the lenses of his bifocals.

"Frelle OverMayor, our wives will not have to be brought here, to suffer the rigours of this endeavour, will they?" ventured Jarel.

Zarvora left to organize the continuing mobilization of Oldenberg behind the project. Dolorian continued the briefing from notes that she had compiled on the train.

"The six Wanderers appear to have been ancient military devices," Dolorian began, her hips swaying slightly as if to the beat of an inaudible tune. It had begun as a nervous mannerism when she had delivered her first public speech, but she soon realized that it was guaranteed to secure the undivided attention of every man in the audience. "The Wanderers' purpose was to detect and destroy such electrical devices of the enemy as might operate on the ground. Electrical devices were of value for those waging war in the ancient times."

"So the Wanderers were weapons that operated for 2,000 years, Frelle?"

"Amazing as it sounds, apparently so. Just before the Ghan invasion began, the OverMayor conducted some experiments that accidentally brought the Wanderers into conflict with whatever controls the Mirrorsun band. Less than a day ago there was a battle in the sky, and Mirrorsun was the victor. We are now able to use electrical devices in war, and the war with the Alspring Ghans is going badly for us at present. Sparkflash radio wagons will give us instant communications, and will free our commanders from the beamflash grid totally. Until now a large part of our forces have been tied down to defending our beamflash towers. Now we can destroy the galleries and abandon those towers if need be, and the sparkflash wagons can move wherever our armies go."

*****

The seven wagons took nearly a month to be made operational, but Zarvora knew that she had to accept the delay. The stalemate in the east was starting to work against her now, as the Southmoors adapted to trench warfare. Winter mist interfered with beamflash links, while the thick cloud often hindered the use of heliostats on the battlefield. Finally the Black Runners brought an unconfirmed report that the Ghans and Southmoors were to merge several divisions for a thrust from Deniliquin down to the Calldeath lands. Rochester was to be split in two.

Five of the seven sparkflash wagons were deployed to the fronts in the west, northwest and northeast, and one was smuggled across Southmoor Territory into the Central Confederation. Troops freed from defending the beamflash towers were moved by paraline to Robinvale, where they were assembled into a new army. Dolorian was assigned to this force, with the seventh sparkflash wagon. The objective was to fortify a strip of land that Alliance forces had managed to capture, a strip that reached all the way to the Central Confederation's border.

It never happened. A horde of Ghan lancers and mounted musketeers descended, seemingly from nowhere. They scattered the disorganized new units before they were ready to move. Zarvora later estimated that some of the Ghan units must have been brought from over a thousand kilometres away in no more than a week. The exhausted but well organized and coordinated Ghans prevailed over the unprepared Alliance musketeers in a battle halfway between Robinvale and Balranald, yet Overhand Gratian somehow gathered the remains of his divisions into an orderly retreat. At Balranald they crossed the flooded river and destroyed the bridges.

"The Ghans must have been warned," Zarvora said as she continued to call to Dolorian from the new Sparkflash Command Centre at Oldenberg. "Someone who knew about the paraline movements was able to deduce that troops were due to be concentrated at Robinvale."

"That spy could be one of thousands," Vardel Griss replied. "The paraline system is a huge structure."

"In three months it will be more secure. We shall have a sparkflash unit on every galley train and in every fort, but until then we have to use the beamflash system, and that system is not secure. The codes were good, yet they were broken and used against us."

"Another calculor, Frelle?"

"Even the Kalgoorlie machine would take two years to break our new codes. No, we were betrayed, as were the fifteen thousand dead musketeers at the Battle of Robinvale. Damn. Still no report of Dolorian and Sparkflash 7."

Griss looked at the wall map, and its seven green pins. The pin marked with a 7 was just north of Balranald.

"She may not be captured. If she is still fleeing she will not be able to transmit. The sparkflash gear takes five hours to set up and tune."

"Let us hope so — uh! That's odd."

Zarvora began to copy out characters from a sparkflash signal. Griss looked over her shoulder, shaking her head.

"Very, very faint, but I've never seen anything like it."

"It's familiar to me, I saw something similar in the fragments of texts that Bouros had at Kalgoorlie. It could be an old representation of letters and numerals known as Morse Code, which represents characters and numerals in two types of strokes, short and long."

Zarvora reached for a book of tables as Griss watched the message repeated.

"It spells DENVER YANG-KI over and over."

"That's not any place I know. It — it could be from beyond the Calldeath lands."

"So it would seem, Frelle Griss. We may not be the only centre of civilization."

"Yang-Ki. It sounds like a name from old China. Will you reply?"

"What can I say? Thanks awfully for calling, but we have a war in progress, so please go away, we can't tune to separate frequencies yet."

"Something simpler, Frelle Overliber. It never hurts to be friendly. Tell them a pre-Greatwinter place name, something big. What is the name of that huge abandon to the south of here?"

"Melbourne. Well, why not?"

Zarvora typed: OVERMAYOR ZARVORA. MELBOURNE. HEARING DENVER YANG-KI.

The ensuing exchange was less than productive, for American and Australian English had drifted some distance apart during two thousand years of isolation. Zarvora keyed END OF TRANSMISSION several times, and presently the transmitter on the other side of the world signed off as well.

"WE something FOR PEACE was their last message," said Zarvora.

"Well they won't find it here. I told them about the war."

"Perchance they do not have wars in China."

*****

Away to the north, Dolorian and Major Hartian, who was commanding her sparkflash unit, were lashing rafts together in the driving rain and floating the radio wagons over the Murrumbidgee River while Alliance bombards on the south bank raked the attacking Ghan lancers and musketeers with grapeshot. The river was well into flood and still rising, and muddy water swirled about the wheels of the last of the wagons as it was hauled up the south bank to safety. It had been a difficult and dangerous operation, and they had been lucky to lose nothing.

"Are you all right, Lieutenant?" the driver of the transceiver wagon called down to a mud-encrusted figure who was pushing against the transverse beam.

"Only just," panted Dolorian, who was soaked to the skin, her long hair partly free of its bindings and plastered to her face by muddy water. "Hairpins at the bottom of the river. Nearly went with them. Safe at last, though."

"Not so, Frelle Lieutenant," called a runner who came stumbling and slipping through the mud toward her. "Word of a Southmoor advance just came. Dispatch rider. Our side can hold 'em for now ... but it's going to be all running battles. The Major wants to know your needs. He's at the pennant pole."

"Six silver hairpins and a Cargelligo orbile comb, dry clothes, hot chocolate, and a month's leave followed by a posting to our embassy in Kalgoorlie — oh, and a rich and handsome suitor who can play the lutina."

"Regret ... can't help, Frelle," panted the runner. "'Specially not with the last." He looked to be all of a weedy and pockmarked eighteen. "I think he wants to know what you need to get this unit transmitting."

"Five hours in secure territory."

"There's a fortified trench square guarding what's left of the bridge pillars at Ravensworth."

"Ravensworth? That's liable to be the place of the next major attack as the Southmoors and Ghans try to link up. Better to destroy the wagons here and now before they're captured. Riding without the wagons we could reach to Central Confederation in ... a day, at most. This rain will give us cover."

"Then it's Ravensworth or flight, Frelle Lieutenant, but think over the former. They're dug in securely, and they have bombards. Their captain fought at Dareton when they broke that cavalry charge. Glasken, that's his name. John Glasken. They say he's a good 'un to be under, Frelle Lieutenant. Brave, a great leader, and seen lots of action."

Dolorian sagged against the muddied wheel of the wagon. Unconsciously she flicked open the top button of her soaked and muddy jacket, then walked two fingers slowly along a spoke as the rain pelted down on her. Bugles sounded the assembly call in the distance.

"More action than you would ever suspect, Fras Corporal," she said huskily, then pushed away from the wheel and began tramping through the red mud towards the pennant pole with him.

*****

Captain John Glasken of the 105th OverMayor's Heavy Infantry was in his command tent when the wagons of Sparkflash 7 and their escort arrived at Ravensworth. Major Hartian sent his adjunct across to fetch Glasken while he supervised the selection of a site for the wagons from horseback. Out of the corner of his eye he saw the adjunct look about for a guard, then enter the command tent. There was a piercing scream, and the adjunct backed out again.

About a minute later Glasken emerged, buttoning his shirt and carrying his sabre and scabbard under his arm. As he approached, a woman darted from the tent behind him with a coat over her head, and vanished behind a pile of logs in the direction of the orderlies area.

"I was, ah, taken with a fever," Glasken explained. "A nurse was tending me."

"A nurse with a paraline conductor's coat over her head?" asked Major Hartian.

Glasken watched the arrival of the radio wagons with perplexity as the Major briefed him on the requirements of Sparkflash 7.

"There are two mast wagons, and then the power wagon and transceiver wagon," he explained as Glasken struggled to understand what the thing was. "The mast wagons must be 50 metres apart, and they extends collapsible masts to a height of 15 metres. Between them is strung a double wire called an antenna, after the ancient Anglaic word 'antenna'."

"But they're the same word," said Glasken.

"Fras Captain, the manual says antenna is named after 'antenna', so antenna is what I says. I 'ad two days of training from the Highliber herself —"

"Yes, all right then. What's it to do?"

"It replaces beamflash towers, that's what. Why a commander can call all the way to Rochester direct for orders."

"But the towers are far too short to be useful. A man on top of one of them might as well be up a tree."

"They're not workin' on light flashes, Fras Captain. They pick waves out of the air itself by that wire."

"Waves? Like on a river or lake?"

"Aye, that's right. Now —"

"But where's the water?"

"Look, are you ignorant or somethin'? Once the waves are picked up the operator sees the message at the spark gap. The little flashes of light are like beamflash transmissions —"

"But you just said it's waves and wires, and now it's back to light flashes and beamflash codes."

"Fras Captain, just listen, will you? This is a major scientific advance."

After a further ten minutes of argument and exposition the two officers parted on less than amicable terms. For the next hour Glasken watched the masts being erected and braced into place with guy ropes. The double wire between the mast-top insulators was almost too fine to see. The cover of the power wagon was removed to reveal ten sets of pedals from a galley train mechanism, with the gearing connected to a barrel-shaped thing with wires trailing off to the transceiver wagon.

Glasken watched the unit at work while he stripped and cleaned his rifle and pistols. More hours passed, and after a tour of inspection he returned to watch during a break in the rain. There was an odd buzzing sound, and the same smell of ozone that followed thunderstorms.

Presently his curiosity got the better of him, and he made his way over to the transceiver wagon. It was dark inside, and filled with a buzzing, crackling sound. A Dragon Librarian sat in one corner. Glasken could see the blue armband of rank, but her head was obscured by a baffle. Her breasts were not, however, and they were alluringly large. He cleared his throat.

"Captain John Glasken of the 105th reporting," he declared. The woman beckoned him in without looking away from the spark gap.

"You are just in time, Fras Captain Glasken," she said in a husky voice. "I am in contact with the great transmitter at Oldenberg, with the Highliber herself."

Glasken slid onto the bench beside her and peered past her into the spark gap box, where a violet light was flickering in and out of existence. The space was confined, and he had to drape his arm over the operator's shoulder to get a view past her head. The sparks had a familiar pattern about them.

"I say, that's beamflash protocol, with standard code," he exclaimed with surprise. "CALIBRATION TEST 5 COMPLETING."

"Good work, Fras Captain, I see you are an experienced operator," his companion purred approvingly.

Glasken realized that although his hand was resting on her left breast, his face had not been slapped. He gave an affectionate, experimental squeeze.

"Just as I can tell distant operators by their keystrokes, I can recognize you by your touch, Johnny Glasken."

"Frelle, I have never worked your switches before, enchanting thought though it might be."

"Ah but you have, Fras Johnny," she said as she turned away from the spark gap.

"Dolorian!" cried Glasken, and he turned to stumble and crash his way out of the wagon at once. "Guards! Guards! Guards! An Alspring spy. Guards! Damn you, here! Quickly."

The Major arrived to find Dolorian standing beside the wagon with her hands in the air and ringed by a dozen of Glasken's infantry while Glasken watched from a distance, calling out for them to be careful and to shoot to kill if she made a move.

"What in hell is going on?" demanded Major Hartian.

"Alspring spy," said Glasken, waving in Dolorian's direction with his sabre. "A personal friend of Lemorel, their maniac leader."

"She's also the most experienced sparkflash radio operator besides the Highliber herself," the Major shouted back.

"All the worse! A spy at the heart of our command."

"I have the Highliber's security clearance," began Dolorian.

"That she does, Fras Captain."

"But she knows Lemorel. Lemorel taught her to shoot, they went shopping in the markets together, they were friends, and well, who knows what else."

Dolorian raised her eyes to the sky for a moment. By now there was an audience of several dozen muddy musketeers gathered around them. "Well I never slept with her, Fras Glasken, which is more than you can say!" she said in a soft yet clear voice.

"*You* slept with the Alspring Horde's *supreme commander*?" asked the incredulous Major.

"Ah, well, just a student dalliance," stammered Glasken. "And only once."

"From July 1697 to September 1699," Dolorian corrected him. "When she discovered that you had been cheating with her she had you sent to the Calculor for life."

"You were *unfaithful* to the enemy's supreme commander?" asked the Major, numbed beyond surprise.

"Three cheers fer Captain Glasken!" called someone in the crowd, and the musketeers cheered loudly.

*****

Since taking the town of Ravensworth Glasken's force had demolished the bridge across the river right down to the stone foundations, then dug in at the edge of the range of their own bombards. Their bombards were finely made, the latest Inglewood type that shot calibrated leadballs with great accuracy, and were thus outside the range of the enemy bombards across the river. The Alspring engineers tried to float their own bombards across on rafts, but the turbulent floodwaters and Alliance bombardment made this dangerous. They gave up after the fifth bombard was lost.

All the while the Southmoors had been pouring cavalry along the roads from Wanganella, and in spite of sabotage and cavalry raids across the border, it was only a matter of time before the gun carriages with their bombards began to arrive. With Balranald in Alliance control and Haytown militarily neutral, the importance of the Ravensworth bridge grew by the hour. A hundred thousand Alspring lancers and their support force were building up on the north side of the bridge. Major Hartian ordered the eight female nurses of the 105th to be escorted north, to the neutral Confederation's border and internment for the rest of the war. All that remained of the hospital unit was the medician and three male orderlies.

Dolorian worked the sparkflash radio constantly, sending estimates of enemy strength to Oldenberg and getting new intelligence through from the transmitters at Balranald and Robinvale, as well as the secret transmitter that had been smuggled into the Alliance embassy at Griffith. Using the Confederation's beamflash system, spies at Haytown notified the embassy when a senior delegation of Alspring leaders arrived from the west. In particular, it was noted that the pennants of the Ghans' supreme commander were flying over the local governor's palace.

"Lemorel's there to demand access to the Haytown bridges," Glasken concluded at once when a runner brought him the message.

Hartian was doubtful. "Why should she bother to talk? She has a division besieging Balranald, and Haytown is not nearly as well fortified. Two days at a forced march, and she could have Haytown in her purse."

"That's tactics, and she thinks by strategy as well," replied Glasken. "To crush Haytown would be to gain the Central Confederation as an enemy. The Confederation has a lot more strength in its lancer divisions than the Alliance, and they match the Ghans in dryland fighting experience. It also has a long and diffuse border near the Alspring supply lines. No, she will bluster and threaten, then perhaps offer them some fantastic compromise that they could never refuse."

Major Hartian looked at the map on the folding table between them, then read through the radio transmissions again.

"Over the river, a hundred thousand Alspring Ghans, who are very anxious to rebuild that bridge. On this side, eleven thousand Southmoors on the roads from the south. Already a build up of five thousand out there, and only nine hundred of us are left — with our three pathetic bombards."

"Those three brass alloy bombards are the finest that my taxes can buy," said Glasken indignantly.

"But there's still only three of them — what's that?"

A rattle of small arms fire broke the peace.

"An attack!" said Glasken, seizing his musket and lancepoint helmet.

The Southmoors had been expected to attack from the Ravensworth side of the Alliance trenches, and to pound the place with artillery first. Instead they had sent nearly the whole force of dismounted cavalry crawling through the open fields to the west and east until they were in a position to attack the Alliance bombard emplacements from two sides. The thin wedge of trenches held at first, then began to take breaches under the weight of suicidal attacks. In a half-hour of fighting the bombards were cut off, and the Alliance troops retreated to a second line of trenches while their trapped comrades fought on in isolation.

Dolorian had been following the developments as a concerned observer from the shelter of the power wagon when a runner found her. He indicated a ragged rally pennant.

"That is the forward command post," he panted. "You are to report there."

Dolorian crawled miserably through the cold, red mud, trying to stay as low as possible and for once in her life wishing that her breasts were a little smaller. Ettenbar called to her from a foxhole, and she made her way across to him while shots flew waspishly overhead. He had risen to the rank of sergeant by now.

"All gone, Frelle Lieutenant," he cried. "Captain and Major ... trapped with the bombards."

"Out there? They're cut off?"

"Frelle, you're the communications lieutenant. You're the senior officer left in charge here." He gave her as crisp a salute as he could manage. "Pleased to give orders, Frelle Lieutenant?"

"Me? But my commission is administrative."

"Orders, Frelle? Please? The men are desperate. They want a leader with orders."

Dolorian raised her head to survey the field of struggling men, gun flashes, drifting smoke and mud-encrusted corpses.

"And I want a pile of cushions on a Northmoor rug, and a warm fire, and my high-heeled boots, and filtered coffee, and caramel cream chocolates."

"Regrettably, Frelle, those things are not in supply here."

"Nothing I want is ever to be found on a battlefield! I want to die in bed, and of old age, and preferably with company —"

A shot kicked up the mud between them, and they crouched down again.

"Ah death, Frelle. Now I *can* accept that in your place. You give order, I lead attack or whatever."

Dolorian could feel tears welling from her eyes and mixing with the mud on her cheeks as she thought. There was a heavy blast in the distance as a spiked bombard exploded.

"Fras Major and Captain destroy the bombards, Frelle."

"Sergeant Ettenbar, when the Southmoors break through, the incendiary charges in the radio wagons must be ignited. In the meantime, I want an attack to relieve the bombard crews."

Ettenbar smiled as he drew a double barrelled flintlock.

"Your orders, my duty, Frelle. And might I suggest that there is a nurse's jacket and headband in the captain's tent, for once the charges are set. Southmoors are chivalrous, a little. A nurse would be treated with honour —"

Dolorian reached out and snatched the gun from him.

"You'd look silly as a nurse, Sergeant."

"No, no, Frelle, I mean —"

"*I* lead the charge, *you* stand by to burn the radio wagons."

*****

The third bombard had just been spiked as another onslaught of Southmoors fell on the doomed position, but the Alliance men were well armed, and the Southmoors were having trouble bringing their superior numbers to bear. They were lancers, trained to fight from horses. Major Hartian lit the fuse to the bombard's touchhole then made a flying leap for the corner beside Glasken. A moment later the barrel jammed with wadding exploded with a shattering blast that left their ears ringing. The Southmoor attack faltered and the line of white cavalry uniforms smeared with red mud began to fall back.

"That's all the bombards, we have nothing they want now," shouted Hartian above the ringing in Glasken's ears.

"They'll have the bridge ready for traffic in ten hours, now that we can't knock it down any more," Glasken replied.

"Let 'em. We'll not last an hour, but the main square could hold out for a couple more days, and the Ghans don't know about the radio wagon. My guess is that they'll pass us by, leaving a small force of bombards to pound us into surrender. Lieutenant Dolorian can call their numbers out to the Highliber for the whole of that time."

"Listen!" barked Glasken. "A Southmoor battle zurna."

"Just tryin' to rally their men."

"No!" exclaimed Glasken. "It's *Campbell's Farewell to the Red Castle*, the 105th's march. That's Ettenbar!"

"They're attacking to relieve us! Fools! The Southmoors will hit their wedge from both sides."

"Major, we should get the men together. Break out and meet them. Major?"

Glasken glanced around, but saw only bodies encrusted with red mud. One of them had to now be the Major. *A stray shot no doubt,* he thought. He was back in command of the encampment. He blew his whistle in the code of the day: RALLY — CHARGE SOUTH — AT MY SIGNAL. The men hastily gathered as the rescue force began to march over from the distant trenches.

"We're to link up with 'em, then retreat to the main square. At my signal!"

Glasken blew his whistle, and they began to scramble out of their trenches and stumble south over the broken ground and corpses. The Major was not dead, however, he was away piling powder barrels together in the powder well, a smoking matchlock fuse between his teeth. At Glasken's final whistle he smashed the top of a barrel in with the butt of a musket. He took the fuse from his teeth and plunged his dagger into a calico bag of granulated gunpowder.

"Good man, Johnny, now here's a send off to hasten ye," he said as he held the fuse above the black granules.

To Glasken the blast was the earth lifting beneath his feet and a brief sensation of flying. It was an almost serene feeling.

*****

Dolorian was picking herself out of the mud in Ettenbar's foxhole when the explosion of the powder dump enveloped her like a thunderclap. Blood was streaming from a cut above her hairline where Ettenbar had clouted her with his heavy brass powder horn. It was running into her eyes and mouth. She mopped at the blood away with a Northmoor silk scarf that she wore to stop the stitching of her collar chafing her neck, then held it over the cut and pulled on her lancepoint helmet. Ettenbar had taken her sabre, she realized. She drew the Blantov 32 flintlock from her belt, slipped and stumbled over the muddy lip of the foxhole and ran crouched over out into the battlefield.

Black smoke was billowing out from the explosion, and dirt was still raining down from the sky. Groups of men were struggling and hacking at each other all around her, and there were no more organized volleys of fire. Off to her left she could see a Southmoor pennant, where an officer was rallying his men, waving his sabre and blowing a tambal. A hundred metres, she estimated, feeling dizzy and dropping to her knees. She cocked the striker of the Blantov, then flopped forward into red mud that was cold, and acrid with human blood. Raising herself on her elbows she took aim, gripping the gun with both hands.

"Must not aim high, must try to hit something," she whispered to herself. As Lemorel had taught her, seven years ago in Libris, she squeezed the trigger gently.

The Southmoor officer toppled, shot through the neck. His men hesitated, then scattered. Dolorian forced herself to stand, her head pounding, then stumbled dizzily through the mud and bodies to where her victim had fallen. She prized the sabre from his fingers, then hefted the weapon. Heavy. The grip was too big for her fingers. She was alone. What to do, what — her whistle! It also marked her as an officer. She blew the three quick blasts of RALLY, and almost at once shapes began gathering around her in the dispersing smoke. Bleeding, limping, battered musketeer infantry with broken sabre blades and muskets with splintered butts.

"Lieutenant Dolorian!" exclaimed a short bearded man.

"Status, what status?" she cried, not knowing what to do next.

The men shambled in closer, their weapons hanging limp, their eyes huge and round through masks of red mud. She noticed two bands on the sleeve of the bearded man. They were not listening to her or responding, she thought in despair.

"Corporal, what status?" she shouted, almost sobbing.

He pointed between her feet, and she looked down to see that she was standing astride the body of the Southmoor officer that she had killed.

"Frelle Lieutenant, that officer —"

"Well so bloody what?" she cried in exasperation. "I shot him. He's the enemy, isn't he?"

"Frelle Lieutenant, he's a Southmoor Overhand. You just broke their attack."

*****

The Southmoors were in too much disarray to mount another attack that day, so the Alliance troops had the battlefield to themselves. An orderly found Glasken in a row of Alliance wounded behind their trenches. He was semi-conscious and crying for black ale with no head and a proper chill. He revived when medicinal rye whisky was poured between his lips, and although he had no deep wounds, he had bad lacerations all down his left side.

"Ettenbar, where is he?" Glasken spluttered. "Damn-fool ordering that attack. I'll have his balls for —"

"Best hurry then, Fras Captain," said the orderly. "Sergeant Ettenbar is dying."

Glasken was helped to somewhere mid-field, where Ettenbar had fallen. His battle zurna was beside him in the mud. The orderly said that he had been shot high in the chest, and that his lungs were filling with blood.

"You bloody dummart!" sobbed Glasken, beating the mud beside Ettenbar with his fists. "I told you not to attack, I told you to defend the radio wagon."

"The Frelle Lieutenant ..."

"Dolorian! Dolorian ordered the attack?"

"Her order ... she tried to lead, but ... I hit her. I lead ... attack."

"You what?" cried Glasken. He carefully raised Ettenbar's head to help clear the blood.

"Can't ... have lady endangered, Fras ... bad form. Besides ... she couldn't —"

Ettenbar began coughing, and blood streamed from his mouth and nostrils. *Just like the captain of the Great Western galley engine,* Glasken realized. The words of the sergeant who had put him through basic training eight years earlier returned to him: *once they bleed from the mouth, don't bother.*

"Just be quiet, don't try to talk."

"She ... couldn't play the zurna ... like me."

Glasken covered his face with his free hand. "In the Deity's name, Ettenbar!" was all that he could think to say.

Ettenbar coughed again, but more weakly. Glasken looked down to see that he was smiling, and his face was no longer contorted with pain.

"Fras Johnny, may Allah ..." Ettenbar began, but he did not manage another breath. Glasken lowered his friend's head to the mud, then sat back on his haunches.

"I know, I know, old friend. Put in a good word for me in the afterlife, whether it is Allah, God, the Deity or whoever. I'll probably need it when I get there, and that's liable to be soon."

*****

With the Alliance bombards destroyed, the Alspring engineers resumed work on rebuilding the bridge. By evening they had the under-structure and beams in place on the stone foundations. Dolorian reported to Rochester that the enemy was working on into the night, laying planks down by lantern light.

There was talk of a ghost, a shadowy Southmoor who carried wounded off the battlefield. Glasken gave the story no credit.

"Think what you will, Fras Captain," said Sergeant Gyrom, "but you were one of those that he rescued."

Glasken's eyes widened. "All this death about us, I'm surprised there's not more ghosts."

"Fras Captain, there's Lieutenant Dolorian coming over."

"Why do I keep bumping into her?"

"Wish she'd bump into me," he said with a nudge to Glasken's arm. "Do you want me to leave?"

"Yes. No. Yes, I suppose so. Check if the medician wants for anything that we can provide, then get some sleep."

"Fras Glasken, I only want to apologize," insisted Dolorian as she and Glasken paced around the sparkflash wagon. Mirrorsun was glowing luridly bright through the dispersing clouds. Its configuration was like three large, bright eyes.

"Apology accepted, now leave me alone."

"I don't have to grovel, Fras Captain Glasken."

"Well don't. Just go away."

"I could have my pick of any man in your 105th!" she snapped, stamping her foot in the mud.

"Sergeant Gyrom!" shouted Glasken, and the sergeant hurried out of the medicians' tent and made his way to them through the Mirrorsun-tinted gloom.

"Fras Captain?" he said as he arrived.

"Sergeant, arrange for Frelle Dolorian to have her pick of any man in the 105th."

Dolorian's temper flared, and she delivered such a slap to Glasken's face that she broke a fingernail and left a short, deep gash in his left cheek.

"Sergeant, leave us!" shouted Dolorian as Glasken reached into his pocket and pulled out some circles of wadding paper to hold against the cut.

"Fras Captain?" asked Gyrom.

"Do as she says," said Glasken. "Dismissed."

Gyrom saluted smartly, turned on his heel and left. He seemed to be hurrying, decidedly glad to be away from them.

"Both of us should feel ashamed," said Dolorian quietly when the sergeant had gone.

Glasken grunted agreement.

"Fras, why are you so cold to me?" she suddenly burst out.

"You showed that you are cruel enough to dangle me on a string, then to let the string go."

"So? You made passionate vows to any number of women, all the while courting others."

"So they did not know about each other. That was all done in affection."

"That was all lies, too. Over the past six years I've met 14 girls who were at University with you. Your line was that you had been celibate for two years past before meeting each of them. Were you really at Rochester University for 28 years? You would have had to have entered the University at four years old."

"Very funny. So what do you want now?"

"To take up where we left off."

"Oh ho, and to raise me to the level of MULTIPLIER 37, FUNCTION 12, FUNCTION 780, ADDER 1048, FUNCTION 9, PORT 97, MULTIPLIER 2114 — and who was that short one with the bald head who liked to use pine-scented bath salts? MULTIPLIER — no, FUNCTION 1680, he served in the original Battle Calculor with me so he must have been a FUNCTION. Then there was that Confederation ADDER, what was his number now? 3016 or 1630?"

Dolorian stamped her foot with anger, but she had been standing in a puddle, and managed only to splash them both. It reminded Glasken of Jemli as she farewelled him on Kalgoorlie's paraline terminus.

"You know their numbers better than I do," Dolorian said sharply.

"I had to watch as you sauntered past with them to the solitary confinement cells. I had to listen while many of them boasted about it later. I had to shrug and shake my head when they asked what I thought of you. I had to look away to my book of conversion protocol codes when they winked and made droopy signs with their fingers."

"Fras, I'm —"

"Let me finish!" exclaimed Glasken, throwing his hands into the air. "I did a little statistical survey, Frelle. Surprised? I may look all cod and muscles, but I have a clever-scale score of 326. I found that all of your known conquests for the last three months of my time in Libris were of components in rostered groups that had direct dealings with me. At the time I thought merely that it meant that I had a better chance with you. Now I know that you were doing it to hurt me, to rub humiliation in my face, and for no other reason than to please your friend Lemorel. For all of my dalliances, Frelle Lieutenant, I never once ever deliberately humiliated or hurt any Frelle that I bedded — although I sometimes antagonized a few for pushing me around. You ought to know that, you seemed to have quizzed a few about me. Now do you see why the sight of your face actually frightens me, and the form of your breasts makes me feel physically ill. In my long years of enforced celibacy at a place called Baelsha monastery, I had to do no more than whisper your name to myself to send my lusts yelping away in terror."

"All right, Fras Captain, all right. Your point is made. I'll go. Good night."

When she did not turn away, Glasken did so instead. He had taken ten paces when she called out to him. He stopped and turned.

"What can I do for you, Fras? I've apologized. I'd be your lover in no more time than it takes to walk to the command tent if you would have me, but you only want me to go away. I have always loved life, Fras Johnny Glasken, but now I want to die."

Glasken's arms hung loose and limp, blood ran from the cut below his eye like a stream of dark tears.

"You forced me into a corner, Frelle, and I lashed out at you. If it is of any comfort to you, I did not want to do that. I know more about your past than I mentioned. Had I wished to, I could have hurt you a lot more. Now please leave me alone."

Glasken visited the medician to have two stitches put in his cheek, then returned to the command tent. Sergeant Gyrom entered sometime later, carrying a sheaf of poorpaper. Glasken looked up from the papers on his pinlamp-lit table.

"I thought I told you to get some sleep."

"NC briefs from Rochester, Fras Captain."

"Leave 'em with me, I'll check them before turning in."

"If ye don't mind me sayin', Fras Captain ..."

"I probably will mind, but say it anyway."

"A ravagin' beauty of a lady is that Frelle Dolorian."

"The word is ravishing, Sergeant, but yes, I agree."

"I think she likes you, Fras, in spite of all that yellin', and that cut. Tomorrow may be the end o'ye, Fras, and ..."

"That's true of every battle, Sergeant. The death rate among officers is highest with captains."

"What I mean, Fras, is that the Frelle Dragon Blue looks to want to ... to ... well, she's in the radio wagon and is cryin' a lot, and I'm sure it's over your cross words, Captain."

Glasken stared up at him for a moment, his chin cupped in his hands, then he reached for his pack and pulled out a jar.

"Share this among the men, and have a swig yourself. It may not make their last night on Earth as delightful as Frelle Dolorian undoubtably could, but it's the best I can do for a few of you."

"But, Fras, you've not cracked the seal yet."

"I don't need any, Fras Sergeant, I want to feel my pain. It proves to me that I'm still alive."

*****

Around 3am the Alspring mortar-bombards were in place, and they began to fire ranging shots into the Alliance square. Glasken woke from an exhausted sleep to the sound of the first mortar shell exploding, and he made his way to the power wagon where a team was standing ready to pedal. Dolorian was already with them, the white bandage around her head seeming to hover in the blackness as it gleamed in Mirrorsun's light.

"The final attack?" she asked.

"No, not yet, but if they have the bridge repaired well enough to take the weight of a siege mortar then they must be pouring their lancers across too."

"How long do we have?"

"Oh, if I were the Alspring overhand, I'd keep us awake like this, then smash a section of our trenches tomorrow morning and send the Southmoor heavy infantry in. They've arrived by now, I could hear their bugle signature before I fell asleep. They'll do what the dismounted lancers could not, and we should be a minor entry in the history books by noon."

"Perhaps a Call will come?" Dolorian suggested hopefully.

"The Alsprings use mobile heliostat towers, they will have warning enough to anchor down. Go to the sparkflash radio now, tell the Highliber our status, and that the bridge has been repaired. Stay with the radio all night, but when the square begins to break tomorrow run to the orderlies. I left a nurse's coat and headband with them for you."

"The coat that belonged to the nurse that had, ah, sat up with you the night before we arrived?"

"I had a fever."

"Thank you, Fras Glasken, but I'm sure the buttons would never fasten across *my* chest. Besides, I'm meant to be a soldier, so I should die like one if I have to."

Glasken sighed. "The offer's there, Frelle. Now, be off to your transceiver."

Dolorian did not turn away, but put a hand out to Glasken's arm. In the light of Mirrorsun, he could see that her face was clean, and that she was wearing her lipstick, ochre face powder and ebony eye shadow below the bandage on her forehead.

"A tiny breach in your defences, Fras Johnny," she said gently. Glasken's shoulders slumped.

"Perhaps I left it for you to find, Frelle Dolorian," he said with his eyes downcast.

Without another word she slipped a hand behind his head and drew him closer. Their shadows blended into one for a moment as they embraced and kissed. A chorus of hoots and whistles broke from the watching pedal crew on the power wagon, then they saw Glasken striding toward them as the distinctive form of Dolorian made for the radio wagon. There was a discreet snickering above the distant thump of mortar-bombards being test-fired by the enemy. Glasken put his hands on his hips.

"Now there's only one thing I want to say to ye buggers before you get pedaling and that's — Mortar! Jump for it!"

The explosive shell scored a direct hit on the wagon, flaying the crew with shards of iron and wood splinters. Dolorian picked herself out of the cold mud, her ears ringing. She scanned the ground in the light of Mirrorsun, after-images of the flash dancing before her eyes. It was a roil of smoke, descending fragments, and running men. Voices were calling for the medician and orderlies.

"Captain Glasken!" she screamed.

There was no reply, not even a groan. She climbed into the sparkflash wagon, and in the darkness pulled a heavy switch across to 'battery' mode. After clenching her hands to steady them and taking several deep breaths, she began to key out her message.

RAVENSWORTH OUTPOST OF 105TH TO ROCHESTER. RAVENSWORTH OUTPOST OF 105TH TO ROCHESTER. POWER WAGON DESTROYED. BATTERY MODE ONLY. NO POWER FOR RECEIVER. MESSAGE TO FOLLOW. ALSPRING ENEMY HAS REPAIRED BRIDGE. SURVIVING ALLIANCE FORCE IN 200 METRE SQUARE AROUND THIS TRANSMITTER. ESTIMATED 150,000 ENEMY WITHIN 10 KILOMETRE RADIUS OF TRANSMITTER. THREE HUNDRED ALLIANCE SURVIVORS. ALSPRING AND SOUTHMOOR FORCES CLOSING IN FOR FINAL ATTACK.

She checked the battery dial in the dim light of her pinlamp. It was nearly down to the red band. Another mortar shell exploded nearby, shaking the wagon.

BATTERIES FAILING. ENEMY BOMBARDMENT INTENSIFYING. ESTIMATE ONE MORTAR SHELL IN FOUR IS NEW EXPLOSIVE TYPE. REPORT BY LIEUTENANT DOLORIAN JELVERIA, STARFLASH 7, FIRST ALLIANCE RADIO CORPS.

She hesitated a moment, then took a deep breath and added SENIOR SURVIVING OFFICER. END OF TRANSMISSION.

As Dolorian stepped from the wagon, she suddenly remembered that there were two fully charged batteries in each of the mast wagons. If what remained of the encampment square held until daylight, she could make another transmission. The OverMayor would at least know what forces were crossing the bridge, and have a last estimate of enemy strength. The batteries had only to be unclamped and carried to the radio wagon. She blew her whistle amid the dim forms of scurrying musketeers and orderlies.

"This is Lieutenant Dolorian," she shouted in a hoarse voice. "I want four strong men here, at the double!"

"Can you hold out for a minute?" Glasken called back from somewhere in the confusion. "We're digging out men here as is still alive."

Dolorian slid to the mud beside the sparkflash wagon, giggling uncontrollably. Somewhere close by Glasken was haranguing whoever was helping him to move a chunk of wreckage.

"Keep your mouth open in case an explosive one comes down, that's what they told me in basics: saves your eardrums. Well the bugger didn't mention the risk of swallowing a half-litre of mud and horse shyte, did he? Gah, I nearly choked, what a foul taste. Hey out there, anyone: is any of my whisky left?"

*****

Glasken had a deep but narrow shrapnel wound in the lower leg. The orderlies cleaned and sewed the gash, and in spite of Dolorian's protests he managed to walk a few experimental steps with a staff and bar crutch.

"I thought you were dead," she admitted as she supported him. "It was such a terrible blast. I — I reported it to the command centre in Oldenberg. I said I was in charge now."

"No matter, Frelle. Leave it a few hours and both of those may come true."

She helped him to the command tent and he lay with his head in her lap while she stroked his hair and teased out the gritty knots.

"When you get the sparkflash going again, could you let the OverMayor know I'm still alive."

"Zarvora? You didn't!"

"Actually, no, I didn't." Glasken laughed, amused at the extent of his own reputation. "She is in contact with a Frelle in Kalgoorlie who is particularly important to me, however."

Dolorian's eyebrows rose in anticipation of more gossip. "How important?"

"She is pregnant by me. Oh, and you could ask Zarvora to get this war over in a hurry so that I can go back and marry Jemli. Being a bastard myself, I'd like that particular family tradition to end with me."

"Now what manner of woman could capture your heart, Fras? I would guess one who is very pretty, but so much as to catch the eye of too many men, one who is bright enough to appreciate your very real talents but not so bright as to overshadow you, well off for funding, and ... you would probably expect a virgin as well."

"Indeed," replied Glasken dreamily. "Well yes, she is pretty, but she is soon to graduate from Kalgoorlie University, very poor, and someone else's wife."

"Fras, my word! I was unfair in my thoughts of you. What is her name?"

"Jemli Milderellen is her maiden name."

It was some moments before Dolorian recovered her breath and composure.

"You know what I am about to ask you, Fras."

"The answer is yes."

"Enough! Too much! Far too much!" she exclaimed with her hands over her ears. "Change the subject, anything else at all."

"Ah ... that was a fine shot of yours that killed the overhand, ah, I'm told," said Glasken.

"Oh, I practised my pistol work for years in Libris. It got me through promotions and regradings, and it also helped keep me out of duels."

"How so?"

"I'm a very good shot now. I've had five challenges to legal duels, but each time I hit the target more squarely than my challengers. That denied them the right to the duel."

"How many were over the poaching of other Frelle's men?"

"Every one of them," admitted Dolorian. "Lemorel's sister," she whispered with her next breath.

Glasken raised himself on one arm, then pressed his forehead against hers in the universal gesture of relaxed affection.

"I'm proud of you, Frelle Dolorian, and I think you lovely. Hardest of all to say, but I forgive you too. Does that help?"

Dolorian put her arms around him and kissed the remains of his left ear.

"Darling Fras, sweet man," she whispered.

"You no longer wish to die?"

"Not unless it's for you."

Dolorian stayed with him until he fell into a deep, exhausted sleep, a pain-killer soak still half-chewed between his teeth. After that she sat up in the tent, riffling through a strategy manual by the light of a pinlamp while the spare batteries were being fitted to the radio wagon.

Suddenly, as Dolorian was on the brink of falling asleep herself, a flickering blue light seemed to illuminate the whole area around the tent. It was followed by a deep hum mingled with a vast crackling in the air. She came back to her senses with a start.

"Callshewt! My batteries!" she shouted, shrugging a rain-drape on and darting outside. At the sparkflash wagon, two technicians were standing staring at the horizon. "It's a short-circuit, you're draining the power!" she called. "Cut the cables, use your sabre."

"We haven't even got the insulator caps off, Frelle Lieutenant," one of them called back.

"You —" There was a distant rumbling explosion, followed by another, and another. "Then what was that noise ... and that smell in the air, like thunderstorms?"

"The sky lit up like lightning, Frelle. Aye, it may be a storm, you can hear the thunder clearly enough." The man did not sound convinced at his own words.

Dolorian looked to the horizon, which was glowing red. "By the Call, are they the Alspring campfires?"

"Can't say as I've noticed, Frelle Lieutenant. Been busy wi'the clamps, as was glued down by some loon back in Oldenberg."

"They's cover fires," speculated a deeper voice behind the wagon. "The blue flash were probably a signal flare, a signal for 'em to all start fires together for smokescreen before dawn. Mark my words, Frelle Lieutenant, they's been told of us as havin' this manner of sparkflash. Those fires are to blind us from reportin' their numbers before they flay us te pie meat come dawn."

Dolorian looked to the horizon again, not fully convinced by the operator's explanation. Still, she had nothing better to offer. "Oh. All right then. I'll note it down for when we can transmit again. Carry on."

"Ah, Lieutenant?"

"Yes?"

"We ... we just wanted to say what a great shot that was you did."

"What he means is, Lieutenant, is that we're with you."

"You an' the Captain, too."

"Go rest now, Lieutenant."

"Aye, when ready we'll call."

*****

When Glasken awoke the sun was just above the horizon, but glowed pale and cold through a pall of smoke. The mortar-bombards had ceased to fire during the night, and there was not even sniper fire. Dolorian briefed him on what had happened while he slept. Glasken sniffed the air.

"Charred meat," he said in a flat voice, as if he was in a dream.

"They must be burning their dead," replied Dolorian.

"No, no ... Strange, silent stillness. Not normal, not real. Perhaps we're dead. Was there an attack? Were we killed?"

The questions caught Dolorian off-guard. She put a hand to her face. "I'm alive, as I can tell." She kissed the wound on his cheek that she had made the night before.

"They should have attacked at dawn, when the sun from the eastern horizon was in our eyes. What happened to their attack? Is the radio wagon working?"

"Some minor coils and joints melted last night, probably because we connected some terminal awry in the dark. My crew should have it live in a quarter hour or less."

Glasken stood up with the aid of his crutch and looked out of the tent into the swirling smoke.

"There's nothing alive out there," he said. "No noises, no shouts, no jingles of gear and harnesses. How long has it been like this?"

"Hours, since long before dawn."

"Your command, Lieutenant," he said as he began to limp toward the trenches facing the bridge. "I'll not be long."

"Johnny, get down!" she shouted, running in front of him and trying to push him back.

For all his wounds, Glasken resisted. "There's no alarm, Frelle Lieutenant," he said dreamily. "They're all dead out there. Your command, mind the square." He limped on.

"All dead?" she said aloud, then beckoned to Sergeant Gyrom, who came over at once. "Go after him, drag him to the ground at the first shot!" she hissed. "We'll stand ready with covering fire."

"Frelle!" said the sergeant with a crisp salute, then he went after Glasken in a crouching run.

They made their way past the dogleg in the trench line, then out into the no-man's land of the previous day's fighting. They reached charred scrubland. Many of the trees were still burning, and the grass was brittle underfoot as they walked from the infirmary tent. Glasken passed several corpses, charred and smelling obscenely succulent.

Dark trenches gashed the red earth ahead, and the reek of roasted flesh was even more sweet and pervasive.

"Captain, Fras Captain, come back!" Gyrom whispered, tugging at his arm. "This is an evil, devil place. The Ghans have unleashed daemons against us."

Glasken shook him off and tried to lift a heavy, charred plank that was lying at his feet. The effort made him reel, and he could feel his stitches tearing.

"Sergeant, help me lay this across the trench," he said softly, as if fearful to break the stillness.

Beyond the trench they walked down the road in utter stillness and silence. Nothing moved, nothing made a sound. Men, animals, insects and birds, all were dead. Smoke drifted and swirled like cream stirred into coffee. They reached the bridge. The railings had been burned away, but the boards had been covered with wet sand and gravel as a precaution against fire bombs. Down on the river a galley wrecked in fighting days earlier was burning where it had been grounded. Around it the floodwaters had dropped quite a way. Bodies floated on the water, both men and fish. Glasken walked out onto the bridge.

"Fras Captain, the bridge isn't safe," called Gyrom.

"Walk in the middle, as I do," replied Glasken, neither stopping nor turning.

"But the Ghans' camp is just beyond the bridge."

"That's where I'm going."

Not far from the bridge was a vast field where the Ghan camp had been made. Glasken looked across the field but did not walk any further.

"Captain, they are all gone."

"Not so, Fras Sergeant, tents burn easily. They are still here."

Gyrom stared more closely at the nearest mound, then took a few steps toward it. "You are right, Captain Glasken, these are all bodies. Thousands of men, with their horses and camels. Look over there, that great hole: thunderbolts from the sky."

"No, that was an ammunition dump exploding in the heat that did all this. Some ancient weapon, perhaps. A glass that concentrates the sun so as to burn ..."

"But this happened at night."

"Then I don't know what to say. Whatever has been turned loose here has made no distinction between Ghan and Alliance warriors, except for a circle a couple of hundred metres in radius ... centred somewhere near our radio wagon." He scratched at his stubbled jaw. "The Highliber's sparkflash transceiver, at the centre of it all."

Glasken gestured to Gyrom to return, then turned away from the blackened field. The sergeant hurried after him and they crossed the bridge again.

"Have the men bring a barrow of gunpowder here," Glasken said as they stepped back onto the south bank. "Tell them to place the barrels low in the supporting framework, make sure that the walkway cannot be as easily rebuilt as last time."

Later that morning the explosion that shattered the bridge echoed out across the charred landscape. A cloud of smoke and debris rose into the air, and the silence returned.

"Annihilated!" the sergeant was crying over and over again as the cart returned to the circle. "It's the Highliber. How did she do this?"

*****

The forty riders that made their way through the charred landscape were evenly divided between Ghan, Southmoor, Confederation and Alliance representatives. A truce pennant fluttered above them on the lance of one of the Confederation officers. They rode uneasily at a brisk trot, surveying the desolation and fearful that it might revisit the place. It was with considerable relief that they arrived at the untouched Alliance square at Ravensworth.

In a sense Lemorel had the advantage at Ravensworth, because she still had 50,000 cavalry just outside of Haytown. It would take but a word from her for the Alspring forces to break the treaty and pour through Haytown unopposed, crossing the river. In another sense time was running out. The constant rain and unending mud and cold were draining the morale of her men, and now this circle of char seemed a warning that the Alliance was favoured by the Deity. The truce delegation was an ideal way to check just what was happening on the south bank at Ravensworth. If the Alliance forces had some huge weapon, then it was all over. If the catastrophe was nothing to do with them, the drive to cut the Alliance in two would go ahead.

"Just as I suspected, no mighty weapon," she said to Overhand Baragania as they approached the Alliance encampment. "This was some natural disaster. My informants tell me that Haytown will offer no resistance if we pour our troops across their bridges without attacking or looting the town. The Central Confederation will demand reparations and an apology, but their OverMayor wants to stay out of the war if possible."

Baragania was wide-eyed and ashen faced. He rode hunched over, as if he expected to be shot at without warning. "Commander, this horror could well have been an act of wrath by the Deity. How can you be so sure of yourself?"

"It's obvious what has happened. The blocking of our way at the Ravensworth bridge meant that a huge build-up of metal weapons and cooking fires took place in a very small area. Why do you think that steam engines and the like are proscribed by all major religions, and why is industry confined to artisans spread thin over the countryside? Metal, heat and smoke. If they become too concentrated in a small area ... well look around you. When my army was compressed into this tiny area, it became like an industrial town in the ancient civilization. The ancient writings are full of talk of industry causing 'greenhouse warming'. Now we can see what that mysterious term 'greenhouse warming' really means."

Baragania looked about him, wide-eyed and incredulous. Her explanation was plausible, but the sheer magnitude of the forces that had been unleashed was still terrifying.

"Why were the Alliance forces spared?" he asked.

"I say they were not. This was but a pocket of a much larger Alliance unit, the rest of which was destroyed. As for this little area, well, why will nine of a city's spires be struck by lightning in a thunderstorm while a tenth is untouched? Pure chance."

"You will have to convince a lot more followers than me, Commander. The men are cold, homesick and frightened. The war has gone from a triumphal promenade to a slow, bloody, hard-fought nightmare on the enemy's home ground. Of late there has been talk of the Deity sending all that rain to blight us as a sign of displeasure. Now ... this."

"I explained it for you!" snapped Lemorel, growing impatient.

"I am an educated man, Commander. I can trace out the mathematics of planetary motion and explain the optics of a telescope. I can accept what you say, but there would be no more than a few hundred like me in all of your remaining army."

"Then the educated elite will have to convince the others."

"This is just my concern, Commander. The elite, as you call them, are the very men with the strongest sense of honour and chivalry. Violate the truce at Haytown or behave dishonourably in any other wise, and you may find that the nails that hold your army together are pulling loose."

"I am a ruthless hammer, Overhand."

"You are a leader, even if your title be Commander. If none follow, you cannot lead."

"That's enough! You're treading a dangerous border."

"Commander, if you do not hear this from me, nobody else will tell you. In the meantime, however, the fears and mutterings will still be there. I shall say this once more because I really am dedicated to your service: behave with honour and do not lose the respect of your officers. We are on the balance, and the needle is finely poised."

"If you want to see honour dragged in the mud, just observe the Alliance captain in this encampment ahead. My informants have warned me that it is John Glasken, the very incarnation of dishonour."

"Captain Glasken. I have heard reports of him too. This cannot be the man you have spoken about. By all accounts he's a brave and popular leader whose men would follow him to hell and back."

Lemorel cut her riding whip across his arms with a sudden swoosh. Baragania flinched at the stinging blow.

"That's enough," she said between clenched teeth.

The incident was not lost upon John Glasken, who was watching their approach with a heliostat telescope.

The small, veiled one in blue, he thought to himself. *Only their Supreme Commander would whip an overhand: it just has to be Lemorel.*

If he could insult her sufficiently, she might just take offence and challenge him to a duel. She was said to be fond of personally executing senior officers who failed her, and killing those who challenged her in duels.

"Let's hope that I live up to your small-arms training, Abbot Haleforth," Glasken whispered as he lowered the telescope.

Dolorian met him back at the command tent. "I made another transmission to Oldenberg," she reported. "I clarified the situation here for them, so far as we understand it."

"You may have to make yet another transmission, and fairly soon. Lemorel's with that delegation, and disguised," he explained hastily with a flourish of his telescope. "When I meet them I'm going to come out with a few choice Glaskenisms. I'll try to goad her into challenging me to a duel. One mention that Jemli and I are lovers should do the trick, and besides, if Jemli ever found out that I missed a chance to shoot her sister she might never forgive me. She doesn't like her very much."

"Duel with Lemorel?" Dolorian said in alarm. "Even if you were Frelle Zarvora I'd advise you to think again, Johnny. And how can you pace out a duel while walking with a crutch?"

"I can now manage without it — but yes, the crutch would be a good prop to give Lemorel false confidence. Then if she bites at the bait, I'll drop the crutch, have my leg bound up with splints and walk flat-footed. As for my shooting, I've had a good teacher over the past few years. If I die, you're in charge. Destroy the sparkflash and make for the Confederation. There are worse fates than internment by neutrals. Anyway, there's said to be no chocolate shortage in the Confederation."

"Good fortune, sweet Fras, and shoot straight."

"Good fortune, sweet Frelle, and do nothing that I would not be proud of."

Glasken chose to meet the truce party beside the sparkflash wagon. The Confederation officer bearing the truce pennant rode up and saluted him. The other thirty nine representatives gathered in a wide semicircle.

"Are you in charge here?" he asked Glasken in Austaric after noting the standards and pennons flying over the camp.

"Captain John Glasken, I'm the most senior officer left alive," replied Glasken, supporting himself with a staff and bar crutch. "What are you doing here?"

"We heard an explosion two hours ago. We made for the cloud of smoke."

Glasken leaned more heavily on his crutch. "I'll put it another way. What are you Confederation neutrals doing out here with those Ghans and Southmoors, and why won't those Alliance officers speak with me?"

"We are here only to observe. We seek facts."

Glasken bit his tongue, barely intercepting an obscene and sarcastic reply. "Is all that out there enough fact for you?" he snarled.

"We rode through it for ten kilometres. They're all dead, tens of thousands. How did you do it?"

"Me? With three hundred infantry, a few orderlies and six signallers? I'm a damn good officer, but I'm not as good as that!"

"Thousands died last night, Captain, roasted in an instant. We thought that you had used a weapon to do all this."

"Us? We were preparing to be overwhelmed. Now I want to speak with the Alliance officers in your party."

"No. That would violate the terms of the truce sealed under that pennant," he said with a gesture upwards. "There will be no exchanging of tactical information that could benefit either side."

"All right then. So, how can I help you? Would you like formal coffee? Dancing girls? A troupe of Alspring eunuchs to draw you a hot bath and lay out a change of undercottons?"

"Fras, I understand what a strain has been upon you —"

"Then get to the point."

The Confederation officer glanced about the encampment again, puzzled and disappointed that there was no mighty weapon to be seen in the scruffy but defiant little outpost. He brought his attention back to Glasken.

"Last night the Ghan commanders summoned us to demand the use of the Haytown bridges. We were in their camp when the sky to the south was filled with a humming sound and a blue, flickering glow, then fires began below the horizon. Whatever did it continued for only a few heartbeats. The Ghans sent scouts out to report on what had happened, and they said that everything was burning within ten kilometres of the bridge near Ravensworth. It seems now that a small circle at the centre of that circle is the site of your camp."

Glasken felt himself go hollow inside, but tried not to show it. "We here had nothing to do with all that."

"The Alspring Ghan delegation cites evidence that the OverMayor Zarvora was experimenting with ancient weapons."

"The OverMayor's experiments involve nothing but pure science." He turned and gestured to the Ghans. "You Ghans, you overran her testing ground at Woomera and killed her engineers and scholars there. Can you swear by the Deity that you found anything like this vast expanse of charring?"

The Ghans remained silent behind their veils.

"All that I know is what I see," Glasken continued. "If this is the work of the Deity, then we were spared while the Ghans and Southmoors were annihilated. Perhaps the Deity is displeased."

An uneasy tone entered the pennant bearer's voice. "Why should the Deity favour you? What special righteousness and virtue does the Alliance have?"

"Look for evil, not righteousness," cried Glasken, turning back to the Confederation's pennant bearer. "Look to the Alspring leader who brought this calamitous war upon us. An Alliance renegade and outlaw, who wins her victories by stealth and betrayal. It is her the Deity is displeased with."

"Fine words from the man who ravished our Commander when she was a girl," Baragania interjected, riding forward from his group.

Glasken rounded on him sharply. "I have never ravished anyone. My charm alone has always been sufficient, and my charm attracted Lemorel. Why look to my own sorry encounter with her, however? In our countless nights together her sister, Jemli Milderellen, told me —"

Lemorel's shot cut him down. An instant later five dozen muskets were trained on the truce delegation, yet several of the Ghans had their own flintlocks trained on Lemorel as well. She extended her arm outwards, then dropped her Morelac to the ground, one barrel still unspent. Glasken lay in the mud, shot side-on, high in the chest. The dark splotch of blood across his left bicep and chest mingled with the red mud that already smeared him.

"Medician!" someone called from the Alspring musketeers.

"Don't bother, I never miss," snapped Lemorel, tearing her veil away and sliding from her horse. Her face was pale and fearful. She had killed to cover her own lies, and now she had to produce a very convincing story.

Dolorian noted her former friend's expression with grim interest, then walked forward to stand protectively astride Glasken's body.

"He abandoned me to the desert," Lemorel shouted in an Alspring dialect to Baragania. "He defiled me, then he defiled my sister!"

"You shot our commanding officer under the cover of a truce!" Dolorian screamed in Austaric.

"Austaric, all speak in Austaric!" demanded the Confederation's pennant bearer.

"As Captain Glasken's second-in-command I demand satisfaction," cried Dolorian. She shrugged off her jacket and stood before them in a blouse stained with river water from several days past. "Name your seconds and have them search me for hidden armour," she said with her hands on her hips and her breasts thrust out.

Lemorel raised her eyebrows, but did not smile. "You should know better than to challenge your teacher. This is a joke."

"Afraid that the Deity will guide my hand?" asked Dolorian.

"Commander accepts!" shouted Baragania.

Lemorel whirled around in fury and glared at him for a moment. He stared back steadily.

"Do you need a second, Commander?" he asked calmly.

"What good is a dead man as a second?" she replied. "I'll fight alone."

She tore off her outer robe, then strode across to Dolorian who held her arms out as she approached.

"Impressive breasts, Frelle Dolorian," said Lemorel as she checked for hidden armour. She stood back and held her own arms up for Dolorian.

"Medician, check her for armour," said Dolorian, folding her arms beneath her breasts as well as she could. Lemorel's face contorted at the slight, and something like a muffled squeal escaped her.

Because a Confederation truce had been violated, the pennon bearer was declared overseer by acclaim. He named four observers.

"As the challenged party, choose the weapons," he said to Lemorel.

"Amnessons. Your officers have them as standard issue."

"Nice choice," Dolorian replied, rolling her hips for the benefit of the onlookers. "Long barrel, lightweight, and a friction trap for the recoil."

Lemorel sneered to hear her own lessons of seven years earlier quoted back to her. Two guns were selected and brought over. Lemorel snatched one weapon and slashed the air with it, feeling the weight and balance. "Your target, Frelle Challenged," urged Dolorian.

Gyrom had found a sheet of poorpaper and some coloured pins in the command tent. The Confederation officers watched carefully as he pinned the paper in place, with a wide, black shield pin at the centre.

Lemorel hefted the gun again, then walked to the target and paced back. Without warning she whirled and fired, and a hole appeared beside the black pin. She was giving Dolorian the chance to better it if she could.

Dolorian pouted. She went down on one knee, supporting her left elbow with it as her hand steadied the long, functional barrel. Slowly she squeezed the trigger. The blast echoed into the silent, charred landscape. The shot smashed the pin.

"That was stupid of you, Frelle," snapped Lemorel, who had never before been beaten at the target. "You bettered my shot, so you have the right to fight me now, but do you think that I'll give you a chance to kneel down and aim like that?"

"No, Frelle, but I'll still try."

"You never learn, do you? Never discuss tactics with your enemy."

They stood back to back. Reloaded pistols were returned to them both.

"Call your distance, Frelle Dolorian," the Overhand said clearly.

"One hundred and fifty," said Dolorian, and there was a faint hiss of breath from Lemorel.

It was a very, very long call. The count began, and took quite some time. "... 149, 150!"

As Lemorel whirled she judged the distance, noted that Dolorian was beginning to kneel, then fired — just as her opponent suddenly bobbed up straight. Her shot took Dolorian low in the ribcage, a little to the left — but below the heart, where Lemorel had been aiming. The image of Dolorian falling was hazy through the gunsmoke as Lemorel lowered her arm. She shook her head, then turned to the overseer for a verdict ... just as the clearing smoke revealed Dolorian lying flat, bracing her elbows in the red mud as she took aim. Her shot hit Lemorel side-on, in the right of her chest, and the ball passed through her heart. She toppled to the red mud, her face a death mask of surprise.

The overseer looked to the observers, who inspected the two women. Lemorel was dead. Dolorian was still alive, and thus declared the winner. The medician tore the fabric away from an ugly wound below Dolorian's left breast.

"Not good with pain," she whimpered through clenched teeth, tears flowing across her mud-stained cheeks. "But ... fooled her. Got her!"

"I checked the Captain during the duel," said the medician as he pressed cotton wadding soaked in eucalyptus oil against the wound. "He's alive. The shot passed through his arm, smashed the shaft of his crutch and deflected, then broke a rib and tore a furrow through his skin. He's in shock and unconscious, but he should pull through. Now just lie still, your bleeding is very bad."

"Tell him ... feared reaching forty. Worse ways to go."

"Don't talk, just relax and you will bleed less."

Dolorian looked into his eyes. "Fras Medician, you can ... rip my blouse ... anytime."

"You're on, Frelle, but not unless you're still alive," he replied, feeling his heart wrench. "Don't drop your pack now. Don't let slip. There's everything for you to live for."

She pouted at the medician, then closed her eyes as he brushed his lips against hers. Moments later she was dead.

"I appear to be in command," Sergeant Gyrom said to Overhand Baragania. *Captain Glasken would be sarcastic*, he thought to himself, *so I must be too*. "Are you through with spying on our defences under the cover of the truce party, or should I line the men up for inspection?"

"We go," Baragania said, folding his arms and looking sadly down at Dolorian's body. "War with honour I understand. Not this. What happened here is ... evil, obscene thing."

"Follow a devil, and such like will befall you."

"Devil has good disguises."

"You should have looked for the forked tail."

The Overhand gestured across to Lemorel's body. "You arrange burial for Commander Lemorel?"

"Why not? I've become good at it, thanks to her."

*****

One of Dolorian's crew was able to transmit the news back to the Command Centre at Oldenberg. Within two days the fighting had stopped everywhere and the opposing armies were pulling back to truce lines. Dolorian's body was taken by wagon to the paraline terminus at Robinvale, and from there to Oldenberg for burial in the family plot at the cemetery. Lemorel was buried on the battlefield, with all the other dead.

The Southmoors ceded a buffer province to the Southeast Alliance that reached to the Central Confederation, while the Balranald Emirate declared itself independent of the other Southmoor nations. Other matters were not settled so easily. The Ghans who were holding the Woomera Confederation's cities refused to give them up. After annexing all independent castellanies as far as Peterborough, Zarvora's army laid siege to the town, then sent three brigades north to Hawker and took that town in a surprise attack.

Tarrin sat in Zarvora's Libris study, listening in amazement while she finally explained the workings of her radio system to him, and how she had used it as a parallel and secure command network in the closing weeks of the war. She also explained her perplexity over what had happened at Ravensworth.

"It was linked to the sparkflash radio, of that I am sure," she said. "The Mirrorsun band was undoubtedly the cause of it, and I think that it was some intense, hollow cone of heat, the same as it used to destroy the Wanderer stars."

"It attacked the radio, yet it spared the very centre, where the radio itself was positioned?"

"Believe me, Tarrin, I have given it a great deal of thought. My feeling is that it could be a matter of aiming. Aim at a target using a drop-compensator sight, and the bead of the sight will cover the target itself."

"But why cover what you are shooting at?"

"The Wanderers were big, and may have been more than 200 metres across. A direct hit would be a kill, even if the centre was spared." She waved her hands in circles, then let them fall. "That theory will have to do for now."

Tarrin was less than convinced. "But the sparkflash transmitters have been used for a short time since the Night of Fire."

"Yes ..." Zarvora frowned at her mechanical orrery as she assembled a few of her speculations into the bones of a theory. "My feeling is that there was some code used that made the Mirrorsun identify the seventh transceiver as one of the Wanderers. That code triggered the response, and it could do it again. Just now I have the Calculor analysing Dolorian's last transmissions for clues, and when the fighting to free Woomera is done, I may conduct experiments in the desert using cleared areas and a single transmitter. Until then, I have had all Sparkflash wagons returned to Oldenberg, where they are to be kept under guard.

"In the meantime, Fras Tarrin, my overhand at Peterborough predicts capitulation within three days at most. I intend to go there to preside over the treason trials, and then to make it the interim capital of the Woomera Confederation until the city of Woomera is set free."

"But Lemorel had the Mayor of Woomera killed when the city fell, Frelle Highliber."

"Correct, but his heir was studying at Rochester University at the time. I intend to create a new office of OverMayor for the Woomera Confederation, and appoint the heir in Peterborough. The youth will be a rallying point, yet it will not matter who holds the old capital. Guard my sparkflash wagons well while I am away, Fras Tarrin. If fools or traitors get hold of them there could be a truly horrendous mess."

*****

Glasken spent the three weeks following the end of the war in a hospitalry near the slave markets at Balranald. His left arm was encased in plaster and burlap, but his leg was soon well enough healed to carry his weight. On the day that he was due to be discharged and return to the 105th he was visited by Vellum Drusas, of the Libris Inspectorate.

"Fras Glasken, the great hero of Ravensworth, and are you recovered enough to be honoured?" boomed the inspector in a mellow and cheery voice.

Glasken was sitting on the edge of the bed and easing his boot on over the bandages. To anyone who knew him, he looked rather subdued.

"To tell the truth I'm feeling just a tiny bit flat," he said as he drew the laces tight. "Most of my close friends in the brigade were killed, and I've been three weeks in an Islamic hospital where I can't get anything stronger than coffee and the only nurses that they let near me are men. My dear Frelle Dolorian was shot while killing Lemorel! Ah, but then she propositioned the medician with her dying breath: it was the way she would have wanted to go." Glasken fell silent, his fingers also idle on the boot laces. Then he looked up at Drusas. "He later told me that it broke something inside him, and he intended to resign his commission and apply to join the Inglewood Maternity Hospitalry. Fras Drusas, all of that sorrow leaves me sickened."

Drusas put a supporting hand on Glasken's shoulder, and adopted the positive tone of a good counsellor. "Well now, Fras Glasken, I can cure a little of that. I'm here to take you to the paraline terminus and hence to Rochester for a great and fabulous ceremony. It's not only your own medal, but the late Frelle Dolorian's parents have asked that you accept her medal and honours on her behalf."

Glasken picked up his packroll. He looked around one last time, as if he was about to leave something of great importance forever, then he limped out of the room with Drusas. "Doesn't seem fair," he said as he signed for his musket, sabre, flintlock and dagger at the locker desk. "There's a lot as did braver than me. I just managed to stay alive."

The hospitalry staff and many of the patients were there to see him off. He was being hailed as the liberator of the Emirate of Balranald, the man who held the bridge at Ravensworth against odds of a hundred to one, the man that Lemorel could not kill, the man who broke the army of the Ghan invaders. Outside, Drusas had a gig waiting, and an escort of a dozen lancers.

"Balranald's a bit like home," said Glasken as they drove along the streets. "It's a paraline terminus town like Sundew, a big place with lots of industry and wind trains taking crates and bales away to places with wonderful names." He gazed about at the turbulent bustle of town life, letting his nostalgia for Sundew wash over the memories of war. "Look there, the slave markets where I was sold for 300 silver rikne — that's nine royals — back in 1700 after I'd escaped the Battle Calculor with Nikalan."

"Hah, a real bargain," laughed Drusas.

"And there, a rail-capping foundry, just like in Sundew. I was born in a lathe and mudbond tenement like that one over there. Until I was seven I grew up with a lot of rough kids among the smithies and railyards while my father worked as a paraline lackey and my mother did weaving. They were saving to buy a share in a vineyard and move to the country. She was a tall, thin, gentle lady with big sad eyes and black, curly hair."

"Well they obviously did find better times," said Drusas, genuinely impressed and trying to show as much. "Saving the fees for University is not common among clerks and weavers."

Glasken seemed hardly to hear him. "Look, a narrow gauge paraline truck with Great Western colours and markings. It must be from their mixed gauge paraline."

"The war scattered rolling stock widely, Fras."

"Aye, like people by the Call. That's how my stepmother died. One day I was in school and the Call rolled over, but we were tethered so it was nothing special. Then some churls I knew burst in and said my mother was taken by that very same Call. It was just like that, no fuss no mess, nothing. I hardly cried, I just felt numb. A few weeks later dad told me that we'd come into a lot of money. He also told me that I was a bastard — a real one, that is. He introduced me to my real mother, and she was a big, jolly lady who cooked well and went in beer races. He married her once we were out of mourning, and bought a share in a vineyard. We all three agreed to live as if we had always been together, and I learned to be a right jolly little terror. First drunk at nine, virginity gone at fourteen. It was odd, though, but I always remember how my first mother used to be so proud of me whenever I topped the class at that ratty little alms-school near the railyards. Whether I rolled home drunk, or bloodied from a fight, or just before dawn after wenching all night, I always got my homework done. I always thought that those big sad eyes of my first mother only got happy when I studied well."

Drusas was unprepared to hear someone with Glasken's reputation speaking like this — and at such length. His own replies sounded awkward and forced, and he was very surprised to find his usual eloquence failing.

"Well then, all to the good. At least you had the scholarly skills to repay your father's investment in your University fees."

"Oh he didn't have to pay, Fras Vellum. I came fourth in the Alliance Certificate exams and won a Mechanics Institute Scholarship."

Drusas had certainly not known this.

"But why did it take you eight years to get a four year degree?"

"Not sure. In Rochester I had a lot of time to myself, and that led to thinking that whatever I did, my first mother would never be there to be proud of me when I graduated. The thought obsessed me, but I found that drink, revels and wenches gave me enough distraction to go on, so that's why I'm what you see here today." The return to his current situation seemed to bring Glasken out of his reverie. He sat up straight and clapped Drusas on the shoulder. "Here now, the paraline terminus."

"And here I must leave you, my remarkable scholar and man of action," said Drusas with some relief. "In your exalted future, spare a thought for old Fras Drusas."

"I'll even spare you a drink, Fras."

With Glasken aboard the train Drusas drove through the city to the new Alliance embassy and then filed a sheaf of forms. Here he also collected a purse, and he spent an entertaining night watching the dance festival in the market sector of the city with two shadowhands ever close behind to guard his purse and back. While they were with him he had no fear of darkened lanes and shadowed doorways.

The night was enjoyable, yet there was no wine to be had in the Islamic city. The dancing was a wildly exciting spectacle, however, starring nomad performers from the north, many of them from Christian and Gentheist tribes. For the first time in many months Drusas felt a stirring at his loins as the show whirled to a climax. At his request one of the shadowhands indicated which streets might harbour harlots, and Drusas hurried along between the narrow, darkened buildings, sniffing at traces of perfume and gaping at forms outlined against gauze shutters.

Suddenly something made him stumble, and he careered into the gloom of a deep-set doorway. Drusas was appalled to find an arm hooked under his chin and his feet free of the ground. By the Mirrorsun light he could make out a dagger point before his eyes, and there was wet blood gleaming on the blade.

"Glasken where?" said an accented voice. "Embassy say returned to regiment. Not so. *Don't* struggle. Shadowhands dead."

"Know — nothing," gasped Drusas frantically, his fingers scrabbling at a thin, hard arm.

"Order for Glasken came from OverMayor. Go to occupation army at Peterborough. Can't find."

"I'm only an inspector. I just filed forms."

The blade point dropped, to begin pressing into the skin over his heart.

"Sergeant Gyrom not see him since in hospitalry. Has been searching. I search too. Business with Glasken."

"I, I can't ..."

The dagger point was through Drusas' skin and pressing deeper.

"Try harder."

"Train. To Rochester."

"With who?"

"Darien. Darien vis Babessa."

Part 6

LESSIMAR

Peterborough had been badly mauled in the siege to dislodge the Alspring agents and sympathizers. Not a single building had escaped damage, yet it was still an important town. — to the extent that it had become Zarvora's new headquarters.

In spite of the ruins and devastation beyond the windows of the Mayor's palace, however, it was a handful of beamflash reports from far away that filled Zarvora and Denkar with disbelief and horror.

SEYMOUR WIPED OUT, EXCEPT FOR A TEN METRE CIRCLE AT THE TOWN CENTRE. HUGE CHARRED CIRCLE, EVERYTHING DEAD, EVERYTHING BURNT BUT STONE AND BRICKS. MARTIAL LAW DECLARED.

"There are more details, but the pattern fits with everything we know about the way Mirrorsun attacks," Zarvora said.

"So it was Tarrin," said Denkar with a scowl as he shook his head slowly. "The Acting Dragon Black of Libris was a spy for Lemorel. No wonder she had the Alliance and Woomera handed to her on a golden platter."

"Not quite. The original plan was that I would be captured, or be cut off in Kalgoorlie. Instead I turned up in the Alliance when the Ghans cut the continent in half. All that he could do was sabotage the Libris Calculor and the networks covertly. If he had been in command, Lemorel would have been OverMayor by the March equinox, and the Central Confederation would be making its last stand by now. That may still happen, of course."

"Impossible!" exclaimed Denkar, now striding about and waving his arms in exasperation. "Lemorel had charisma, but Tarrin is just a glorified lackey."

"Lackey or not, Tarrin has a powerful weapon at his command. You see from these reports what he did at Seymour. All that he has to do is smuggle a sparkflash wagon into a town and then have it broadcast whatever that trigger code happens to be. Total annihilation will follow."

"Four wagons, Zar, not one."

"Not so, Fras Husband. The research effort in Oldenberg has been continuing, although at a less frantic pace than for the first month. By the end of the year Tarrin will have a transmitter that will fit into a one-horse gig, and be powered by a single operator with a pedal generator. He could smuggle that into Kalgoorlie, this place, anywhere. Look at this report: the central circle is only ten metres across. He must have found away to fine tune what Mirrorsun can do with its weapon."

"We're not defenceless!" exclaimed Denkar, appalled by her sudden depression. "We can seal every road and paraline from the southern Calldeath lands to, to ..."

"To where? The Northmoors? The Carpentarians, who are the subjects of the Alspring Ghans anyway? Disassembled transmitters could be carried on camel caravans across the deserts and we would have no way of knowing."

"But that's not the case yet. Tarrin's position is weak."

"Not so. Most of Woomera is in Ghan hands, and the Southmoors could be rallied. The Alliance would come close to civil war if forced to choose between myself and Tarrin. Look at these demands. Full control of all operational beamflash towers, and links to Woomera and Kalgoorlie to be restored under the supervision of his engineers. All paralines to be restored, and all Alliance galley trains to be allowed total freedom of movement with no inspections."

"No! Galley trains can carry the transmitters even at their present size and weight!" cried Denkar, wide-eyed and appalled at the idea. "They would allow him to kill whole cities with what he already has."

"So you think that we should try to buy time?"

"Yes! Definitely yes!"

"I think not. Tarrin is just another ruler, little different from me. Why kill thousands, even millions, just so that I can have the title of OverMayor?"

"Because Tarrin killed a town just to test his weapon!" Denkar was shouting now, frantically trying to revive some sense of aggression in his wife. "He could have just as easily chosen a tract of scrubland or desert somewhere. The scrublands east of Lameroo, for example."

"Yes, you are right, but that does not make him any easier to defeat. Do you have any constructive suggestions?"

"Challenge him to a trial. The circle of char is ten kilometres in radius, so its centre could be observed in safety from the gallery of a high beamflash tower. Tell Tarrin that you will accept his terms unconditionally if he can put a char circle exactly eleven kilometres south of the Culleraine relay tower. We could watch in safety from there, we could use the telescopes to observe that he can call down annihilation at will on our cities. Even then, that may not be the end."

"What do you mean?" asked Zarvora, some tone and interest creeping back into her voice.

"Mayor Bouros has been experimenting with sparkflash radios for far longer than we have, he can now fit a radio into a one-horse gig. If Tarrin sends a four-wagon sparkflash to Culleraine we could monitor the code. If we also have a dozen gig-sized transmitters ready —"

"No!"

"We could be ahead of Tarrin within a single day!"

"No! I'll not hold my people or any people to that sort of ransom."

"Tarrin is a lackey, he has no guts for a fight. Offer him a duel and he will back off unless he has a champion. Look, you could have a gig-sized transmitter smuggled into Rochester or Oldenberg within a fortnight, ready for the code. Once the operator has the code, it would only be a matter of your order."

"My order, precisely. What happens if the operator becomes tired and misreads a coded message, or panics as the Constable's Runners close in? Oh, Denkar, I am proud of you for devising a way to fight back, but this is too much for me. I shall take heed of your first suggestion and challenge the wretch to a demonstration south of the

Culleraine tower. If he can manage that, I shall surrender. King Connolly the Wise will be my example."

"Who was he?"

"A good and merciful monarch of the late Twentieth Century who was brave enough to lead his own soldiers into battle. Nothing is known of him beyond a single chronicle, and a crowned portrait in the Sundew Mayoral Gallery of Fine Art that dates back to the 1980s. The chronicle, which is one of our more reliable accounts of the period, mentions him as flying a huge metal war machine over that city now known as the Brisbane abandon and dropping tons of horse manure on the place instead ravaging it with shrapnel mines and nuclear winter bombs."

"I begin to see ... a humane yet humiliating demonstration of his overwhelming military superiority. But Tarrin's demonstration was just the opposite, he annihilated Seymour."

"I never said that Tarrin had either the wisdom or mercy. In any case, that king's role in that ancient conflict is not the one which I am faced with today. You see, Denkar, he is later mentioned as entering the city in triumph and amid great rejoicing, so the rulers of Brisbane must have had the courage and humility to surrender to him without pointless bloodshed."

Zarvora looked out over the shattered and fire-blackened buildings of Peterborough, her hands clasped behind her back. "In our haste to revive the military technology of the pre-Greatwinter people, let us not forget to learn from their triumphs of mercy and humanity as well. If Tarrin has an overwhelmingly superior weapon, and if he can demonstrate that he can target it with ease and speed, I shall try to muster the courage to surrender."

Denkar put an arm around her shoulders and stood with her for sometime, looking out over the ruins. Her head slowly bent across until it was resting against his.

"If it's any help, Zar, I'm proud of you too," he said without turning away from the window.

"It is a lot of help. I have never felt so weary or hopeless in my entire life."

*****

Glasken's blindfold and gag were removed once he was within the walls of Libris. Just as had been the case eight years before, he was driven from the Rochester paraline terminus through the still-familiar soundscape of the city and lifted from the cart once the gates of the library had boomed shut behind it. When he was finally unbound he found himself in the very induction room that he had been taken to in 1699, except that this time it was Tarrin waiting to meet him, flanked by two Tiger Dragon guards.

"Welcome home, FUNCTION 3084," said Tarrin as Glasken rubbed his wrists and looked about.

"I thought there was a law against this sort of thing," replied Glasken.

"Not in your case."

"Who say so? The OverMayor —"

"OverMayor Zarvora was assassinated in Peterborough on the day that you left the Balranald hospital. As the Ghans suddenly took heart and renewed their invasion with the remains of their army, I was forced to negotiate a truce. I do not have the late Frelle Zarvora's talents to wage war."

Glasken shook his head in silence. The news was like a slap across the face. To him Zarvora had seemed unkillable.

"So, why am I here in the Calculor again? I'm a damn good captain, but a pretty average component."

"For your own safety, Glasken, and for the good of the Alliance. The Ghans want you dead. The duel that killed Frelle Lemorel was fought in your name. You held up their advance at Ravensworth when victory was within their grasp, and you are assumed to have had something to do with that huge circle of char that annihilated two thirds of their army and a large number of Southmoors."

"The mute Dragon Librarian, Darien, showed me a confidential report on the train — before your Black Runners trussed me. It *is* true then, Mirrorsun charred our enemies ... but nobody is sure why." Glasken scratched at the newly-emerging stubble along his jaw line. "As for your first two facts, I suppose they are truish."

"Suppose! You're willing to entertain the proposition as a matter worthy of further debate! Well let me tell you that the Ghans and Southmoors have no such doubts on any of those three ideas. The Southeast Alliance is alive with assassins, all looking for you."

"So you brought me to the Libris Calculor?"

"It's secure enough, for now. If the Alliance falls to its enemies, you will probably be strung up by your testicles and lowered head-first into a vat of boiling banegold."

"That makes a firing squad sound humane."

"You begin to catch on. Now, we do have a chance, and you may be the key to that chance. If we had the text of Frelle Dolorian's last transmission, the transmission just before the char, we might have a chance to direct Mirrorsun to send such annihilation at will."

"But you must have the message yourself."

"Not so. There was a thunderstorm over Oldenberg on that night. We got parts of the message, but not all. As you know, Dolorian is dead, but you were in the tent with her until dawn, Glasken."

"You would do better to check the transmissions log from the transceiver wagon."

"She never logged that last message, probably because you were in such a hurry to bundle her out of her trews and into your bedding. There must have been pillow talk. What did she tell you?"

"I was wounded, I fell asleep."

"Lies!"

"Not lies! You've never been under fire or wounded, you would not understand. Even a shallow flesh wound from a small-bore musket can leave a man gibbering for days. I was blown up twice in the one day, I had nine gashes down one side, a broken arm, and a piece of metal the size of your thumb pulled out of my leg."

"All right, all right. The question is not one of dalliance, the message is all that matters. You were her commanding officer, she must have told you what she transmitted to Central Command. Think! The Alliance is hanging by your words."

Glasken scratched his head, then folded his arms and eased into a shallow meditation, as he had learned to do at Baelsha.

"When Dolorian sent the message, the mortar had just hit the power wagon and she was using batteries. She thought I was dead when she sent the message. She typed that she was in command, and that the Ravensworth bridge was repaired and the Ghans were joining with the Southmoors to wipe us out. That was all."

"We have the gist of that already. She added positions and estimates of troop numbers. Was there anything else that she did? Some extra transmission, some experiment?"

"I would help if I could. The trouble is that I can't."

*****

Tarrin met the fully re-instated Mayor Jefton of Rochester in Zarvora's old study. Jefton looked about in distaste. Tarrin had let the room slide into a chaos of files, scrolls, maps and punched paper tape, while some Calculor display mechanisms and mechanical animals were out of adjustment or broken. Plates of food scraps and coffee mugs were all over the place, and Jefton shuddered at the mouse droppings and trails of ants.

"Glasken was no help with the text of the message, damn him," Tarrin reported, apparently oblivious to the disorder his occupancy of the room had created.

"Then just try sending combinations of what we do have until we have a result," said Jefton as he cleared some files from a chair, dusted it with his fly-whisk, then sat down. "We only lack a dozen or two letters."

"No. Zarvora will be monitoring us with the receivers from Kalgoorlie. If we seem to be bumbling about, she will suspect the truth at once and be down on us like a train load of mortar shells."

"Transmit all the combinations one after another until one works, it will take less than a day."

"No!"

"I order you to!"

"Nobody gives me orders! I gave you back Rochester, but don't forget that I retain the post of Highliber and the new rank of OverMayor. You report to me, Fras Jefton, don't forget it."

"And do not forget that Zarvora is still alive, whatever you told Glasken!" Jefton reminded him, sitting forward and gesturing with his fly-whisk. "You are no more Highliber or OverMayor than I am until you have Mirrorsun at your beck and call." He sat back and smiled accommodatingly. "Why not do as I say?"

Jefton smashed his fist down on the keyboard. A blow from Zarvora would have splintered the wood, but Jefton's fist just bounced off. He gave a yelp and sat rubbing the reddened skin, his eyes tightly closed.

"Well, why not?" asked Jefton again.

"Because I may not have all the combinations, and I'm not good enough at codes and mathematics to be sure that what the FUNCTIONS and regulators tell me is true."

Jefton sat back, impressed yet appalled by the admission.

"Well give it to the University's edutors."

"Then *everyone* will have the full text. If we manage to master the true code, it will only take one with one transmitter, and I too could join most of this city as a lump of bloodied, charred roast."

*****

Denkar re-read the text of Dolorian's last message before the char, then shook his head.

"Tarrin must be better at coding than I thought if he can get some pattern out of this," he said to Mayor Bouros, who had just arrived on the first galley train from Kalgoorlie since the restoration of the paraline.

"There was a little interference, but our filters and directional antennas are very fine, Fras Denkar. The duty operator was convinced that she got the full text."

"There is something so sad, so compelling about it," said Denkar, handing the transcript back to Bouros.

The Mayor of Kalgoorlie clamped his spectacles to his nose and read the text again. As he finished he flicked the edge of the page. "I have seen this so many times that I'll soon be able to recite it, my friend."

"Pah, I already can," said Denkar with an elaborate orator's flourish. "Listen to this: RAVENSWORTH OUTPOST OF 105TH TO ROCHESTER. RAVENSWORTH OUTPOST OF 105TH TO ROCHESTER. POWER WAGON DESTROYED. BATTERY MODE ONLY. NO POWER FOR RECEIVER. MESSAGE TO FOLLOW. ALSPRING ENEMY HAS REPAIRED BRIDGE. SURVIVING ALLIANCE FORCE IN 200 METRE SQUARE AROUND THIS TRANSMITTER. ESTIMATED 150,000 ENEMY WITHIN 10 KILOMETRE RADIUS OF TRANSMITTER. THREE HUNDRED ALLIANCE SURVIVORS. ALSPRING AND SOUTHMOOR FORCES CLOSING IN FOR FINAL ATTACK. BATTERIES FAILING. ENEMY BOMBARDMENT INTENSIFYING. ESTIMATE ONE MORTAR SHELL IN FOUR IS NEW EXPLOSIVE TYPE. REPORT BY LIEUTENANT DOLORIAN JELVERIA, STARFLASH 7, FIRST ALLIANCE RADIO CORPS. SENIOR SURVIVING OFFICER. END OF TRANSMISSION.

"Splendid work," said Bouros, applauding briefly.

"Ah, you never met her, Fras Mayor. She was very full of figure and had long, lustrous hair, although nothing like that of Frelle Jemli. She had style, and a roving eye, yet she was discriminating."

"You had a little dalliance with her perhaps?" enquired Bouros.

"Quite a memorable dalliance. She was a Dragon Yellow then, and the Libris Calculor had just been commissioned. Just after Zarvora had some regulators shot for negligence, Dolorian called in on our cell to flirt with MULTIPLIER 8. It was about then that the medician's report on MULTIPLIER 8 was found to report a dose of the pox and she suddenly became less than enthusiastic for the man. I had come to have a few words with her in the meantime, however, and she presently managed to have me sent to the solitary confinement cells for some not entirely solitary confinement. That was before the Highliber and I had got together, of course."

"So ... you were once a component, a slave."

Denkar considered his slip-up for a moment. With so many components who had known him already liberated, it would not be easy to maintain any of the current lies for long.

"I began my years in the Calculor as a slave, but in time I came to think of myself as more of a volunteer. The Highliber came to love me too, yet I was too important to spare from the register of active Calculor components."

"I see. So you stayed in a prison with an open door for love of your jailer. Hah, what a strange and wonderful romance it was between you and the Highliber. Poor MULTIPLIER 8, though. He was unlucky indeed."

"Unluckier than you think, for medician's reports on all staff had just been added to the Calculor's data store. I spent the entire night awake with my cell abacus in the dark until I broke the internal transmission code. On my next shift I carefully inserted a report of pox into a certain component's personal records."

"The devil you did!" exclaimed Bouros, who laughed until he was in real pain.

"When next she visited the cell in the course of her normal duties Dolorian had cooled towards MULTIPLIER 8, but the dashing and urbane FUNCTION 9 offered her a half dozen hard-won Northmoor chocolates on a tray that I presented using my bunk pillow as a cushion. Needless to say she was impressed. She sauntered off, presumably to check my own medical records on the Calculor, and would you believe that I was banished to the solitary confinement cells that very night."

"A splendid stratagem, with an inspired guess about the liking for chocolates," Bouros chortled.

Denkar kept his own tone serious, but he was having difficulty twisting the wide grin from his face. "That was no guess. The personal records of the regulators turned out to be just as easy to access, and they included a few words on interests and preferences."

Bouros was nearly exhausted with laughter by now, and was incapable of a reply.

"She was worth fighting for, Fras Mayor. When I was roused by your lackey and given the transcript of that message, why my heart nearly broke. I wanted to rush across all those thousands of kilometres with an army to save her. Hours later she was back, saying that a miracle had indeed saved them, and that even Glasken was still alive. A few hours more, and she was really dead."

"Ah, Fras, we all wished we could have gone to her side to fight the Ghans, even I, who never laid eyes upon her. Name me anyone who would not have —"

Denkar had slammed both hands down on the desk, and was staring at Bouros with his eyes protruding as if pushed from behind.

"I cannot, Fras Mayor, and you are a genius!" he exclaimed, staring at the Mayor as if he had just discovered one of Glasken's caches of gold.

Bouros looked at him doubtfully. "If you have some brilliant insight, my friend, then you are the only genius in this room, for I can certainly not see it."

Denkar grasped him by the shoulders and shook him gently as he spoke, his voice bright with excitement. "She reached out and touched my heart, and yours — and Mirrorsun's as well! The greatest of the ancient calculors were said to be sentient, and the Mirrorsun band may be controlled by the last of such ancient calculors. It heard her transmission, and came to her aid."

Bouros stared at him, dumbfounded, then he snatched up a piece of chalk and began scratching on the nearest slate. "The area of char is the same as that she defined the enemy to occupy in her message, with a circle at the centre where she was said to be! Yes, yes indeed, Fras Denkar."

There was a knock at the door, the three quick, sharp raps that Zarvora always used. Denkar walked over and lifted the latch.

"Frelle Zar, you must have read my mind," he cried.

"Fras Den, darling," she said, sliding her arms around his neck and hugging him until their foreheads touched. "Hear my news first."

"Good news, dearest Zar?"

"Wonderful news, but without your support I would have given up already, without bothering to check certain matters in depth. I got a message through to the aviad town of Macedon, and asked them to go to a border peak in the Calldeath lands that has a clear view of Seymour. They took their most powerful portable telescope and did some spying. Seymour is untouched, although sealed off by units of the Alliance army. They also noticed the burned-out ashes of huge bonfires in practically every paddock."

"A bluff, by Greatwinter!" exclaimed Bouros.

"A bluff indeed, the cunning little rat! I have ordered a total blockade of the Mayorates under his control, and I suspect that he would probably have trouble holding anything other than Rochester city for more than a day or two. I shall do what Lemorel did at Alspring: lay siege and bombard only the Mayoral Palace."

"Libris is close by," said Denkar. "We owe the people of the Calculor too much to risk their lives."

"Starving Tarrin out could take years, and many others will suffer before he does."

"There may be a better way. Glasken is back in the Libris Calculor as a FUNCTION, according to Frelle Darien's reports. The aviad friend of his, Ilyire, is familiar with Libris, and he knows Glasken by sight. Can you get Ilyire smuggled into Libris?"

"Loyal double agents are a problem, but Frelle Darien is one who is known to Ilyire. She could deliver the necessary papers and instructions and help him gain access to Libris. She operates under the name Parvarial Konteriaz when working for me as a double agent, but goes under her own name when about Tarrin's business."

"Is she trustworthy?"

"I think I trust her — and so does Tarrin. She accidentally delivered Glasken into his hands just before he revealed his duplicity. She has been a personal friend of his, but ... what else can I do?"

"If she is the best, then she will have to do. Make ready to do all that we have discussed, but first get me to Phillip Bay and Theresla with one of the new sparkflash transmitters on a gig. It's also imperative that I not be delayed for genototem games at Macedon, by the way."

Bouros sat up and waved both arms in the air. "Don't forget to tell her your theory on Mirrorsun, Fras."

*****

Guided by Zarvora's other agents, Darien had found Ilyire at a tavern in a hamlet just east of Echuca. She was cautious yet eager as she approached the tavern. Tales of his transformation had been filtering through to her over the months, and in spite of the heated exchange that had seen them part, she did have an underlying affection for him. She had been worried that he had only been spreading rumours of his reform to lure her into contacting him again, but now even Zarvora had confirmed his transformation. If Ilyire had lost some of his fanatical protectiveness, Darien was eager to give him another chance.

The Bargeman's Jar was a low, rambling, ancient place that served as the hamlet's hostelry as well. Darien paused as she caught sight of the sign, staring into a polished draper's plate to comb her hair and smear a film of scarlet on her lips. In spite of the winter chill and mist she wore her travelling cape thrown back, and she even undid two buttons of her blouse.

At the taproom she presented a card to the maid, but the maid could not read. The maid fetched the vintner, who managed to slowly and painfully work out that Darien could not speak, that she wanted a private room, and that she wanted Ilyire sent there. As she sat waiting, a Call warning bell began to ring in the distance. Ten minutes to a Call. She reached down and wound her timer, then clipped her tether to a rail in the gloomy room. The latch of the door clacked. Ilyire entered.

Darien held up her hands and began to sign a greeting, but Ilyire shot out a hand and twisted her arm up behind her back. As she struggled silently, her face distorted in obvious pain, he grasped her other arm and bound her hands behind her. He walked around in front of the Dragon Silver librarian. Her eyes were wide with fear, and she was shaking her head from side. He began to speak to her in the Alspring Ghan language that she understood.

"No? You shake your head for no. The one word left to you, Frelle Dragon Silver Darien. My little assassin, my dangerous vixen. Your voice is crippled, but you are still deadly. You betrayed Fras Glasken, my Master. Drusas delivered him to you on the train, and you gave him over to that pretender, Tarrin. Poor Master, betrayed after fighting so valiantly and suffering so much."

Darien shook her head again and struggled against her bonds.

"Darien, Frelle Darien, I am disappointed in you, and in myself. You are a traitor, but I love you still. Still, I must kill you. You once wanted me to break my slavish, perverted adoration for you, and I have done just that. Fras Glasken helped me to get a proper perspective on the arts of living, would you guess it? Alas, you will die because I have changed into what you wanted me to become."

He examined the papers in her sling bag, and in her pockets. There were the sealed orders for Glasken, which appeared to be genuinely from Zarvora, but when he broke the seal the contents were in some military code that he could not follow. Other papers and border passes were made out to himself, and there were detailed instructions for breaking into Libris unnoticed and locating Glasken. Most of the papers referred to Parvarial Konteriaz.

"Who is Frelle Parvarial, and how did you kill her? Poor girl. You had a mind to lure me to Rochester with genuine papers for my Master from Frelle Zarvora, then deliver both papers and myself to Fras Pretender Liber Tarrin, it is clear enough. Well then, the papers will reach my Master, but your Tarrin will be disappointed."

He pocketed the papers.

"A Call is close, Frelle Darien. Very soon your mind will be lured away, and I shall unbind you and turn you loose to wander south to your death. Perhaps the Deity will spare you as he spares one in a thousand, that is the only chance I can give you. By rights I should plunge a knife into your heart — but I cannot do that."

He closed his eyes and concentrated for a moment.

"Not long now. I — I want to kiss you goodbye, but that would be such a horrible act, for it is I that am about to kill you. Darien, Darien, do you not wish that I was the way I used to be?"

The question was rhetorical, but to his surprise Darien gave a weak smile, stared straight at him and shook her head. A moment later the Call blotted out the intelligence behind her eyes, and she was mindlessly striving to go south. Ilyire untied the cord that bound her wrists, then freed her from the Call tether that held her to the room's railing. He led her outside, held her facing south down the street, then released her. She walked away at a steady pace, never once looking back.

"Even facing death you loved me just a little," he said to her distant back, then he turned away, his face in his hands.

*****

Glasken looked up from his *Systems Enhancement Abstracts* as the hooded regulator turned his key in the lock of his cell. Without a word he beckoned Glasken to follow, but not any of his cell-mates. They went to an empty tutorial room, and the regulator latched the door and turned to face Glasken — who exclaimed in disbelief as the hood fell back.

"Ilyire!"

"No less, Fras Master. My humble self."

"Theresla, she sent you."

"Her? My silly sister? Hah!"

"Just wait a minute! What's all this Master bit, and who sent you after me?

"Zarvora ... little bit, Fras Master."

"Zarvora was assassinated."

"Zarvora spoke to me ... three day past."

"Tarrin! That lying fykart told me she was dead."

"Not so, but more than Zarvora. Monks after you. Men in cassocks and sandals. Come to Kalgoorlie, go everywhere, even palace. Want you."

"Baelsha and its bloody abbot, I should have known. Nobody ever escaped from Baelsha before me. Are they far behind you?"

"Long way, Master. Killed all five."

"You managed to kill five monks from *Baelsha*?"

"Not easy, but yes. Spending weeks to recover injuries. I thinking, Fras Master be traced by monks. Came after you. Found you at Woomera. Shadowed — I think is word — you until Balranald. Helping."

"Can you get me out of Libris?"

"With difficulty, but stay first. Zarvora instructions for to follow."

"I was afraid of that. Well then, Fras Ilyire, tell me all your story, for it will certainly not take as long as mine. Much has happened to me since we last met."

"Not so, Fras. I with you since Woomera."

"What?"

"I see you rescue Highliber at Peterborough, lead charge against Southmoors at Ravensworth, and even kiss lovely Frelle Dolorian. I carry you from battlefield, Master, I keep you safe. You bury Ervelle's bones at Maralinga, Master. In secret I watch you speak words over her mound, fire a shot in respect for her royal blood. A brave and good man, Fras, you are that."

"Me? Did you really trail me in secret, protecting me?"

"I said to myself, if any man betrays my master, I cut out his heart. Alas, too late I discovered what Vellum Drusas, that false swine of a Dragon Librarian, did at Balranald."

"So what did you do?"

"I cut out his heart."

"Oop — That's it, no more! Just tell me what I have to do for the Highliber, and how we can escape."

Ilyire handed across the coded instructions to Glasken, who read it all slowly and carefully.

"A bold and delicate scheme, Fras Ilyire, and quite a role for you as well. Listen carefully now."

*****

Glasken sat at the specialized FUNCTION desk in the Calculor, trying not to look suspicious or guilty, but feeling as conspicuous as an emu in the stocks. Contrary to the falsely-embellished tales of continual grinding work in the great machine, there were extended periods of inactivity for many of the components during a normal shift. An algorithm written in by Highliber Zarvora in 1696 rotated the workload across components to keep the loadings even. The algorithm had not been updated in twelve years, even though the Calculor had become 46 times bigger. Glasken knew that he would have five or ten minutes of slack once a particular pattern of work had been disposed of.

The bypass scheme that Denkar had developed in 1698 had not been updated in over a decade either, and Glasken had doubts about whether it would still work. Sighing as if he had been hard done by, Glasken began to set patterns of values in his transmission registers according to the instructions that Ilyire had passed on to him. It took two minutes, according to the reciprocating clock above the observation gallery, and he silently thanked whoever had installed a minute hand since he had last worked there.

At three minutes of time left, the status flag snapped to the ENTER position, giving him such a start that he flinched on his seat and muttered "Fykart" under his breath. FUNCTION 12472 looked around. Glasken muttered "No fykart peace for wicked" by way of explanation as he flicked the beads back and forth to code a message that existed in his mind alone. FUNCTION 12472 wrote his name in her disruption complaints log and put a cross against it. He dumped the last of the code patterns to the output registers, then added the routing protocols for Rushworth, Seymour and, and...

He could not remember the name of the beamflash tower that sat on private land south of Seymour, on the edge of the Calldeath lands. There were nine such towers, he did remember that much. Only one thing to do, he decided as his input register flag snapped up to signal that legitimate work had arrived: he followed SEYMOUR with COMMON.

A request from Highliber Zarvora to Theresla via Macedon went out to nine stations. This is it, thought Glasken as he worked the beads for a paraline routing problem between wind and pedal trains at the Euroa intersection. There was a half hour to go before the end of the shift, then he had study time and a morning meal before cleaning out his cell and sewing inserts into an undersized uniform to make it a better fit. It would take only minutes for the message to reach each of the outpost towers, and while the farmers' lackeys were scratching their heads over the odd code one tower in particular would be sending it on to Macedon. By the time he was leaving his shift a decoded transcript would be strapped to the back of an emu running from the township to the Melbourne abandon where Theresla lived. How long would that take? Hours? Days? Glasken was uncertain about distances beyond the Calldeath boundary. And if she was not home? Then what?

"Can a bloody bird work a letterbox?" he asked out aloud, and FUNCTION 12472 frowned and put another cross against him in her disruption complaints log. Glasken did not notice.

His mind returned to the other eight outpost towers while his fingers and feet did their Calculor work. By now the more conscientious farmers' lackeys would be reaching for their code books. Ten, fifteen minutes at most. A few would give up, assume it was a military transmission gone astray, and destroy it. Someone would return it. It would have returned to the beamflash tower above him by the time he was walking out of the hall. Someone would put it aside for the Inwards Anomalies basket, and after an hour, or two, no more than four, it would be put to the Calculor for identification. In very little time it would show up as anomaly, and in a little more time it would prove uncrackable to the decoding routines. After that there would be a trace of the message, which would end up back at the output buffers of the Libris Calculor itself. *Then the fun starts,* he thought to himself. *They'll either shoot me at worst, or at best make me scrub the seats and do everyone's laundry.*

The System Herald declared the shift ended. Glasken stood up and stretched after locking his registers. He winked at FUNCTION 12472, who coloured and made to put yet another mark against his name in the log before she realized that he had not actually caused a disruption.

In his cell again, Glasken found that his cell mates were out on other duties. He waited until the guards and prisoners had ceased to walk past before extracting a snapwire from its hiding place and turning to the lock. After several minutes the door to his cell was still locked, and his patience was beginning to fray badly. He carried on a running dialogue under his breath as he continued to work the lock.

"What sort of fykart administrator wouldn't change the fykart algorithms in twelve years? There's plenty of free fykart FUNCTION and Regulator programming time. They're otherwise up to fykart in the solitary confinement block. Instead the fykart administrator spends a bleeding fortune of my fykart taxes on new fykart locks. For what? To keep dummart programmers in fykart cells that they're not wanting to leave for fear of having a fykart musket rammed so far up their arses that the thing could be fired without spilling a drop of fykart blood as long as they had their mouths open —"

"I have key, Fras Master," murmured a voice under his bunk.

Glasken leaped aside, bringing his guard up, then collided with the cell wall and fell across his writing desk.

"Ilyire! Damn you! Come out, hurry. We have to go. The bloody place will be down about our ears in four hours."

"Did you get the message out to my sister, Master?"

"That I did, but I had to do it in a pretty sloppy way. Four hours before the screaming starts about the security breach, I estimate. It should be just after mid-morning coffee break. The security regulators had better be wearing their brown trews, that's all I can say."

"I don't understand, Fras."

"Ach, just get us out of here. You've got a key, but do you have somewhere we can hide for however long it takes?"

"Both I have, Master Johnny."

When they were securely hidden in a stores loft Glasken began to relax.

"Nothing to do but wait now," he said. "One matter, though. Where is the agent that Zarvora sent with you? Is she safe and secure somewhere for when the chaos starts."

"Not so, Fras. She was a traitor, under the guise of a dead agent, Parvarial Konteriaz."

"Dead? But that's terrible, I met her as long ago as 1698, she was a steady friend."

"I avenged her, Master. I turned the traitor loose into a Call, even though I loved her."

Glasken suddenly went pale in the dim light. "You did what?"

"I —"

"Gah, shaddup, fargh Alspring fykart dummart. Did you read what the Highliber said in my instructions?"

"The code was beyond me, Master."

"But, but — no, I'm not about to tell you in case you do some fykart dummart thing as is worse."

Glasken sat in silence, thinking and weighing up risks. Ilyire became increasingly restive.

"Johnny?"

"How many guns have ye?"

"Two twin barrel Morelacs."

"The Lemorel special, I should have known. Give 'em here — and that throwing knife."

"Master, what are you to do?"

"Get myself killed, dummart, that's what."

"You not getting killed without I help too."

"That bloody Austaric grammar of your — hey, who's that?"

"Where?"

Glasken brought the butt of a Morelac down on Ilyire's head as he turned away. He caught the Ghan as he fell, and eased him to the floor.

"Call's touch, but it felt good to do that. Pays you back for what you did to me in the Maralinga stables in 1701."

Duty in the Libris Calculor was never so pleasant that components would go out of their way to do two shifts in one day, so there was no procedure to catch a component returning for a second shift. He hurried down the corridors, then slowed at the sight of the registration desk. There were four Dragon Orange guards on duty, and a Dragon Red seated on the corner of the desk.

"And where might ye be goin'?" he asked as Glasken smiled and made to go past.

"I, ah, had to see the medician. Ah — headache."

The Dragon Red turned to the register. "No names listed as is taking leave of the Calculor hall during this shift."

"I was, that is, I was in so much pain that I was carried out, I couldn't sign out."

"Were that the case yer escort would have signed for ye, and there's no signature by anyone. Where's yer escort?"

"He stayed with the medician, he's ... got a headache too."

"And now ye haven't?"

"Ah, well it's a good medician you've got in here, nothing but the best for us components."

The Dragon Red slid from the desk and advanced on Glasken. Garlic was strong on the breath that he exhaled up at the much taller component. Glasken backed away until stopped by the wall. The Dragon Red's eyes were close set and red rimmed, and when he held a hand up to wave his finger in Glasken's face, he exposed a dotted line around the wrist with 'Cut here, Southmoor Callbait' tattooed beside it.

"I think ye're just late, FUNCTION 3084, I think that ye're so late that ye'll break the record set in 1699. Get over to that book and sign in under the red line on the Inwards column!"

Glasken signed. The five who were guarding the door were enjoying themselves, and were probably not likely to search him.

"Ye'll get a demotion at next Humiliation Day," said the Dragon Red as Glasken straightened. "Now get in there and rattle the beads."

Instead of making for the FUNCTION desks or the relief pool room, Glasken went straight to the toilets and entered the door reserved for FUNCTIONS. It was nearly four hours into the shift, and not far from the beginning of the staggered coffee break. He took DISABLED signs from the mop closet and hung them on all privy doors but one. In this one he waited until the sound of approaching footsteps announced the first FUNCTION. There was an exasperated curse from outside then the door was pushed open. Glasken's fist slammed into the man's midriff, then he hit a precisely chosen spot on the FUNCTION's jaw with the point of his elbow. It took only seconds to remove the DISABLED signs from the other doors, then Glasken was back in the cubicle to tie his unconscious victim and appropriate the desk identification badge from his tunic. He had just fixed the latch from the inside and jumped the door, when he realized that it might have been more humane to unlace the man's trews before leaving him propped over the dump-hole. There was no going back by then, however.

The desk assigned to his victim was in lock mode, and as Glasken returned it to ACTIVE he glanced to the FUNCTIONS either side of him and tapped his forehead. They nodded back, satisfied that he was from the spares pool and replacing a component with a headache.

A quick scan of the registers indicated that heavy diagnostic work was in progress using decoding algorithms. They were already onto him, and he suspected that traps had been set for the code pattern that he had used to send the message to Seymour. There was no choice, however. He had to use the same pattern again, and even the same addressing, if he wanted to contact Macedon. His fingers flew over the beads, then he set the registers, broke into the data transmission stream and began to set up his output registers to transmit to the beamflash network. They were sure to stop the message at the gallery above him, he realized — then he stopped and thought: was there a direct link to Euroa? He set up a routing string through Euroa that might have only existed in his conjecture. Reaching under his tunic, he pulled back the strikers on both Morelacs. There was an emphatic click as he despatched the contents of his output register.

Glasken's legitimate work was piling up by now, and it would not be long before a regulator was sent to check on him. He tried to drag recollections of beamflash procedure manuals out of a memory that had never been particularly willing to accept them. In normal routing practice — no, but this would be war routing, and there would be a contingency check before any transmission. The follow-up would catch his use of the same anomalous code, and they would send a HOLD command directly to Seymour. Unless, of course, something distracted them. He frantically typed the first two lines of a Rochester University drinking song in the code pattern, routed it directly to Seymour and the nine towers beyond. He despatched it.

Almost at once a bell began to jangle somewhere high above him in the observation gallery. They had picked up the message. Regulators would be sent to detain him within seconds. What else to do? He drew a Morelac and fired at the gearbox of the main reciprocating clock.

Amid the screams and cries that erupted with the echoes of the shot, something whizzed past Glasken's ear and smashed into his output register. Automatically he turned and fired the second barrel at the observation gallery. A guard tumbled over the stone railing, screaming as he fell, and crashed to the desks below. The senior components were now dashing about in a panic, while the lower-level components were struggling to hide under their desks and benches. Another guard fired, dropping a FUNCTION to Glasken's left. *They're shooting at random,* he thought as he took out the second Morelac and checked the strikers. His shot hit another guard in the gallery, who collapsed over the stone railing. The others backed off out of sight. Another figure appeared at an access hole cut in the brickwork of extensions that had never been continued because of the Kalgoorlie calculor's success. A Dragon Librarian clothed in black. Tarrin! Glasken took aim and squeezed the trigger. The flint striker shattered, but the gun did not discharge.

"Fargh dummart gunsmiths, pox 'em all!" shouted Glasken as he frantically unclamped the flint from the other striker. By the time he was ready for another shot, Tarrin was nowhere to be seen ... and a fantastic head-dress of gunmetal barrels and wooden stocks ringed Glasken's scalp, all with guards or regulators at the other end. Glasken lowered his Morelac to the floor very, very slowly.

It was late in the afternoon before anyone saw fit to get back to Glasken. Two guards and one FUNCTION were dead. Over a hundred components had been injured, and a lot of damage had been done by trampling feet and components smashing mechanisms under desks as they sought cover. The Libris Calculor was still for the longest time since its commissioning. All of those who wanted to question Glasken were needed for the repairs, and once the great machine was finally operating again, it was in only a limited mode.

*****

Glasken's first message reached Theresla on the shores of the Phillip Bay. Its simple instruction was BEGIN, because the aviads were ready in Rochester. She entered the water at once to communicate with the dolphins, and relay to them a request for help. The dolphins deliberated, then decided: the Call rolled over Rochester for the first time in recorded history.

The city had not been designed for safety during a Call, and there were no mercy walls, Call-rails or watchbirds and terriers. Nobody wore an anchor and timer belt. Ilyire raced through the corridors of

Libris opening doors and unlocking gates amid crowds of mindless, shambling people who had interest in nothing but walking south. Librarians, technicians, guards, senior staff and readers wandered into the streets of Rochester, and joined the crowds making for the south of the city. A ring road inside the wall led to the south gate and out across a wide stone bridge over the shallow lake and into the suburbs. The main gate was closed, and only a trickle of people were managing to get through the access door beside it. Ilyire hurried to the gatehouse where he threw levers and chopped ropes until he could raise the dropgate. Once it was two metres clear of the ground he jammed the windlass, using the gate captain's halberd of office.

This Call did not last the two or three hours, as it did everywhere else on the continent: it continued for five. Libris emptied, the Mayoral Palace emptied. The Constable's Watchhouse, the markets, the University, the shops, the houses, the hostelries, taverns, the brothels, the blockhouses of the fortifications, every part of the city was purged of its citizens. A few were left, trapped in blind laneways and corners, or locked in watchhouse cells or the stocks. Those locked in the cells of the Mayoral Palace and Libris were all of unquestionable loyalty to Zarvora, and were mainly Dragon Librarians.

Ilyire wheeled a cartload of gunpowder into the middle of the main bridge after four hours had passed, then he released the main dropgate and secured it. The cart blew a span out of the heavy stone bridge. There were other bridges across the lake, as well as dozens of boats, but the south bridge was wide and strong, a perfect route for a massed attack.

Suddenly the aberrant Call vanished. Most of the people of Rochester, Oldenberg, and all of the small towns in the null zone that was the Rochester Mayorate, found themselves in open fields, between twenty and thirty kilometres from home. All at once a rush began in the opposite direction. Tarrin managed to rally several hundred Dragon Librarians and lead them to the forefront of the horde of citizens. Their only weapons were pistols and sabres: those with muskets had dropped them the moment that the Call arrived.

"Nothing like it ever happened," panted Tarrin as he jogged along with the others.

"Is it related to Mirrorsun, Fras Highliber?" asked a Dragon Gold.

"That's not worth asking," puffed the already winded Tarrin. "We just need to be first back. At least nobody else will be any better prepared."

But the loyal Dragon Librarians that Ilyire had just released from the Libris and palace cells were far better prepared. Ilyire had freed and armed them as soon as the Call ceased. The Calculor components had been just as safe, being imprisoned as well, and Ilyire had disarmed and chained up their regulators already. The Dragon Librarians loyal to Zarvora were outnumbered, but they had the advantage of being behind high walls, having all the bombards and muskets that they could use, and the leadership of a hero of Ravensworth bridge, Captain John Glasken.

Someone else had been ready. Zarvora had stationed small sparkflash transceivers at the four compass points around Rochester. As soon as the extraordinary Call began she was informed, and commenced moving her troops in from loyal centres by galley train. For several days the fighting continued in the outer suburbs of Rochester and on the lake's bridges, but once Zarvora's troops had fought past paraline centres under Tarrin's control the end was a foregone conclusion. Tarrin was no warrior, and for once the situation needed tactical rather than strategic skills. He was caught, tried and sentenced in very short order, and was already hanging dead on the scaffold by the time Jefton was found hiding in a farmyard shed near Euroa. The Mayor-Seneschal of Rochester could only be tried and executed by his peers, and it would be many months before the assembled Mayors of the Southeast Alliance sat in judgement over him, then knelt in their splendid robes and raised their muskets at the command of the OverMayor, Zarvora Cybeline.

*****

The street-to-street fighting was still raging in Rochester's suburbs when Zarvora entered inner Rochester across one of the footbridges. With her were Denkar, Bouros and several dozen Tiger Dragons. Glasken was nowhere to be seen, but was said to be directing bombard fire at rebel concentrations in the lakeside suburbs from the inner city walls. Zarvora's group split up after a hasty conferral, and Bouros made for the artillery position. Bouros had never actually set eyes on Glasken, and he also had the idea that his own fame was so widespread that everyone knew him by sight.

"Where is Fras Glasken, who got my sister with child?" he thundered.

Muskets appeared from everywhere, pointing at Bouros.

"You leave Captain alone, an' back away," snarled someone with an east Highland accent.

"Yes, you just mind your place, Kalgoorlie Callbait," added an educated Rochestrian voice. "Touch our Captain and we shall blow your ugly head off."

Bouros thought for a moment. *Rule one in engineering,* he thought to himself: *meet the functional requirements.*

"Fras Glasken!" bellowed Bouros at the top of his lungs. "Your lady's in labour. Get to the beamflash tower! Now!"

A large, well-proportioned man detached himself from the group, and the patter of running feet slowly faded in the distance.

*****

Glasken stepped out of the lift into the beamflash gallery.

"Glasken!" shouted Zarvora from the beamflash transmitter mechanism. "Do you take Jemli Milderellen, recently Cogsworth, as your lawful primary wife?"

"Who, me? Yes!" Glasken called back.

Denkar took him by the arm and led him to where Zarvora was tapping out a beamflash transmission and speaking aloud as she worked.

"JEMLI PAUSE JOHN GLASKEN SAYS YES PAUSE JEMLI MILDERELLEN RECENTLY COGSWORTH PAUSE DO YOU TAKE JOHN GLASKEN AS YOUR LAWFUL PRIMARY HUSBAND STOP." She sat back with a sigh. "And now we wait."

"Wait for the beamflash to Kalgoorlie?" cried Glasken. "The child will be born, grown and halfway through University before the reply returns."

"Not so, Fras," Denkar assured him. "I had a sparkflash transmitter set up at the base of the Kerang beamflash tower and linked in to another at the palace in Kalgoorlie. It's minutes at most."

Zarvora was trying to massage a migraine from behind her left eye and seemed to have aged several years in a matter of weeks.

"I am doing this because I owe you a lot, Glasken," she said hoarsely as Denkar stood beside her and patted her shoulder, "but in the name of the Deity will you please settle down and sort out your love-life in future?"

*****

Jemli screamed and squeezed Varsellia's hand as the contraction racked her.

"Try talking or singing, Frelle. Count to a thousand, anything."

"Can't count. Too much — ah, letting me go again."

"Then don't think about next time."

Someone came running in behind Jemli's range of view. Varsellia rustled a sheet of poorpaper.

"Do you, Jemli Milderellen, recently Cogsworth, take John Glasken to be your lawful primary husband?"

"What do you mean, recently Cogsworth, I still am! Ach, Who cares, what the hell, yes, yes."

Varsellia scratched at the paper with a charblack stylus. "Take this back to the sparkflash operator, hurry!" she told the messenger.

Minutes passed. There were more running feet on the flagstones of the Kalgoorlie Mayoral Palace. Varsellia came to sit beside the bed and rustled more papers.

"Zarvora Cybeline, OverMayor of the Southeastern Alliance has just pronounced you and Johnny as primary wedded, with the right to invel-spouses to be decided between yourselves," Varsellia paraphrased hurriedly. "Here's a kiss, passed on."

"You can come out now, your father and I are married," Jemli called to her abdomen.

"Ach, that's the water gone," said the midwife.

*****

Zarvora gazed patiently through the eyepiece of the beamflash telescope as Denkar rubbed a wet towel across the back of her neck. She read the sparkles of code from the distant tower's heliostat out aloud, not bothering to work the key of the tape punch.

"Baby girl, perfectly formed. Jemli well. Weight at birth — 6.1 kilograms! Glasken, how could you? The poor woman."

"What do you mean?" asked Glasken, who was now lying against a nearby pillar.

"That's over twice what my twins weighed together. Had it been me instead of Jemli, I'd be dead by now. There's more coming in ... hmm, wrong blood type for Ilyire but right for you. Yes, you are definitely the father, Glasken."

"Ilyire?" exclaimed Denkar. Both Zarvora and Glasken ignored the question.

"And an aviad, Fras Johnny Glasken — just between you, me and Denkar," she continued, looking the worse for her headache with each passing minute. "It finishes YOUR CHOICE GLASSY. Is that about invel-spouse rights?"

"No so, it's about the naming," Glasken explained. "If it's a girl, I choose. That's what we agreed. Tell her, ah, LESSIMAR JEMLI and, and, ah, I LOVE YOU JEMMY."

"Do not be embarrassed, Fras, just think of me as a machine."

"Lessimar, eh?" said Denkar. "Very pretty. She will be grateful for a name like that when she's older."

"My step-mother was Lessimar, it's after her."

Denkar rattled the door of the medician's closet. When it did not open Glasken called "Stand away," drew his Gimley 40 bore and fired at the lock. Zarvora slowly lowered her hands from her ears, then drew a key from her jacket and tossed it to the flagstones beside Glasken. Denkar shook his head as he pulled the shattered lock away and took a litre jar from the closet. After pouring some whisky into two measure-glasses he tossed the jar to Glasken.

"Lameroo Medicinal Rye?" Glasken exclaimed as he removed the cork."What's this for? Changing my bandages?"

"To Lessimar Jemli Glasken and her proud parents," declared Denkar, holding up his measure-glass. Zarvora delicately dipped a fingertip into her measure-glass and licked it. Glasken swallowed several mouthfuls.

"Jemli and I tested as human," gasped Glasken, once he had finished coughing.

"So did my parents," Denkar assured him. "It's rare, but aviads can be born to humans. Genototem scholars can explain it to you."

"I forgot to tell you, the Black Runners located Cogsworth last week and smuggled him out of Rochester," said Zarvora as she rubbed her temples. "He signed an adultery admission after I gave him 100 royals and put a gun to his head. Denkar also had several backdated receipts in his name forged from, ah ..."

"The Perfumed Whirlpool," mumbled Denkar staring intently at a fragment of lock tumbler on the floor.

Zarvora took a deep breath. "The things that I make him do in the line of duty."

"Don't you wish you were her invel-spouse?" asked Denkar.

"Thought not," said Zarvora as Glasken opened his mouth. "Besides, I have already given my invel-rights to Denkar. Now, as

OverMayor I also have a magistrate's authority. I picked up these blank divorce certificates on the way here, so ..." She began to scratch away at the parchments with a goosequill from beside the gallery's attendance roster. "Will yesterday's date do?"

"Aye," said Glasken.

Zarvora dusted some powder on the wet ink. "Here is Jemli's copy," she said as she rolled up the parchment. Glasken stretched across to accept it, then put it in his tunic pocket.

"Thank you, Frelle, thank you from both of us. Lucky you found the old coot in time."

"Hah, it wouldn't have mattered," Denkar assured him, "we could have backdated everything then claimed any contradictory documents were forgeries. You can do things like that with calculor records. Can we come to your invel-wedding too?"

"I'll have to ask my wife," replied Glasken before taking another drink.

The output punchtape began to click out a message from below in Libris. Zarvora put a hand to her ear to listen. "Some folk down on the Libris roof want to see you," she said, getting to her feet. She helped Glasken up. "Take the drop-lift to level fourteen, and take this too," she said as she handed him her Morelac Twin-50. "It is very noisy," she added.

With Glasken gone Denkar sat at the Receiver eyepiece and checked the logistics messages that were now coming in from the Kerang beamflash tower. "Boring," he said after a moment, then snapped the shutter down. Zarvora sat on the floor beside his chair and put her head on his lap. He began to massage the muscles at the back of her neck.

"It is so peaceful with him out of here," she said, closing her eyes.

There was a distant cheer, followed by two gunshots, the word "Girl!", then more cheering and gunshots.

*****

There were many treaties and arrangements signed over the weeks following Tarrin's defeat. The Southmoors broke into a number of small Mayorates and emirates, leaving the Emir of Cowra in charge of his immediate emirate and nothing more. Many of the new and smaller states were well disposed to the Southeast Alliance.

The Alspring Ghans began returning to their desert cities, not so much in defeat as with the promise of something better than conquest. Six months of trying to order the staff and crews of the Great Western Paraline Authority about had backfired very seriously. Many Ghans had become hopelessly entranced by broad gauge wind and galley trains, and they were scouring the desert for the remains of ancient iron rails and track routes. A 7 foot gauge paraline was to be built across the deserts to link Alspring to Woomera, but in the meantime the camel trains were opening up a flourishing trade. Zarvora also agreed to sell a radio wagon to them to decrease their isolation, and to educate some of their military engineers in the latest tuned circuit radio technology.

The strange annihilation at Ravensworth was the subject of a great number of studies, and early in August an interMayorate conference of edutors at Griffith concluded that it had been caused by an excess of conductive smoke from the volume of cooking fires combined with ionized paths traced by their mortar shells and the proximity of a great deal of metal weaponry. All of that combined to induce a type of massive and localized lightning. In effect it provided physical proof that the prohibition on steam engines was based in physics and not religious mysticism. Metal, steam and smoke were seen to be a deadly combination, and it was seemingly unwise to concentrate heavy industry in any one place or use steam engines to power trains.

Zarvora, Denkar and Bouros knew differently, but chose to remain silent. They knew that Mirrorsun, the huge band with a potential surface area greater than that of the entire moon, was alive and conscious. It had been generated by an old technology, the machine technology from before the Call. It was a calculor of a type, and it was sentient. With the war over, they turned to the problems of communicating with it.

Zarvora's rocketry experiments had provoked a conflict between the band and the Wanderers, this was confirmed very early in the strange new alliance of intelligences. The Mirrorsun band was damaged, but it had won. The Wanderers were destroyed, and no longer shot their unseen forces at any electrical devices that those on the surface of the earth experimented with.

What nobody had realized was that the Mirrorsun band would hear their radios in an otherwise lonely cosmos. When Dolorian sent out her last message from Ravensworth about defeat and death being so close, Mirrorsun interpreted the words as allies of the Wanderers attacking one of its fellow radio beings. It focussed a massive blast of microwave radiation on the area that Dolorian had radioed as being covered by enemy forces.

Nor was Mirrorsun the only voice on the radio bands. Other continents that were known from ancient texts to exist on Earth suddenly came alive after being isolated by the huge lakes called oceans and the creatures of the Call. China, Col-Arado, Siberiac and Zurig were the first four that were contacted, and the piecing together of the ancient civilization's surviving legacy accelerated beyond even Zarvora's wildest dreams.

"Nobody but you should hold to key to Mirrorsun," Denkar told her as early as August in 1708 GW. "I was willing to use its power as a weapon, but you were not. That earned you the right to deal with it as none of the rest of us can."

"That may have just been weakness on my part," she countered.

"Then it's a weakness that we can all learn from. Where do we go from here with the band?"

"Oh, more study and better communication with it. I intend to use a calculor as an interface, in fact I shall put it in the old Calculor hall."

"But the Calculor hall still contains the Libris Calculor, Zar."

"It can be decommissioned. It is no longer sufficiently fast or accurate when compared to the electric relay switch calculors. The components can be given a general amnesty and some gold royals to get them back into society."

"But Zar, many don't want to go, remember? Tarrin tried to disband them on the eve of the war, and they barricaded themselves inside. They saved the Libris Calculor for you to use in your war with Lemorel. Take out those who do want to leave, and the dangerous felons who ought to be in jail anyway, and there are still 5,000 components who want to stay. That's a lot of talented people, Zar, and they all know the workings of a calculor."

Zarvora looked at him as if she was seeing him for the first time. It took her some moments to gather together the words of a reply.

"To me it was just a tool ... yet you are telling me that it is a whole world to those living within it."

"Perhaps not a world, but home, at least."

"All right, all right. I did not fight the war to throw my troops out of their home. Tell me what would please them."

*****

The components of the Calculor were subdued and morose as they obeyed the SYSTEM HALT command and gathered, along with those off-duty, to attend Zarvora's briefing. When it had been the Rochester and Southeast Alliance Human Rights Association attempting to destroy the Calculor they could imagine that there was a mistake. With the Highliber, there could be no doubt about it.

"Wish it was some new configuration," said PORT 3A sadly as they sat waiting for Zarvora.

"We could always get together outside once in a while," MULTIPLIER 17 suggested. "You know, get a few of us together with abacus frames and run the machine."

"Oh yea, it could be in the meeting hall of the Echuca Library, and we could invite some Dragon Librarians to walk among us with canes, hitting anyone who makes a mistake and dragging an occasional component off to the broom closet for some solitary confinement."

"A few of us have not thought it such a stupid idea — ah now, here's the Highliber."

This time there was applause for Zarvora instead of cowering and terrified silence. The Highliber was surprised by the reaction, and it showed in her face. She mounted the rostrum, and spoke in a much more muted voice than they were used to. Many cupped hands to their ears to listen.

"Components of the great machine known as the Calculor, today is a day of destiny for you all. Today you will all be made free, there is no doubt of that. Being free does not mean that you can no longer work in the Libris Calculor, however.

"Some of you may know of the new electric calculor that is being assembled here from imported components. It is a thousand times smaller than the Libris Calculor, yet a thousand times faster. Now, just imagine the Libris Calculor in its current form being expanded a thousand times. The demand for regulators and technicians would be enormous, and in a way, the electric calculor is no different. I have great need of experienced people to convert Libris Calculor programs written in Calculor Conversation Protocol to the electric calculor language, CIND, or Calculor Instruction Numeric Dialect. This will be a massive task in itself, yet there is more again. Mayor Bouros of Kalgoorlie estimates another increase in calculor speed of 200 by this time next year.

"Put another way, all of those who stay in Libris will be paid as regulators and tend the new, electric calculor. It will be harder, much harder. No more blindly following instructions, you will have to think from now on. I can give you five days to think about it, during which you will be under limited supervision. Do take the offer seriously, we do need you. Thank you once more for all the work that you have done here in the Great Calculor of Libris. You really have helped to change the world."

When she had gone the ranks of components were in confusion, yet very few were depressed.

"So, it was a new configuration after all," said PORT 3A.

"New configuration, be buggered, it's a complete rebuild," replied MULTIPLIER 17. "Do they have any manuals or diagrams, I wonder?"

"Look there, by the door, it's FUNCTION 9, who used to be in charge of our cell when you were an ADDER."

"Hey there, FUNCTION 9!" called MULTIPLIER 17 as they both hurried over to where Denkar was standing. "Where have you been for the past eighteen months?"

"3A, 17, the day's fortune to you. What did you think of the announcement?"

"Gah, too fantastic to credit," said PORT 3A. "It's all very well in theory, or for a toy-sized model, but not on the scale of the Libris Calculor."

"But we've had models working for years," said Denkar. "I've been developing the CIND language myself. It's faster to develop programs because you can write out the whole thing in numerical symbols."

"All in numerical symbols?" said MULTIPLIER 17. "When could we see it?"

A crowd was beginning to gather around them by now, both regulators and components.

"We have a small working model here and six galley wagons with generators to provide power. First we need components to carry in the boxes, pedal on the galley wagons, and to chop up a few hundred desks to make room. Who will volunteer?"

A forest of arms shot up at once. The Great Calculor of Libris thus came to an unceremonious end, with its components chopping away the desks, wires, frames and mechanisms while others carried in boxes of relay units, plugs and insulated electrical cables. Assembly began under Denkar's direction, and continued for several days until the first test calculations brought the relays clattering into life.

With the help of the electric calculors in both Kalgoorlie and Rochester, Zarvora composed a string of messages in the ancient ASCII representation and keyed them through her sparkflash transmitter to the Mirrorsun band. This rendered the exchange impenetrable to eavesdroppers elsewhere in the world. It was unrewarding work at first, with hesitant and confusing transmissions between two intelligences very alien to each other, but slowly some exchange of meaning took place. The band had to work in Japanese, then English, then extrapolate the English into Austaric, which was why it had taken so long between Dolorian's desperate message to Central Command, and Mirrorsun's microwaving the greater part of the Southmoor and Alspring armies. Under Zarvora's tuition the standard of its Austaric improved, yet the concept of life at ground level was difficult for the Mirrorsun band to comprehend. In the end it was Zarvora who provided the solution.

*****

Glasken peered through the curtains of his room in the Rochester Mayoral Palace. Four floors below, in the Courtyard of Triumph, the OverMayor was presenting medals conferred during the war. Ilyire stood behind Glasken, hearing only the cheering and band music.

"Oi, there goes one of their secret agents, wearing a mask," said Glasken. "Can't see the medal from here. Mind the pin, Frelle Zarvora. Now the Tiger Dragons have whisked her back into the palace." Glasken turned back to Ilyire. "Come and see, you don't know what you're missing."

"My place is here, Master."

"Still guarding my back, Fras?"

"It has enemies, Master."

"And your own back?"

"I guard it to guard you."

Glasken parted the curtains again and looked down to where Sergeant Gyrom was accepting medals from the OverMayor on behalf of himself and Dolorian's family. There was a medal for Gyrom as well.

"What a life. I can't accept a bloody medal in public for fear of Baelsha monks in the crowd, I can't go to my family in Kalgoorlie for fear of Baelsha monks a-watch for me. How can I have a public invel-wedding to Varsellia without appearing in public?" He looked back to

Ilyire, who was standing relaxed yet alert, his eyes always on the move for threats. "You don't have to be part of this, Ilyire. I'd prefer to see you free."

"But, Master, I am free."

"You're not free from an obsession to protect those who you worship."

"Not worshiping you, Master."

"I have replaced Theresla as your mad god."

"No. Mad god you are, but ... duty is —"

"Absolute balls! Tell the truth."

Ilyire looked either hurt or guilty, Glasken was not sure which. His hands went through several gestures before he could add the accompanying words.

"Master, I protect you because — nothing else. You are linking to evil mistakes I make."

"Go on."

"I help Lemorel abduct you, go to Alspring cities. Then she tore world apart. Frelle Dolorian died to stop her. All fault is my own."

Glasken gave Ilyire a reassuring slap on the shoulder, forgetting how little his aviad friend really weighed. Ilyire stumbled, but Glasken caught him by the arm.

"Sorry, I keep forgetting. Funny, I also blame myself for all that Lemorel did. Highliber Zarvora probably feels the same too. So, you want to live as a fugitive, protecting me because I am the only one that you wronged who is still alive. You really need Darien to occupy your time, don't you?"

"Master, what is done is done."

"Do you still worship Darien?"

Ilyire was standing with his hands clasped and his eyes cast down, while Glasken paced before him. "I killed her, Master. No more worshipping. Evil mistake, now only memory to love."

Glasken turned away from him and looked through the curtains again. "Oi there, the herald stumbled while backing away from the OverMayor! Bouros caught him. Now he's up again, but his hat's on backwards. What a laugh." Glasken closed the curtains. "Ilyire, I must admit that I enjoy having someone as adept as you around to deflect the blades and bullets from my unworthy body, but I'm not selfish — well, not all the time. You called me a god before. All right, then: were I god, were I able to bring Darien back from the dead, would you leave me and be a match for her?"

"Master, do not blaspheme."

"Answer my question."

"Master, yes, but speak no more of this. This talk puts needles through my heart. Needles of sorrow."

Ilyire closed his eyes, and Glasken knew that he was shutting out the topic. He stood watching for a moment with his hands on his hips, then drew a curtain aside a little to reveal a small Dragon Silver Librarian standing with her hands pressed against her cheeks and her lips parted in an unfathomable expression. There was a gleaming medal on a green ribbon pinned above her left breast. Glasken put an arm around her shoulders and gestured her to enter.

"He's a bit of a sop, Darien, are you sure he's really your type?"

Darien nodded shyly as Ilyire opened his eyes. At the sight of her he reeled, clutching at one of the newly-installed brass Call rails. Darien rushed forward, and they embraced.

"Darien? Alive? Master, master, you bring her back from dead," he said, hardly daring to admit that what was happening was true.

"Ilyire, your Frelle will be unimpressed if she hears you call me 'master' again. I'm your friend, nothing more. At least I hope I'm your friend, married men go a bit funny about their old friends."

"Real, warm, breathing," Ilyire crooned to Darien. "No ghost."

"No ghost, Ilyire," said Glasken. "When you told me that you had turned your Frelle into the Call, I clouted you and went back to the Calculor. I slipped an extra message into the beamflash network to Macedon. I asked the aviads there to set up a watch on the Call paths, and gave them a description of Darien. As you well know, the aviads' way is not to help humans passing through the Calldeath lands on the way to the sea, but in this case an exception was made."

"Fras Glasken, bless you. May Deity bless you."

"The Deity, God, call him what you will, but he seems to have put his martial monks onto my trail, so I must disappear. That's for the best, as folk like you seldom want an audience. Look after each other now, after all that trouble I went to. Lovers are easy to find, love is rare indeed."

After what seemed no more than moments Ilyire and Darien realized that Glasken was gone. They rushed outside, and Ilyire called to the guards, but none reported seeing him ... including the tall, broad-shouldered guard who was the well-disguised John Glasken of Sundew.

The shadowy figures from Baelsha continued to keep watch around Libris for several days after the ceremony. A confirmed sighting of Glasken at Elmore eventually drew them south to that little town, but before they could close in on the fugitive the Call swept over the little railside town and lured Glasken away. The monks followed the trailing edge of the Call, keeping an anchorless figure of Glasken's build in sight of their telescope. They broke off the pursuit upon reaching the Calldeath lands. Glasken was as good as dead.

*****

Zarvora watched the sky above Phillip Bay, while Theresla's dirkfang cats prowled about, guarding her. The sky was clear blue, with not a cloud or bird to be seen. She did not know what to expect, but Mirrorsun had agreed to this very time and place. Thunder rumbled somewhere in the distance. Thunder from a clear sky. That had to mean something. She scanned the area over the bay again with her brass and silver twinoculars.

When at last she caught sight of the object it was already quite low, and perhaps two kilometres away. A tiny white sphere was descending beneath a red, umbrella-shaped thing, like the seed of some featherdown plant floating on the wind. It approached the horizon, stood out sharply against the waves, then splashed undramatically into the water.

About forty minutes later a school of dolphins became visible as they towed what looked like a vast red tent through the water toward the beach. Some distance behind it a white sphere bobbed sluggishly in the dark water. Zarvora could see scorch marks on its surface. Theresla was visible as a dark figure being towed by one of the dolphins.

"What do you want done with this thing?" asked Theresla as she waded ashore, white skin showing in places through the grease and blacking.

"The ball should weigh 200 kilograms, that is enough for us aviads to carry."

"We must carry away the cloth that broke its fall as well. It's as smooth as glass to the touch, and my dolphins are disturbed by it. They gripped it and dragged it here only to get it out of their water."

They dragged the white sphere from the water and carried it to the nearby ruins of a house that had collapsed from sheer age and decay.

Zarvora tapped an array of numbered studs near where the parachute was attached, and the top part of the sphere hinged open. Inside were white, cube-like packages, which she removed and began to put into her rollpack.

"What are those packages for?" asked Theresla as she helped Zarvora fold the parachute. The inner surface was dark blue, in contrast to the red exterior.

"They are devices to communicate better with Mirrorsun. This cloth can generate electricity if left spread out in sunlight, electricity to power the devices from the sphere. Even the cords that attach it are electrical cables. It is ancient technology, Frelle Invel-sister, a type of radio that no other can spy upon. Mirrorsun and I are about to explore each other's worlds."

Zarvora studied the markings on several of the boxes, then opened one and took out something like a bracelet. It was a plain, coppery colour, but slightly flexible to the touch and had a number of studs and square panels inset.

"This is for you," said Zarvora as she read instructions on a sheet of smooth, skin-like material. "Hold out your hand."

Zarvora cleaned the grease and lamp-black off Theresla's left wrist with medicinal rye whisky and a cotton cloth. At the touch of a stud the band shrank and bonded with her wrist.

"So this is all that you told me about?" said Theresla holding her wrist up and regarding the unlikely looking machine with scepticism. "This is the same as a sparkflash transceiver the size of a wagon?"

"It transceives sounds and pictures, and draws power either from your blood and body heat, or from sunlight. When you want privacy, you turn it off thus, with this stud."

"So I am linked to you wherever I go, Frelle Invel-sister?"

"And to Mirrorsun, just as I am to be."

Zarvora attached her own bracelet, and they went through a few trials of using the ancient devices in local mode. Finally they changed mode to give Mirrorsun its first view of the earth from a human perspective.

Some hours later the two invel-wives sat together in a darkened room of Theresla's house, watching a grey landscape covered with machines that were nothing more to them than fantastic geometric forms. Above was a black sky, sharp with stars, yet the scene was bathed in sunlight.

When they finally turned off their bracelets and went upstairs, the afternoon was well advanced.

Theresla studied Zarvora as she poured the tea. She had lost some of the lines in her face, yet she still seemed slower, less driven.

"Now I understand the term Greatwinter," said Zarvora as she lay back in the weak sunlight and breathed in the scent of the tea. "At least I think I do. It did not come from some ancient war between humans."

Theresla huddled deeper into her covering of robes and dirkfang cats, then extended a thin, white arm to pick up her own cup.

"So what was Greatwinter?"

"The old climate," said Zarvora. Theresla arched her eyebrows, but said nothing in reply. "From our own records, and from what limited information Mirrorsun can provide, I would say that the sheer size of industrial production by the Anglaic civilization was changing the climate. When the Call first appeared, the temperatures were already climbing, and Mirrorsun was a project to give the world a huge sunshield. Only one self-replicating machine, the first of thousands, was on the moon in 2021, when the Call brought the old civilization down, but it faithfully worked away, making copies of itself and making whatever was needed to complete the band. Now the band can cool the earth, but we have grown used to the hotter climate. The coastal cities are partly drowned, but who cares? What was the normal temperature in the Twentieth Century is Greatwinter for us."

Theresla returned her cup to the table and began to stroke a tabby dirkfang. "The band has been contracting lately. Was that at your request?"

"Yes. I have been making coded transmissions using the new tuned transceiver at Oldenberg. A hotter world is normal for us, so I have asked Mirrorsun to configure itself narrow, and to allow us to have our present climate. The band is anxious to serve us, but is confused about its role. It keeps on calling me some untranslatable term called 'sensei'. It seems to have a single mind, spread across the band and the lunar machines and factories. It could be persuaded to manufacture a wide variety of helpful machines and deliver them to the surface of the earth for us to use."

"You carry a heavy burden of power and responsibility, Frelle Invel-sister," Theresla observed, her face very solemn. "All of this will change the world."

"I was fortunate to have practice as OverMayor. Could I talk about the Call now?"

"Talk. I am said to be an authority."

"Logic's Arrow," Zarvora said simply. "Apply Logic's Arrow to the Call and what do you get?"

The magnitude of the task made even Theresla hesitate.

"The Call draws off fodder from the land to feed sea-creatures. It has done so for two thousand years," she said at last.

"Before that?"

"There was no Call, there was a mighty terrestrial civilization. It dominated the earth ... it dominated the seas as well."

"Which would make it hard for a civilization to arise there and become sufficiently advanced to develop something like the Call."

"Perhaps not. From what I have heard in the epics of the Bay Dolphins, humans were encroaching on the seas, and the Call was an ancient weapon that a species known as cetezoids dusted off to defend their home."

"Perhaps indeed. We know that the people of the ancient Anglaic nations were experimenting with the genototems of sea creatures, just as they experimented on themselves to produce us. Let us say that they built a race of creatures with enhanced powers and intelligence that we cannot even guess at."

"To what end? Why breed more intelligence into a creature?"

Zarvora sighed and shrugged. "We do it ourselves. We breed more intelligent emus so that they can be better trained to restrain their masters and mistresses when they are in the grip of the Call. Perhaps these sea-creatures were meant to herd and tend fish in the same way as our sheepdogs and drover emus look after herds and flocks on land. Taking that as the premise, what follows?"

"The experiments got out of hand, the creatures learned to use the Call."

"And?"

Theresla paused, trying to untangle the threads of possibilities. "The creatures used the Call to free themselves of human control. But that doesn't make sense. A sheepdog has no reason to rebel against the shepherd."

"But if all shepherds were consistently cruel to all sheepdogs, it might be different. Fragments of books mention that vast stocks of fish were drawn from the seas with things called driftnets. There was a practice called whaling by which the largest sea creatures, perhaps those called the cetezoids, were harvested in a manner so cruel that even humans fought among each other about whether it should continue. My own feeling is that some group of human edutors altered the genototem of these cetezoids so that they could have the intelligence to fight back. The cetezoids were so bitter after centuries of being butchered, however, that they turned upon humanity as a whole, developed the weapon we know of as the Call, and they won the war that followed."

"But what about the wars between humans, the nuclear bombs that caused nuclear winters?"

"I have examined maps of the entire continent, and I have found only two sites where the ground was turned to glass, as the bombs are reputed to do. Extend that to the rest of the world and you have a terrible war, but not a catastrophe. I would say that there was great confusion and panic, with humans blaming each other for the Call at first and sending their metal flying machines to bomb the suspects. The sea creatures learned to generate the Call between 2021 and 2022, according to my best estimate — based on the sudden plunge in ancient manufactured goods with dates stamped on them."

Theresla had been educated in many of the religious beliefs regarding the Call when she was younger, and had learned the scientific theories. In essence, there was nothing new in what Zarvora was saying, yet she was unsettled by the conversation.

"Apply Logic's Arrow again," Zarvora suggested when Theresla had remained silent for a time. "How are we aviads like those cetezoids and dolphins?"

"We ... are products of an ancient experiment in genototem transformation."

"What else?"

"We are — immune to the Call."

"Which means?"

"I cannot follow you."

"We have a property that humans do not have. Take away the Call and what will happen?"

"We would have no special advantage."

"More than that, Frelle Invel-sister, we would have a great number of disadvantages. We breed more slowly, yet we are stronger and longer-lived and even our average intelligence is roughly that of the brightest humans.

"Thus aviad individuals tend to be killed as soon as they appear in any population. They are called devil-children in some religions, and in others are feared so much that there is not even a term for them. We have too many advantages over humans to be trusted. Yet a few of us survive. We are lured by the Call when children, and only discover that we can resist it at puberty: that allows us to survive childhood at least."

Theresla sat up, showering heavy cats onto the floor. She wrapped her arms about her knees.

"Invel-sister, I have never heard how you survived."

Zarvora closed her eyes to conjure up the scenes of three decades earlier. Theresla noted that she was not smiling, and that she was gently beating a fist into her palm.

"Pure luck. When I was nine I had a secret boyfriend who was a little older than me. He was the son of a blacksmith, and I was from one of the lesser noble families. We exchanged locks of hair, all that sort of thing. Then one day he came to me and said that he was no longer affected by the Call. He proved it by producing a ring that he had taken from my finger that afternoon during a Call. He said that it would be the making of his fortune, that he could hire himself out as the town's protector during the Calls. He went to the market common beside the river and declared that he was immune to the Call, and when he had everyone's attention he held up the ring of office of the Christian Overbishop and the seal of the Mayor to prove it. I was there, I was so proud of him. I was also about ten paces from the militiaman who drew his flintlock and shot him as smoothly as he might have lifted a tankard from the table of an inn. That militiaman was escorted from the market common shoulder-high, and was later made an alderman. There was a court of enquiry, of course, but he was exonerated for shooting a thief.

"Thus by the time that I reached puberty I was aware of what might happen should I lose susceptibility to the Call. Sure enough, a week before my first issuing of blood, I noticed that my mother was straining on thc end of her Call-tether, while I had felt nothing more than a tingling in my head. I kept it a secret, yet I began to go exploring during Calls. I learned a great deal of forbidden information, and I used it to advance myself beyond what I was: the daughter of an Inverell refugee nobleman with limited wealth. A few aviads could live very well at the expense of the vast mass of humanity."

"And the vast mass of humanity is not happy about it," Theresla added. "Yes indeed, I resorted to tricks to hide my own abilities. Remember when I had Ilyire dress up in that suit of living green vines?

People believed that was why he could resist the Call. Someone even stole it from him."

"Remove the Call, and we lose the single advantage that sets us apart."

"But what about the Calldeath regions? Surely —"

"Why should the permanent Call in the Calldeath regions be any different to the one that sweeps over the countryside further inland? With the Calldeath lands gone the aviad communities at Macedon, Lilydale, Warragul and Leongatha will suddenly be within reach of human armies. I estimate that there are as many as 9,000 aviads living along the Calldeath strips, yet the Calculor has accounted for between 9 and 11 million humans living inland. Those are bad odds. We would be wiped out in any confrontation. As grim as it may sound, we need the Call."

"Then why did you go to so much trouble to build the Calculor and launch those rockets at the Mirrorsun band?"

"I was feeling my way, I have to admit it. At first, I was alarmed that the Mirrorsun band would cause a new Greatwinter. I knew that the Wanderers shot invisible forces that killed electrical devices, so I wanted to trick them into shooting at the band. Then the band began to repair itself, and I knew that it might be able to fight back. The Wanderers might well be destroyed by Mirrorsun, so I made ready the electrical devices that Bouros had been developing underground. At first I had no plan past the launch of my rockets. Theresla, I had intended to settle back in my offices of Mayor and Highliber, happy that I had saved the world from Greatwinter."

"Now you rule the world."

"The world, Frelle? What of the seas?"

"The sea creatures rule the seas, and they want nothing more than that. As long as the land dwellers are well behaved, they will leave us alone."

"And beyond the seas?"

"Unknowable."

"Unknowable? I wonder. My sparkflash operators report a growing traffic from beyond the seas. It has standardized on an archaic form of data transmission called Morse code, and the language seems to be an evolved form of Anglaic."

The concept took some time for Theresla to assimilate. She brewed up more tea, and laid out seedcakes and fruit while the shadows of late afternoon quickly lengthened.

"So, we can talk with people that we can never meet," she said as she sat down again. "What does that mean?"

"We can probably teach each other a vast amount. The world is opening up, and I have been Highliber for only a dozen years. There was a time when humans thought that they had no other intelligent life to share the world with. Now they have us, the sea creatures, and even Mirrorsun. We aviads hold the key to all four intelligences."

Theresla gestured to the little grey cube that had been projecting images from the moon onto a downstairs wall not an hour earlier.

"What a paradox. We now know more about the moon and Mirrorsun than the bottom of Phillip Bay, for all the help and love that my dolphins give me. As Fras Glasken taught me, when you are most comfortable you are probably most in need of a change. I may go north for a while, to the Sydney abandon. The cetezoids know of it as what we might call a holy place."

Zarvora was surprised by this. "The Sydney abandon. We know it to be very big, but nothing else is known to connect it to the sea-creatures."

"All the more reason for me to go there."

*****

Glasken had surrendered himself to the Call at Elmore, and wandered south in an unresisting, mindless rapture, safe from the pursuing monks of Baelsha within the sweep of the Call. A prearranged beamflash signal had already been sent south. Like Darien, he was rescued by the Macedon aviads and escorted through the Calldeath lands in safety. He came to his senses as if walking through an invisible curtain, and found himself at the edge of a small fortified town. It was a clear, cool winter's mid-morning with the sun bright in a cloudless sky. The place was a gaudy splash of terra cotta, orderly and incongruous against the green fields and bushland of the Calldeath. There to meet him was Theresla.

"This is a null zone like Rochester," she explained as they walked the streets, "except that it is within the Calldeath lands. I ... arranged it with certain friends of mine."

"So I cannot leave unaided?"

"No, but neither can any Baelsha monk enter to do you harm. Until now the aviads had to bring up their children among humans until they reached puberty and grew immune to the Call. Now we have a safe haven here. We don't need humans at all."

Glasken noted that Theresla spent a lot of time with her left hand up to her neck or shoulder, and that there was a cheap but strange looking bangle on her wrist.

"A pleasant town, and some pretty good wives," he commented, trying to show enthusiasm for Macedon.

"Yes ... yes. Actually that brings me to the subject of your parents. Your father, Narmorti Glasken —"

"Scrawny old goat, but he breeds good vines."

"— is a share-farmer in the vineyards at Sundew, and is married to Jolene d'Taklenam."

"Fine figure of a woman, my mum. Tips the scales at 114 kilos and bakes the finest butter pastries in Sundew. Won the bakery award at the Goldentongue Drinkfest in 1686, 1689 —"

"She is not your mother."

"She won the beer races, too, in 1691 — what? The devil you say!"

"The devil has nothing to do with it. Your real mother was married to Narmorti and you were their only child. Her name was Lessimar Pandoral, appropriately enough for having turned *you* loose on the world. The records in Sundew shire show that a month after the birth she was lured away by the Call."

"I know all that," said Glasken. "But you have it wrong. I really was the child of an affair between Jolene and my father. His wife agreed to bring me up as her own. The records show it, I've checked."

"The records are incomplete. Lessimar Pandoral was being beaten by an angry mob just before the Call took her. Your father told me that, and that he later married Jolene and had the town records altered to show that you were the child of an adulterous liaison."

"But why? What had she done?"

"She was accused of being an aviad by a jealous neighbour on falsified evidence. During the mob's attack a Call came past. Her timer and anchor had been smashed and she walked away to the Calldeath lands, which, as you know, are very close to Sundew. The trail of blood led straight there, even through bramble walls. Thus she was proved innocent because the Call took her, but she died in the proof. Your father was awarded a massive fine from the neighbour, who had actually been one of your mother's suitors years before. Narmorti used the money to buy his share in the estate."

Glasken suddenly stopped and sank to a wall, his hand over his mouth. Several people began to gather around. A rubicund man offered a pouchflask of orange brandy to him. Glasken took a swig and coughed, then handed it back without noticing that the Mayoral crest was on the side. A thin, greying woman with bushy hair like the Highliber's bent over and stroked his head. She was wearing the robes of a Liberal Gentheist bishop.

"We all understand your grief, young Fras, nearly all of us have been victims of human fear and hate," said the bishop.

"My mother, my real mother!" exclaimed Glasken, springing to his feet and confronting Theresla, who was standing back with her arms folded. "I remember her eyes, how sad they were, but how happy she was when I studied well. She never knew that I got a degree, about my chain of taverns, or that I've had two medals —"

"And over a hundred women," added Theresla.

"One more like that and I'll set my wife onto you!" he quipped lamely, but his emotions were already draining his control.

Glasken was not particularly vengeful by nature, but this was all too much. "Who was that neighbour who denounced my mother?" he suddenly burst out, his voice contorted by the sobs he was fighting to keep down. "I'll kill him, that's what I'll do! Do you have his name? You must have his name." He seized Theresla by the shoulders when she did not answer. "What about a sketch, Frelle, please, you must have seen a portrait, they have a big tradition of portraits at Sundew. I'll find Ilyire and go back there with him, he can cut the bastard's heart out and I'll ram it up —"

"Fras Glasken! Such language, and in front of your mother, our bishop!"

"I —"

"I told you he was big and excitable, Frelle Lessimar," Theresla said to the thin, greying woman in the bishop's robes.

Lessimar Pandoral's expression hovered somewhere between pride and adoration as she gazed across at her son. "My Johnny, they say you're as hard to kill as I am."

She held out her arms, but Glasken's knees buckled. They finally embraced kneeling together in the dusty street. Theresla stood by with her arms folded, her left wrist facing outward.

"Lessimar was conscious during the Call," Theresla continued as mother and son were helped to their feet. "She was bleeding and bruised, and had a broken arm, but she walked a straight line as if in the grip of the Call. She reached the safety of the Calldeath lands, then an aviad patrol found her. She — you're not listening, are you?"

Theresla wandered off with the Mayor as the crowd around the reunited mother and son grew bigger.

"An impressive sort of fellow," the Mayor declared. "A pity that he turned out to be human. We could, ah, use him here."

"True. His hair is wrong and he is not as strong as most aviad men. Although he has been trained to resist the Call in a limited way, he is as susceptible to it as any human."

"Well, he should be a great asset to human society, whenever it becomes safe for him to return. He's a marvellous example of just how good mere humans really are and what they can do, for all their faults and weaknesses."

"He is Alpha 2 Positive Gamma Negative."

"His genototem? Well, that's no surprise. We must monitor his offspring among the humans to see if any turn out to be aviads."

"Gamma Negative, Mayor, remember what that means? With humans there is a small but significant chance that he can sire an aviad child, as he did with Jemli. Any couplings he has with aviad women, however, will result in aviad children exclusively."

The Mayor's eyes suddenly widened, and his mouth hung open as he stroked his chin. "I ... shall get the medician to draw up a little list, I think. Thank you, Frelle Theresla. Thank you well indeed."

An hour later Theresla was packed and ready to leave. She called past Lessimar's house, where the preparations for an evening revel to celebrate Glasken's reunion with his real mother were under way.

"You should stay for the evening at least," Glasken insisted as Theresla kissed him on the cheek and tweaked his moustache. "You're the real guest of honour here, after all that you did."

"I am not one for revels, Fras, unless you have marinated mice and roast bats on a stick. Do contact me in years to come, though."

"Frelle, Frelle, I may be a filthy, overbearing, drunken lecher, but I'm still a gentleman. What about tomorrow, a couple of quiet half-litres and a game of kneesies under the table for old times' sake? They have a couple of taverns here, praise the Deity for that, and I'm not going anywhere with Baelsha bogeys after me. Wonder if Jemli will like it here in Macedon?"

"It may not be necessary for her to come here. Mayor Bouros will be off to see Baelsha in the weeks to come. He has some strong bargaining points in favour of them lifting that death-order on you, should you reappear alive in Kalgoorlie."

"Aye now, that's fantastic news. Weeks, you say? And I'll be able to leave this place? Pah, that's good. Only two taverns, and with all the women married and their husbands living in. Can't wait to get out of the dummart-boring place, and anyway, I'm missing Jemli and I've never even seen my daughter. I rather suspect that Varsellia does not want her invel-wedding over either the beamflash or the sparkflash. Ach, but enough of all that. Are you or are you not for a drink tomorrow?"

"Fras Johnny, remember how you vanished as soon as Ilyire and Darien turned their backs upon you?"

"Aye."

"Well I am about to do the same to you, for I have work to do, and I have to go a long way to do it — and in secret. Let us say goodbyes now, quickly, a last Glasken grapple."

"Look to yourself, and don't eat any strange mice," he said as they hugged each other.

"And you stay out of trouble. It is my turn for stupid heroics now. Ah look here, the Macedon medician, his lovely wife Vivenia — and their beautiful little daughter who is walking already! Hullo, hullo," she said, sweeping the child into the air. "Look at all those ribbons you have. This is Fras Glasken, he has a little daughter too. Here now, Fras, get used to carrying cuddly little possums like this one."

"Fras Glasken, you will be staying some weeks in Macedon, I hear, so Vivenia and I were wondering —" began the town medician, but Theresla cut in.

"Fras Medician, this man does not yet know of the term 'Genototem Hospitality', or of the difficulties you have been battling to keep inbreeding out of the aviad genototem, but I could think of no better edutors than yourself and Vivenia to acquaint him with the theory and practice. Why don't you take our newest refugee for a walk in the gardens of the beamflash tower for some theory first, while I say goodbye to Frelle Vivenia? Oh, and I shall give her a little message for you, Fras Johnny, one that I dare not deliver myself, lest you think badly of me."

"I — a message?" said Glasken, handing the child back to her mother. He bowed to Vivenia. "Frelle Vivenia, when we return my ears will be eager for whatever your lips have to offer."

The two men walked away, the medician already tracing genototem lines in the air. Vivenia put her daughter down.

"Vivenia, listen carefully," Theresla hissed as soon as the men were out of earshot. "I shall be away from my house for a very long time. Months, perhaps even longer. I want no searches made for me. Understand?"

"Yes, Frelle, but — Jekki! Leave the cat alone!"

"Tell the Mayor. Please."

"Of course, Frelle. Rely on me."

"Now, what do think of my present to the Macedon genototem?"

"He seems too good to be true, and he's the son of our Bishop Pandoral as well. Look, I know it is presumptuous of us, but ... everything has been prepared at our house for the afternoon, starting with a light but tasty lunch, then Kaldarri is taking the little one for a boat-ride on the reservoir. I can have Fras Glasken back at the house of his mother before sunset, Frelle Theresla, it will not interfere with the evening revel in his honour. Do you think that he will consent to come to our house, Frelle, to accept our genototem hospitality?"

"It is hard to tell, he has changed — mellowed, perhaps. I suspect that he really is lonely for his family, and that could be a problem. Still, we cannot have Kaldarri's theory without your practice, so try telling him that Baelsha requires proof that he is half-aviad, proof in the form of offspring with true aviads."

"Who is Baelsha?"

"It is a place. Just tell him."

"But, Frelle, one is either aviad or human, there are no half-aviads. Fras Glasken is a true human who carries an aviad genototem of —"

"Vivenia, tell him none of that if you do not want to ruin your chances. He can be upset easily, nobody knows that better than me. Remember, tell him Baelsha needs more proof, and it must be with true aviads."

" 'Baelsha needs more proof, with true aviads.' All right then, but Frelle, what am I talking about?"

"It does not matter. Besides, it is not true, and after a fashion it is revenge." Theresla embraced Vivenia, pressing their foreheads together. "Good fortune, and when I return be sure to tell me what he is like," she said with a wide, malicious smile.

"Oh, Frelle Theresla, what a tease you are," Vivenia said as she was released, playfully batting at Theresla with her long, bushy, aviad hair.

Theresla was gone before Glasken returned. She travelled swiftly north through the Calldeath lands, escorted by creatures that struck fear into the hearts of everyone else. Two days later she emerged into the farmlands of humans, and changed into the robes of a Libris Inspector before entering the town of Seymour. That evening, as Mirrorsun and the full moon rose together over the winter landscape she was on the paraline railside of Seymour, studying copies of ancient maps from the Libris vaults by the lamplight as her pedal train was shunting for the night's journey north. Beside the name of the Sydney abandon she had written extensive notes with a char stylus. It was a long way to travel, but the paraline reached all the way to the Calldeath border at Goulburn. After that, she would be on her own.

Epilogue

Theresla sat in the ruins of a building with 'Miocene Institute' carved into the stonework above its entrance. It was a warm, muggy evening in mid-spring. She had her wrist propped on one knee as she projected an image from Zarvora's bracelet onto a nearby wall, and listened to a faint trickle of sound.

Varsellia was walking down the aisle in the Gentheist Cathedral of Kalgoorlie, with afternoon light streaming in through the windows. Behind her were Glasken and Jemli, so tall by comparison that Varsellia looked more like their daughter than an invel-bride. Glasken looked slightly distracted, then Theresla realized that the tune being played by the band in the loft was *Campbell's Farewell to the Red Castle*. Behind them came two Gentheist bishops, one of them being Lessimar Pandoral. She was carrying a well-behaved baby a few months old, who was batting at a pair of medals pinned to her blanket.